The Romanov Ransom

TITLES BY CLIVE CUSSLER

DIRK PITT® ADVENTURES

Odessa Sea (with Dirk Cussler)
Havana Storm (with Dirk Cussler)
Poseidon's Arrow (with Dirk Cussler)
Crescent Dawn (with Dirk Cussler)
Arctic Drift (with Dirk Cussler)
Treasure of Khan (with Dirk Cussler)
Black Wind (with Dirk Cussler)
Trojan Odyssey
Valhalla Rising
Atlantis Found
Flood Tide
Shock Wave
Inca Gold
Sahara
Dragon
Treasure
Cyclops
Deep Six
Pacific Vortex!
Night Probe!
Vixen 03
Raise the Titanic!
Iceberg
The Mediterranean Caper

SAM AND REMI FARGO ADVENTURES

The Romanov Ransom
  (with Robin Burcell)
Pirate (with Robin Burcell)
The Solomon Curse (with Russell Blake)
The Eye of Heaven (with Russell Blake)
The Mayan Secrets (with Thomas Perry)
The Tombs (with Thomas Perry)
The Kingdom (with Grant Blackwood)
Lost Empire (with Grant Blackwood)
Spartan Gold (with Grant Blackwood)

ISAAC BELL ADVENTURES

The Cutthroat (with Justin Scott)
The Gangster (with Justin Scott)
The Assassin (with Justin Scott)
The Bootlegger (with Justin Scott)
The Striker (with Justin Scott)
The Thief (with Justin Scott)
The Race (with Justin Scott)
The Spy (with Justin Scott)

The Wrecker (with Justin Scott)
The Chase

KURT AUSTIN ADVENTURES
Novels from The NUMA® Files

Nighthawk (with Graham Brown)
The Pharaoh's Secret (with Graham Brown)
Ghost Ship (with Graham Brown)
Zero Hour (with Graham Brown)
The Storm (with Graham Brown)
Devil's Gate (with Graham Brown)
Medusa (with Paul Kemprecos)
The Navigator (with Paul Kemprecos)
Polar Shift (with Paul Kemprecos)
Lost City (with Paul Kemprecos)
White Death (with Paul Kemprecos)
Fire Ice (with Paul Kemprecos)
Blue Gold (with Paul Kemprecos)
Serpent (with Paul Kemprecos)

OREGON® FILES

The Emperor's Revenge (with Boyd Morrison)
Piranha (with Boyd Morrison)
Mirage (with Jack Du Brul)
The Jungle (with Jack Du Brul)
The Silent Sea (with Jack Du Brul)
Corsair (with Jack Du Brul)
Plague Ship (with Jack Du Brul)
Skeleton Coast (with Jack Du Brul)
Dark Watch (with Jack Du Brul)
Sacred Stone (with Craig Dirgo)
Golden Buddha (with Craig Dirgo)

NONFICTION

*Built for Adventure: The Classic
  Automobiles of Clive Cussler and Dirk Pitt*
*Built to Thrill: More Classic Automobiles
  from Clive Cussler and Dirk Pitt*
The Sea Hunters (with Craig Dirgo)
The Sea Hunters II (with Craig Dirgo)
Clive Cussler and Dirk Pitt Revealed
  (with Craig Dirgo)

CHILDREN'S BOOKS

The Adventures of Vin Fiz
The Adventures of Hotsy Totsy

The Romanov Ransom

CLIVE CUSSLER
and ROBIN BURCELL

MICHAEL JOSEPH
an imprint of
PENGUIN BOOKS

MICHAEL JOSEPH

UK | USA | Canada | Ireland | Australia
India | New Zealand | South Africa

Michael Joseph is part of the Penguin Random House group of companies
whose addresses can be found at global.penguinrandomhouse.com.

First published in the USA by G. P. Putnam's Sons 2017
First published in Great Britain by Michael Joseph 2017
001

Printed in Great Britain by Clays Ltd, St Ives plc

A CIP catalogue record for this book is available from the British Library

HARDBACK ISBN: 978-0-718-18468-1
TRADE PAPERBACK ISBN: 978-0-718-18469-8

www.greenpenguin.co.uk

MIX
Paper from
responsible sources
FSC® C018179

Penguin Random House is committed to a
sustainable future for our business, our readers
and our planet. This book is made from Forest
Stewardship Council® certified paper.

CAST OF CHARACTERS

CRIMEA, 1918

Dowager Empress Maria Feodorovna—Russia.

Pyotr—a servant.

BUENOS AIRES, 1947

Klaus Simon—twelve-year-old nephew of Ludwig Strassmair.

Dietrich Simon—Klaus's older brother, killed during World War II.

Ludwig Strassmair—Nazi prison camp commander, Klaus's uncle.

Greta—companion to Strassmair.

Herr Heinrich—Nazi officer.

Joe Schmidt—plane passenger.

Lennard Lambrecht—pilot.

Eckardt Häussler—cryptographer.

THE PRESENT DAY

Fargo Team

Sam Fargo

Remi (Longstreet) Fargo

Selma Wondrash—the Fargos' research assistant and go-to person.

Professor Lazlo Kemp—assists Selma with research, from Great Britain.

Pete Jeffcoat—Selma's research assistant, Corden's boyfriend.

Wendy Corden—Selma's research assistant, Jeffcoat's girlfriend.

Former DARPA Members

Ruben "Rube" Hayward—case officer, CIA's Directorate of Operations.

Nicholas Archer—owner of Archer Worldwide Security.

Friends of the Fargos

Albert Hoffler—Selma's cousin.

Karl Hoffler—Albert's oldest son.

Brand Hoffler—Albert's youngest son.

MOROCCO

Rolfe Wernher—German businessman.

Gere Stellhorn—Wernher's driver and henchman.

Tatiana Petrov—Russian businesswoman.

Viktor Surkov—Tatiana's bodyguard.

Zakaria Koury—Brand and Karl's guide.

Lina—Zakaria's cousin.

Kadin—Lina's servant.

Durin Kahrs—acquaintance of Brand and Karl.

KALININGRAD

Sergei Vasyev—Archaeology major.

Andrei Karpos—historian, Amber Museum guide.

Miron Pushkaryov—Königsberg castle groundskeeper.

Leopold Gaudecker—head of the Wolf Guard.

POLAND

Renard Kowalski—miner and expert on Project Riese tunnels.

Gustaw Czarnecki—miner and expert on Nazi Gold Train.

Tomasz Gorski—lieutenant, Internal Security Agency.

Nika Karaulina—Russian agent.

Felix Moryakov—Russian agent.

GERMANY

Helga—head caterer.

Ambassador Halstern—American Ambassador to Germany.

Mrs. Halstern—the Ambassador's wife.

Wilhelm Schroeder—furniture restoration expert and attorney.

Laurenz Hippler—Anholt castle's manager.

ARGENTINA

Nando Roberto Sandoval—jungle guide.

Dietrich Fischer—descendent of Ludwig Strassmair and young Klaus.

Julio—helicopter pilot.

The Romanov Ransom

PROLOGUE

I

The old woman stood with tears in her eyes as two men loaded the last of the three wooden trunks onto the back of a hay wagon. The first was filled to the top with strings of pearls, loose diamonds, and precious stones. Gold bars and coins in the second. The third contained the jewelry gifted to the royal family over the last three hundred years, diamond-studded tiaras, necklaces, and rings. She ignored all of it, her gaze only on the much smaller chest that her maid was carrying to the wagon.

"Wait!" she commanded.

Her maid turned toward her. "What's wrong?"

How could she voice her feelings at such a time? The jewels and gold meant nothing to her. But that last chest . . . She watched as the man, Pyotr, took it from her maid. "One last look."

Pyotr deferred to the other man, a stranger to her, who climbed into the front of the wagon, taking the reins of the two horses that were champing at the bit. "We're already late."

She turned toward Pyotr. "Please . . ."

"Be quick." He set the small chest on the back of the wagon, stepping back to allow her access.

Dowager Empress Maria Feodorovna lifted the latch, opened the lid, then pulled off the layer of lamb's wool, revealing four bejeweled eggs that she'd managed to take with her when she went into hiding after the Bolsheviks took over Russia. Her breath caught as she lifted the Royal Danish Egg, cradling it in her hands. It had nothing to do with the beauty of the moonlight reflecting on the precious stones set in gold, surrounding the white and light blue enamel, nor the meticulous workmanship by the jeweler, Fabergé, who wrought each so that it was a masterpiece of beauty and delight to any who beheld it.

"Enough," the driver said coldly.

"Give her a moment," the maid told him.

"They're just jewels."

"To you," Maria said, taking in every facet. "To me, these hold memories . . ."

This particular egg contained a surprise of miniature portraits of her parents. Given to her by her late husband, they were the stories of happier times with him, her children, and later her grandchildren, who were still so very young.

"You'll see your family again," her maid said. "I know it."

She nodded, swallowing the lump in her throat, and lowered the egg into its lamb's wool nest next to the other three. "Thank you . . ."

Pyotr, about to close the lid, suddenly looked at her. "Do they know how many eggs are here?"

Maria shook her head. "No. Only that I was going to include them."

He eyed the small case, then removed the egg she'd held, fluffing up the downy wool and repositioning the others so that it looked as though the case had only contained three.

She took it from him, holding back her tears. "I have no way to repay you. Thank you."

"Tell no one. Ever."

"I won't," she said as he covered the cargo under the hay in the wagon, then climbed into the front. "I promise."

He gave a nod as the driver shook the reins, the horses racing off with a king's ransom in the back of the wagon. Watching until it disappeared, Maria Feodorovna hugged the egg to her chest, equal parts of hope and terror filling her heart.

"YOU SHOULDN'T HAVE done that," the driver told Pyotr as the wagon jarred across the hardened dirt road.

"Why not?"

"Because it belongs to the people."

"They won't miss one small thing. Not with everything that she turned over to us."

"That's not for you to decide."

Pyotr saw the firm set to the man's jaw. He didn't pretend to know what the revolution was about, beyond the Bolsheviks' belief that the Emperor and his family had lived in excess and splendor while the masses faced hunger and an uncertain future. The people's wrath carried over, even after Nicholas II had stepped down from the throne and the royal family was imprisoned.

Some of it, he understood. Much, he did not. "What difference does it make if we allow her a few happy memories in her time of fear?"

"The difference? You sound as though you sympathize with her."

"She's just an old woman."

"You'd be wise to keep those thoughts to yourself, lest you end up like her family."

Having worked for the Romanovs for a number of years, the last thing Pyotr wanted or needed was for anyone to think of him as a sympathizer. In these times, that line of thinking led to death. "I wasn't thinking. You're right."

The man said something below his breath, then urged the team of horses faster. For the next several days, Pyotr never mentioned the

Romanovs, and he hoped that the incident with the Dowager Empress was long forgotten. It was nightfall by the time they reached Yekaterinburg, but instead of driving toward the governor's house where the Romanovs were imprisoned, they turned left.

"Where are we going?" Pyotr asked.

"Meeting someone to drop this off."

Panic set in. "If we don't deliver this in time, they'll kill the royal family."

"What do you care? Their fate is *not* your business."

"But—the ransom . . . The Dowager Empress entrusted us with it. To buy their passage."

"Ransom?" the man laughed. "You don't really believe they were ever going to let them go, do you?"

"We promised."

"You fool. What'd you think would happen? That the Bolsheviks would take this as payment, then set them free? Soon, Maria Feodorovna"—he turned and spat, his expression one of disgust at the mention of the Dowager Empress's name—"will meet the same fate as her son and his disgusting spawn."

Only then did Pyotr realize they were too late. The entire Romanov family had been killed. The children's faces flashed in his mind—the last time he'd seen them, before the clash of war, they'd been so happy . . .

"Where are we going, then?"

"To bring that as proof." He nodded toward the back of the wagon. "When they see what the old woman stole from Russia, trying to buy her son's freedom, she and every last Romanov will be hunted down, as will anyone who supports them."

Of all the royal family, Maria Feodorovna's life meant something. Unlike her son and his wife, she'd served Russia well. This war was her son's making. His failure to lead.

But if, as he said, they came after *everyone* who supported the royals, Pyotr was bound to be high on that list, especially once they learned he'd left Maria with one of the eggs. The very thought frightened him, especially when he realized where they were going. The old barn where a number of royalists had been shot. "Are you going to tell them what I did?"

"Of course. Your fate is for the people to decide."

They were going to kill him.

Pyotr's hands shook and he tucked them at his side, stealing a glance at the man beside him, eyeing the pistol at his hip.

The wagon wheels hit a rut, jarring the vehicle and throwing him against the driver. He grabbed the gun and pushed away, pointing it.

The driver turned, trying to grab the weapon. "What—"

Pyotr fired.

The shot hit him in the chest. He fell to the side, letting loose the reins. Pyotr shoved him from his seat and he tumbled down to the ground. Grabbing the reins, he stopped the team, then turned them around, pausing beside the fallen man.

He looked up at Pyotr, his face turning gray. "Why?"

"Saving my life. And Maria Feodorovna's."

"They'll bury you right next to her. The moment they find you or anyone else with that treasure."

"They'll never find it." He shook the reins, then headed toward the castle. He knew of a hidden panel in the Amber Room. The Bolsheviks would have to disassemble the entire place to find it. Somehow, he'd get word to the Dowager Empress that she needed to leave, that they intended to kill her.

And maybe one day they could come back for the treasure.

II

BUENOS AIRES
DECEMBER 1947

There must be something we can do. We're not asking for much. I'll pay it back. Every cent."

The desperation that twelve-year-old Klaus Simon heard in his father's voice twisted at his heart and he edged closer to the kitchen door, straining to hear the conversation in the front room.

"Please, Ludwig," his father continued. "If you could find it within you to help us this once."

"Actually, there is something . . ." For several seconds, the only thing Klaus heard was the ticking of the kitchen clock behind him. Finally, his uncle said, "I'm in need of help during a short trip to Santiago. If you agree to my conditions, I'll make it worth your while."

"I'll do anything. Anything at all."

"Not you. Your boy."

Surprised, Klaus pressed his ear against the door. "I don't understand," his father said. "What would Klaus have to do?"

"Nothing much. More companion than anything else. These trips can be tedious."

"How long would he be gone?"

"A few days at the most. More important, we're willing to pay well."

A long stretch of silence followed before his father answered. "I don't know. Perhaps we'll find another way—"

Klaus pushed open the door, bursting into the room. "I can do it. I can."

His father's brow furrowed. "I told you to wait in the kitchen."

"I'm sorry," Klaus said, stealing a glance at his uncle. He barely remembered the man from when they'd lived with him in Germany. Only that his Uncle Ludwig Strassmair had argued with Klaus's mother when he'd brought notice that Klaus's older brother, Dietrich, had been killed in the war. Dietrich, apparently, was not fighting for Germany, as everyone thought, but for the resistance against Nazism. His mother never recovered from Dietrich's death—or the scandal— and after selling everything to buy them passage to Argentina, she'd cut off all contact with her brother. "Let me go. Please, Father."

Uncle Ludwig smiled at Klaus. "See? Even the boy is willing."

His father, however, was not so quick to agree. "Let me talk it over with him. I'll telephone to let you know my decision."

"*Danke.*"

His father waited until Uncle Ludwig drove off, then turned a troubled glance down the hall toward the bedroom where his wife slept. With a tired sigh, he looked at Klaus. "You heard what he said. It's only for a few days. To Chile and back."

"I heard." Klaus watched his father, trying to figure out what he wasn't telling him. "He only wants a companion. That doesn't sound too hard."

"There's something you should know . . ."

"What, Papa?" he asked when his father didn't continue.

Again, that sigh. This one more weary than the last. "Your uncle . . . He's a Nazi. As are his friends."

Hope fled at the realization that his mother would *never* allow this. It didn't matter that Dietrich had chosen to fight for the resistance, she blamed the Nazis for his death.

His father glanced down the hallway once more, then back at Klaus. "Still . . . the war is over. No need to tell her. *Or* your sister, who blabs everything."

"But—"

"It would break your mother's heart." He put his hands on Klaus's shoulders, looking him in the eye, giving a half smile. "If there was any other way, we would find it. Yes? But there isn't . . . You understand?"

Klaus understood all too well. He and his father could overlook the source of income if it bought the medicine his mother desperately needed. What did it matter if a few Nazis slipped into the country? And, as his father said, the war was over. Those men were simply Germans like him.

Besides, it was only for a few days.

Somehow, though, his mother must have overheard, because when he went to visit her, she tried to dissuade him. "I'm going to die anyway," she said from her sickbed. "What good will that money be then?"

"I won't let you," Klaus told her, trying not to see how frail she'd become. These days, she barely got out of bed.

"Dietrich had no choice, fighting against Hitler. We didn't leave soon enough. But I taught *you* to do what is right. In this, *you* have a choice."

"This is right. For you."

She said nothing, merely closed her eyes and drifted off to sleep.

That night, when he went to say good-bye, he thought she was still asleep. But when he turned to leave, she opened her eyes. "Klaus . . ."

He came into the room, sitting on the edge of her bed.

She reached out, took his hand in hers, her grasp weak, her skin cool. "Promise me . . ."

"Promise what?" he asked, having to lean close to hear.

"Follow your heart . . ." She reached up, touched his chest, then lowered her hand, closing her eyes. "Dietrich . . ." Maybe she was hallucinating, seeing his dead brother instead of him. Thinking she'd fallen asleep once more, he started to rise. But she opened her eyes, her soft smile melting his heart. "Do that, Klaus . . . You'll be rewarded . . . Promise me?"

"I promise," he said, wondering if she even had two days to live. What if she died before he returned . . . ?

No. He refused to think such a thing. He had to do this. If he didn't get the medicine, she would die.

With a heavy heart, he leaned down, kissed her forehead, seeing that she'd fallen asleep again. "I love you," he whispered, then left with his Uncle Ludwig Strassmair to Buenos Aires.

"HERR STRASSMAIR. Good. You're here. Come in. Come in."

Klaus, his uncle's suitcase in hand, was about to follow him into the office when he thought he heard something behind them. He stopped and looked down the darkened hallway. The wind, he decided, then trailed his uncle into the office, where Herr Heinrich, a gray-haired man in a military-style jacket, sat behind a battered wooden desk, his hand lying atop a brown folder. A blond-haired woman about the age of Klaus's uncle, mid-forties, stood behind him. She eyed Klaus. "This is the boy?"

"Klaus," Ludwig said. "My sister's son. Good German stock." He took the case from Klaus, then guided him to the door. "Wait outside. We'll be just a few minutes."

Klaus walked into the hallway, remembering his father's warning to mind his own business. But Ludwig had left the door open, and he couldn't help overhearing the conversation.

"Were you followed?" Herr Heinrich asked.

"No," Ludwig replied. "I was very careful."

Klaus glanced down the darkened hall, suddenly worried about that noise he'd heard when they'd entered. What if they *had* been followed? He edged closer to the open door, wondering if he should say something.

"So," Ludwig said, "we're proceeding?"

"We are. But first I want to see what you've brought before it's all sold. Open it."

A moment later, Klaus heard Herr Heinrich give a low whistle, while the woman said, "Amazing. I have only heard tales of their magnificence."

Unable to resist, Klaus peered through the crack in the door. Herr Heinrich held a bejeweled, egg-shaped object. The green iridescence reminded Klaus of a small jade pendant his mother used to wear. Gold filigree vines wrapped around the egg, and diamonds sparkled along the vines like bright flowers. "Which one do I have?" Heinrich asked, turning the piece back and forth, the light catching on the diamonds.

"This," his uncle said, "is the Empire Nephrite Egg."

"How many eggs do you have?"

"Only three. But also several other chests that Maria Feodorovna managed to smuggle out of Russia when she fled to the Crimea. One contains many of the crown jewels belonging to the Dowager Empress, the others are filled with hundreds of loose diamonds, precious stones, and gold. It's clear that she paid well for the release of her son and his family."

"And yet the Bolsheviks killed them anyway," Herr Heinrich said. "Rather fitting that we're using the Romanov Ransom to fund our strike against Russia." He turned the egg about in his hands, the diamonds glinting in the overhead light. "A shame your men couldn't have gotten the Amber Room as well. A sight to behold."

"Hard to play refugee while smuggling something that size. These were difficult enough to get out of Germany without leaving a trail."

"And that pilot? I heard he was working with the Allied Forces."

"Lieutenant Lambrecht?"

"Yes. What if he talks? He could lead them right to us."

"Unfortunately for him, he's dead. My men sabotaged his plane. The last word was that it crashed somewhere in Morocco."

"What if someone finds the plane? Our plans—"

"—are in code. By the time someone does find them—assuming they ever do—we'll be in Santiago, setting everything in motion. It'll be too late."

Klaus had no idea what they were talking about, nor did he want to know. As he started to back away from the door, Herr Heinrich looked up and saw him staring. "What's this? You! Come here."

He froze.

Ludwig turned, saw him, then gave a sharp nod. "Klaus!"

He entered, worried what his uncle would do, when his glance strayed to the egg, even more beautiful up close. "I didn't mean to see. I just—"

The woman laughed. "You want to hold it?"

Klaus shook his head, afraid he'd drop it.

Herr Heinrich handed the egg to Ludwig, who wrapped it in a square of gray wool cloth.

"Beautiful, isn't it?" the woman said.

Klaus nodded, unable to look away, as Uncle Ludwig carefully returned the egg to its case. He saw two more egg-shaped forms beneath their wool wrapping.

"Fabergé," she said, though the name meant nothing to Klaus. "Do you know what they're for? Why you're taking them to Chile?"

He shook his head. He only knew he was to dress warm because they were flying over the Andes Mountains. And that the money he would make would keep his mother alive. "No, fräulein."

"To bring in the Fourth Reich—"

"Greta!" Herr Heinrich started to rise.

Ludwig, clearly upset over the interruptions, or perhaps Greta's revelation, snapped the case shut. "We should go. The hour grows late, and our plane awaits. You have the papers?"

"Of course," Herr Heinrich said, sliding them from the folder. Ludwig was reading the pages when Heinrich's phone rang. He answered, listened, then said, "Yes. He's right here." Heinrich held the phone toward Uncle Ludwig. "For you."

Ludwig set the papers on top of the suitcase. As he took the phone, his coat brushed the topmost page onto the floor.

It landed at Klaus's feet and he reached down to pick it up, seeing the words *Unternehmen Werwolf* at the top. Before he got past the first lines, trying to figure out what Operation Werewolf was about, Greta took the paper from him, setting it facedown on the stack.

"Hold on," Ludwig said into the phone. He covered the mouthpiece. "Greta, I'll meet you at the car. Take the boy and close the door."

The woman put her hand on Klaus's shoulder, guiding him into the hallway. "Come with me, Klaus."

He followed Greta outside, where Ludwig's sleek black Mercedes sedan gleamed beneath the bright moon. As she led him to the car, he glanced back toward the office, thinking of the papers that Herr Heinrich had given to his uncle. His father might be willing to overlook Uncle Ludwig's past, but Klaus didn't think he'd turn a blind eye to reviving the Nazi Party and starting the Fourth Reich. His mother, he knew, would be horrified.

She'd want him to tell his uncle that he couldn't go with him. Especially after what he'd read on that document.

"*. . . blame the Americans for a bomb strike on Russia . . .*"

Surely his father would understand why he couldn't go?

Someone shouted as the office door burst open. Ludwig raced out, suitcase in one hand, gun in the other. "Get in the car!"

A shot split the air, and Ludwig turned, firing into the doorway. *Crack! Crack!*

Klaus froze. Uncle Ludwig ran to the driver's side, shot twice more, then threw the suitcase in. "Hurry!"

Greta pushed Klaus toward the car. "Get in."

He jumped into the back, Greta the front, as Uncle Ludwig started the car, cursing as the engine sputtered, then kicked in.

The vehicle sped off, making a sharp turn, throwing Klaus against the door.

Heart thudding in his chest, he finally dared a look, seeing nothing but a cloud of dust behind them. "What happened?" he asked. "Why were they shooting at you?"

Several seconds passed before his uncle responded. "Robbers. After the treasure. They came in from the back as I was leaving."

Greta said, "Herr Heinrich?"

"Dead. They killed him."

"What about the papers?" she asked.

"In the suitcase."

"Good," she replied. "If they found those—"

"Enough!" Uncle Ludwig looked at Klaus in the rearview mirror, then back at the road.

"Take me home," Klaus said, his voice cracking. "I don't want to do this."

"No," Uncle Ludwig snapped, driving even faster. "Too late."

"I—I don't understand. Why do you need me?"

Greta answered. "Because no one looks twice at a man and woman with their son."

The only reason that would make sense is if they knew they were being watched. They were using him as a prop.

Klaus wondered what Dietrich would do if he were in this position. Was this why he'd died? Surely it was none of Klaus's business. Besides, he was only twelve.

Follow your heart . . .

In his heart, he knew that his mother would choose death rather than allow the Nazis to come back into power. And if his presence made it easier for his uncle to succeed?

He knew the answer.

Keeping an eye on the back of his uncle's head, he edged his hand toward the door. As soon as the car slowed for a turn, he threw the door open, jumped out, tumbling into the street. Ignoring the pain, he scrambled to his feet, then ran. Tires screeched as his uncle slammed on the brakes, bringing the car to a stop.

"Klaus!"

He didn't turn, just barreled on. There was a light in the building at the corner, and he darted toward it, seeing an open door. Music drifted out—an Italian folk song—along with loud voices and laughter. "Help!" he screamed. "Please! Someone help me!"

He reached the doorway just as his uncle grabbed him by the shoulder. "Klaus!"

"Help me!" he said, trying to pull free.

A man, holding a wine bottle, looked out at them.

"*Mio figlio*," his uncle said.

The man nodded.

"No!" Klaus shouted as his uncle dragged him away. "No *mio figlio*! I'm not his son! I'm *not*!"

"Shut up!" Uncle Ludwig backhanded him across the face. "Do that again and I'll *kill* you. Understand?"

Pain mixed with terror as he read the anger in his uncle's eyes. Klaus glanced toward the bar. The man who'd come to the door lifted the wine bottle to his mouth and took a long drink, then walked away. The street was empty, dark, and Klaus was utterly alone. He looked at his uncle and silently nodded.

"Good," Ludwig said, digging his fingers into Klaus's arm, holding tight. "Now, walk quietly back to the car. Not a word."

Heart racing, Klaus nodded again. Somehow, he'd find a way out of this. For Dietrich. For his mother.

"Get in," his uncle ordered when they reached the car.

The woman turned toward him as he slid into the backseat. "You shouldn't run, Klaus. It's only for a few days. And we *know* where you live."

After they arrived at the airstrip, his fear grew as they loaded the chests from the trunk into the hold, then boarded the four-engine Avro Lancastrian, Uncle Ludwig not letting go of the suitcase. The plane had been used as a bomber during the war, later imported to Argentina and converted for passenger use. Although there were nine seats, single file, there were only five passengers. His uncle directed Klaus to sit, then took the seat in front of him, setting the case with the eggs and the Operation Werewolf papers on the floor beside him.

Such an ordinary suitcase . . .

What was in it was anything but ordinary, Klaus thought as someone shouted from outside the plane.

There was a commotion at the door, and he turned, saw a man, wearing a tan overcoat, enter.

"Sorry," the man said, out of breath. "Didn't mean to hold up everyone. Joe Schmidt," he said by way of introduction. He spoke perfect German, but the accent was something Klaus couldn't place. There was a sheen of perspiration on Schmidt's brow, and he reached up, wiped it with the back of his hand. Winded, he stood there a moment, looked around, his gaze catching on Klaus, and then his uncle, before taking the seat just behind Klaus.

Once the door was shut, the engines started, and the plane moved down the runway. Klaus gripped the edge of his seat as they lifted off. He closed his eyes, trying to take even breaths. He was scared. Part of his fear came from the fact that he'd never been in a plane before. He looked down at that suitcase, thinking about what Greta had said about the Fourth Reich, the papers and the cases of jewels his uncle was carrying, and the men shooting at them as they fled. And then there was Greta's comment about needing Klaus with them. To keep from being noticed.

Who would be watching them?

Something made him look back at the man who'd boarded last. Joe Schmidt. Their gazes met. The man gave a slight nod, and Klaus turned away. Somehow, over the roar of the engines, he fell into a fitful sleep.

Something jarred him awake. Klaus opened his eyes, confused by his surroundings. He looked around, then behind him as he felt his seat shudder and saw that Joe Schmidt had Uncle Ludwig's suitcase. When the man realized he'd been caught, he raised his finger to his lips.

They *were* being watched. His heart sped up a little at the hope that someone was going to stop the Nazis. He dared a slight nod, wanting to reassure the man that he wasn't about to tell, and he glanced toward his uncle's seat, noticing his head tilted to the side. Sleeping. Or so he thought until Ludwig dropped his hand down toward the floor where the suitcase had been, his fingers reaching at nothing. He jumped from his seat, looking around, frantic. The moment he saw Schmidt with his suitcase, he lunged.

Schmidt shoved the case upward. His uncle blocked it with his arm, then slammed his right fist into Schmidt's jaw. Schmidt grabbed Ludwig by his shoulders, pulling down as he brought up his knee.

Ludwig staggered back, then reached beneath his coat, drawing his gun. Klaus turned toward the other passengers, willing them to get up and help, but they cowered in their seats. Only Greta stood, gripping Klaus by his arm. He looked back as Schmidt threw himself at Ludwig, ramming him with all his weight. The two men tripped over the suitcase, crashing to the floor. The gun flew from Ludwig's grasp, landing near Klaus. Greta pushed him aside. She grabbed the gun while Ludwig overpowered the man, pummeling at his face until he lost consciousness. "Kill him!" Greta said.

His uncle pulled a knife from his boot. In a flash, he rammed it beneath the man's sternum.

Klaus stared in shock at the growing red stain on Schmidt's white shirt. His stomach roiled with nausea, and he took several deep breaths trying to calm it. "Why . . . ?"

Greta must have heard him over the roar of the engines. "He's a spy sent to stop us."

Turbulence jolted the plane, throwing Klaus and Greta against the seats. She dropped the gun as she tried to break her fall. Klaus grabbed it, his hand shaking as he pointed it at her.

She tried to stand, grabbing for the gun, but he shoved her back into the seat. She reached for him. "Klaus. You don't want to do this."

Ludwig's brows went up a fraction when he realized that Klaus had the gun.

"Give me the gun, Klaus . . ." Uncle Ludwig took a step forward. "It's over now. There's no reason to fight."

Tears clouded Klaus's vision as he backed away. "I'll shoot you."

"It won't do any good," his uncle said. He glanced at Greta, giving her a sharp nod.

She stood, taking a step toward Klaus. He pointed the gun at her and she stopped.

His uncle moved to her side. "When this plane lands, those papers *will* be delivered. But if you help me get them there, you'll be rewarded. You *and* your father will have all the money you need. Think of your sister."

Klaus blinked away the tears, seeing the dead man, wondering if it was worth dying for . . . Was this how his brother died?

"Klaus . . ." Uncle Ludwig held out his hand. "Your mother wouldn't want anything to happen to you. Give me the gun."

Follow your heart . . . Do that . . . You'll be rewarded. Promise me . . .

His mother's voice sounded so clear in his head. Heart beating, he backed away from them, turning the gun toward the two passengers who tried to stop him. "Get out of my way!" he shouted as he continued backing up until he bumped into the ladder that led up to the cockpit.

"Klaus!" Uncle Ludwig yelled. "Get over here!"

He kept the gun pointed at them. "Stay away," he said, grabbing at the ladder, climbing with one hand, as he kept an eye on them. He poked his head into the cockpit, saw the pilot at the controls, either unaware of what had transpired at the back of the plane or too busy trying to fly it to worry.

Klaus took a deep breath, looking down at his uncle.

"No!" Ludwig yelled, running forward. "Stop him!"

Someone grabbed Klaus's leg as he swung around. Too late. He shot the pilot. The man slumped over, and the plane jolted. Klaus fell into the cockpit. The black sky turned white as they spiraled toward the snowy mountainside, the roar of engines drowning out the screams.

In those few moments, Klaus's last thought was not of death but of his mother.

And that he would see her again very soon.

1

To the left!"

"Copy that. Moving to the left. Five . . . four . . ."

The helicopter hovered near the sheer rock face, the tethered basket swinging from the cable, as one of the rescuers radioed, "Don't come any closer. You're one-zero from the wall."

"Copy that."

Sam Fargo watched as the two search-and-rescue volunteers, a man and woman, both wearing khaki uniforms and yellow helmets, guided the helicopter basket closer to where his wife, Remi, lay on an outcropping of rock, her left leg stabilized with a makeshift splint. The turbulence from the rotors whipped her auburn hair about her face, her green eyes tearing up from all the dirt blowing around. The man glanced up at the hovering helicopter. "We got it!" he radioed.

Sam took note of every move they made, resisting the urge to step in and take over. And even though he knew his wife was in good hands, it was difficult to stand there and do nothing. Within a few minutes, they had her secured in the basket, then stood back as she was lifted from the mountainside. No sooner was she safely on her way than his phone rang. He wanted to ignore it, but when he saw it was Selma Wondrash, the head of his and Remi's research team, he answered. "Selma."

"How's Mrs. Fargo?"

"Doing better than the rest of us. She at least gets to ride out of here. The rest of us have to climb."

"You can always volunteer to be the victim next time," she said, then got right to the point. "You recall my cousin's nephews you and Mrs. Fargo were backing for that documentary they were making on the ratlines?"

Because he and Remi sponsored so many educational and archaeological ventures through the Fargo Foundation, the charitable organization that they had founded, he sometimes lost track of who they were funding. In this case, though, being a World War II history buff, he distinctly recalled the young men and their project, a documentary on the ratline—a system of escape routes used by the Nazis and Fascists who fled Europe after the war. Even so, it took him a moment to bring up their names. "Karl and Brand. I remember. Why?"

"Their uncle hasn't been able to get in touch with them for a couple of days. He's worried. Especially after getting an odd message on his voice mail."

"Any idea what it was?"

"Something about them finding a lost plane in Morocco, and people were after them. He can't get any help from the authorities, because the boys didn't register with the consulate, and no one seems to know where they are. I told him that you might be able to pull some strings and get someone to look into it. I know you and Remi have a date tonight, but—"

"Your family's our family," he said, grabbing his backpack from the ground and slinging it over his shoulder. "Have our plane ready to go. As soon as Remi and I get home, we'll pack and head to the airport."

SAM AND REMI FARGO were not the usual multimillionaires content to rest on the laurels of good business decisions that had netted them more money than they could spend in several lifetimes. Sam had earned an engineering degree from Caltech, spent seven years at DARPA, the Defense Advanced Research Projects Agency, then left to start his own company, where he'd made a fortune developing a number of inventions used by the military and intelligence agencies. Remi, an anthropologist and historian with a focus on ancient trade routes, graduated from Boston College. Her background came in handy during the pursuit of their particular passion, searching for lost treasures around the world. It also helped that she had a near-photographic memory, was proficient in several languages, and was a world-class sharpshooter when it came to firearms. As many scrapes as they'd been in over the years, there was no one Sam would rather have as his partner than Remi.

There was, however, one slight issue about leaving tonight. It happened to be the anniversary of the day they met at the Lighthouse Cafe, a jazz bistro in Hermosa Beach. To them, it was even more important than their wedding anniversary, and they honored it each year by having a date at the very table where they'd spent their first evening talking the night away.

Remi was waiting for Sam at the car when he finally got there after the climb up the cliffside with the volunteers.

"Took you long enough," she said, looking at her watch. "We're going to get stuck in commuter traffic if we don't hit the road soon."

Sam tossed his climbing gear into the back of their Range Rover.

"Any chance you wouldn't mind a slight change of plans . . . ?" He left the question hanging, noting the disappointment on her face.

"We've never missed date night at the Lighthouse."

"Maybe we could mix it up a bit. A week of date nights somewhere else? Like Morocco?" Before she had a chance to respond, he added, "Selma's family might be in trouble."

"I love date night in Morocco."

2

It was late morning, the bright sun shining on the snow-peaked Atlas Mountains in the distance, when Sam and Remi landed in Marrakesh. They rented a black four-wheel-drive Toyota Prado, then drove out to meet Selma's cousin Albert Hoffler, who was waiting in front of the hotel as they pulled up.

"He looks like Selma," Remi said as Sam turned the key fob over to the valet. "At least in the eyes."

In fact, he was also about the same age as Selma, in his fifties, with brown hair, and a neatly trimmed beard and mustache flecked with gray. His smile seemed strained—understandable, considering the circumstances. "Mr. and Mrs. Fargo. I can't thank you enough for flying all the way out here."

"Please. It's Sam and Remi. Save the formalities for Selma," Sam said, shaking his hand.

"Cousin Selma's been that way her whole life." His smile was fleeting, and he gave a tired sigh. "We can talk over lunch. I've reserved us a table."

He led them through the hotel's spacious courtyard lobby, with a fountain and reflecting pool in the center. The restaurant was on the far side, the tables overlooking the pool. When they were seated, he said, "How much has Selma told you?"

Sam replied, "Something about a voice mail you received while the boys were here working on the documentary. And that you haven't gotten much cooperation from the authorities."

"It's not that they're *not* cooperating, more that they have nothing to go on. The truth is, they're not officially missing yet, since they're not due back for a day or so. But after that voice mail . . ."

"What can you tell us?" Sam asked.

"They landed here after finishing up in Spain, documenting the lines of escape taken by some high-ranking Nazi officers who were fleeing to South America. I believe this is the project you were funding. They were looking for shipping records in Casablanca but got sidetracked after hearing a legend about a Nazi pilot rescued after the war. Apparently, he'd parachuted from the plane before it crashed, wandered the desert for days, and was rambling on about a map."

Sam noticed Remi perk up at the mention. Maps intrigued her. "What was it of?" she asked.

"That's just it. Nobody knows if the story's even real. The boys thought it might be a map of the ratline route. Naturally, they wanted it for their documentary. They left Casablanca for Marrakesh, and, from there, to a few villages located below the Atlas Mountains, to determine where the legend originated from and who knew of it. The last I heard, they were following a very promising lead on locating the plane. I've called their cell phones but it goes straight to voice mail, and they haven't called back. The hotel staff here has been very gracious, letting me into their room to look for anything that might help. Their suitcases, extra cameras and equipment are there, but their backpacks and climbing gear are gone. They're excellent climbers." He stopped to thank the waiter who poured water infused with mint leaves into their glasses. When they were alone again, he said, "Their rooms are booked until the end of the week, and the hotel manager feels that if they don't return by then, he would be more concerned. They told him they were going to be gone for a while."

"How long ago was this?" Sam asked.

"He thinks about five days. I know what you're thinking. They said they were going to be gone. But if you'd heard that message . . ."

"Do you have it?"

"I can play it for you. I think their reception was poor. Some of it cuts out. It's in German, though."

"Remi speaks German."

He took out his cell phone, pulled up the voice mail message, then hit PLAY, laying it on the table.

They leaned in close to listen. Remi asked him to play it a second time so that she could write it down for Sam. "We found it! The plane! At camel . . . not sure. Shooting at . . . Maybe someone . . . out there . . . days."

"You hear the excitement?" Albert asked her.

"Or panic," Remi said.

"Panic. That's what I meant. And why I came. With the spotty reception, who knows what really happened."

Sam asked, "When did this message come in?"

"Maybe two days after they left the hotel for the trip to the mountains." He picked up the phone, giving a ragged sigh. "That's the last I heard from them." He looked away a moment, his gaze drifting to the lobby. Suddenly, he stiffened. "That's who they were with! I'm sure of it!"

"What?"

He pointed through the potted palms into the lobby. "That man in the blue shirt talking to the girl at the desk." Albert accessed the pictures on his phone and showed them a photo of three young men sitting on a rough-hewn wooden bench, each lifting a beer mug in a toast. "My nephews," he said, pointing to the men seated on the right. Sam eyed the photo, noting the two boys, one wearing a red jacket, both with sun-streaked brown hair and brown eyes. "This man on the left," Albert said. "That's who they hired to take them out to the Berber Villages."

Sam compared the photo to the dark-haired man at the desk. "Definitely him. Let's find out what he knows."

The three got up and walked toward the desk. When the man saw them heading toward him, he bolted out the doors.

3

Sam gave chase. Remi was right behind him, ignoring the curious stares of the other guests milling about the lobby. Sam ran to the right, across the cobbled drive. The man darted around the corner, then down a side street, racing toward a red Renault as he dug the key from his pocket. He held out the key, and the doors beeped as the car unlocked. Just as he opened the door, Sam caught up to him, grabbing the back of his shirt, then swinging him around, slamming him against the car.

"Please!" the man said in French. "I don't know anything."

Sam shot his hand up to the man's neck, gripping it. "You speak English?"

He nodded. "Some."

"Your name?"

"Z—Zakaria."

"Zakaria. We're looking for Karl and Brand Hoffler."

"I—I've only spoken to them on the phone."

"We have a picture that says otherwise."

"A very old picture. I swear, I don't know anything."

Remi wandered closer to the faded-red Renault. She peered into the window as Sam asked, "You're saying you talked to them by phone, but you never met with either of them on this trip?"

"I think they took up with another guide. They didn't tell me who. Maybe they didn't want to hurt my feelings. I don't know."

Sam eyed the twists of cables on the backseat, turning back toward Zakaria. "What do you know about audiovisual equipment?" he asked.

"Just the camera on my cell phone."

"Then why do you have a bundle of AV cords in the back of your car?"

A sheen of perspiration appeared on Zakaria's brow as he shook his head. "I—I don't know."

Sam leaned into him, pressing his fingers into his neck. "Maybe you need a little help with your memory. Where are they?"

His eyes widened in fear. "I don't know! I swear!"

"We don't like being lied to," Sam said. "Not when it comes to our family being endangered." He glanced at Remi. "In French, in case there's any question."

The young man's gaze shifted to Remi's as she translated. When she finished, Sam added, "And they're making a film that we're paying for. If anything happens to them—"

"Wait. *You* are the Fargos?"

Sam loosened his grip on Zakaria's neck. "You know who we are?"

He nodded, then his gaze caught on Albert. "Who's that?"

"Their uncle."

The young man closed his eyes, sinking down as though suddenly relieved. "Please. You have to understand. I only wanted to protect them."

"From who?" Sam asked, finally letting him go and stepping back.

Zakaria reached up, rubbing his neck, trying to swallow. "I don't know. They called me and said they were being chased. Someone was shooting at them, but they got away. They thought it was because of their search for the plane."

"How long ago was that?"

"About four days ago."

"They're not back?"

"That's what I came here to find out. I was hoping they'd been back by now. Or called. We expect them anytime."

"We?"

"Durin Kahrs. A friend of theirs from school in Germany. He was with them when they took off to look for the plane. He came back early, and when I told him what happened, that they were shot at, he warned me not to talk to anyone. He worried about someone trying to find them. He thinks someone doesn't want them to find the plane."

"They're okay?" Albert asked.

"They were when I talked to them."

"Maybe," Sam said, "you should start at the beginning."

He nodded, looking at each of them, in turn, as though to assure himself they weren't about to attack him further. "They hired me to act as a guide, to take them out to some of the remote villages, because they'd heard the story about this downed World War Two pilot dragging his parachute through the desert."

"How'd they get your name?" Sam asked.

"I wrote an article about the pilot that was published in the university paper when I was a student. They found a reference to it on the internet and looked me up."

"There had to have been a lot of soldiers traipsing around the continent after the war," Sam said. "What makes this story stand out?"

"The legend is that the pilot offered a great reward if someone could find his downed plane and take him to it. But he died, and the plane was never found. Naturally, everyone assumed it must contain gold stolen during the war. But after talking with the villagers, it seems more likely that the story was embellished over the years. None of them mentioned gold."

"And no one's looked since?"

"Of course they have. There are even groups that advertise it as the highlight of their tour."

"I have a question," Remi said. "How is it that Karl and Brand found it when no one else could?"

"I think because their interest differed from everyone else's," he said. "Everyone else, without exception, wanted only to know where the plane was located because they hoped to find gold. The villagers were always very happy to point them in the right direction. Of course the direction varied, depending on which villager they happened to ask. What all these people failed to realize was that anyone who saw the pilot is no longer alive. I think that's why the directions varied so greatly." He glanced toward Albert, then back at Sam, saying, "Unlike everyone who came before them, Karl and Brand weren't interested in the plane right off. They were thinking documentary. Filming candid responses. They're the first to ask if anyone was related to the villagers who actually found the pilot or those who spoke to him."

"They were filming?" Sam asked.

He nodded. "They wanted to document how the legend was passed down from generation to generation. But later, when they went through the film footage, they realized that these particular villagers spoke of a specific place in the upper desert mountains where the pilot was found. One villager even produced the parachute. And so they thought that it was worth pursuing." He gave a tired shrug. "No one thought they'd find it, but they did."

"Where is this place?" Sam asked.

"The villagers called it Camel Rock. It's somewhere up in the Atlas Mountains."

"Can you take us?"

"That's just it, I don't know where it is. I wasn't with them when they found it. But I think Durin went out with them, at some point. He might be able to show you."

"How do we get in touch with him?"

Zakaria tried calling. "It goes right to voice mail. He's usually with his sister. She's very sick. Cancer. But he's supposed to call me this evening when he returns from visiting her. I'll set up a meeting."

They exchanged numbers, Zakaria telling them he'd telephone as soon as he heard anything at all. As promised, he called later that afternoon, saying that Durin would meet them in the main square at the *medina* that night at seven.

4

The scent of grilled meat and diesel fuel permeated the air as Sam and Remi neared the open-air market. Soon, the faded orange-red clay buildings on either side of the narrow cobblestone streets were filled with the *souk* and its covered stalls with vendors hawking their wares, everything from clothing, jewelry, and baskets to the finest spices. Motorbikes sped past, the whir of their engines mixing with the constant beat of drums and *rhaita* flutes as snake charmers played for their cobras, trying to lure an audience. In the main square, Sam expertly stepped between Remi and a vendor who tried to put a snake around her shoulders. "Trust me," he told the man. "She's not interested."

"Playing hero, Fargo?" Remi asked as they continued on, avoiding a woman who tried to grab her hand, offering to paint henna on it.

"If he knew your aversion to snakes—and how quick you are with a knife—I doubt he'd be so eager to put one near you." They stopped halfway down the row of shops facing the square, taking a look around. "He did say meet by this café?"

"There he is," Remi said, nodding in the opposite direction.

Zakaria Koury saw them and waved as they approached. "Mr. and Mrs. Fargo," he said, then gave a wide smile. Apparently, he'd forgiven Sam for roughing him up. "You found me. Good."

Sam shook hands with him. "Where's Durin?"

"He's on his way. First, some refreshment."

He drew them past a stall with skewers of meat and vegetables set out to another that served drinks, then, without waiting, said something in Arabic to the vendor, who indicated they should sit at the table along one side. "Better this way," Zakaria said quietly. "In case someone's watching. Right now, we're just a few tourists stopping for coffee. Durin is worried about being followed."

Sam took a casual look around. No one seemed to be paying them the least bit of attention. "Why would anyone be watching?"

"Durin thinks that Karl and Brand aren't the only parties interested in this downed plane. He tells me there have been—how should I say it?—some less than savory inquiries."

"Did he say who?"

"No. And he wasn't happy that I'd talked to you after he told me *not* to talk to anyone. It wasn't until I explained that you were funding Karl and Brand's project that he relaxed enough to agree to meet with you. He should be here anytime."

"You think he'll agree to take us out to the site where he last saw Brand and Karl?" Sam asked.

"I don't see why not," he said, as someone placed cups of coffee on the table in front of them. "He says he tried to talk Karl and Brand from going out alone. Even if they did find it, considering how long that plane's been up there, and all the weather it's endured, he doubts there's much left to find."

Their strong coffee nearly finished, Zakaria nodded out toward the open square. "There he is now."

Sam saw a tall blond man about the same age as Zakaria, mid-twenties, smoking a cigarette as he walked. He looked over his shoulder several times as though looking for a tail. When he saw Zakaria, he seemed to relax, slowing his pace.

Sam paid for the coffee, and the three joined him.

"At last," Durin said as Zakaria made the introductions. He dropped his cigarette, grinding it out with his foot. "Maybe my imagination is getting the best of me. Every person I saw seemed to be watching me."

"I warned the Fargos that you were worried about being followed."

"It's true," Durin said, taking another look around. "I hope I'm wrong, but it's best to be careful."

Sam checked the area he'd seen Durin walking from, his gaze catching on a dark-haired man in a gray-striped *djellaba*, who looked in their direction as he walked past. He met up with another man in similar garb, and both continued on, never looking back. Though neither had done anything out of the ordinary, the first man's casual glance, then immediate disinterest, bothered Sam. "What about those two?" he asked Durin.

"Where?"

"Near the stall selling mint tea." Sam pointed, but by the time Durin focused in the right area, both men were lost in the crowd.

"Probably nothing. I'll keep an eye out," Durin said. "So what is it you're here for?"

"Zakaria tells me you might be willing to escort us out to the site?"

"In the Atlas Mountains, nothing is easy to get to. I can at least take you to where I last saw them. I had to leave early. My sister's been ill, and I had made plans to be with her."

"How long do you think it'll take to get where Brand and Karl thought the plane might be?" Sam asked.

"One, maybe two days. A deep gorge to get across, and steep terrain on the other side of it."

"What about a helicopter?" Remi asked.

"No place to land. Trust me. We looked at every possibility. The best-case scenario is to drive out as far as we can, then go the rest of the way on foot. I have to warn you, though. It's dangerous. A lot of bandits roam the upper desert. I don't think it's a good idea—"

"How soon can we leave?" Sam asked.

"First thing in the morning, if you have a car with four-wheel drive. You can follow me. Once there, I can point you in the right direction. Beyond that, you're on your own. If I didn't have to get back to my sister, I'd take you all the way."

"Don't worry about it. We'll make it work."

"Good. You're staying at the same hotel as Brand and Karl?"

"We are."

"I'll meet you there before sunrise." He looked at Zakaria. "How about you?"

"I'll be there."

Durin eyed Sam. "You realize the weather's taking a turn for the worse? Series of storms lined up."

"All the more reason." Sam had checked the weather forecast as they were flying in. Their only window of opportunity was early tomorrow or late the next day, and he wasn't about to wait. "See you in the morning."

After he left, Zakaria said, "I'll walk you to the gate." They started in that direction, weaving their way through the crowd. "Keep your hands close, Mrs. Fargo. The ladies who do henna tattoos are sometimes aggressive."

"So we found out," she said.

There was a commotion behind them, someone yelling, and then a loud crash. They turned to see a cart knocked over, small trinkets and cheap jewelry spilling to the ground, the vendor, shaking his fist, shouting. Someone pushed Remi and she stumbled.

"Sam! My purse!"

He glanced back just as a man raced off with Remi's handbag tucked beneath his arm.

5

S tay with Zakaria," Sam called, taking off after the thief. He
pushed through a group of tourists posing for pictures with a
tame monkey, then past a stall selling fresh orange juice.

The thief darted into a narrow alley, barreling over anyone who
got in his way. Soon, the colorful *souk* and eager vendors hawking
their wares gave way to a maze of dark doorways and high walls, the
noise from the crowded marketplace fading in the distance. The only
sounds came from the thief's and Sam's footsteps, echoing through
the tunnel-like streets.

The man glanced behind him, saw Sam gaining, and quickened his
pace. He shot around a corner, jumping over a wooden crate filled
with empty burlap sacks. The alley twisted to the left, and he pulled
an empty garbage can out, swinging it around at Sam, who was midair
over the crate. Sam dodged the can as he landed, hearing it rattle down
the alley behind him. When he looked back, the thief was gone. Although he could hear the sound of running, the alley was empty. There
was only one direction the thief could have gone, but any number of
doorways.

Sam stopped and listened, trying to hear the footsteps, when someone laughed from a window above. He looked up, saw a boy and a girl, grade school age, looking down at him, their dark eyes alight with curiosity and amusement. One of them pointed, not down the alley but at an arched doorway about ten feet away. Sam walked up to it, and the boy nodded. Sam returned the nod.

The heavy wooden door hung on iron hinges, and when he pushed, it swung open, not to a house but to another alley. The thief, his chest heaving from exhaustion, was about twenty yards ahead, fishing through Remi's purse, pulling out the wallet and opening it. Recognition hit Sam as he realized this was one of the two men he'd seen following Durin. When the guy looked up and saw Sam, he dropped the purse, kept the wallet, and took off again.

Sam closed the distance, was nearly on him, when the thief suddenly turned and threw the wallet at Sam. The man stumbled as he turned back, and Sam pounced, slamming him to the ground. They rolled together, the thief trying to twist free. Sam held tight, using their momentum to swing the guy around, until Sam was back on top, vaguely aware that someone was running toward them. Sam drove his fist into the man's face. The thief lay there motionless, his stunned expression moving from Sam to someone just behind them. Sam grabbed the guy's shoulders, rolling away just as a club came crashing down, missing Sam and striking the ground.

Sam shoved the thief to the side just as his partner kicked at Sam's ribs. The blow knocked the breath from his lungs. Sam saw the man's boot coming at him again. He spun around, scissor-kicked, sweeping the guy's feet from beneath him. His attacker fell to the ground.

The first thief scrambled to his knees, lunging. Sam caught the glint of a knife arcing toward him. He blocked the blow. The thief swung again. Sam caught his arm, gripped the knife hand, twisting the weapon from his grasp. It clattered to the cobblestones as Sam swung, slamming his fist into the man's eye socket.

"Police!" someone shouted from the gate.

The thief dragged his partner to his feet, pulling him away.

They raced through the alley, and Sam jumped up, about to give chase, when he saw Remi and Zakaria coming through the gate.

No police. Regardless, their ruse worked. The thieves were gone.

Remi picked up her purse, then her wallet.

"Everything there?" Sam asked.

"Seems to be." She looked at Sam, her gaze sweeping over him from head to toe. "You okay?"

"Fine." Beyond the bruises likely to develop on his ribs and knees, his worst injury was a few scraped knuckles. "Had you given me a few more seconds, I might have won the round."

"Close enough, Fargo. Or did you forget we have an early day tomorrow?"

"Good point," he said, glancing down the street in the direction the thieves had fled. Tonight's events seemed entirely too coincidental. Durin being followed, and then the distraction in the marketplace moments before Remi's purse had been stolen. He examined the five-inch folding knife left behind by one of the thieves. Sharp, well-balanced, quality German carbon. Not the sort he'd expect a couple of Moroccan street thieves to be carrying. And, now that he thought about it, that was a pretty elaborate and deadly scheme to steal a purse.

Only one reason for all this that he could think of. Someone didn't want them to get out to that plane.

6

―――――

Rolfe Wernher slid a knife around the wine bottle seal, pausing when someone knocked on the door. He set the knife on the counter and rested his hand on the Glock next to it. It didn't matter that he was in his private suite of rooms on the fourth floor of his *riad* or that he had armed guards on each floor below should anyone breach the security of the first floor. In his business, preparation was always the key to staying alive.

"Come in," he called out, picking up the gun, keeping it at his side.

Gere Stellhorn, his eye swollen and a bruise forming, walked in. "You wanted to know as soon as we returned."

"I'll be right with you." Rolfe returned the gun to the counter, glancing out to the patio, where Tatiana Petrov waited. She either didn't hear the knock or she wasn't interested, her attention solely on the unparalleled view of the night lights below. Normally, he would've taken this meeting with Gere in his study on the second floor of his *riad*. But he wasn't about to leave so important a guest as Tatiana by herself. And so he finished opening the wine, poured two glasses, then carried one of them out to her.

"Forgive me, Tatiana," he said as he walked up.

A light breeze stirred at her long brown hair, which skimmed the back of her low-cut red dress, the fabric shimmering as she turned. Her opalescent blue eyes regarded him with mild curiosity.

It occurred to him in that moment that he'd never seen her smile, something he attributed to her Russian upbringing in a strict household. He held the glass toward her. "An unexpected business matter. It shouldn't take too long."

She took the glass. "The weather's lovely and the cityscape amazing. Take your time."

He glanced out, trying to see it through her eyes. The fourth-floor patio commanded a view of the entire city, the soft lights accentuating the stars above. He far preferred the vista during the day when he could see the snowcapped Atlas Mountains in the distance. That at least reminded him of his homes in Germany and Austria—and where he hoped to get back to very soon, once this business was concluded.

He left her and returned inside, leaving the patio doors open. Gere had not moved from the entry. Like Rolfe, Gere was German, though at the moment he looked more like a local Moroccan, with his wavy dark hair and the long, loose-fitting gray-striped *djellaba*.

"What happened to you?" Rolfe asked, giving a pointed glance to the injuries on the man's face.

"A run-in with someone that Durin met."

"So you were able to follow him after all. What'd you find out?"

"It appears he was telling the truth. Zakaria is with an American couple and plans to take them out to the plane."

Rolfe was careful not to show emotion. As one of the few people alive today who even knew what was really in that plane, he wasn't about to let someone else possess what he believed was rightfully his. He'd first learned of the plane's existence through his father, who'd learned about it through his. In fact, Rolfe's father had spent most of his adult life searching for it, only to finally give up, declaring its existence to be mere legend. The truth was, the man had been possessed by the hunt, allowing it to consume his mind and his fortune. Rolfe was not about to let that happen. After rebuilding that fortune, he'd been far more careful than his father, putting out feelers, and, yes, pursuing a few false leads, but never letting the search take over his life. Though Rolfe had spent far more than he'd anticipated, he wasn't about to end up like his father, broken and near penniless.

He glanced out toward the patio, saw that Tatiana was still absorbed in the view, then turned back to Gere. "This couple—you think *they* are somehow involved in looking for this plane?"

"We suspect so. Unfortunately, we couldn't get close enough to hear what they discussed without bringing undue attention."

"Apparently, you got close enough to meet up with someone's fist," Rolfe said.

"It was the only way we could think to find out who they were. We set up a ruse to steal the woman's purse to look at her identification."

"And what have you learned?"

"The woman is Remi Fargo. I heard her calling out to someone named Sam. We assume he's her husband." Gere held out a folded notepaper.

Rolfe took the sheet, reading the two names. "What do we know about them?"

"We're not sure yet. We've only just returned."

"Find out and get back to me."

"We will."

Rolfe set the paper on the table next to the gun. "Anything else?"

"Not yet. We'll know more tomorrow when we meet up with Durin."

"Call me as soon as you do."

After Gere left, Rolfe took his wineglass out to the balcony, where Tatiana waited, her back to him as she looked out toward the city.

He paused a moment to admire her. In her Christian Louboutin red stiletto heels, she stood nearly as tall as he. Her red silk dress draped softly over her lithe figure. She was exquisite. "How is your wine?"

She turned toward him, her expression calm. "Perfect," she said, lifting her glass in a toast. "To good fortune."

"Agreed." He touched the edge of his glass to hers.

She sipped, then turned her attention back to the cityscape. "That very bright area out there. What is it?"

"The marketplace. Some evening, perhaps, we can venture out there. The *medina* is quite a sight to behold."

"If I'm here that long." She turned, leaning back against the stone parapet, to look at him. "Tell me, Rolfe. Do you think this is *the* plane? The one you've been searching for all this time?"

Her question surprised him. "Why would you ask that?"

"Because your father was so obsessed with it. Why else would you be here, of all places?"

His father. Of course. "And why are you here, Tatiana?"

"Visiting one of my favorite German businessmen, of course." She swirled the red wine about in her glass, her expression softening. "If I'm not mistaken, you were just about to convince me why I should stay on here . . ."

"Why don't we discuss the matter over dinner," he said, guiding her to the patio table that had already been set.

A couple of hours later, when he walked her out, he saw Gere's note had fallen to the floor. The breeze must have swept it from the table.

Tatiana reached it before he did, leaning down to pick it up. She handed it to him. "Something to do with your impromptu business meeting at the start of our dinner?"

"Apparently, someone who's also interested in the plane."

"You'd better move fast, then."

"I intend to," he replied, guiding her to the door. After she left, he looked at the names written there.

Sam and Remi Fargo.

It wouldn't be the first time someone had disappeared from the face of the earth after getting in his way.

7

Having to make a last-minute trip to Marrakesh had not been on Tatiana's agenda, but there was little she could do once she'd gotten word that Rolfe had arrived and was very close to finding the plane. And so it was that she'd taken the first flight from Russia to meet with him. Getting him to invite her over for dinner was the easy part. Keeping him from discovering her interest in the plane while trying to find out what he knew? That had been a challenge.

She'd taken a calculated risk this evening, asking about the plane, but, in the end, it seemed the only way she could think to get the information as quickly as she needed. It surprised her, though, that Rolfe had given it up so easily, and she wondered if his undue interest made him prone to the same mistakes his father had made. For a man with so many successful criminal enterprises, Rolfe hadn't struck her as someone so careless as to leave a note such as that out in the open where anyone could see it. Then again, maybe that had more to do with her part in carefully nurturing a relationship with him over the last six months in order to keep tabs on his hunt for the missing courier pouch.

His loss, her gain, she thought after Rolfe's driver dropped her off. She took out her telephone and made a call the moment the car drove off.

"I'm back at the hotel now," she said, speaking Russian, as she walked through the lobby. "I think I stumbled across something that I wasn't meant to see. Two names. Remi Fargo. The other name is Sam, I assume same last name. I want to know everything on them as soon as possible."

"Has to be the American couple we saw them meeting with tonight when we followed Rolfe's men. They stole the woman's purse, no doubt to find out who she was. I'll get started on it. How'd the dinner go?"

"Flawless. Although he knows that I'm aware of his interest, I believe it will work to our advantage."

"You let him know you knew about the plane?"

"I felt it was necessary."

"And he didn't seem suspicious? Or even suspect that you're the other buyer that Durin Kahrs had contacted?"

"Not in the least." She glanced at the three clocks over the hotel's front desk, each giving a different time for that part of the world. Here, in Marrakesh, it was past midnight. "Keep me informed. I have a feeling that we can trust Durin Kahrs as much as we trust Rolfe. Not at all."

"On that we agree," he said, then bid her good night.

She dropped the phone into her purse and took the elevator up to her room. Finally, she thought, all this time searching was going to pay off.

8

Sam and Remi left before dawn the following morning. Rain wasn't expected until late in the afternoon, giving them some hope that they'd have a chance to find the Hoffler brothers before the height of the storm. And though Sam wanted to believe that Karl and Brand were merely running behind schedule and that nothing was wrong, between their frantic voice mail message, and then the theft of Remi's purse last night, his instinct told him that the best-case scenario was a rescue mission and the worst-case was a recovery mission. As much as he hoped for the former, he and Remi were prepared, the back of their Toyota four-wheel drive filled with climbing gear and a trauma kit, as they followed behind Durin and Zakaria in Durin's silver Nissan X-Trail.

The drive took them through the countryside, where the fields of cactus seemed at odds with the Atlas Mountains in the distance. Eventually, the desert landscape gave way to rolling foothills, which turned to craggy peaks and valleys before leveling off to a high-desert plateau. After several hours on the road, Durin slowed, then stopped on a road that paralleled a steep ravine to their right.

Sam pulled up behind him. He and Remi got out, joining Durin and Zakaria at the edge of the roadway. Durin lit a cigarette, though it took him a few tries as the wind whipped across the plateau. He nodded toward the mountains in the distance. "That's where they went."

Sam took his binoculars to have a look, but saw nothing on the other side except high-desert scrub. "Mind narrowing it down a bit?"

"Across the gorge. You see that rock that looks like a giant camel's head on the crest of that ridge?" Durin stepped closer to him, pointing. "Looks almost like it's balancing on the edge."

Sam saw an outcropping of rock that jutted up and out. Not quite a camel's head. More like stacked wedges of Swiss cheese. "Got it."

"That's what the boys were talking about. Something called Camel Rock. It's where they were heading when I left them here."

Sam adjusted his focus, noticing it looked more like a camel's head when it was blurry. He glanced over at Remi, who was searching for it with her own binoculars. "See it?"

She nodded.

He glanced at Zakaria. "We should probably get started."

Zakaria eyed the steep cliff leading down to the valley below and the steeper climb up the other side. "That's a long fall. You sure they went that way?"

"*Ja.*" Durin Kahrs used his cigarette to point out a possible path to their left. "Series of steep switchbacks. You can see the zigzag of a trail on this side leading down. That's the path that Karl and Brand took. I'd guess a day and a half to get there and back."

"Sure you don't want to go with us?" Zakaria asked.

"If my sister were better, I would." He looked at his watch. "I really have to get going. Good luck to you."

As Durin drove off, Sam peered through his binoculars following the route Durin said the brothers took. The trail seemed treacherous, the switchbacks steep in some places, with a sheer drop down to the ravine below. At least a several hours' trip to the bottom. Going up the other side didn't seem much better, and he turned his attention to the sheer rock wall below so-called Camel Rock. Durin was right. There didn't appear to be a direct route to the rock formation. The trail Durin pointed out would end up way above it. That left a lot of places that Brand and Karl could have fallen.

A movement near a boulder to the west of the site caught his eye as he panned the area. Mountain goat, he thought, trying to find it again until he spied something red on the rock below that. Adjusting the focus, he took a better look. "Wasn't one of Albert's nephews wearing a red jacket in the photo he showed us?"

Zakaria put his hands over his eyes, trying to see for himself. "Brand wore a red jacket. But if it's his, where are they?"

"That," Sam said, "is what we're going to find out." He studied the area from top to bottom. "For that jacket to be there, we at least know they made it to the other side."

Remi surveyed the area. "There's got to be a quicker way across this gorge than going down that trail."

"That's what I'm hoping for," he said, sweeping his binoculars across the far side. "Over there." He pointed in the opposite direction than the one Durin had indicated. "I think if we approach from the east instead, we can rappel down that rock wall and cut the time in half getting to the bottom of the gorge."

"Starting from where?" Remi asked.

"About a half mile from here. See those two trees below the crest near that outcropping of rock?"

She turned her binoculars in that direction. "Got it."

"Let's drive over for a closer look."

THE AREA WAS even farther from the road. There was about a fifteen-foot descent to the trees, where they could anchor. An easy rappel from there to the bottom would cut significant time from their journey. "This'll work."

"What about when we get to the other side?" Remi asked.

Sam pointed. "We could scale up that rock face to the ledge where the jacket is. Or close to it. There's a fairly even vertical crack running up from the bottom."

"You think we can get to the ledge?" she asked, lowering her binoculars.

"Possibly, but that's not what we're aiming for." He lifted his glasses, studying the crack line leading up the cliff.

She took another look, adjusting her focus. "What then?"

"If we climb past the height of the ledge and come in from above, we'll have a better view."

Zakaria stood near them. "What if they're not there?" he asked. "Maybe they've already started back."

They could only hope, but Sam doubted it. "If so, there should be some signs—assuming we can get there before the rain starts. We'll see if we can track their direction. If they're there, we should find them."

A solid plan, he thought, glancing over toward Zakaria, who looked a bit pale as they slid into their harnesses and buckled on their helmets. "You're sure you're going to be okay here by yourself?"

Zakaria nodded as he eyed the gear hanging from their harnesses. "I'm more worried about you. That way seems dangerous. And the storm is coming in much faster than anticipated."

"If they're hurt," Sam said, sliding his pack over his shoulders, "we need to get to them as soon as we can."

Zakaria gave a dubious glance toward the sheer rock wall on the other side of the gorge. "How will I know if I need to go get medical help?"

A good question, since they had no idea if they'd have cell coverage at the bottom of the gorge or on the other side. This side was sketchy, the signal strength depending on where they stood. Remi had also packed a satellite phone, but they'd have to be out in the open.

The last thing they wanted to do when time was of the essence was discover they had no way of calling for help.

"If," Sam said, raising his arms above his head, then crossing them into an X, "you see either of us doing this, it means we need medical assistance or help getting to them."

"And if you find them and they're okay?"

"You watch American football?"

"Touchdown!" Zakaria's eyes lit up as he raised both his arms over his head. A moment later, his expression turned serious. "Let's hope you score."

Sam tossed him the key fob, and Remi left him her extra pair of binoculars, before they started out. The dry red dirt crumbled beneath their feet as they made their way around the large boulders to the trees where they anchored their ropes. Just before they started down, Sam glanced back at Zakaria, and then the horizon, eyeing the dark clouds gathering in the distance.

Zakaria was right. The storm was coming in fast.

9

The gusting wind sent their ropes spinning, slamming them against the cliff face, making their descent even longer than anticipated. They reached the bottom, leaving the ropes in place for their return. Sheltered from the wind now that they were at the base of the ravine, they picked their way over scattered broken boulders and rocks down to the creek bed.

Thunder cracked in the distance as they hefted their packs, walked along the creek, when Sam pointed toward the edge of the water where a trail of waffle boot prints moved in the same direction. "Someone's been here recently."

"I'd feel better if there were two sets instead of just one," Remi said.

He looked up toward Camel Rock, then back toward the area that Durin had said they'd traveled. "If they took that other trail that comes out above the ledge where we saw that jacket, these might not even belong to one of them."

He rested his hand on the butt of his holstered Smith & Wesson, thinking of the panicked voice mail and the mention of someone shooting at the boys. The sole set of footprints bothered Remi as well because he saw her doing the same with her Sig.

Finally, they reached the area below the ledge. Sam craned his head back, looking up at the wall in front of them, before moving back to get a better view. "This looks doable."

"That's pretty high."

He smiled at her, then turned toward the wall. The crack, running vertically up the rock sheer, varied in size from a finger's width to wide enough to step into. Sam took the lead, placing the cams and anchoring the rope, as Remi took up the slack from below. Getting to the ledge where they saw the jacket was going to take a bit more finesse. The cracks they were using to ascend angled to the right away from it.

The first fat drops of rain started to fall as they made their ascent. The higher they climbed, the stronger the wind blew. Rain lashed at their faces, soaking through their fingerless gloves.

Sam placed a cam, tugging to make sure it was secure, when a wind shear blasted down, knocking them against the rock. Remi, in the midst of reaching up, lost her grip on the wet rope, slipping. Her harness jolted as the rope went taut, breaking her fall. He saw her dangling below him, the wind spinning her like a top.

"Remi!"

Lightning flashed overhead, followed a few seconds later by the crack of thunder, as the storm raged over them. He tried not to think of all the metal cams hanging from their slings, turning them into human lightning rods.

Remi reached out, stopped her spinning by grabbing at the cam jammed into the crack.

"You okay?" he shouted, barely able to hear the words himself.

She nodded, then pointed up.

As if they had a choice of any direction but. They were forced to climb at a much slower pace, the wind and rain turning what should have been an easy climb into a treacherous one. Sam realized they were going to have to take cover. The only possible place was the ledge where Brand's jacket was found. He looked down and called out to Remi. "The ledge!"

They slowly made their way over. Sam climbed up over the edge, then reached down, grasping Remi's arm, helping her up. Safely on solid ground, they looked at the red jacket, noticing its unusual appearance as the wind rippled the nylon material.

"Sam!" she said, shouting to be heard. "Rocks inside."

"To keep it from blowing away."

Which meant someone had knotted the sleeves to hold the stones . . .

A sense of relief swept through him as he looked up, trying to see what, if anything, was on the cliffs above them. Surely that meant they were up there. Whether hurt, hiding, or both, it was definitely a sign put out to let *someone* know where they were.

He cupped his hands around his mouth and called out their names.

The only thing they heard in return was the sound of the wind whistling through the craggy rocks above them.

"If they're near the top," Sam said, "or tucked in some crevice, they might not be able to hear over the wind gusts."

He scooped up the jacket, dumped the rocks from the sleeves, stuffed it into his pack, then joined Remi beneath the cliff's overhang. It offered some protection, though not much, the wind still gusting. They huddled together to wait out the worst of the storm. At one point, Sam checked the other side to see how Zakaria was faring. Rain splattered against the binocular lenses, making it difficult to see clearly.

"Is he there?" Remi asked.

"In the car."

"At least someone's warm and dry."

He tucked the binoculars away, then took out some beef jerky and water. By the time they finished their quick meal, the wind and rain had lessened. Within a half hour, the sun actually broke through, though black clouds still threatened. "Let's get up there while we can."

They reached the crest, walking until they saw the camel head. From the other side, it had appeared to be one solid rock. As they neared, though, it looked less like a head and more like a jumble of boulders and crevices. A clear path at the back of the so-called head led right up to the edge of the gorge. Sam looked down, saw that the cliff jutted out, preventing them from seeing down to the ledge where they'd just taken shelter. "They didn't drop the jacket from here. Has to be the other side of the head."

Remi eyed the jumble they'd have to get across. The wet rocks were slippery, the edges sharp, and it would be slow going. "We might have to reassess our dinner plans by the time we get them out of here."

"Let's find them first."

Finally, they reached the other side, where a few pines stood sentinel between the boulders. Sam held on to one of the trees, peering into the dark crevice. Lightning flashed, and, in that brief moment, he caught a glimpse of rope puddled on the ground about twenty feet below.

10

Thunder rumbled above them as Sam pointed toward the rope. "Down there!"

Remi took a quick look, then stepped back as Sam leaned over, shouting, "Karl! Brand! Can you hear us?"

He waited.

Only the wind and rain. He dropped to his belly for a better view. Unfortunately, the angle prevented him from seeing much of anything. Sam anchored his rope to one of the trees, lowering himself into the crevice. "Karl! Brand!"

One of the boys stepped into view, brushing his wet hair from his face as he looked up toward Sam. "Mr. Fargo? What are you doing here?"

"Your uncle called. Where's your brother?"

Brand stepped in beside Karl, soaked through.

"Either of you hurt?" Sam asked.

Karl shook his head. "We're fine. Cold, wet, hungry, but good."

He rappelled down, glad to see the two still wore harnesses, recalling that their uncle said that they were experienced climbers. That would make their return much easier. "What happened here?"

"We're not sure," Brand said. "We were up on the ridge, on our way home, when someone started shooting at us."

"Did you see who it was?"

"No," he said. "We came back down here to get away. The only thing we can think is that whoever it was followed us and unknotted our rope so we couldn't get out. The good news is, we found the plane."

"Where?"

"Behind the camel's head. It's a bit of a climb down."

Sam looked up at Remi. "See if you can get a call to their uncle. I'm going down to take a look at that plane."

A light rain started to fall as he followed Karl and Brand along the ledge, then down the rocks toward the aircraft. No wonder the plane had never been found before now. It had crashed behind the massive rocks that formed the base of the camel's head. The left wing had been sheared off. What was left of the fuselage was protected by the overhang of the massive rock outcropping it rested beneath. Between that and the scrub that had grown up around it, it was well camouflaged.

Whether or not anything left inside had survived the decades of weather remained to be seen. "Have either of you been in it?"

"Not any farther than the hold," Brand said. "We used it for shelter from the rain. It doesn't seem very stable."

He was right about that. The plane was wedged beneath the outcropping, the right wing, what was left of it, having dropped into a deep crevice, with the body of the plane perched precariously over the same space, the nose tilted down.

Sam took out a flashlight and aimed it inside. Karl moved next to him as they peered into the opening where the tail had sheared off. The area near the door was slick with red mud where Karl and Brand had taken shelter from the rain. Beyond that, the interior was surprisingly dry, protected from the elements by the overhang. A thick layer of red dust covered the floor, marred down the middle by waffle boot prints. "Those yours?" Sam asked, recalling the footprints down by the creek bed.

Karl shook his head. "They were already there."

Sam followed the trail with his light. "Wonder if he found anything."

"If so," Karl said, "he left something behind." He pointed to what looked like a book stuck between the pilot and the copilot's seats. "We wanted to get to it, but didn't think it was safe."

Sam placed one foot against the plane, pressing on it, thinking that even if it did fall, it wasn't going far. The crevice it was wedged in seemed too narrow. Still, no telling what might happen, and so he retrieved Karl and Brand's rope, then, brushing the rain from his face, waited for Remi, who was rappelling down from the boulders.

"Your uncle is anxiously waiting your return," she said when she joined them, taking a closer look at the plane. "That thing looks like it's going over any second."

"I don't think it'll go far. It's wedged pretty tight, never mind someone's been in there." Sam showed her the boot prints. "Same as down in the ravine."

"If you're wondering, that doesn't make me feel better," Remi told him as he attached the rope to his harness. Brand and Karl, with well-muscled arms, took up the length. Remi stood near them, directing.

He ducked down, then entered the plane, testing his weight, the rain beating down on the fuselage. It was clear that this particular craft had been used for small cargo loads since the only seats were the pilots' and one behind the cockpit. The hold was empty, and the downward tilt wasn't too severe, but Sam's wet shoes turned the dust into slippery mud. He slowly made his way toward the nose, until a loud grating noise brought him up short.

"Careful, Fargo," Remi said.

"Always." The footprints he'd seen didn't extend much farther than he was now—for good reason, he thought, eyeing the empty space that once housed the glass nose and the missing cockpit windows. The plane might not entirely fit down that crevice, but he certainly would. Taking a tentative step forward, he aimed his flashlight toward the cockpit, seeing the thin book between the pilot's and co-pilot's seats.

He edged forward. The hull creaked. Suddenly, the entire plane shifted nose downward, throwing Sam against the fuselage. Flashlight flying, he crashed into the cockpit, grabbing at the seat. His feet dropped through the missing window, nothing but air beneath him.

Remi looked ready to jump in after him. "*Don't* move."

"Wasn't planning to." He hugged the pilot seat, the rope taut, as the plane slipped farther. Metal groaned and twisted against the rocks. He grabbed the book, then tucked it into his waistband. Rain sluiced into the opening, rivulets of water streaming along the floor, his feet slipping as they hauled him up. The plane shifted again, the metal screeching as it scraped on the rocks. Karl reached in, grabbed his arm, and Sam climbed the rest of the way out. When he was on solid ground, they all turned, looked into the tail end of the plane, seeing nothing but blackness through to the cockpit.

"Living on the edge, Fargo?" Remi asked.

"A little excitement's good for the ticker."

"And your prize for risking your life?"

"Possibly a logbook." Not nearly the significant find he was hoping for, after hearing the plane's legend, but perhaps historically worthy just the same. He slipped it into his backpack to keep it dry. "We'll take a look at it in the car once we get out of here."

After Brand coiled his rope and slung it over his shoulder, the four climbed up the boulders to the top of the ridge. A reprieve in the weather buoyed Karl's and Brand's spirits, especially after they learned Zakaria was waiting for them.

Brand searched the other side of the gorge, trying to see him. "How'd he know where to find us?"

"Durin showed us the way," Sam said, focusing until he saw Zakaria seated in the front passenger seat of the Toyota. Zakaria must have been watching for them because he suddenly threw open the door, jumped out, binoculars in hand, as Sam raised both arms straight up in the air. Touchdown.

There was nothing more exhilarating than a successful search and rescue—even for the one waiting on the other side. Unfortunately, that exhilaration died at the sight of the swollen creek in the gorge below. Worried about the possibility of flash floods, Sam hurried them along the ridge. By the time they reached the bottom of the gorge, the creek had doubled in size and speed, the cold current pulling at them as they crossed. They were almost to the other side when they heard a loud rumble like a stampede. Within seconds, a giant wave of reddish brown water swept down the gorge toward them.

11

A deafening roar grew in intensity as the water neared. Racing to the cliffside where they'd left the ropes hanging, Sam and Remi helped the boys first, giving Brand the backpack with the logbook. The boys safely up, he and Remi grabbed the ropes, attaching their own harnesses, as the water hit. The surge swept their feet from beneath them. They gripped their ropes as the current pulled, the spray lashing at their faces. Sam looked up, saw the boys watching in fear, as the water raged past. Finally, it crested, then started to recede, allowing them to continue their climb. Soaked and exhausted, they reached the top. Sam and Karl gathered the ropes as Remi and Brand hiked up to the Toyota. A moment later, Remi was back. "I can't find Zakaria."

"He's not in the car?"

"No. The key fob's on the seat next to the binoculars, but he's gone."

Sam examined the area near the trees, wondering if he'd somehow slipped in the mud and fallen into the gorge. Nothing appeared disturbed around that area, and he returned to the Toyota to have a look around. What he didn't expect to find was a cigarette butt half buried in the mud near the front tire.

He crouched down, noticing a distinct waffle boot print next to it. "How well do you and your brother know Durin Kahrs?"

Karl looked over at Brand. "He's your friend, isn't he?"

"Mine? I thought *you* knew him."

"What? No. I thought—"

They both turned perplexed faces toward Sam and Remi, Brand saying, "Now that I think about it, when we ran into him at the bar, he acted like he knew us. Everything he brought up was more open-ended questions."

"Yeah," Karl said, nodding. "Vague things that seemed legitimate. 'How's everyone at home?' or 'Remember that class we had together?' We were the ones supplying him with all the information."

"Classic con technique," Sam said. "What was his interest in the plane?"

Karl shrugged. "He just offered to help us find it. I'm not even sure how he knew—"

"He said he read that article on our documentary, remember?"

"There was an article. He could've found out that way . . ." Karl looked at Sam. "You think he's the one who untied our rope and left us stranded there?"

"Hard to say, right now. But if I had to lay odds, it's a safe bet."

"What about Zakaria?" Brand asked. "He wasn't involved, was he?"

Remi and Sam exchanged glances, Remi saying, "He seemed genuinely worried about you."

"I agree," Sam said, pulling out his phone. He tried calling. When Zakaria's phone went to voice mail, Sam texted *Where are you?* He waited a few seconds for a response. When there was none, he tucked the phone in his pocket. "Let's finish loading the gear, then take a look around."

As he suspected, Zakaria's footprints veered through the mud away from the gorge and toward two other sets of footprints, and tire tracks that didn't match the Toyota's.

"He definitely went off with someone," Sam told them as a return text finally came in.

Almost there. Do you have the courier bag?

"Not the response I was expecting." He showed them the text, asking, "Anyone ever mention anything about a courier bag to either of you?"

Karl shook his head.

"What courier bag?" Brand asked.

"Exactly what I was thinking," Sam said as Remi pointed to something in the distance.

"That's got to be Zakaria," she said, handing him her binoculars.

He focused in, seeing Durin Kahrs's silver Nissan racing toward them. Someone stood, popping their head and shoulders out of the vehicle's sunroof, then lifting up an automatic rifle.

Sam grabbed Remi's arm, pulling her behind the Toyota. "Get down!" he yelled to Karl and Brand. A bullet whistled past them, striking the ground nearby.

Two more shots hit the side of the Toyota.

Sam and Remi crouched behind one wheel, Karl and Brand the other. Sam drew his Smith & Wesson.

Remi unholstered her Sig. "Makes me wonder what's in that courier bag we supposedly found."

"I'm more interested in a plan to get out of here."

Another shot was followed by the hiss of air from the front tire. So much for driving away, Sam thought. He looked back toward the trees. Their only route of escape was into the gorge. If they could reach the outcropping of rocks below, they had a chance to find cover. "Hope you're ready for another hike?"

"I thought you'd never ask."

"After you."

Remi crawled toward the ravine, careful to keep the Toyota between her and the approaching vehicle.

"Brand, Karl," Sam called out. "Follow Remi." They scrambled after her. He followed. Seconds later, he heard the sound of the Nissan rumbling across the rough, muddy ground. Sam quickly surveyed the outcropping, spying a couple of boulders jutting up through the wet brush that seemed large enough to provide cover. He pointed. Remi nodded, drawing the boys behind the larger of the rocks, ducking down beside them. He dove behind the other.

"Where are they?" a man at the top of the ridge asked.

"They had to have gone back down."

Sam braced his gun against the right side of the boulder, leaning over just far enough to see through the brush around it. Two men, both with scarves over their noses and mouths, stood at the crest, rifles at the ready.

They wore traditional *djellabas*, and he recalled Durin's warning about local bandits in the area. If one of the men *was* Durin, he'd changed clothes.

"Come on out!" the taller of the two called. "We won't hurt you!" For local bandits, their grasp of English was very good.

"Footprints," the other said, his eye on his scope, following Remi's tracks through the mud with the barrel of his long gun. He lifted his rifle, aiming toward the rock where Remi and the boys were hiding.

Sam fired.

The man's shot went wild as he stumbled, then fell, the rifle flying from his grasp. The second man jumped back out of sight. "Don't shoot!" he called out. "He shouldn't have fired. It was a mistake."

"Like the shots you took at us?"

"Just a warning."

"Some warning," Remi muttered.

"What is it you want?" Sam yelled.

"Don't shoot, or I'll hurt your friend!"

Sam kept his gun aimed that direction, straining to hear what was going on up there. A moment later, he saw someone moving up on the crest. Recognition hit, and he let up on the trigger. Zakaria, his face bloodied and a gag around his mouth, was now a human shield for his captor. "I'm listening," Sam shouted.

"Bring me the courier bag and I'll let your friend go. If you call the police, I'll kill him, then come after you."

"What courier bag?"

But the man dragged Zakaria back. A moment later, they heard an engine revving as the vehicle sped off.

Remi looked over at Sam. "They *are* gone, aren't they?"

"Wait here and I'll find out."

He made his way up the hill, staying low, gun ready. The dead guy was sprawled facedown in the mud on the hillside, his hand outstretched and, just beyond it, his rifle. Sam reached out, grabbed it by the barrel. "Remi!" He slid it, butt first, toward her.

She retrieved it, covering the hilltop, while he made his way toward the crest.

He ducked behind a stand of brush. The car was gone. He checked inside the Toyota, then all around it. "Clear!" he yelled, returning to the ravine, making his way to the body as Remi, Karl, and Brand climbed up the hill toward him.

The first thing Sam noticed was the dead man wore hiking boots with the same waffle pattern as the prints they'd seen in the plane. When he rolled him over and pulled down his muddied face mask, he wasn't at all surprised. It was Karl and Brand's supposed friend, Durin Kahrs.

Remi eyed the body. "It'd be nice to know what's really going on here."

"And what Zakaria knew." He dug through the man's pockets, found his ID, and took a photo with his cell phone. Finding nothing else of interest, they climbed back up the hill to their Toyota—and the flat tire. At least the keys were in the ignition. "Don't suppose AAA makes international calls?"

"Sorry, Fargo. I think we're on our own out here."

Sam changed the tire while Remi stood guard. Karl and Brand were too shell-shocked to do much more than watch.

She glanced down at Sam before returning her gaze to the horizon. "We shouldn't have left Zakaria here."

"It wasn't like we had a lot of choice."

"It's our fault," Brand said.

"No," Sam replied. "It's Durin Kahrs's fault. You couldn't have known he was playing you."

"You think it could be the logbook they're after?" Brand asked.

"Hard to say. We've definitely got to take a better look at it." He finished tightening the lug nuts, going over everything that Zakaria told them. He gave the last lug nut a final twist, then stood. "Something's bothering me about all this."

"What's that?" Remi asked.

"If this courier bag was on that plane when Durin went out to the crash site, it's a safe bet that he took it."

"Which doesn't make sense," Remi said.

Karl added, "If he already had the courier bag, why have us come all the way out here?"

"Exactly." Sam took one last look around to make sure they hadn't left anything behind, then closed the tailgate. "Only one reason I can think of. A setup, to begin with. He'd already been out to the plane, found this courier bag, didn't want you or Zakaria to know he was in possession of it, and decided to use you as the means to an end."

"Unfortunately for him," Remi said, "the plan backfired."

12

Gere kept one hand on his prisoner as he kicked at the door, then yanked Zakaria in by his arm. The man murmured something through the gag around his mouth. Whatever it was, Gere wasn't interested. He dragged him upstairs, then locked him in the office. When he came back down, he started to go over what he was going to tell the boss. For a man who liked the outward appearance of only being semi-interested in the whereabouts of this plane and the courier bag that was supposed to have been on it, Rolfe Wernher was definitely into micromanaging.

That meant if he didn't call him right away, the guy was likely to have a heart attack. But before he could think of a good story, Rolfe walked in. As usual, he was dressed in a silk suit—gray today—his only concession to the heat was the open collar of his crisp white shirt. "I expected a call before now," Rolfe said.

"The bag wasn't there."

A vein pulsed in Rolfe's temple, and his nostrils flared slightly. Several seconds of silence passed before he spoke. "Where is it?"

"I'm not sure."

"What do you mean you're not sure?"

"We got there just as the Americans returned from the downed plane. They didn't have it with them. Durin thought maybe they'd already been out to the plane. It makes sense, since they got back far sooner than it should've taken. At least according to what Durin told me."

"Where is he?"

Gere glanced away before meeting Rolfe's gaze. "Dead."

"How?"

"The American killed him."

"Fargo killed Durin?"

"To be fair, Durin tried to kill them first."

Rolfe's lips pressed together as he processed the information. "You're a fool. Durin set us up. The Fargos couldn't have had the bag. They flew in the night before. When would they have had time to get out there?"

Gere was almost afraid to ask the obvious. "Then who has it?"

"Durin, you idiot. Which presents a big problem, since he's dead." Rolfe's gaze bored into him. "You're the one who handled him. You don't find it odd that he didn't take you out to the plane before now? Why would he have let the Fargos go searching for those two brothers without being there himself? Especially when he knew how valuable that bag was to us?"

Gere shrugged. "I don't know."

"He already had it."

"He couldn't," Gere said. "He had to go visit his sister. She was sick or something."

"And how long was he gone?"

"A couple of days . . ." Gere felt his face heat up at the apparent realization that Durin *had* played him.

"Where does he live?" Rolfe demanded.

"I don't know."

Rolfe drew his gun, pointing it at Gere. "Then you're completely useless to me. Aren't you?"

His eyes went wide. "I—I . . . Maybe Zakaria knows where it is. I brought him here."

Rolfe lowered the gun, waiting.

"Durin took their friend Zakaria hostage. I have him upstairs," Gere said. "Durin accused him of going to the plane and getting the bag, but Zaharia told me he didn't have it. The Fargos, either." Realizing all this did was prove Rolfe's point that Durin had played them for fools, he added, "I did, however, tell the Fargos if they wanted to see Zakaria again, bring the courier bag to us."

"Wait here," Rolfe said. He walked up the stairs. Gere heard the walls shake from whatever Rolfe was doing up there. Gere worried about the safety of anyone getting in the man's way—including himself, he thought, seeing the look in Rolfe's eyes as he stormed down the stairs, gun in hand.

"This is your fault," Rolfe said, then shot him in the thigh, the gunshot echoing in the confines of the room.

He fell to the floor, crying out, his ears ringing.

Rolfe narrowed his gaze. "If you weren't my nephew, I'd kill you. I still may." He strode to the door and opened it. "When your hostage regains consciousness, see if you can't get Durin's address out of him. If not, you better hope the Fargos find this courier bag and bring it to you."

13

While Sam drove, Remi read the logbook to them, ending with, "Casablanca, January nineteen forty-six. No cargo. Very odd . . ."

Sam checked his rearview mirror, then glanced over at Remi. "What is?"

"Those were the last entries. Didn't the plane go down six months after that date? Or did I misunderstand?"

"You're right," Karl said. "At least that's the way we heard it."

"Then why no entry?" she asked.

"Good question. Karl and Brand can take the book and talk to Selma about it," Sam said as his phone rang.

It was Ruben Haywood, a case officer for the CIA's Directorate of Operations, returning Sam's call. They'd met after Sam was recruited by DARPA and attended the CIA's Camp Perry training facility during covert operative school.

The two had clicked during the six weeks of intense training in weapons, fighting, and survival skills. They'd been fast friends ever since, never mind that Rube was the closest thing they had to a concierge international law enforcement connection. "Where are you now?" Rube asked.

"Driving back to Marrakesh," Sam replied. "We're heading to the hotel where Karl and Brand's uncle is waiting. They're here with us. On speakerphone, by the way."

"Okay. I'll get in touch with one of my contacts out there and start a quiet investigation into the shooting. If we're lucky, we'll find something in the background on the dead guy that'll help lead to the kidnappers. Does Zakaria have any family in the area?"

Sam glanced at the brothers in his rearview mirror.

"A cousin," Brand said. "Lina."

"You catch that?" Sam asked.

"Got it," Rube said. "What about talking to her in the morning? See if she knows anything that'll help?"

"We'll do that."

"In the meantime, try to get some sleep. I'll let you know as soon as I hear something."

"Likewise," Sam said.

THE NEXT MORNING, Sam, Remi, Karl, and Brand drove straight to the *riad* where Zakaria had been staying with his cousin. They got out of the car, Karl staring at the salmon-colored walls of the three-story home. He turned to Sam. "What are we supposed to say? Lina's going to know something's wrong the moment she realizes he's not here with us."

If Zakaria's cousin was overcome with worry, chances were that she'd be too emotional to give them the information they needed. "Let's take it slow. See what, if anything, she knows."

They walked up to the blue keyhole-shaped door, and Sam knocked.

The man who answered the door spoke only Arabic, but he recognized Karl and Brand and stepped aside to let them in. Like many of the grand houses in the area, the residence was built around a wide courtyard, this one paved with blue and white tiles in a beautiful mosaic pattern and shaded by palms. In its center, a fountain bubbled. An open arcade hall surrounded the courtyard, each arch framing a door or window that led into the house.

Sam thanked him, then said, "Is Lina home? We need to speak to her."

Remi repeated his question in French.

He replied something unintelligible, then lifted his hand slightly as though directing them to wait. A few moments later, Lina walked in. About a head shorter than Remi, she wore a white *sefsari*. Sure enough, when she saw Karl and Brand, she looked toward the entry, searching for her cousin, her smile fading when she didn't see him. "Zakaria's not with you?"

"No," Sam said. "Have you heard from him?"

"Yesterday. Just before he left with Mr. Kahrs on this expedition. He told me they'd be home today." Her gaze landed on Karl and Brand. "Zakaria was very worried about you both. You're okay, then?"

They nodded, Brand replying, "Yes."

Sam stepped in before either of them could say a word. "Do you know anything about what Durin and Zakaria were working on together?"

She glanced at the Hoffler brothers, then back at Sam. "Only what Zakaria told me. That Durin was a friend of theirs. He was helping them search for an old plane from World War Two, I believe. Zakaria invited Durin to stay here on a couple of occasions because there were times he had to leave very early in the morning—to see his sister—and staying here was much more convenient . . ." She looked at each of them, in turn, before focusing on Sam again. "I don't understand. What's going on?"

"Did either of them mention anything about a messenger bag? Or a courier bag?"

"No. Why?"

He realized then there was no way to avoid the truth or lessen the shock. Not if they wanted to get to the bottom of this. "Durin Kahrs is dead, and Zakaria was kidnapped."

Her face turned pale, and her hand went to her throat. "I—I think I need to sit." She sat on a bench near the fountain, taking a few moments to gather herself. "The police? You called them?"

"Not officially."

"I don't understand."

Sam explained about Durin's part and the warning not to call the police.

"Thank you. Not that our police aren't trustworthy. But what if the kidnappers found out? They might kill him if they're crossed."

"Our thoughts exactly."

"There must be something I can do to help?"

"Would you mind if I had a look in Zakaria's room? And Durin's when he stayed here?"

"Please." She turned toward the door she'd come through. "Kadin?"

The man who'd let them in stepped out from the shadows of one of the arches. She spoke to him in Arabic and he nodded, indicating that Sam should follow.

Zakaria's room was on the third floor. There wasn't much to look at. A bed, a small table, and a wardrobe. It took less than five minutes to search the room, and nothing to show for it. Durin's room was the same. Sam returned to the courtyard, where Remi and the others were sitting by the fountain.

Remi smiled at him. "Anything?"

"Unfortunately, no." It occurred to him then that if Durin had conned Brand and Karl, he'd probably done the same to Zakaria, and even Lina. "I don't suppose you know anything about Durin Kahrs?" he asked her.

She glanced at the Hoffler brothers. "Nothing, other than he visited a few times after he and my cousin began working together." She gave a pained smile. "I shouldn't speak ill of the dead. He was always polite, but there was something about him that I didn't care for."

"Such as?"

"My only interaction with him while he stayed here was when Zakaria was present. To me, though, he always seemed too secretive. Especially after Karl and Brand thought they had possibly found the area where this plane might have crashed. Zakaria told me that Durin argued with them about it."

This was news to Sam, and he turned to the boys. "What argument?"

Karl said, "About going out to the plane. We wanted to leave the very next day, but he wanted to go *after* he visited his sister."

Brand nodded. "That's when he told us she was dying of cancer. He just needed a couple of days to go see her, so we promised to wait."

"Durin was with you when you thought you'd discovered the location of the plane?" Sam asked.

"Yes," Brand said. "Or, rather, the location of Camel Rock. So after this big guilt trip about waiting for him, when we do get all the way out there, he suddenly announces that he can't go across the gorge. He has to get back to his sister."

"That," Lina said, "was what Zakaria told me as well." She stared at the fountain, giving a tired sigh. "I'm afraid that's all I can tell you about him. Perhaps Kadin might know something." She called his name, and once again he stepped out from the arcade behind her. She asked him a few questions, listened as he answered, then translated. "The last day he saw Mr. Kahrs he had just returned from a two-day trip visiting his sister. As usual, he was holding a backpack, but this time, when Kadin offered to carry it for him, he declined."

She looked at Kadin, who continued with his story, before turning back to them. "In fact," she said, "Mr. Kahrs was very protective. He went up to his room, gathered the few things he'd left here, then departed. One thing Kadin did notice, though, was that Mr. Kahrs's boots were covered in red dust, the same as he saw on their shoes after he, Karl, and Brand returned from their trip to the mountains after first discovering the location of Camel Rock."

That certainly fits with the time line, Sam thought, as Remi asked, "Have any of you ever met his sister?"

"No," Lina said.

Karl shook his head. "Looking back, it's so obvious. We only first heard of her after he tried to get us to put off hiking out to Camel Rock."

"What about where he lives?" Sam asked Lina. "Do you or Kadin know?"

She asked Kadin, who shook his head. "No."

With nothing further to learn, they thanked her and Kadin, then left, driving Karl and Brand back to their hotel. The moment Sam dropped them off, he got a text from Rube: *Have an ID on your DG.*

14

———

"D G?" Remi asked when Sam showed her the text.

"Dead guy," Sam said.

"Quite the top secret code."

"Gets the job done." He pulled to the side of the road and called Rube. "What do you have?" he asked, holding the phone so both he and Remi could listen.

"Durin Kahrs *is* his real name. Definitely has a record. Believe it or not, jewel thief."

"A jewel thief?" Sam repeated.

"Part of an international ring. At least according to the file the FBI has on the guy. He's suspected in a number of heists in Europe and the U.S."

"Guess you can clear his warrants."

"What've you found on your end?"

Sam told him what they'd learned from Zakaria's cousin. "I'm guessing whatever was in that backpack is what we're looking for."

"You think he had it the whole time?" Rube asked.

"Looks that way."

"But why come after you?"

"Undoubtedly, our untimely arrival," Sam replied. "If I had to guess, Zakaria and the Hoffler brothers weren't the only ones he was double-crossing. He hoped to use us as a distraction."

"Pretty bold."

"When you think about it," Sam said, "what'd he have to lose?"

"His life," Remi replied.

"What about the weapon he used?" Sam asked. "You get anything back on that serial number I sent you?"

"I was getting to that next. Stolen from Frankfurt a few days before a big heist in the same area. Same group suspected in a number of other heists throughout Europe."

"You have an address on the guy?"

"Two. One's in Germany. Locally, we show an address in Marrakesh." He read it to them. "Current as of three months ago."

"That's pretty recent."

"Look, Sam. You shouldn't be involved in this. Too dangerous."

Remi raised her brows at that. "You do realize who you're talking to, Rube?"

"I do," Rube said, his voice filled with resignation. "Just hoping that he might listen, for once."

"Appreciate your concern, old friend," Sam said as he started the car and shifted it into drive, pulling into traffic. "But Zakaria was kidnapped on my watch. And unless you can miraculously come up with a rescue team in the next ten hours without going through all the red tape, the least we can do is check out that address."

"Just be careful."

"Will do," he said, disconnecting the call. He glanced over at Remi. "You're okay with that?"

"I'll check my calendar and see if I have anything more important scheduled." She picked up her phone, typing something on the screen.

He glanced over, saw she was actually entering the address into the map. "Any luck rescheduling that manicure?"

"Very funny. Make a right at the next intersection."

DURIN KAHRS lived in a four-storied apartment complex about twenty minutes south of the hotel. Typical of the buildings in the era, the only windows facing out were high, to allow a breeze in, and narrow, to protect against the desert sun. In other words, there was no chance of breaking in from the outside. Sam drove past the address twice, checking the area, before parking down the street. They entered through a wrought iron gate that led into a fairly large courtyard in the center of the complex where children played under the watchful eyes of their mothers. Each apartment door faced into the courtyard, the upper floors accessed via two enclosed staircases in opposite corners. Sam and Remi smiled at the women, then climbed the nearest flight of stairs to the second floor, walking around the balcony until they came to Durin's apartment.

Sam knocked on the door, not expecting anyone to answer, more to determine what sort of lock was installed and if there was an alarm. There was not. "Let's go," he said, taking note of the rest of the complex as he and Remi walked toward the staircase. No way to get into that apartment without being noticed. Not in the daylight at least.

"See what you needed to see?"

"So far."

"And?"

He smiled at her. "Date night. Dress in black."

Remi linked her arm through his as they took the stairs down. "I love date night."

15

Sam and Remi returned to Durin's apartment complex after ten that night, parking far enough away not to be noticed but close enough to watch and get an idea of who came and went from the building. This time, Remi drove, since she'd be keeping watch while Sam broke in. Both were armed with handguns. They planned to communicate using Bluetooth earpieces and their phones.

It was easy to pick out Kahrs's apartment. The two slit-like windows were the only ones not lit. As the night passed, the surrounding lights went out one by one until there were only a few stragglers still awake, two on the ground floor and one on the third floor. Finally, after midnight, all was dark. Sam waited another twenty minutes just to be sure.

Remi called Sam.

He pressed the button on his earpiece. "Let's get started."

"Have fun."

He leaned over and kissed her before getting out of the car, gently closing the door. Once he crossed the street, he kept to the shadows as he walked toward the complex. "See you in a few."

"Do you think other couples have this much fun on date night?"

"In their dreams, maybe." That was one of many things that had attracted him to Remi. Dinner and a movie was what other people did on dates. He and Remi were more likely to be climbing mountains or trekking through jungles in search of treasure. Or, in this case, breaking into someone's apartment on their way to rescue a friend who was in trouble. Looking back, he tried to remember if there was a time when they'd ever had a normal date. Well, besides the night they'd met at the Lighthouse, and, of course, the times they'd returned on the anniversary of that meeting . . .

He pushed through the wrought iron gate, the courtyard lit only by a dim light at each stairwell. Just before he entered, he glanced back toward the car, barely able to make out the silhouette of Remi, watching from the driver's seat. He gave a nod, quietly closing the gate behind him, listening to the sounds, determining what was normal, before proceeding up the stairs. "Still there?" he asked, putting on his gloves and slipping a lockpick from his wallet.

"Still here."

He paused when he reached the second floor, looking down into the courtyard, where a cat, eyes glowing green, padded across. Nothing else moved, and he continued on to Durin Kahrs's door, inserting the pick into the keyhole, teasing it in and out, until the lock turned.

Once inside, he dimmed his flashlight to its lowest level and took a quick look around, glad to see that nothing appeared disturbed. That, he hoped, meant he was the first in—and this courier bag, if it even existed, was actually there.

The apartment was sparsely furnished with a couch, coffee table, and flat-screen television in the front room, and a small table and two chairs in the dinette area. The faint smell of stale beer drifted in from the kitchen, no doubt from the dozen or so empty bottles dumped in the trash can near the counter. After looking around, he moved to the first bedroom, which was used as an office. A desk and chair were positioned just below the high and narrow window. There was only one drawer in the desk, filled with assorted pens and pencils. A few bills on the top, but nothing important. The other room contained a bed, side table, and footlocker secured with a padlock. It took him less than a minute to pick the lock.

"Sam, you need to get out of there."

"I may have found something."

"Whatever it is, forget it. Two cars just pulled up. Four guys, definitely a couple with guns."

He opened the shutter of the window and saw two compact sedans parked across the street with four men walking from them toward the apartment building. Two held guns down by their sides. No doubt, the other two were armed.

So much for getting out through the front.

He'd come this far, and he wasn't about to leave without looking. Kneeling, he opened the trunk, dismayed to see nothing but neatly folded clothes inside. Then again, who locked up clean laundry? He reached in, dug around until he felt something stiff beneath the several layers of shirts. Whatever was hidden in there was wrapped in a white sheet. He pulled it off, revealing a narrow, brown leather courier bag. Definitely World War II era. If that wasn't enough to convince him this was the item taken from the crashed plane then the residue of red dust on the inside of the sheet was.

He slung the strap over his shoulder and returned to the window, looking out. The street was empty. "Where are they?"

"One's standing guard out front, the other three are splitting up."

Definitely not what he was hoping for. "On my way out now."

"How?"

"Still working on that part." He walked to the front door, pulled it open about an inch, listening. When he heard them in the courtyard below, he closed and locked the door. Plan B it is . . . Back in the bedroom, he grabbed the sheet that had been wrapped around the bag, knotting it around the metal rail of the bed. Sheet in hand, he climbed onto the sill of the open window—not an easy feat, considering how narrow the space was.

"Sam . . . ?"

"A little crowded in the courtyard. Tell me when it's clear your way."

"Clear. For now."

He squeezed through and balanced on the sill as someone kicked open the front door. Two men rushed in. They saw him as he jumped over the side, the friction heat burning through his gloves as he slid down the sheet.

One of the men leaned out, trying to grab him. When he missed, he shouted something that sounded like Russian. The man at the gate ran toward Sam, gun pointed. Sam swung, then dropped on top of him. They landed on the concrete, Sam on top, the gunman stunned. Sam grabbed the gun, rolled over, and fired at the window.

The two men jumped back. Sam got up, ran in Remi's direction. "Start the car," he yelled.

Crack! Crack! The gunshots echoed down the street. Sam fired back as he took cover in a doorway.

Tires screeched as Remi backed the car toward him, the smell of burnt rubber filling the air. Sam fired at the building, then jumped in.

"Cutting it close, aren't you?" she said, taking off, the back end skidding out as she hit the gas.

"Timing's everything." Sharp pings sounded as bullets hit the back of the Toyota as Remi turned the corner.

"So what'd you find?" she asked, looking over at him, then back at the road.

"World War Two courier bag," he said, noticing red and blue

emergency lights flashing in the distance in front of them, the sirens growing louder as the vehicles neared. Remi made the next turn, and Sam watched in the side mirror as two patrol cars raced past.

"Where to?" Remi said.

"Hotel. Time to open this thing and see what everyone's after."

16

Sam slid the strap from his shoulder, holding up the leather pouch so Remi could see. It measured about eight inches wide and ten inches long. A steel buckle secured the front flap. The leather was dry and cracked, with embedded traces of red dirt. When he unbuckled it, it cracked even more, bits of dried leather dust drifting to the tabletop. Considering the number of years it had been sitting in the wreckage of that plane under varying temperatures, it was in surprisingly good condition.

"Look at that," Remi said as Sam lifted the flap. She pointed to a name written in ink on the inside. Lennard Lambrecht.

"Wonder if he was the pilot."

The front of the pouch had a space for pencils and a compass. The main compartment was divided into two. One side held a folded map and two posted letters. The other side held a small pale yellow tin about two inches square.

"That's it?" Remi asked, picking up the tin and opening it. Inside was a perfectly preserved World War II–era typewriter ribbon.

"So it would seem." He turned the bag upside down and shook it. Bits of yellowed, almost translucent paper fell out. A few pieces seemed to have pencil marks on them. When he picked one up, it disintegrated into even more pieces.

"A bit disappointing, considering." She took the spool of typewriter ribbon, unwinding it. "Maybe a secret message wound up inside?"

"Worth a look." He opened the map and spread it out on the bed. Someone had penciled a circle around the city of Königsberg. He sifted through his knowledge of World War II. The Allies and Russia had bombed Königsberg near the end of the war. Other than that, he couldn't say why it might be significant. He looked over the letters, noting they were addressed to C. Eburhardt. At least the letters had survived, he thought, handing them to Remi. "Don't suppose you can read any of this?"

She rewound the ribbon, then looked them over. "Definitely German . . . Some are . . . garbled, almost. The sentence structure doesn't make sense. Maybe Selma can make something out of it." Selma was their go-to for all things needing to be researched. In her mid-fifties and Hungarian-born, she was also multilingual. If she couldn't come up with a translation, she knew someone who could.

"Let's get pictures of everything," Sam said. He and Remi photographed the items from all angles before making a video call to Selma. She answered from her computer, looking at them through her dark-framed glasses.

"Mr. and Mrs. Fargo. Good to hear from you. Back from your expedition? Anything exciting?"

"Interesting date night," he told her. "More important, someone got to the plane before us, which brings me to my point. Assuming we have the full story here, the only thing found at the site of the downed plane beside the logbook pictures we sent was a leather courier bag containing a typewriter tin with a ribbon, map, and two posted letters dated nineteen forty-five. They look to be written in German, but Remi thinks something's odd about them. You should have photos in your email now."

As Selma looked down at her keyboard and typed, the desk lamp highlighted the spikes of her short hair that she'd recently started dying a subtle shade of blue and pink—something they attributed to her burgeoning romance with Professor Lazlo Kemp, who, because of his knack at cryptology, also worked for the Fargos. She nodded. "Right here. Where do you want me to start?"

"Translation, to start," Sam said. "See if it has anything to do with the map. We've got an errand to run, so we'll get back to you later."

"Anything I should be aware of?" she asked Sam.

"Other than Zakaria being kidnapped, and breaking into a building to steal the courier bag being used as ransom to pay the kidnappers? Can't think of anything."

Remi leaned in, saying, "Unless you count the guy Sam killed and the bullet holes in that Toyota we rented."

Selma eyed them over the top of her glasses, then focused on Sam. "That's it?"

"Night's still young, Selma."

"Let me know if you need the cavalry sent in."

"Will do."

Sam disconnected. "Let's get this over with," he said, texting Zakaria's phone.

I have the bag. Call for delivery.

The phone rang less than a minute later. "What took you so long?" the kidnapper asked.

"Having to dodge a few of your gunmen, for one."

"What kind of fool do you take me for? My men are right here."

"You're saying you *didn't* send anyone?"

"If we'd known where to go, we wouldn't have needed a hostage, would we?"

Couldn't argue with that. But if they weren't the only ones looking for this thing, who else was? "Where do you want me to take it?"

He named the location. "And make sure you come alone."

"Who do I ask for?"

"Gere."

"Well, Gere. I want to know Zakaria is okay. Or no deal. Put him on the phone."

A muffled sound as though the phone was being handed off to someone, then, "Sam? Are you there?"

He recognized Zakaria's voice. "You okay?"

"Fine. I'm sorry. I—"

His captor was back on the line. "You got what you wanted. One hour, if you want him alive."

The line went dead.

Sam slid his phone into his pocket, then took extra ammunition from his gear bag. "They want the pouch? Let's give it to them."

17

Remi looked up the location on the satellite map. "Right here," she said, showing it to him.

"I like it," Sam said. "At this hour, deserted. Now, how to get him *and* us out of there . . ."

She'd heard enough of Sam's stories from his time at DARPA to be able to cite a few. "What about that trick you and Rube used back in Curaçao? You know, with the bottles?"

"That could work. As long as the rain holds off."

"I didn't think about that. I'll check the weather report." She accessed the weather app on her phone. "Looks like rain's not expected until early in the morning."

"Let's hope that's accurate." He studied the satellite map. "You think you're up to it?"

She gave a slight smile at his purely rhetorical question. "O ye of little faith."

Once they finalized their plan and got the bottles they needed, they headed out. Sam drove, and when they reached the street, he shut off the headlights, idling slowly down it. The area was industrial, no one around this time of night. All the buildings were dark except for one about halfway down the block.

Sam stopped the car about two buildings away. "This looks like a good place. Direct line of sight."

Remi noticed a recessed doorway to her left, shadowed. Even better in her mind, the front door was barred from the outside and locked with a padlock. No one would pop out unexpectedly. "Looks good to me."

What didn't look good was the light drizzle that had started. At least it was evaporating as soon as it hit the windshield. Maybe they'd have a chance after all, she thought, adjusting her Bluetooth earpiece.

As they did at Durin Kahrs's apartment, they planned to communicate by phone. Sam called her cell, making sure they had a connection. "Ready when you are."

He turned on the headlights, switching to brights, not only to light up the front of the building but to make it difficult for anyone to see Remi as she hid in the background. She got out, unsnapped her holster, pausing by his open window. "Be careful."

"Likewise."

She waited in the shadowed doorway, her Sig aimed toward the brightly lit building, looking for any open windows where someone might be hiding, waiting to take a shot at them. Sam opened the car door, remaining in the driver's seat as he let the car idle forward before stopping it in the middle of the road. Without getting out, he leaned over, setting two water bottles on the ground, one empty, one full—and, next to them, the courier bag, flap open, with the letters and map partially showing. Driver's door open, he backed up the car, angling it so the engine block was between him and the building, then glanced in Remi's direction. She eyed the setup. "Perfect," she said.

"I'm calling now." He turned back toward the building, and she heard the ringing from the three-way call.

A moment later, someone answered, "Fargo?"

"Who's this?"

"Gere."

"Gere. Send out Zakaria if you want the courier bag."

The man laughed. "You want to see your friend? You bring it in."

"*Not* going to happen," Sam said. "Let me tell *you* how this works. Send out Zakaria. When he's safely in my car, we drive off, you get the bag."

"We could shoot you right there."

"You could. But your courier bag and everything in it will burn."

"My men are watching you right now. You think you can get it before we get you?"

"Look out your window. Let me know when you're there."

From the corner of her eye, Remi saw movement in an upper window, then heard Gere saying, "What of it?"

"Notice the courier bag and two bottles," Sam said, putting a cigarette in his mouth, lighting it. The drizzle turned to fat raindrops as he sat in the driver's seat, the door still open. He puffed on the cigarette a couple of times until the end glowed bright orange. When he tossed it, sparks bounced up as it hit the street, then rolled about a foot in front of the courier bag. "Watch the empty bottle on the left."

Remi fired. The bottle flew forward, bouncing toward the curb.

"That other bottle," Sam said, "is full of gasoline. The laws of physics say it's not going as far as that empty bottle. In fact, I'd lay odds it lands on top of that pouch, soaking your map, then spreading out to that lit cigarette. We know what happens when gas and fire meet. Your choice is this. Send out Zakaria or we destroy the map."

18

Remi held her breath as scattered raindrops hit the pavement, somehow missing the lit cigarette. A muffled discussion followed, some of it sounded like German, at least from the bit that Remi heard, then, "How do I know everything's there?"

"You have my word," Sam replied. "Everything we found is there. A map, two letters, and an old tin with a typewriter ribbon."

Another muffled discussion, then Gere saying, "He's coming out the front door."

The skies let loose, soaking the pavement. Remi hoped they weren't paying attention. Finally, the door opened. She pressed slightly on the trigger, ready. When a man stepped out, his hands up, Sam said, "It's Zakaria."

She moved her finger from the trigger but kept aim on the doorway, scanning the windows above, as Zakaria walked toward Sam's car, then ran the rest of the way, into the front passenger seat. Sam shifted the car into reverse, then backed toward Remi.

Gun out, she sidestepped to the car and got in the backseat. Sam hit the gas, tires squealing as he backed away. Just before he turned the corner, Remi caught sight of two men running through the pouring rain, one with a gun pointed their direction, the other going straight to the courier bag.

Sam looked at her in the rearview mirror. "Nice shooting, Mrs. Fargo."

"You think they'll be upset when they discover it's really iced tea in that bottle?"

"I guess that depends on whether they try to light it or drink it." Sam glanced at Zakaria. "You okay, my friend?"

He nodded. "Thank you. I don't know what I would've done if you hadn't come for me."

Though the inside of their car was dark, Remi could tell his lower lip was swollen, and there was dried blood below his nose and mouth.

"I'm curious," Sam said. "How'd all this happen, to begin with?"

Remi, noticing Zakaria taking a shaky breath, said, "Why don't we get him back to his cousin's house, give him a chance to rest up a bit, before we start grilling him."

THE FOLLOWING MORNING, Sam paced the courtyard, looking at his watch. "How much sleep does a guy need before he gets up?"

"Considering what he went through," Remi said, "we can forgive him for sleeping in." She was seated on a bench beneath the palm, enjoying the morning sun that angled into the courtyard over the eastern roof, lighting up the fountain in the center.

Lina walked in, her smile kind when she addressed Sam. "Zakaria asked me to give his apologies and to let you know he's on his way down."

When he showed a few minutes later, his face still bruised, his lower lip slightly less swollen than last night, Sam stopped his pacing. "You're up."

Zakaria smiled, then winced at the pain it caused him. "Sorry to keep you waiting."

"No worries," Remi said as Sam took a seat next to her. "It's not like we have anything going on this morning."

"You okay?" Sam asked.

"Yes." Zakaria pulled up a wrought iron chair and sat across from them. "I know I already thanked you, but—"

"No thanks needed," Sam interjected. "We're glad we could help."

Lina excused herself so that they could talk in private.

Zakaria glanced back, checking to make sure they were alone, before saying, "This is my fault. I realize that now. After I saw you had found Karl and Brand, I texted Durin to let him know the search was successful. I told him that you were on your way back." He gave a deep sigh. "I swear, I had no idea what he was up to or I'd never have let him know anything."

That explained the timing of it all, Remi thought, as Sam asked, "What happened?"

"Maybe a half hour after I texted, Durin and this other man, Gere, drove up. For them to arrive that quickly meant that they must have been well on their way at the time they got my text."

Remi glanced toward Sam, certain he had to be thinking the same thing she was. That Durin had intended to ambush them all along. Probably to protect his secret, that he'd already been out to the plane and found the courier bag.

Zakaria absently touched his bruised cheek as he continued his story. "Durin's friend had an assault rifle slung across his back. I saw another rifle in the car. I—I was shocked. Confused . . . And Durin had this wild look in his eye, and I realized I had to get out of there. But he caught up to me. The next thing I knew, he's smashing me across my face. He kept asking what we'd found in the plane. When I told him I hadn't gone out there with you, he accused me of lying, and his friend tied my hands behind my back, forcing me into their car."

"Did you hear any of their conversation?" Sam asked.

"Some. They were speaking mostly German. Too fast for me to

understand more than a few words here and there. One I kept hearing was *Lösegeld*."

"Ransom," Remi translated.

He nodded. "That must be it. Durin told me they were going to hold me for ransom."

"What about who they worked for?" Sam asked. "Can you tell us anything about the people he was involved with?"

"I heard a name . . . Rol . . . Rolfe . . ." He stared off into the distance a moment, gathering his thoughts. "I'm certain that's the name I heard. I think he's the one who came in and tried to get Durin's address from me. And demanded to know where the courier bag was. Big, bald man in a fancy suit. That's all I can tell you about him."

Sam pulled his phone from his pocket and looked at a text message on the screen. "We need to get going," he said to Zakaria. "You're sure you'll be okay here?"

"Definitely. Kadin might look harmless, but he's not. No one's getting past the front door."

He walked them out, thanking them again for coming to his aid, and promised to call if he remembered anything else that might be useful.

Remi waited until they were at the car to ask Sam about the text.

"It's from Selma," he said. "She thinks that one of the two letters found in the pouch might be in code."

"She give you any idea what it said?"

"That's what we're about to find out."

19

D efinitely an interesting mix," Selma said when they called her back.

Remi raised the volume on her iPhone so that they could hear over the road noise. The Toyota wasn't exactly the quietest vehicle they'd ever rented. "Interesting how?"

"A German plane carrying a letter dated half a year after the war ended."

"Coded?" Sam said, intrigued. "War-related?"

"Not exactly. The only thing we've been able to glean from it is a mention of Königsberg and a date from the war, mentioned in the body of the letter," she said as Sam's phone buzzed in the center console.

"Hold on, Selma," he said. "Another call coming in."

Remi picked up his phone. "It's Rube," she said, putting him on speakerphone as well.

"Hi, Rube," they said together, Sam adding, "What news?"

"Got a hit on your name—assuming Zakaria heard correctly," he said. "Rolfe may be Rolfe Wernher. His criminal history goes back a few decades, but nothing too serious. Mostly minor stuff like a few drug violations, and a burglary charge that was dropped to petty theft. It's the stuff they weren't able to prosecute him on that worries me. Money laundering, tax evasion, drug trafficking, conspiracy, et cetera, et cetera. There seems to be a lack of direct witnesses who can be found. The few who have stepped forward end up missing."

"Well, now you can add kidnapping to his list of charges," Sam said.

"Assuming we can keep Zakaria safe and tie Rolfe to it."

"Anything on the men who hit Durin's apartment?"

"One of my Moroccan contacts tells me that the plates on the two cars abandoned at Kahrs's apartment came back as rentals. The interesting thing is, the credit card used to rent them. They seem to belong to a fictitious business in Russia."

"The kidnapper said he didn't know who was shooting at me," Sam said. "It'd be nice to know who's behind this fictitious business. Even nicer to know if there really is more than one group involved."

"I'll see what I can find out. Anything else you can tell us about the group who came after you at the apartment?"

"I'm not certain, but I think they were speaking Russian. That's about it."

"Not much, but it's a start."

After Rube disconnected, Sam said, "Sorry, Selma. Thought it'd be quicker. You catch all that?"

"I suppose it explains the bullet holes in your rental car. Not sure I'd want to be the poor guy checking in the returns," she said over a rustling of papers on her end. "I have a few notes here on what we've been able to come up with so far. Like I said, we have a date and a city. Königsberg, the eighth of April, nineteen forty-five. Beyond that, we're not sure. Yet."

"Is the date significant?" Sam asked.

"The Russians invaded Königsberg right around that time, rousting the Nazis. So, it could be. Beyond the general knowledge that

Hitler ordered the removal of all the looted art and treasures stored there, we know they got some of the art out."

"Please," Remi said, "follow that up with a confirmation that the Amber Room was on that list of what they got out."

"Wish I could, Mrs. Fargo. Whether or not they were able to disassemble and move the Amber Room in time has been a hot topic of debate ever since. Lazlo's fairly certain the letter refers to something else entirely. He just needs a little more time to verify his preliminary findings. Hold on. He's right here."

"Quite the find, these letters," Lazlo said, his English accent evident. "I'm not sure about this first letter. In fact, it's so banal I wonder why someone would even bother to mail it, considering how much airmail cost back then. That led me to take another look after trying to read the second letter. At first, I thought it may be the key to break the code. But that doesn't seem to be the case at all. I'm not even sure either letter is really in code. More, that it's all purposefully written out of order for some odd reason. Just no order I can discern."

Lazlo rarely got right to the point, and, as expected, today was no different. "Long story short . . . ?"

"One of the letters has a pencil notation circled on the top. Not in the letter writer's hand but in a script that matches the logbook, or, rather, the *R*'s that appear in the words *Romanov Ransom*, scrawled in the margin of the logbook that you found on the plane. I'm waiting on better photos of the pages from Karl and Brand. The cell phone photos they sent—"

"Back up a bit," Sam said. "Romanov Ransom?"

Remi added, "As in the murdered royal Romanovs?"

"The only Romanovs I can think of."

"I wasn't aware there was a ransom involved," she replied.

"Neither were we. There aren't any historical references to any ransom being paid by, or on behalf of, the Romanov family. At least not that we've been able to find. That'll take a tad more research."

"What about the map?" Sam asked. "What do you make of it?"

"The map," Selma said, "indicates you need to make Königsberg your next stop. Or, to be more precise, Kaliningrad, as it's now called."

"What do you think?" Sam asked Remi. "A quick detour?"

"Kaliningrad? What are you waiting for? It's a destination I've always dreamed about."

20

The phone Tatiana held discreetly in her lap buzzed with an incoming text, and she glanced down at it, reading the one word on the screen: *Call*.

Finally, she thought as Rolfe perused the wine menu. "Will you excuse me for a moment?" she asked, slipping her phone into her clutch, also on her lap, then sliding her chair out. "I should have stopped by the ladies' room on my way in."

He made a cursory rise from his chair as she stood.

"I'll be right back," she said, then turned toward the lobby. Once in the ladies' room, she pushed open each toilet stall door to make sure it was empty before calling Viktor. Her foot tapped a cadence on the polished marble floor as the phone rang.

Eventually, Viktor picked up. "I have the update you wanted," he said.

"A bit late, don't you think?"

"A few complications. The police towed the rental cars, and one of our men was injured in a shooting. I needed to tie up some loose ends so that nothing comes back to you."

"What happened?" she asked.

Viktor hesitated, which in her experience always meant bad news.

"Someone got to the apartment first," he said at last. "We think it was the Fargos."

"And?"

"The pouch was gone when we got there. Either they got it or someone did before them."

The only other people who even knew the thing existed were Rolfe and his men, Durin being one of them. Who would've guessed that when she paid Durin to bring the courier pouch to her instead of Rolfe, he was double-crossing all of them? She should've known better. That, however, mattered little. He was dead, and she still didn't have the courier bag. "Do me a favor. See if you can learn any more about the Fargos. I'd like to know what they're up to."

"That's what I was calling about. The Fargos arrived in Kaliningrad. This morning."

"What on earth are they doing there?" Tatiana asked.

"There's only one reason I can think of. They're looking for information on the Romanov Ransom. They had to have recovered the courier bag from Durin."

"Interesting. If anyone had it, I would've guessed Rolfe."

"It's possible that he got it from the Fargos. Regardless, the timing of their visit shows they have some knowledge of what that bag contained or they wouldn't be here. I'm not sure how much you know about them, but they have the expertise and the wealth to self-fund their search."

She took a moment to absorb that information. "How hard would it be to follow them?"

"With the men I have working for me? Shouldn't be a problem."

"Good. I want to know everything the Fargos are doing while they're in Kaliningrad. Between their search and Rolfe's, maybe all we'll have to do is sit back and let them do the work."

"Understood. I'll set it up."

After he disconnected, she dropped her cell phone into her purse, checked her makeup in the mirror, then returned to the table in the restaurant where Rolfe was waiting. "You ordered already?" she said, noticing a bottle of Argentinian Loscano Private Reserve Torrontés chilling in an ice bucket.

"I hope you don't mind. Unfortunately, I have to catch a plane."

She gave a small pout, hoping it was convincing enough. "And here I thought we'd be able to meet for dinner. You were supposed to take me to the *medina*."

"Something came up," he said.

A courier pouch, no doubt. "And where are you off to this time?"

"Home. Business matters that need attending to."

She lifted her wineglass, taking a sip, looking at him over the rim, deciding that once again she was going to have to take the direct approach. "Any luck on your plane?"

He gave a neutral smile. "Unfortunately, the person I hired to find it was recently killed."

"Oh. So that's it, then? You're giving up?"

"I didn't say that. Just that I'm pursuing different avenues at this point."

"What do you suppose is in it?"

"The plane?" He gave a slight shrug. "I suspect the usual World War Two regalia that's so prized by collectors."

"Nothing extraordinary about this particular regalia?"

"That's what I hope to find out," he said, then looked at his watch. "You'll forgive me if I cut our time short. The bill is paid. So, please, enjoy your wine. I really do need to get going." He stood, moving to her side, giving her a kiss on the cheek. "Good-bye, Tatiana."

With a perfunctory smile, he departed.

She sat there a moment, eyeing her wineglass, wondering if he really did have to leave or if she'd pushed him too far. A waiter, apparently noticing Rolfe's departure, approached, asking if she was ready to order.

"Never mind," she said. "I've lost my appetite."

21

Originally known as Königsberg, the *oblast* of Kaliningrad became part of the Soviet Union at the end of World War II. When the Soviet Union collapsed, Kaliningrad remained part of the Russian Federation even though it was physically separated from Russia by Lithuania, Poland, and the Baltic Sea. Sometime in the 1990s, it went from being a closed state that restricted access of any foreigners to an open state that now allowed tourists to visit—as long as they had the proper visas. Sam and Remi, being semi-frequent visitors to Russia for various philanthropic events, kept current Russian visas and flew into Kaliningrad Khrabrovo Airport the following night.

Although Remi was fluent in a number of languages, Russian was not at the top of the list. As usual, the ever-efficient Selma made arrangements for a translator. "Sergei Vasyev," she told them over the phone after they checked into their hotel.

"Vasyev?" Sam asked. "Any relation to Leonid?"

"His second cousin, if I'm not mistaken." Leonid Vasyev, a Russian archaeologist, had worked with them on an expedition to the Solomon Islands. "Leonid informs me that Sergei is highly reliable, and, based on what Leonid knows about your . . . I believe he said 'propensity for trouble,' there's no one else he'd recommend."

"Then we look forward to meeting him."

SERGEI WAS WAITING for them in the lobby of the hotel the next morning. There was a slight family resemblance to Leonid. Sergei was a bit taller, with dark hair, and blue eyes, and was much younger—closer to Sam's age. His face lit up when he saw them step off the elevator and walk toward him. "Mr. and Mrs. Fargo. It's an honor to meet you."

"The pleasure's ours," Sam said. "And, please, Sam and Remi."

"Sam and Remi, then," he said, shaking their hands. "Leonid's told me so much about you and your sponsorship of his expeditions. I look forward to working with you."

"Likewise," Sam said, noting his accent was almost nonexistent. "Your English is excellent. Where'd you grow up?"

"Name the country. My parents worked for the Russian embassy, and we moved around a lot. They insisted I learn the language of each country we lived in. I also went to graduate school in California. UCLA."

"Majoring in?" Remi asked.

"Archaeology. Leonid was a big influence. I wanted to be able to travel like he does."

As they pushed through the lobby doors, Sam said, "We have a rental car."

"I can drive." Sergei held up his keys. "Easier that way, since I know the streets. You have names of who you need to talk to?"

"Selma said she'd forward the information to us as soon as she found someone," Remi said, checking to see if there were any updates on her phone. There weren't. "I don't suppose you know anyone who can talk to us about Königsberg castle."

"What are you looking for there?"

"Some of the more obscure history of the castle during World War Two," she said. "Preferably, a local historian who might know something about what the Germans stored there before it was bombed. Or someone who could give us anecdotes that didn't make it into the textbooks or internet lore."

"I know right where to start."

"Lead the way," Sam said. "We're open to suggestions."

"So where is it we're going?" Remi asked Sergei from the back of his car.

"The Amber Museum. There's someone there who knows everything there is to know about what was smuggled into the castle during the war. If anyone can talk about what else was stored there, he can."

The museum, housed in one part of an old Teutonic castle, held thousands of amber displays, one of the more unusual pieces containing an entire lizard. While fascinating, he and Remi both gravitated toward the display on the history of the Amber Room, an entire chamber in the Catherine Palace made of amber panels backed with gold leaf. An enlargement of a photo from 1931 showed how the room appeared before the Nazis had discovered it at the palace after invading Russia. They disassembled and carried it off to Königsberg, where it remained and was most likely destroyed when the Allies bombed the castle in 1944. No one had seen it since, though there were rumors that the Amber Room had somehow survived the bombing and the Nazis had smuggled it out of the castle prior to the end of the war.

Next to the photograph of the original was a photo of the reproduction of the Amber Room, re-created in the same chamber at the Catherine Palace near St. Petersburg. Remi compared the two photos. "Imagine finding the original. That would be the discovery of the century."

"One thing at a time, Remi," Sam said, noting that Sergei had moved off to talk with one of the curators. After a brief discussion, he waved them over. "Let's go see what he's found." Sam and Remi turned at the exact moment that a man and woman walked in, nearly running into them. "Sorry," Sam said.

The couple gave him a cold stare, both making a sudden about-face to look at a different display.

"Not very friendly," Remi said, glancing back at them.

"Sergei," Sam said. "I take it you've got news for us?"

The young man gave a wide smile. "Pay dirt! That's how you say it, yes?"

"I believe so," Sam said, figuring he'd reserve judgment on the end result.

"This," Sergei said, turning to a tall, thin man with gray hair, "is Andrei Karpos. Historian and guest lecturer at the university."

"Pleased to meet you," Remi said.

Sam shook his hand, asking, "On what subject?"

"The lost treasures of Königsberg castle," Andrei said.

"Definitely pay dirt," Sam said.

22

Andrei suggested they take a walk outside since he was about to go on break. He guided them toward the vendor stalls located in the front of the museum, where tourists shopped for amber trinkets and jewelry. "Cheaper than in the museum shop," he said, greeting one of the vendors as they strolled past. "Sergei tells me that you're here about the Amber Room. That's what they all come for."

"Actually," Sam replied, "we heard the Amber Room might not be the only thing moved from the castle. We're more interested in the other treasures that might have been smuggled out before the bombing."

"Anything in particular? The Nazis moved a lot of stuff."

"The Romanov Ransom."

He glanced over at them, somewhat surprised. "Not many people know that story."

"So you've heard of it?"

"More on the legend side of things . . . but, yes," he said, continuing on until they reached the park.

Sam waited a few moments, and when Andrei didn't volunteer any more information, Sam asked, "What legend?"

He stopped, his gaze landing first on Sam, then Remi, as if to convince himself they were worth his time. "First, how is it you learned of the ransom?"

"Documents from a downed German plane in Morocco."

"It's finally been found, then?"

"You know of it?" Sam asked, surprised.

"Not so much the plane as the pilot who flew it."

"Lennard Lambrecht?" Remi said.

Andrei's brows went up a fraction. "You *have* done your homework."

"Who is he?"

"Lennard Lambrecht, a Nazi officer, was a double agent, working for Russia and the Allies, even after the war ended."

Sam was always interested in World War II history, especially when it was something he wasn't familiar with. "In what way?"

"He helped arrange passage from Europe to Morocco for the Nazi war criminals fleeing prosecution. What those German officers didn't know was that he was also reporting their whereabouts to the authorities."

"A ratline spy," Sam said, thinking that Brand and Karl would definitely want to interview Andrei for their documentary.

"Exactly. Because of his assistance, a number of high-ranking German officers were arrested before they were able to set sail for South America. It was during his work there that he'd heard rumors of a plot against Russia being concocted by a group of Nazi officers. They were going to bomb Russia and blame it on the Americans. You can imagine what something like that would have done."

"World War Three," Remi said.

"Quite possibly."

"How," Sam asked, "did this Romanov Ransom come into play?"

"If rumors are to be believed, the ransom was stolen from Russia at the same time as the Amber Room, then stored by the Nazis at Königsberg castle. Once the Germans realized they were losing the war, it was smuggled out. The ransom was to be their fail-safe plan. Or—how do you Americans say it?—the Hail Mary plan. They planned to use the stolen treasure to finance the sabotage of the peace efforts."

He paused for a moment to look around, then back at the group. "My understanding is, Lambrecht died a hero. He knew he'd been compromised. His handlers felt the benefit outweighed the risk and sent him in one last time to get the names of those involved and the route they took to smuggle the ransom out of Königsberg castle. He was bringing that information back when his plane went down in the Atlas Mountains in Morocco."

He glanced over at them. "What is it you two plan to do with this information?"

"To start," Sam said, "we document it for historical value."

"Let's say you do find the Romanov Ransom?"

"Return it to its rightful owners."

Sergei nodded, saying, "That's what the Fargos do. Trust me."

Andrei directed his attention to Sam, saying, "I've had other people make inquiries. People I don't trust. And neither should you."

"Understood," Sam said.

Remi asked, "What do you think the Romanov Ransom is?"

He looked at his watch. "Time to turn back. My break is only fifteen minutes." They made an about-face, heading toward the crowded stalls once more. And just when Sam doubted that Andrei was going to say anything more, he spoke. "It was rumored that Maria Feodorovna, the Dowager Empress, paid a vast fortune in jewels to free her son and his family from the Bolsheviks."

"Any idea how much or what it consisted of?" Sam asked.

"As far as a dollar amount? I have no idea since no documentation exists. She kept a diary, but there's no mention of a ransom paid. A peer of mine suggests the ransom was stolen by someone in her own household before it ever made it to the Bolsheviks. Another believes it was paid, but the Bolsheviks never intended to release the imperial family to begin with. And, as we all know, they were murdered. As to what was in it? Depends on who you ask. That it was paid explains why her fortune was nonexistent when she fled the Crimea."

"Humor us," Sam said as they weaved their way through the growing crowd of shoppers. He noticed the couple from the museum shop a few booths away to admire some of the amber trinkets.

"Naturally, everyone assumes there were a few Fabergé eggs gifted to her by her husband, Alexander. After all, it would explain why a handful have never been found or accounted for. She would also have kept any jewelry he'd given her over the years. There are numerous photographs of her wearing tiaras and necklaces that have never been seen since." Andrei nodded at someone he knew, as they walked, then glanced over at Sam and Remi, saying, "I'm sure that if you're aware of any of the history surrounding the murders of the Romanovs, you know they'd amassed a fortune of loose stones that were meant to tide them over once they escaped the country. The royal family had sewn them into the lining of their clothes. It would have been no different for the Dowager Empress when she fled to the Crimea. In my opinion, if this ransom truly exists, it would be worth hundreds of millions of dollars."

"Do *you* believe the stories?" Remi asked. "That the ransom really exists?"

"I do," he said, pausing beside the booth where he'd greeted one of the vendors. Strings of amber beads hanging from hooks glistened in the sunlight. "I believe the Bolsheviks had it, and then the Nazis took it when they invaded Russia."

"Took it from where?" she asked, running her fingers along one of the long strands.

"Originally? Catherine Palace, St. Petersburg. Same time they took the Amber Room." He gave a slight shrug. "Doesn't matter. No one's ever seen it or the Amber Room since. So, whether it really exists or not is anyone's guess. My opinion counts little."

Sam eyed the couple just a few booths away. The woman picked up a small amber frame, turning it about in her hands. The man stood with his back to them. Their actions seemed normal, tourists doing the tourist thing, but something about them didn't seem right. Keeping his eye on the couple, he asked Andrei, "What was it you were saying about others making inquiries into this?"

23

ometime last year," Andrei said as they continued on toward the museum, "I was approached by two men who asked if I knew anything about the Romanov Ransom having been taken to Königsberg castle along with the Amber Room. I told them the same as you."

"Earlier, you said you didn't trust them. Why is that?"

"These people wanted exclusive access to my notes. They offered to pay because they didn't want what I'd found out in the public realm. Thousands more than I'd ever make publishing my book. I refused."

"It's your passion," Remi said. "There is no price."

"Exactly," he said, sounding surprised. He glanced over at Sergei. "You were right. They do understand."

"I told you," Sergei said.

"What happened next?" Sam asked.

"When I turned them down, one of the men threatened that if I did publish the book, they'd come after me. The publisher I had lined up suddenly went out of business. Another small academic press I had submitted it to was sold, the new owners no longer interested."

As they walked past, Sam watched the couple from the corner of his eye. Neither looked their direction.

"At the time," Andrei continued, "I assumed it was just my bad luck. But when I decided to self-publish it, the shop belonging to the printers I hired burned to the ground. That's when I realized that whoever they are, they were intent on keeping my work out of the public domain."

"These people," Sam said. "Anything you can tell us about them?"

"Beyond that they're dangerous?" He shrugged. "I was never able to prove anything. The more I talked about it to the authorities, the more I looked like a crazed man spouting a conspiracy theory. Even I was beginning to disbelieve what was happening."

Remi said. "Weren't you worried for your safety?"

"At first, no. But after the printing press disaster, I realized that others around me might be hurt. That's when my wife suggested that I put all of my work on the internet instead. She felt that once it was out where everyone could see it, they'd lose their leverage." Andrei gave a deep sigh. "At the moment, it's still an obscure academic paper that takes a bit of searching, but, as my wife pointed out, with social media these days, should anything happen to me, people would be bound to do a search of my name. If they did, that paper would shoot to the top of the search results. So much for keeping the information private." He gave a cynical smile. "The very next time they contacted me, I let them know."

"Did it work?" Remi asked.

"They've left me alone ever since. Of course, it also gave them access to everything I'd gathered, but what could I do? One day I may try again to get it properly published, but, for now, there it sits on the internet for anyone who cares to look for it. So, please. Help yourself. And if I were you, I'd take a good look at the bibliography—something I didn't pass on to those charlatans. Some of my most amazing finds were from a diary kept by the groundskeeper of Königsberg castle."

Remi took out her phone and opened a text to Selma as they talked. "Notes," she said. "So I don't forget."

When they neared the front of the museum, Andrei stopped, saying, "Duty calls. Even for us volunteers."

They thanked him for his time, and Sergei walked him back to the museum entrance.

Sam waited until they were out of earshot before asking Remi, "You happen to notice we were being followed?"

"The man and woman who nearly ran us over inside the museum?"

"The same."

She put her hands on her hips, her expression one of mock seriousness. "An appalling lack of etiquette, that they'd follow us around without a proper introduction."

"Agreed. Time we introduced ourselves."

24

The woman, Remi noticed as she weaved her way through the tourists and shoppers admiring the various amber knick-knacks, had questionable taste. She tried on a hideous necklace interspersed with plastic gold beads, then a pair of dangling earrings. As she held them to her ears, she checked herself in a handheld amber mirror, undoubtedly searching for Sam and Remi in the reflection.

Sam caught up with Sergei to let him know that they'd meet him at the car. Remi swept past the couple, never giving any indication that she noticed them at all, keeping close to the crowd for safety. She stopped to admire an amber elephant figurine about two inches high. "How much?" she asked the vendor.

"For you, only twenty-five hundred rubles. Genuine Baltic amber. The finest anywhere."

Whether it was the finest was debatable. It was, however, charming, and she turned it over in her hands, admiring the way the light caught in the inclusions. "Two thousand," she offered as Sam joined her.

"Twenty-two." He gave a firm nod.

A little over thirty dollars. Very reasonable. "Twenty-two it is. Sam?"

He took out his wallet and paid the man, who wrapped the elephant in tissue and put it in a small cloth bag, handing it to Remi.

"*Spasibo,*" she said.

He gave a broad smile in return. "You're very welcome."

Remi tucked the bag into her purse as Sam led her back toward the park. "And where are our new friends?" she asked.

"Right behind us."

She again linked her arm through Sam's, eyeing the crowd, breathing in the scent of freshly mown grass, as they walked. Other than the people following them, everything seemed normal. Children ran past, laughing as parents called after them to wait. Several teenage girls giggled at a nearby booth as they tried on amber necklaces. Up ahead, armed police officers strolled near the park, keeping a watchful eye on everything around them. That, she realized, was one of the things Sam would be watching for. Less likely for anything serious to happen in an area like this—especially if the pair following them was armed. "Do we have a plan?"

"I'm thinking we go with the up close and personal, didn't know you were here approach."

"Like the time in Mykonos?" she clarified since they'd been in a number of scrapes together.

"Exactly," he said as they strolled along. "Now."

They turned, saw the man and woman about ten feet away, both suddenly very interested in the items at the booth. The woman placed her purse down on the shelf beside her as Sam and Remi quickly closed the distance between them. When they were nearly on top of the couple, Remi threw up her hands in surprise, stepping between the woman and the booth. "You're right, Sam. I wouldn't have believed it if I hadn't seen it with my own eyes." Remi put one hand on the woman's arm, drawing her attention, while reaching behind her to scoop up her purse. "What on earth are you two doing here?"

Sam moved in, putting his arm around the man's shoulders. "How are you?" he asked as he and Remi walked alongside, sweeping them in the direction of the two armed police officers. "So, lunch? Dinner? What do you say?"

The pair tried to distance themselves, but Sam and Remi stepped closer. The woman looked around, suddenly worried, as the man said, "We—we don't know you."

"Sure you do. Sam Fargo. My wife, Remi. And you are?"

The man hesitated, then said, "Ivan Ivanov."

"Ivan Ivanov?" Sam stepped back to open a wallet, reading the ID. "I would've guessed something like . . . Ilya Aristov."

"That's mine!" He tried to take back his wallet.

"So you're not Ivan Ivanov?"

The woman turned toward the booth in a panic. "My purse!"

Remi held it up. "You really have to be careful in places like this," she said, opening the bag, seeing a small handgun next to a wallet. "Leaving it right where anyone could grab it. So careless."

The woman reached for the bag.

Remi took a quick step back, gripping the weapon, careful to keep it hidden as she aimed it at the couple. "I'd hate to blow a hole through the bottom of a Louis Vuitton. Wait. It's a knockoff. No worries."

"You're making a big mistake," the woman said.

"Right," Sam said. "And yet, here you are. Exactly why are you following us?"

The man's glance strayed toward the police officer, then back at Sam. "I—I don't know what you're talking about." Other than his slight Russian accent, his English was impeccable. "As your wife said, you have us mistaken for someone else."

"Could be," Sam said, stepping close to Ilya, expertly removing the man's gun before he even realized what had happened. "Follow us again? We won't be this nice."

"What are you going to do?" he asked. "Shoot us?"

"Remi, see if those nice officers are busy."

"Politsiya!" Remi called out as the man and woman bolted in the opposite direction. "Hmm. You'd think they'd at least accept our lunch invitation."

"BOTH NAMES ARE ALIASES," Selma announced later that afternoon. "Their IDs are professional fakes."

"Who are they?" Sam asked. He'd taken a photo of their IDs before Remi turned over everything to the two officers, reporting their suspicious behavior in a mixture of English and broken Russian. The police declared it a robbery attempt, something Sam and Remi highly doubted.

"According to the information I was able to find," Selma replied, "your would-be robbers are associated with a Russian crime family run by Tatiana Petrov, who took it over from her father after he was murdered by a rival crime family."

"What are they known for?" Sam asked.

"According to the newspaper articles I was able to find, drug trafficking, sex trade, the usual."

"Even I've heard of the Petrovs," Sergei said. "Very bad. I recommend you leave Kaliningrad. They're worse than your American Mafia."

"Why us?" Remi asked.

"Because of Durin," Sam replied. "They have to be part of the group who attacked us at his apartment. It definitely confirms that there are two separate groups after this Romanov Ransom."

"One more thing," Selma said. "After going through the bibliography on Andrei's internet book, I was able to dig up some interesting information on that retired groundskeeper of Königsberg castle. Andrei was right. You're definitely going to want to interview the man."

25

The once splendid Königsberg castle had completely burned after the Allied bombing in 1944, leaving only the thick walls. After the war ended, Königsberg was annexed by the Soviet Union, renamed Kaliningrad, and the castle remains were leveled by a government that wanted to erase any reminders of its Prussian past.

It was this last fact that made the presence of a groundskeeper a bit of a surprise—at least in Remi's mind. There wasn't much left of the grounds to keep, unless one happened to be an archaeologist. The empty rectangular courtyard was now surrounded by gray boards blocking off the area from the public. A large section of the boarded wall had fallen and a temporary chain-link fence stood in its place, allowing a view into the castle property and, at the far end, the recent excavations.

Sam checked his watch as the three stood on the sidewalk, waiting. "He did say meet here near the parking lot?"

No sooner had the words left his mouth than a taxi pulled up. Remi saw a gray-haired man holding a cane get out, pay the driver, then hobble in their direction. "That's got to be him."

"Miron Pushkaryov?" Sam asked as he approached.

"You must be the Fargos," he said with a thick Russian accent. "And Sergei. Forgive me for being late. I stopped by to see Andrei before I came out here."

"No worries," Remi said. "You're here. That's what counts."

"But I do worry. Ever since Andrei wrote that book, he's had many things go wrong. I wanted to make sure you were who you said you were. Therefore, it was necessary to do so in person." The man placed both hands on the brass head of his cane, eyeing them. "Andrei mentioned what happened to you at the museum. So you see, they're still watching him. They're probably watching me. They may even be watching you."

Sam scanned the vast parking lot that ran the length of the castle grounds, not seeing anything suspicious. "Were you followed here?"

"I hope not." He gave Remi a thorough appraisal. "Andrei never mentioned how beautiful you are."

"You're very kind, Mr. Pushkaryov."

"Merely observant. And, please, call me Miron," he said, then turned to Sam. "What is it you're looking for, Mr. Fargo?"

"Information."

"On?"

"The treasures that might have been stored at Königsberg castle."

"You mean the treasures that were *taken* from the castle after the bombing?"

"Precisely," Sam said. "What is it you know?"

"Only what my grandfather told me. The most valuable treasures were kept belowground, out of the public eye. They survived the Allied bombing and remained there up until Hitler ordered their removal."

"The Amber Room?" Remi asked. "Any chance it survived and was moved?"

"We can always hope. Unfortunately, recent excavations of the subterranean levels *have* turned up bits of amber . . ." He nodded toward the castle grounds, his smile bittersweet. "Still, being that my grandfather told me tales of a line of trucks waiting in the courtyard to be loaded at the end of the war, one never knows. Perhaps they got the Amber Room out in time. But I was under the impression that you were interested in something else entirely."

"We are," Sam said. "Have you heard of the Romanov Ransom?"

"Of it, yes. What was in it . . . ?" He shrugged. "I don't precisely know."

"Is there *anything* you can tell us?" Remi asked.

"A bit. My grandfather remembered seeing Nazi officers loading crates from the castle onto numerous trucks one night. Two officers inspected each truck, then removed four smaller chests from one. They opened the chests to see what they contained, then carried them to a different vehicle. The last truck in the line."

He stared through the chain-link toward the excavation site, taking a deep breath, then letting out a sigh. "So long ago . . . My grandfather used to bring me here when I was a boy, telling me what the castle looked like before the war. The pictures. They don't do it justice." He lifted his cane, pointing with it. "Over there, you can see the fence surrounding the excavation where some of the treasure was believed to have been stored. And over there is where the trucks pulled up and the men loaded everything from the castle's remains. I loved hearing the tale from my grandfather." His soft smile faded when he looked back at them. "As a boy, I dreamed of following the trail that my grandfather had seen on their map. I was going to find the treasure."

"Map?" Remi asked.

"I assumed that's why you were here. You had to have found the map."

A loud screeching of tires caught their attention. Sam spun around as a blue sedan sped through the adjoining parking lot toward them. Bright sunlight glinted off the black-tinted windows as the car slowed and the rear window rolled down—and someone pointed a handgun in their direction.

26

"Get down!" Sam yelled.

He grabbed Miron, pulling him behind a parked delivery van. Remi and Sergei dove behind a Fiat as the first shot was fired. A second shot ricocheted off the ground just a few inches from Sam's leg. The car sped off, its tires squealing on the pavement as it whipped around the corner. Sam peered around the side of the van. The gunman's car sped through the parking lot, the back end fishtailing as the driver whipped it around for a second pass.

Sam helped Miron to his feet. "We need to find cover."

"The excavations," Miron said as Sergei supported him from the other side. They reached the chain-link fence that surrounded it. Plywood and tin walls encompassed the perimeter, but the gate was open for the workers, who were climbing up from the dig site to see what was going on.

Sam looked back, saw the blue car stopping near the gate. The gunman in the backseat threw open the door, about to follow, when the high-low whine of police sirens sent him scurrying back. The car sped off as the police arrived just in time to give chase.

"That was close," Remi said.

Miron gripped his cane, his hand shaking. "I suggest we get out of here before the police come back. Unless you don't mind being questioned for hours about why someone was shooting at us."

"I like your way of thinking," Sam said. They'd already dealt with the police that morning after the incident at the museum. Having their names come up again was likely to result in a lot more red tape and valuable time lost.

"Where to?" Sergei asked, pulling the keys from his pocket.

"My house, if you don't mind. It'll save me a taxi ride."

It took about twenty minutes. Sergei drove while Sam, gun in hand, kept an eye on the side mirror and on every car they passed. Finally, they pulled up to an ivy-covered gabled house on a cobbled road. A brick walk led to Miron's front door, which he unlocked, allowing them in. After locking the door behind them, he leaned his brass-headed cane against the wall, then took off his gloves, scarf, and hat. "I'll turn on the heater to take the chill off. Make yourselves comfortable," he said, crossing the room to the thermostat.

"Earlier," Sam said, "you mentioned something about a map? You assumed that's why we were here."

"The map . . . Yes." Miron tapped the button and the heater kicked on, bringing with it the scent of burnt dust, leading Sam to believe that he didn't run it all that often. Judging from the peeling paint and general state of disrepair, Sam gathered that money was tight. "Rather a long story, so perhaps you should take a seat." He directed them to sit at a round, scarred mahogany table, protected, oddly enough, with a glass top, which did nothing to hide the markings and gouges on the surface.

"According to my grandfather, the map—I'm assuming it's the same one you found—showed the route they were plotting for the trucks to take the treasure that had been stored up until then at Königsberg castle."

"There wasn't a route drawn on the map we found," Sam said. "Königsberg was circled, but that was it."

"If I'm not mistaken, the route was actually traced onto paper from the original map."

"That explains the bits of brittle yellowed paper we found in the courier bag," Sam said. "A shame it didn't survive."

"The tin?" Miron asked.

"You know about that?"

"Only because my grandfather wrote about it in his diary." He nodded to a black and white photo on the bookshelf of a dark-haired man who bore a striking resemblance to Miron. "He, apparently, turned the map, the tracing paper copy, and the tin over to someone named Lambrecht, who was supposed to get everything to the Allies."

"Any idea as to the tin's significance?"

"None. My grandfather seemed to think the items had some importance beyond the gold. Of course, some of that was to finance the escape of the Nazi officers who planned to flee the continent. But he always suspected that there was something more going on. Even before Hitler ordered that all of the stolen art be removed from Königsberg castle, my grandfather believed these officers were making plans for the treasure—he just couldn't figure out what for. It's why, when he found their map, he copied their route, at great risk to himself. And it's why he kept this table. It was in their office when they made their plans," he said, running his hand across the smooth glass surface.

"The Romanov Ransom?" Remi asked. "Did it have something to do with that?"

"Indeed it did, Mrs. Fargo. It's what's behind all this violence. These people trying to keep Andrei from publishing his book all these years believe his writings will help others find the treasure before they do. And yet what they don't realize is that they're all chasing the wrong lead."

"Why is that?" Sam asked.

"The evidence my grandfather found and turned over to Lambrecht and the Allies. It's all right here."

He patted the tabletop.

Sam glanced down at it. "I'm not sure I understand."

"Mahogany. Very soft, as you probably know."

Sam examined the dark wood, noting the scratches and other marks. "What, exactly, are we looking at?"

"The route that was traced from the map. The same route on the bits of paper you found in the courier bag. Not that you'd realize it unless you know where to look," he said, trailing his finger across some unseen mark on the table.

Sam leaned in close, seeing a faint indentation in the dark wood in the shape of a large jagged Z. "That's the route?"

"I believe so. The only reason it's never been examined any closer was that the original map was missing. As many times as I've tried to re-create the route on a modern map, it's never worked. I expect it's because of the size difference. But since you have the original, all we need do is overlay the tracing that I made on top. That will tell us where the treasure is."

"One problem," Remi said. "We no longer have it."

Sam pulled his cell phone from his pocket. "But we do have photos. If you have a computer, we can print it out."

27

Unfortunately, they had to approximate the size of the map since the photos Sam took with his phone had nothing to reference the map's original size.

"A little bigger," Sam said.

"Are you sure?" Remi said. "A little smaller, wasn't it?"

Sergei, standing behind them, said, "Maybe we can find something similar online. There's plenty of World War Two memorabilia around."

"No time," Sam said. "That looks pretty close. Let's print it out and put it together."

Remi sighed. "The things you don't think about when you turn over the original . . ."

"This will have to do."

Fortunately, Miron had an accurate sketch on acetate paper that he'd traced directly from the route drawn on the tabletop. He brought it out, laying it on top of the newly printed map. "I can't tell you how many times I've tried to overlay it on various World War Two maps of Europe. So far, no luck."

Sam positioned the tracing paper so that one end of the Z mark rested atop Königsberg castle. "The moment of truth."

Remi watched as he turned the tracing paper about, trying to match the other end of the Z to some city. "And what truth would that be?"

"That we still don't know where it leads. Not unless we can figure out how the map was positioned on the table when that tracing was made."

"Actually," Miron said, "I believe we can. It makes sense that the map would be positioned with north at the top, and the person making the tracing would be standing at the south."

"Agreed," Sam said. "But it's a round table. How do we know where they were standing?"

"Because the same man who drew the route on the original map that my grandfather copied, signed his name on the requisition order for the trucks to take the treasure there. Chances are good that, being in charge, he sat in the same chair each time. That would be here," he said, pointing to the edge of the table near Sam's right elbow. "You can see his signature. Obermann Ludwig Strassmair."

Almost at once, Sam, Remi, and Sergei leaned in, examining the tabletop, trying to see what it was Miron was talking about. Sure enough, the signature, though faint, was there for all to see. Signed and dated 31 January 1945. Sam moved the map so the bottom was positioned near the man's signature, then slid it up so that the edge of the bottom of the zigzag line started where Königsberg castle was circled on the map. The top of the zigzag landed between the two German cities of Breslau and Waldenburg, both now part of Poland and currently known as Wrocław and Wałbrzych.

"Ludwig Strassmair," Miron said, "commanded one of the prison camps in that area. It makes sense he'd move the treasure to somewhere familiar to him."

"What else do you know about him?" Sam asked.

"At the end of the war, he was one of several officers instrumental in the deaths of thousands of German civilians. Strassmair and the others refused to allow them to flee Königsberg before the Russians invaded." Miron let out a tired sigh. "The treasures stored at the castle were another matter entirely. That, he made sure, was saved before the Russians came. Most, my grandfather believed, was to finance something called *Unternehmen Werwolf*. Have you heard of it?"

"Operation Werewolf," Sam said. It was supposed to be an elite troop of Germans trained to use clandestine guerrilla tactics against the Allied Forces behind enemy lines. "Everything I'd read suggested that the program failed. More propaganda than reality."

"It definitely existed," Miron said. "Not quite how they planned or how history painted it. At the close of the war, those operatives who weren't discovered by the Allied Forces ended up helping run the ratlines to assist the Nazis' escape. The reason I bring it up is that I believe Obermann Ludwig Strassmair, the officer who requisitioned the trucks, was a member of this group. The trucks with their treasures, with the Romanov Ransom, were meant for this operation. More important, the Nazis intended that there'd be no survivors. They executed every person who was aware of the trucks' existence."

"But your grandfather . . . ?" Sergei said. "How did he survive?"

"The bullet only grazed him," Miron replied, touching the left side of his chest to indicate where his grandfather had been shot. "When a Nazi guard fell on top of him, he played dead, staying beneath the body until the last truck was gone."

"And Obermann Strassmair?" Sam asked.

"Declared a Nazi war criminal after the war. Never arrested—not that they didn't search, mind you."

"What do you think happened to him?"

"I think he succeeded in his mission. To secure the Romanov Ransom and the other treasures, laying the groundwork for their retrieval after the war. Their sole purpose was to make sure they could recover it all when they needed to for *Unternehmen Werwolf.*"

He tapped the map. "History paints the *Werwolf* members as more a nuisance than any real threat. To his dying day, my grandfather believed the *Werwolf* guard continued on, passing their secrets to subsequent generations for one sole purpose: to watch over the stolen treasures of the Third Reich for whatever purpose they've deemed. What that is, I don't know."

"And what do you think?" Sam asked.

"I believe the threat of the Guard is real, even to this day. I think they're behind the attacks on Andrei and his book. They're dangerous. And that doesn't take into account anyone else on the search for this treasure. There could very well be others."

"So we've found out," Remi said.

Sam eyed the tracing paper, with its route landing right between both cities. There was a lot of space between the two, and the accuracy of the location depended on guesswork. "Bottom line. Where would you be looking for this treasure? Wrocław or Wałbrzych?"

"Personally, I'd go with Wałbrzych. It is, after all, home of the legendary Gold Train in Poland."

"But so many have looked," Sergei said. "They found nothing there."

"And yet, the rumors still persist. There must be a reason." He removed the tracing paper from the map, then took a pen and circled one area. "Here, near Książ castle, is where I'd start. It was part of Project Riese, a network of tunnels and bunkers that the Nazis built throughout the mountains, including beneath the castle."

"Great," Remi said to Sam. "More tunnels."

"Show me a country in Europe that doesn't have them," Sam said.

"Still," Sergei added, "it's a good place to hide a treasure."

Remi made a scoffing noise. "What about a good old-fashioned desert island?"

"Ignore her," Sam said. "She's a little tunnel weary after getting lost in a few below Nottingham." They'd been searching for King John's Treasure at the time. "About this Castle Książ," he said, returning his attention to the map and Miron, "why there and not at the sixty-fifth-kilometer marker on the line from Wrocław to Wałbrzych? If we're going with rumors, isn't that where everyone else thinks the Gold Train is? Even our attempt at placing the route on the map shows it's somewhere in between."

"And maybe it is. But Renard Kowalski, an expert on the tunnels of Project Riese, works at the castle. At least he was still working there a couple of years ago when I spoke to him. He's the one you'll want to talk to."

Sam picked up the map, where Castle Książ was circled, showing it to Remi. "Date night in Wałbrzych?"

"So romantic. Tunnels, flashlights! I can wear my designer boots again!"

28

Tatiana stepped outside the airport doors into the crisp autumn air, took one look at Viktor's face, and knew there was a problem involving the Fargos.

Taking the suitcase from her, he placed it into the trunk, then opened her car door, closing it for her after she was seated.

"What happened?" she asked once he was behind the wheel.

He checked his mirror, pulled out, before answering. "I won't bore you with the details other than to say we underestimated the Fargos. They realized they were being followed and managed to lose our tail."

"The Fargos bested you?" she said, looking over at him in surprise. "What happened to all these highly trained men working for you? Surely you had more than one set of eyes on them?"

"We did. But they were . . . distracted by the shooting at Königsberg castle."

"I thought I told you—"

"It wasn't us."

"Then who?" she asked.

"No doubt Rolfe or someone from his entourage."

"He's here? How?"

"If I had to guess, he flew into Gdańsk, then drove over the Polish border. Had he flown directly into Kaliningrad, we would've known."

If the Fargos were here, it stood to reason that Rolfe would also be here. He had the courier bag, after all. "I should have anticipated."

Several seconds of silence passed. She glanced over at him, saw his jaw clenching and his knuckles turning white on the steering wheel. Clearly, he was blaming himself.

"Where is he?" she asked.

"Rolfe? We followed him to a house about thirty minutes' drive outside of town."

"And the Fargos?"

"They've left Kaliningrad."

"To where?"

"We're still working on that."

She weighed her phone in her hand, thinking about how to salvage this mess. "I have an idea." She called a number, letting it ring. "Rolfe, darling . . ."

"Tatiana? To what do I owe the pleasure?" he said, sounding anything but pleased.

"I've just arrived in Kaliningrad for business. I understand you're here as well."

"How is it you know this?"

"Did you really think that a man of your reputation can just waltz into my territory without anyone noticing?"

There was a slight hesitation on the line, then Rolfe asked, "What is it you want?"

"To meet, of course. I feel we have unfinished business. When is a good time for you?"

"I'm currently busy with—"

"Later this afternoon, then?" she said, not giving him a chance to back out. "It's important, or I wouldn't ask. Shall I come to you, or would you like to meet me?" she said, naming a location far enough away from where she was told he was staying so as not to arouse suspicion. "I'm just leaving the airport."

As expected, he chose to meet her at his location and gave her the address.

"I'll see you in a couple of hours," she said.

SHE AND VIKTOR drove out to the secluded house and were met at the door by Gere, who limped as he led them down a hallway toward a dark-paneled salon. Rolfe was seated in a leather armchair, drinking what she assumed from the gold flakes floating in the clear liquid was Goldwasser vodka.

"Tatiana," he said, rising.

"Rolfe." She walked up to him, smelling the strong alcohol on his breath as she let him kiss her on both cheeks.

He glanced at Viktor and, as expected, promptly ignored him. Looking at Tatiana, he waved her toward the matching chair opposite him.

She sat, looking around the room. The heavy, dark wooden furnishings appeared expensive, including the paintings on the wall: bloody battle scenes from the Middle Ages. "Charming," she said, eyeing the artwork with distaste. "How did you find this place?"

He returned to his chair, picking up his glass. "It belongs to a business associate of mine."

"You have business associates in Kaliningrad?"

"I have business associates all over Europe."

"Perhaps you should introduce me to some of them."

He took a sip of his drink, then set it on the chairside table. "What is it you're doing here, Tatiana?"

She studied the man for a moment. There was a definite change about him. Normally, he was eager to see her, wanting to foster a relationship that he hoped would tie their two businesses together. That thought always amused her mostly because she was the one who'd planted the idea in his head. Today, though, his eyes held a slight annoyance, and there was a stubborn tilt to his chin.

It galled her that she had to handle it this way, but she had no choice and so she just came out with it. "I've come to make a deal. I want in on the Romanov Ransom."

His brows rose slightly as he picked up his glass, swirling the liquid so that the gold flakes spun about. "That's not going to happen."

"You need me."

"The moment I find out what I want to know, I won't need anyone."

"I thought that's what the contents of the courier bag were supposed to have told you?"

This time, he couldn't hide his surprise. "How do you know about that?"

"I make it my business. Your man—what was his name?"

"Gere?"

"Not him, the other one." She glanced over her shoulder at Viktor, who stood stock-still behind her. "What was his name?"

"Durin," Viktor said.

"Yes. Durin . . ." She focused on Rolfe. "The courier bag he stole from the plane was supposed to be on its way to me. Had he not been killed, I'd have it now, not you."

Rolfe stared at her for several seconds, the only reaction was the bulge of a vein beating fast at his temple. He drained his glass, then set it on the table, as a muffled thump came from the room next door.

It sounded to her as though someone had fallen against the wall. "What was that?" she asked, standing.

"Nothing."

She eyed Rolfe's telling temple vein pounding away. Before he could object, she walked over to the door and pulled it open, surprised to see the tall, bearded man holding an old man by his throat.

Tatiana, recognizing the aggressor as Leopold Gaudecker, stormed into the room, stepping over a brass-headed cane on the floor, as Leopold raised his hand, about to strike.

"Stop!" she demanded, grabbing Leopold's arm. "What are you doing?"

Leopold, still holding the old man by the throat, glared at her. "I'd suggest you remove your hand from my arm before I hit you instead."

"Try it," she said, whipping out a stiletto, holding it just below his sternum. "Exactly what is going on here?"

He looked down at the point piercing his shirt, then at Rolfe. "Your Russian princess annoys me."

"Regardless, I'd do what she says," Rolfe said. "I've heard assassination is one of her specialties."

She pressed the point farther, drawing blood. "Let him go."

Leopold stepped away, both hands raised. "You're crazy."

"So they say." She waited until Viktor entered the room before closing and putting away her knife in its hidden sheath. When he positioned himself between her and Leopold, she rounded on Rolfe. "You have *no* idea what you're involving yourself with by bringing that man here."

"The groundskeeper? You know him?"

She wasn't about to admit that she had no clue as to who he was. "You forget what country you're in. I make it my business to know. Why is he here?"

"He knows where the Fargos are."

"Does he?" She looked at the old man with renewed interest. "And you think beating him is going to work? As old as he is, you're likely to kill him first."

"You have a better way?" Leopold asked. "By all means. Show us how it's done."

"Clear the room," she said, "and I'll be glad to."

No one moved.

She leveled her gaze on Rolfe. "I'm sorry. Was my German a little rusty?"

He studied her a moment, then gave a sharp nod to Leopold. "Go," he said.

The man stalked out, not happy about taking orders from her.

Rolfe hesitated.

"You, too." She walked up to him, putting her hand on his arm, guiding him from the room.

"Just curious how you plan on getting this information."

"We have our ways," she said, then turned to Viktor. "You know what to do."

He gave a slight nod.

She glanced at the old man, his eyes widening in fright as Viktor approached. Closing the door, she returned to her seat. Leopold stood, arms crossed, glaring at her. Ignoring him, she turned to Rolfe, who was pouring himself another drink. "It shouldn't take long," she said.

Five minutes later, Viktor opened the door. The old man sat in a chair, his gaze on the ground. Viktor walked up to Tatiana and whispered the information in her ear.

"Thank you," she told him, then to Rolfe said, "I now know where the Fargos are."

Leopold eyed the old man through the open door. "How?"

Tatiana took her time, pleased to see that Rolfe's gaze was fixed only on her. "Here in Kaliningrad, it's easy to forget you're in Russia. But being Russian, we know it's not the beating or killing that buys cooperation. It's the threat of what can be done to their family once they're no longer around." She glanced at Leopold, who quickly looked away. Apparently, he was sore at being bested. She turned her attention back to Rolfe. "I have contacts everywhere, including the police and the government."

"Impressive," Rolfe said.

"As I mentioned, Rolfe, you need me."

"For now."

"Perhaps I should clarify. You need me if you want to do business in my country. Ever." When he said nothing in response, she knew she'd won the immediate battle and nodded for Viktor to remove the man from the room. "Should there be any more information to be had, we'll find out and let you know. Assuming we have a deal?"

Rolfe watched as Viktor led the old man toward the front door. "What did you learn?" he asked after they were gone.

"As I said, I know where the Fargos are." She waited a beat to let that settle in. "That *is* what you were trying to discover, was it not? Of course I must assume you know that the Fargos are also searching for this treasure. They have a map in their possession with a specific location marked on it. In Poland."

"Poland?" He eyed the vodka in his glass, mulling it over. "Forty percent."

"Half or I find the Fargos and the map on my own."

"You forget that you don't have the Guard working alongside you. Considering that Russia no longer controls Poland, the advantage is mine."

"Guard?"

"Perhaps you know them by their older name. *Werwolf.* Leopold's men are as bloodthirsty as their title implies."

Trying to hide her surprise, she flicked her gaze toward Leopold, then back at Rolfe. "And what makes them special?"

"The Guard," Leopold said, his cold blue eyes staring at her as though he'd be glad to rip out her throat right there, "have men in every country in Europe. You tell me where in Poland and I will have twenty men ready at a moment's notice waiting for the Fargos before they even arrive."

She studied the bearded man before returning her gaze to Rolfe. "Fine. Forty percent. But I'm coming with you."

"You don't trust me?" Rolfe asked.

"I expect the feeling is mutual. Like you, I've been searching for this for too long. I'm not about to let it slip away." She made a point of looking at her watch. "It's late. I have a few business matters that can't wait."

"You can't leave," Rolfe said, following her to the door. "You haven't told me where in Poland the Fargos are headed."

She wasn't about to pass on that information, yet. "Since Leopold said he only needed a moment's notice, I insist on waiting until we're ready to leave. I'm sure you understand. That whole trust issue. Shall we meet back here in, say, two hours?"

He reluctantly agreed, and she left. Outside, she found Viktor waiting, the engine running. "Where's the old man?"

"In the trunk."

"Any problems?"

"Turns out, he was far more cooperative than I could have hoped for. What happened after I left?"

"I'm in for forty percent."

"Forty?"

"I wasn't in a position to bargain. How can I, when I know nothing about this Wolf Guard? *Werwolf.* Did you know they still existed?"

"I'd heard rumors of them in Germany, and even Poland. But not in Russia."

"Well, Leopold, obviously, runs them. He came from somewhere." She glanced at the house as they pulled away and saw the very man in question watching from a window. "I want to know everything there is about this Leopold Gaudecker and his group. He claims given any location, he can send men to find the Fargos with very little notice."

29

The Fargos' flight to Wrocław early the next morning took a little over two hours. Sam invited Sergei, who happened to be fluent in Polish, to come along with them.

As usual, the ever-efficient Selma had their rental car waiting for them the moment they cleared the airport. From there, they drove straight to Wałbrzych, catching sight of the majestic pink and gray thirteenth-century cliff-top Castle Książ as they neared the city. It was even more impressive up close as they walked through its vast courtyard and ornamental gardens.

Sam looked around the gardens, then into the castle. "Divide and conquer?"

"Good idea," Remi said.

While she knew enough Polish to get by on her own, Sam was going to need Sergei's help. "You check inside, Remi. Sergei and I will see if we can find someone out here who knows him."

She left. Eventually, he and Sergei found a gardener, tending a bed of roses.

"Excuse me," Sam said. "We're looking for someone named Renard Kowalski."

The gardener glanced over, his gaze taking them in, before turning back to the flowers, clipping off the faded red blooms.

Sergei repeated the question in Polish. Their conversation was short and, apparently, from the expression on Sergei's face, surprising. He turned to Sam, lowering his voice. "Didn't see that coming. The guy's dead."

"Kowalski? What happened?"

"A hunting accident. He says they don't talk about it. No one does."

Sam eyed the man who seemed a little too eager to get back to work. "That's it?"

"That's it. He wouldn't even give me the name of anyone who knew him."

"Let's find someone else who can help." But the pattern repeated with the next two employees. "It'd be nice to find out what's going on. Maybe Remi's having better luck." He texted her, and she answered, saying she'd be about fifteen more minutes. When she did emerge from the castle, walking down the stairs, it was with a group of tourists led by a guide.

Remi waved them over. "Very knowledgeable," she whispered as Sam and Sergei joined her at the back of the group. "Talking about access to the tunnels being out here. Maybe when she's finished, she'll be able to tell us something."

The young woman waited for everyone to gather around. "Here," she said, her English thickly accented, "at the conclusion of our tour, in what is called the Honorary Courtyard, is another of the access points to the chambers. One is fifteen meters down, the other fifty. Both were part of Project Riese, a vast series of tunnels built by the Nazis using prisoners of war from the nearby camps. The headquarters for the project was located in the castle. Beneath our very feet," she said, sweeping her hand in front of her, "the Nazis built a lift that led to the chambers below. The shaft has since been filled. To this day, no one knows the true purpose of the tunnels." She answered several questions from the group, told them to enjoy the gardens, then waited patiently as they wandered off. Finally, noticing Remi, Sam, and Sergei still standing there, she smiled. "Is there something I can help you with?"

"Yes," Remi said. "We're looking for someone who might have known Renard Kowalski."

An almost imperceptible look clouded the woman's eyes. Sam couldn't tell if it was fear, sadness, or a combination of the two. "I honestly can't tell you," she said.

"Can't?" Sam asked. "Or won't? The man worked here. I'd think someone might know something about him."

"I'm afraid you're mistaken. My understanding is, it was more that his presence was tolerated. He came many days out of the year, searching the castle and the grounds for evidence of the Gold Train— which he never found. He became something of a legend around here for it. But, no, he never worked here."

"He was killed, though?" Sam asked.

"A hunting accident. Tragically, his hobby searching the woods for evidence of this train is what killed him."

She started to turn away, clearly in a hurry to get out of there.

Remi reached out, touching her arm. "Please. Is there anyone who might help us? Anyone who knew him and what he was working on?"

The woman hesitated, looking around—perhaps to see who was watching—before focusing on Remi. "There is one man who knew him well."

"How do we get in touch with him?"

"You don't. He doesn't talk to anyone. He's—how do you say it . . . ? The word for someone who lives alone, avoiding society . . . ?"

"*Recluse?*"

"That's it. But . . . crazy. Dangerous, even. Some even say he's the one who killed Renard Kowalski."

"Does he have a name?" Sam asked.

"If you were to ask in town about the crazy recluse, someone might know."

"Where would—?"

"I'm sorry, but that's all I can tell you. I really have to go."

She quickly walked up the stairs and into the castle, never looking back.

"Odd," Remi said.

Sam agreed. "Makes you wonder if that hunting accident was really a hunting accident."

30

In the neighborhood below the castle, everyone seemed to know who the man was—Crazy Gustaw—but no one seemed to know where he lived. Sam was grateful that enough people in the area spoke English to make it easy to ask questions. Unfortunately, no one wanted to talk about the man. Their best source was at a newsstand. "You don't find him," the man working there said. "Gustaw finds you. If that happens, watch out."

"How?"

The man shrugged.

After a frustrating morning of their polite inquiries being avoided, Sam pulled out several bills, placing them on the newsstand counter. "Is there anyone who can help us locate him?"

"Possibly at the pub," he said, picking up the money and pocketing it, then pointing down the street. "After they closed the mines, some of the old miners still meet there. You'll recognize them. They sit at the tables in the corner, playing dice. Gustaw used to drink with them. Not anymore. Not since his friend was killed."

"We appreciate your help."

"You may not. They aren't too friendly to strangers."

Sam agreed with his assessment when they walked into the dark-paneled pub. The group of men in the corner, ranging in age from mid-fifties to late sixties, continued playing their game, ignoring them, as Sam asked if anyone knew where to find Gustaw.

Sergei repeated the question in Polish. A gray-haired man sitting closest to them swept his gaze across the room, before landing on Sergei, then Sam, in English, saying, "Better you leave."

"We're looking for a guide," Sam said. "Someone who knows the history on some of the tunnels in the mountains and who might be able to interpret an old map to current locations."

"Sorry you wasted your time. The government has moratorium on digging in area. Too many people trying to find Nazi Gold Train."

"We're not after the train," Sam said. "Just trying to find some information—"

"No information. The Guard always watching." He turned his back to them, reaching for the dice cup.

"What can we do to change your mind?"

"Nothing," he said without turning around. "You should leave. Before anything happens."

"Like what?"

"Getting shot." He covered the top of the cup and began shaking it, the dice rattling inside. No one else at the table would even look at them.

Sam glanced around the dimly lit bar, noticing the handful of other patrons sitting about, their expressions wary, looking the other way when Sam tried to make eye contact.

The bartender, drying glasses with a white towel, watched the proceedings in silence.

"Let's see what he knows," Sam said quietly. They crossed the room, taking a seat at the bar. "Three pints of whatever lager you have on tap," Sam said. "And some information."

"Americans?"

Sam nodded.

"The pints I get you. Information . . . ?" He went back to wiping the counter down. "What is it you want to know?"

"We're looking for a guide who knows something about the tunnels in the mountains. A friend of Renard Kowalski," Sam said. "Some describe him as a recluse who lives in the woods."

The moment Sam mentioned Renard's name, the bartender stilled, then went back to wiping the counter. "The man you look for. Crazy Gustaw," he said as a loud scrape came from behind them. "Better you not to go."

Sam glanced back, saw a tall, dark-haired man from a table near the door eyeing them as he rose from his chair. "We'll take our chances," Sam said as the man walked out the door. He slid several large bills onto the counter.

"Your life." He tossed the towel over his shoulder, picked up the money, then took a napkin and drew a map. "Be smart, wait for morning. Gustaw might shoot. Actually, that's true all time. To him, everyone is enemy."

"What sort of enemies?"

"You ask Gustaw. If he not kill you first." He slid the napkin toward Sam, then filled three mugs from the tap.

They took the beer to an empty table.

"So where does he live?" Remi asked.

Sam showed her the napkin. The castle was drawn at the top left corner for reference. "Not too far from here, apparently."

They finished their drinks, then left. As the three crossed the street, Sam saw the dark-haired man from the bar standing in front of a store, talking to someone else. Something about the way both men were watching them bothered Sam. "I'm getting the idea that we're the subject of their conversation."

Remi glanced over, then back. "Any earlier in the day, I'd say let's give them something to talk about. Right now, I'd rather get to the hotel. I hear a hot bath and a glass of champagne calling my name."

"Why, Remi. How absolutely decadent. Couldn't think of anything better." With the reception they seemed to be receiving in town, it was probably best to get off the streets before dark. They checked into their room, Sergei occupying one down the hall.

That night, before they went to bed, Sam turned off the lights, then stood by the window. They were on the second floor, facing the street. A man with a dog on a leash walked past, his glance straight ahead. About a block up, his dog alerted on a parked van. Any number of things could have caught the dog's attention, even the scent of another dog. Sam, however, liked to operate on the theory that a dog's nose should never be ignored. Despite the crisp, cool autumn weather, he opened the window, closed the curtains, then informed Remi that he'd be taking the first watch.

About two hours later, he heard the slightest sound outside their window. Glancing over, he saw the faint light from the streetlamp filtering through the part in the curtains. He got up and, standing to one side, peered out. Two men stood across the street by a car, and two more were crossing toward the hotel.

"Remi." He leaned over, touching her on her shoulder.

She stirred.

"Wake up."

"What's wrong?" she asked.

"We have company. Better get dressed. Time to get out of here."

They'd barely slipped their shoes on when he heard a creak in the hallway. There was a fifth person because no way could they have gotten up there that fast. Another floorboard creaked, this one farther down the hall. Make that six.

Didn't matter.

They were trapped.

31

Sam knew what they were after.

They wanted Miron's map. He hoped that meant they were bypassing Sergei's room completely. His gun gripped in one hand, he stood at the open window, spying through the slit in the curtains. The men in the street seemed to be watching the front entry of the hotel. They weren't the ones he was worried about.

He looked over at Remi, pointing toward the bathroom. She nodded, grabbed her gun and phone, while Sam slipped Miron's map from his pack, circling the other locations in the vicinity of the Project Riese tunnels. Hoping it would buy them some time, he left the map on the table, placing his pack on top, making sure it was visible beneath it. After a quick look around, he joined Remi behind the bathroom door, leaving it open far enough to reveal the toilet and empty shower.

The soft clicks as someone picked the lock gave way to the sound of the knob turning and the door opening. The security chain rattled, then went tight. For several seconds, the only sound Sam heard was Remi breathing beside him and the ticking of the furnace blowing heat into the room.

Whoever was out there wasn't moving.

No doubt testing the waters, making sure their victims weren't wakened, before they busted through.

Sam gripped his gun, ready to fire.

He heard the chain move, then the sound of screws ripping from wood as one of the intruders shoved his weight against the door. The men rushed in, flashlights sweeping the room.

"They're gone," someone said in English, his German accent thick.

Loud footsteps crossed the room. "They went out the window," another said, his accent sounding more Russian.

"They knew we were coming."

"Dump their bags. Find the map."

Sam heard them ruffling through their things, then someone saying, "I have it."

"What's that?" Silence, then, "A siren?"

"Go! Go!"

As quickly as they came in, they left.

Sam didn't move. He and Remi remained behind the bathroom door for several seconds until the heavy footsteps receded down the hallway. The faint siren grew louder.

Outside, he heard the sound of men running and car doors closing, followed by the rev of engines as the vehicles sped off.

Sam moved to the window, looking out. The street was clear. "Have to say, that was a very convenient siren."

"Sergei got my text," Remi said, holding up her cell phone.

He eyed the gun she held at her side. "You can text with one hand?"

"Can't you?"

He almost laughed. If it weren't for autocorrect, his texts would probably be unreadable. And that was using two hands. "Nicely done, Mrs. Fargo." He glanced out the window again. "Cops are here. We should probably stash the guns."

"And let Sergei know we're okay."

———

THE POLICE LEFT sometime after sunrise, with a stern warning that this was the very reason why the government was set against people looking for this Gold Train. Sam, Remi, and Sergei packed up their things, found an open café, and sat down to an early breakfast. They were walking to their car when Remi pulled out her phone.

"Who are you calling?" Sam asked.

"Miron," she said, putting the phone to her ear. "I tried to reach him last night after dinner to let him know about his friend. He wasn't home."

"No voice mail?"

"Unfortunately, no." She ended the call and put the phone in her pocket. "Still not there. After what happened at Königsberg castle, I'm a little worried."

"Try again later. Right now, we need to see if we can find Renard's friend before our map thieves figure out where we're going."

Gustaw Czarnecki lived in the very forest that once overlooked one of the prisoner-of-war camps that housed the Project Riese workers. The winding foothills road led through a thick stand of trees, the pavement turning to gravel the higher they drove. A dog barked as they neared the cabin, and Sam saw someone pull back a curtain inside, then drop it. A moment later, the door opened slightly.

The second Sam saw the rifle barrel, he slammed the brakes. A shot hit the dirt about five feet in front of them. He glanced in the rearview mirror. It was a straight line down that hill, making them an easy target. They had nowhere to go, he thought, as the door swept open. A stocky gray-haired man stepped on the porch, a rifle in one hand, the barrel pointed downward. The way he held himself and watched them, there was no doubt in Sam's mind that he was ex-military. A black German shepherd appeared at his side.

Sergei gripped the back of Sam's car seat. "Why aren't you backing up?"

"Because if he wanted to kill us, he would have. Sit tight," he told Remi and Sergei, putting the car in park. He got out, resting his hand on the butt of his Smith & Wesson. "Mr. Czarnecki? Sam Fargo . . ."

The man stared at him.

"Sergei," Sam said. "Come on out, keep both your hands where he can see them."

He heard Sergei's door open behind him and, from the corner of his eye, saw the young man stepping out, holding both his hands high. "Now what?" Sergei asked.

"Tell him who we are."

Sergei did. The man responded, and Sergei translated, saying, "He wants to know how you know who he is."

"Tell him we were looking for Renard Kowalski. We found out— well, that his name came up as a friend of his."

Sergei repeated the answer.

Gustaw gave them a thorough appraisal, not moving for several seconds. Finally, he leaned the rifle against the porch railing, told his dog to stay, then walked out to meet them. "My apologies for that greeting," he said, his heavily accented English perfect. "I don't tend to have a lot of friendly visitors."

"Military?" Sam asked.

He nodded. *"Wojska Specjalne."*

"Special Forces," Sergei repeated.

Gustaw nodded, then gave a short whistle. The dog bounded down the steps, sitting at his side. Reaching down, he scratched the dog's head. "What brings you up here?"

"A tunnel," Sam said. "We heard you're a local expert."

"In other words, you're looking for the Gold Train. I can tell you it's supposed to be out on the sixty-fifth kilometer. I'm sure you can find someone to take you out there. Just not me."

"We're actually looking for information on Obermann Ludwig Strassmair."

His brows went up a fraction. "What makes you believe this area has anything to do with him?"

"Someone from Kaliningrad had a map that showed a possible route he took after he fled Königsberg castle, trying to escape the Russian invasion. It led us here."

"Sorry you came all this way. I only work alone."

"We're prepared to pay."

"It's not about the money." He crossed his arms, his expression cold, hard. "It's too dangerous. Leave."

Sam realized that this was a man who'd made up his mind and wasn't about to give in—not in the usual way. Taking a gamble, hoping the man might change his mind, he said, "Based on the number of people who've tried to kill us trying to get here, you're probably right. But thanks for your time."

And then he opened the car door as though he were about to leave.

32

Just when Sam thought his ploy to take off wasn't going to work, Gustaw asked, "What happened? Who tried to kill you?"

Sam rested his elbow on the car door, then gave a quick version of the armed men and the break-in at their hotel. "I'm only assuming it's related. We know very little about all this. Which is why we're hoping you might be able to help."

The man's stance relaxed. "You were lucky. The Guard doesn't usually leave witnesses alive."

"The Guard?"

"Wolf Guard, is what we call them around here. Assuming that's who came after you."

The fact Gustaw mentioned this same group told Sam they were on the right track. "Any chance there's a connection with *Unternehmen Werwolf* from World War Two?"

"My opinion? There's no other explanation. Once the government officially announced that this area was one of the possible locations of the Gold Train, strange things started happening around here."

"Like what?"

Gustaw looked in the car at Remi and Sergei before asking, "Who did you say you were?"

"Sam Fargo. My wife, Remi, and our friend, Sergei," he said. The man nodded at each of them, and Sam took that as a sign of acceptance, motioning for Remi to get out of the car, while he continued the conversation. "You were saying something about strange things happening?"

"*Strange?*" Gustaw gave a cynical laugh. "Maybe that's not quite the right word. What would normally be a pleasant weekend hobby, looking for historical artifacts, has turned dangerous—even deadly. The government might deny their existence, but they're definitely taking precautions about closing off certain areas."

"Anything you can tell us about this group?" Sam asked.

"More a theory, but I believe some present-day members of the Guard are related to Nazis enlisted into *Unternehmen Werwolf* during the war. Given their history, and their increasing numbers, I'm sure they've recruited criminals and the like to help. Which is why I'd suggest you turn back around. It's one thing if you know the risks. I do."

Remi eyed his cabin and the surrounding woods. "Aren't you afraid to live alone out here?"

"I saw you coming up before my dog alerted me," he said, patting the German shepherd's head.

"Cameras?" Sam said. "I didn't see any on the way in."

"Hidden. I received an alert on my phone the moment you left the paved road and hit the gravel. Other areas as well."

"Set off by the weight of the car?"

"Or someone walking through the woods too close to areas I happen to be exploring in."

"That sounds like a sophisticated system," Sam said, hoping they might get more information with flattery at this point. "You set it up yourself?"

"Most of it."

Remi, picking up on Sam's lead, smiled sweetly. "I'd love to see how it works."

Gustaw studied her a moment, glanced at Sergei, then looked directly at Sam. "You seem like nice people. Go home. I don't want to be responsible for anyone else getting hurt."

"What do you mean anyone else?"

"My partner, Renard Kowalski, was killed by the Guard."

Sam realized he'd misread the man. His desire to work alone had nothing to do with the treasure. "I'm sorry about your friend. We'd heard it was a hunting accident."

"It wasn't."

"After what'd happened to us, we didn't think so. Even so, my wife and I are well prepared to handle anything that the Guard throws our way."

"You'd take your wife, knowing how dangerous it is?"

"There's more to her than meets the eye."

Gustaw nodded at Sergei. "What about you?"

"I know what the danger is," Sergei said.

The man looked at each of them, in turn. "If I can't talk you out of it, I suppose there's nothing left to do than make sure you don't get into trouble out there. Come on in. I'll show you what you need to know."

He led the three to his cabin, the wooden floorboards creaking beneath their weight as they entered. The scent of pipe tobacco filled the air, the pipe burning in an ashtray near a blue armchair. A cast iron woodstove radiated heat, and the dog wandered over, curling up on the floor in front of it.

"Over here," he said, indicating a computer monitor on a desk in the corner. Displayed on the shelves behind it were a few World War II artifacts, including a helmet and several tarnished coins. He turned the monitor so they could see it. "My security system."

Sam watched the rotation of smaller-framed camera views on the larger monitor, seeing the cameras leave the pavement for the graveled road before switching to the front of the cabin and then the back. "You were saying something about cameras on other areas you wanted to keep an eye on? I only see three active frames here."

"The views of the house and the road leading to it are always on. It keeps me from jumping up every time I let my dog out. Or if I have to leave her here when I run into town. My phone alerts me if one of the other cameras activates. Right now, nothing's going on out there."

"Definitely an impressive system. How many cameras total?"

"Twelve." He woke up each camera, giving them a view of the surrounding forest.

"Twelve?" Remi said. "All to watch your cabin?"

"Other than the road and my house, most of them are pointed toward the two areas I'm currently exploring."

"Not the tracks near the sixty-fifth kilometer?" Sam asked. "We heard that was one of the places they suspect the Gold Train was hidden."

Gustaw looked up from the monitor. "I thought you weren't interested in that?"

"Not specifically. We're interested in one of the men who may have been responsible for hiding it. Or, rather, the route he took when he fled Königsberg. I have a map I can show you."

Sam accessed the photo of the original Königsberg map on his phone. "The route we were looking for isn't on here," he said. "We found out about that from a friend in Kaliningrad."

"Considering how large this area is, I'm surprised you were able to find me."

"We're persistent, if nothing else. So why is it that you're discounting the sixty-fifth kilometer as being legitimate?"

"It's still a very good theory. Renard got a hit on the area with ground penetrating radar. Definitely something down there about the size and shape of a train car."

"You weren't able to dig there?"

"The government wouldn't let us." He looked away a moment, eyeing his dog. "We were searching for the entrance when Renard was killed . . ."

Remi reached out and touched his arm. "I'm sorry. We all are."

He nodded, took a deep breath, looking back at them. "There are several other areas not yet explored. But with the number of tunnels down there, who's to say which one leads where? This hill here," he said, pointing to the top far-left frame on the monitor, "has definitely held a lot of Nazi activity. That's where I found the coins and the helmet." He woke up another camera, two frames over. "Here, this is the other side," he said, tapping the frame between them. "This brook originates at the tunnel and runs down between those two hills. I believe the Nazis diverted that water. That means they had to have done so inside the mountain."

"You're sure?" Sam asked, intrigued.

"Very. I found an old, hand-drawn map of the area from before the end of the war." He pulled out a present-day map of the area, showing a location closer to the town. "The brook ran from the mountain into town on this side prior to the Nazi occupation. The farmers were able to use the water for their livestock. Once the explosions and excavations of the tunnels occurred, the brook was diverted here to the other side of the ridge." He pointed to another location on the map. "The perspective and distance are somewhat misleading until you see the area in person. But once you're there, you can easily see how a short diversion up at the top of the hill makes such a difference."

Remi leaned in for a better view. "I'm not sure I understand. There have to be several water sources originating in these mountains. What makes this one special?"

"Because that's where I found this." He reached for something on the shelf next to the old German helmet, then held out a lapel pin with a small skull and crossbones on it.

Sam recognized it instantly. The insignia of *Unternehmen Werwolf*.

33

As Rolfe listened to Leopold Gaudecker's men arguing over where to start their search, Tatiana and Viktor, her ever-present bodyguard, walked in the door. She looked around at the chaotic scene before zeroing in on him. "What's going on?"

"Leopold's men are trying to pinpoint where the network of tunnels starts and how the Fargos plan on getting in."

She glanced over at the table and the men leaning over the map. "Where did that come from?"

"The Fargos."

"How?"

"The Guard broke into their hotel room last night and took it."

"Are you insane?"

He looked down at her, surprised to see the fury in her eyes. "We have the map. That's all that matters."

"I warned you to leave the Fargos alone."

He was surprised by her vehemence. "Nothing happened. If they're smart, they're on their way to the airport. What I don't understand is why you care?"

"In case you're too stupid to realize, the Fargos are known world-

wide. If anything happens to them, it will be more than the local police investigating. You may not care that Interpol is breathing down
your neck. I prefer that my business dealings are not under that much
scrutiny."

"Calm down. As I said, they got away. Now, do you or don't you
want to be involved in the search?"

Tatiana eyed the men standing around the table, then looked back
at him. "I do."

"Then pay attention. These men know the woods."

She crossed her arms, clearly annoyed with the proceedings. Or,
as he'd surmised before, annoyed that she wasn't running the search,
which made him wonder if that crime boss father of hers ever told
her no.

He turned back toward the table, listening to what Leopold was
saying.

". . . We set up here and here."

"Why?" one of the men asked. "How do we even know that's the
right location? The sixty-fifth-kilometer marker is here. It's circled.
That's where we need to be."

Tatiana wedged herself between Rolfe and the man standing next
to him in order to see. "*This* is the map you stole from the Fargos?
Why are so many places circled?"

"Because," Rolfe said, "that's how we found it. No doubt Fargo's
buying time."

"So you don't even know where the tunnel entrance is?"

"We know it's somewhere in the forest between here and the castle."

"Well, let's hope you can narrow it down. There's a lot of forest
around here."

"She's right," the first man said. "Why are we spreading ourselves
so thin?"

A dark-haired man shook his head. "You're all wasting your time.
I know exactly where the Fargos are going."

"How?" Leopold asked.

"When the Fargos were in the pub, we heard them asking about Crazy Gustaw. The bartender confirmed it."

"Who is this person?" Rolfe asked Leopold.

"The only other man who knows the woods better than my men."

"Do we know where this Gustaw lives?"

"The general location." The man pointed to it on the map.

"That's within one of the circled areas," Rolfe said.

"I've heard he has the entire area under surveillance."

"I don't care if he sees us," Rolfe said. "I care about finding what's in that tunnel before he or the Fargos do."

"We can come in from here," Leopold said. "If it's the tunnel I believe, then it probably lets out here." He pointed toward another spot on the map. "The sixty-fifth kilometer. Or it could be here." This location was farther along the tracks. "We should have men waiting."

"Why?" Rolfe said. "Isn't it more important to stop them before they find the tunnel?"

"In case we miss them."

Thinking ahead. He liked that. "Good. Let's get started."

"What about me?" Tatiana asked, then angled her head toward her bodyguard. "And Viktor?"

Leopold clenched his jaw, telling Rolfe, "She and her man can go out with the roving patrols. Your call."

Apparently, Leopold was still sore over Tatiana pulling a knife on him. "Patrol it is," Rolfe said. Not wanting to alienate her completely, he added, "With me."

"What about the Fargos?" she asked.

Rolfe was regretting his desire to expand into Russia. "She makes a good point," he told Leopold. "We need to do this without bringing attention to our actions. Try not to harm them. Anything else you want to add?" he asked her.

"That should do it," she said, then nodded to Viktor. "We'll be outside, checking our weapons."

Rolfe waited until the two walked out, shutting the door behind them. He glanced out the window, watching until they were out of earshot, before turning toward Leopold and the rest of the men. "She may be afraid of Interpol stepping in, but I'm not. You see the Fargos, kill them."

34

The brook was about half an hour's walk from Gustaw's cabin, starting from beneath a pile of large rocks and rubble that looked as though someone had set explosives in order to close off a cave entrance. They moved past the rocks to the other side of the ridge, where Gustaw nodded toward the top. "Up there."

Sam shielded his eyes from the sun, seeing scattered birch trees that had taken hold in the barren rocks.

"You see the one birch," Gustaw said, "about twenty feet up? From here you can't tell, but up there, at its base, you can hear the water running below. There's a space between the rocks next to the tree. I think it's an air shaft. Possibly a better way in than removing all these rocks down here at the base to open it up."

Sam turned back to the solid rock cliff, looking up at the tree and the possible air shaft. "Some reason you haven't gone in before now?"

"I have no idea if it leads anywhere or if it's simply a cavern. Mostly, I haven't had the heart. Not since Renard was killed. We were going to go down together. Now . . ." He looked away, not saying anything for several seconds. The only sounds were the birds chirping around them and the leaves rustling overhead in the breeze. "You're here now. I say we go in."

They climbed to the top, and though Sam would have preferred to anchor off the trees higher up, the rope he'd brought wasn't long enough for a simple two-line rappel, especially after he cut off a six-foot section to improvise a harness.

Returning his attention to the air shaft at the base of the lone tree, he decided it looked more natural than any man-made opening. Still, as Gustaw had described, they could hear the water running below.

Remi pushed against the birch. "You think it'll hold our weight?"

He kicked at the papery white trunk, feeling a slight vibration beneath his boot. Though thin, the tree seemed to be solidly rooted. "I think so," he said, grateful that both Sergei and Gustaw were experienced climbers. "I'll go first."

Years of fallen leaves cushioned the floor, the scent of must and mold rising with each step as Sam turned around to examine the cavern. Sunlight filled the shaft but also filtered in through the few cracks near the bottom where Gustaw had removed some of the rocks from what had once been the entrance. Behind him, water trickled down the rock wall, then disappeared below into a crevice.

Sam turned again. If there had been a cavern, it looked like the explosion had sheared off a massive wall of rock across it. His first inclination was that they'd reached a dead end. But as he shined his flashlight around, he saw darkness at the top of the rock wall, making him think the cavern continued on the other side.

"Everything okay?" Remi called down.

He looked up, saw her silhouetted at the shaft opening above him. "Fine. Come on down. Not much here. Hoping there's something deeper inside." After an easy climb up to the top, he swept his light across the area. All that was left of the cavern entrance was a V-shaped passage leading off into the darkness. That's what told him there was more to see, and he waited for the others to climb down. Once there, Sam led the way, over the broken rock, past all the destruction from the explosion, then into the narrow opening that eventually widened into a fully finished tunnel. Twin steel rails of train tracks emerged from the rubble behind them, continuing on into the tunnel, where they disappeared into the darkness. The size and scope of the tunnel reinforcements gave Sam pause, trying not to think of the horrors suffered by the men forced to build it. The others must have felt the same. No one spoke as they followed the tracks until they ended at the entrance of two separate tunnels.

"Which way?" Sergei asked.

Sam shined the light down the right tunnel, noting the bricked arch and supports as far as the eye could see. The left was about the same size but had not been reinforced. "Good question."

"The left," Gustaw said, checking his compass. "That seems to be the general direction of the castle. Maybe it even leads there."

"What about the right?" Sergei pointed that direction. "At least it's finished."

"Actually, neither," Remi said from behind them. All three turned. Remi was pointing toward something on the wall. What at first glance appeared to be an uneven portion of the reinforced bricked tunnel wall was actually a sliding door set on a rusty track. The brick was carefully layered over it as camouflage.

"Good eye," Sam said, returning to her side. He pushed, then leaned into, the door, but it held firm. When Sergei joined him, the door squealed in its track, finally opening. Sam handed his flashlight to Remi. "You found it. You get the first look."

Remi entered, and Sam nearly ran into her when she stopped short. "What's wrong?" he asked.

"There's a dead guy on the ground."

35

Sam aimed the beam of his flashlight into the space. Even though Remi had warned him, the sight of a mummified Nazi soldier was not what he'd expected. The man had been shot in the forehead, his body mostly preserved by the cool air circulating in the tunnel. *"Totenkopf,"* Sam said, noting the skull and crossbones insignia on the man's collar. It was a duplicate of the insignia that Gustaw had found near the forest entrance. "Could have been a prison camp guard brought in to oversee the work. I wonder who killed him?"

"And why?" Remi added.

"Russians, maybe?" Gustaw said. "When they were rousting the Nazis after the war?"

"Interesting theory," Sam replied, shining his light around the cavern, noticing the stacks of wooden crates filled with canned goods. "If it was the Russians, they would've stripped it of anything of value. Definitely the food. There's enough canned goods here for an army." In fact, the crates, lined up several deep along the wall, were about the shape and size of a railcar. Gustaw looked over at Sam. "I suppose this explains why we saw what we did on the ground penetrating radar. That Renard lost his life over canned food—"

"He lost his life," Sam said, "because there are evil people in the world."

"I know . . ."

"Look at this," Remi said, her attention fixed on the floor beside the desk. "An Enigma machine. A shame someone destroyed it."

Sam glanced over to see a splintered crate and, within it, the remnants of the machine, some of the wiring exposed near the front, the keys and rotors smashed to bits.

Sergei walked up next to Sam. "What's an Enigma machine?" he asked.

"For codes," Sam said, leaning down and picking up one of the smashed rotors. "Sort of like a typewriter to send out ciphered messages." He showed the rotor to Sergei, pointing out the few letters that hadn't been scraped off the circumference. "Each rotor had the alphabet on it," he said. "This machine used three rotors at one time. Some of them used four. A message was typed in and coded by the rotors. The person on the receiving end needed to know which rotors were used and in what order to decode the message."

Remi moved to the desk, picking up a green book, opening it. "Maybe the dead Nazi was in charge of inventory control . . ." She turned a page. "A list of what's in the cans."

Sergei looked over her shoulder. "I don't suppose there's a listing of treasure chests . . . ?"

"Unfortunately, no." She glanced at Sam as he tossed the broken rotor onto the Enigma pile. "If I had to guess, they were preparing the ultimate bomb shelter. With what's listed here, and the water they diverted, they could live for months." She set down the book, then opened the top desk drawer. "Fountain pen, pencils . . ."

Sam walked over to the dead soldier, crouching down beside him for a closer look. "I'd say he was executed."

"Maybe he was an embezzler," Sergei said. "Lesson learned."

"Doesn't make sense," Sam replied. "Why seal the chamber, break the Enigma machine, and leave all that food behind . . . ?"

Gustaw reached into one of the crates, pulling out a can. "Only one explanation. They didn't want anyone to find it or know what it was for. There has to be a reason."

"If," Remi said, "this is the location from the Königsberg map, maybe he was killed for the same reason that all those guards were killed at Königsberg castle. Dead men tell no tales."

Sam looked up at her. "That is the best explanation yet."

She smiled.

"Don't let your head swell. If you're correct, we still have to figure out what secret he was protecting." He patted the dead man's pockets. Finding nothing of significance, he stood, looking around the room. "Let's do an inventory. Maybe something will turn up. Remi, finish going through the desk. We'll search the crates."

After looking through a half dozen, Sam glanced over at Remi, who was crouched beneath the desk. "What's wrong?"

"Trying to get this drawer out," she said, pushing at it from beneath. "I'm hoping there's a false bottom. It won't—" There was a soft click, and the drawer slid out. "Bingo."

She scooted out, then stood, a slight frown on her face as she reached into the drawer. "One gold bar—"

"Not bad," Sam said.

"If it's the rumored Romanov Ransom, there's not much of it here," she replied, pulling out a thick stack of bills and placing it next to the gold. "A key. And this . . ." She held up a familiar-looking square tin, placing it on the desk. "Typewriter ribbon . . . Clearly, this is the favored Nazi brand." She opened the tin. "Surprise! Typewriter ribbon."

Sam picked up the tarnished brass skeleton key, turning it over in his hand. "A key and money."

"Do you know what I don't see?"

He glanced at the tin and realized the moment she said it. "An office with no typewriter."

Sergei and Gustaw stopped their search, Gustaw asking, "Why would that be important?"

"Not sure." Sam handed his pack to Remi and she placed the found items inside it. "But we have someone who can research it for us. Let's finish up in here and get moving."

They went through every last crate but found nothing but canned goods inside. A few minutes later, they left. Once they hit the railroad tracks, Sergei stopped to look back.

"What's wrong?" Sam asked.

"Who knows what else is down there. It's a shame we can't explore farther."

"We can always come back another time."

"Of course," Gustaw said. "You know where I am. Anytime you want to come back, you come see me."

They reached the cave entrance, climbing over the boulders that had bridged the creek bed. A shaft of sunlight lit the floor, dust motes floating up and around the rope they'd left hanging.

They climbed out, emerging into the bright sunlight, but the peaceful sound of the water trickling beneath them was broken by the buzz of Gustaw's phone. He pulled it from his pocket, looking at the screen. "Someone's here . . ."

Sam scanned the area in the forest below, not seeing anything. "Where?"

"Everywhere." Gustaw looked up from his phone in shock. "We're surrounded."

36

H ow many men out there?" Sam asked, his eyes on the woods. Gustaw swiped through the various screens on his phone, each showing a different area where the alarm had tripped. "Eight. No, ten. Four, just coming up to the cabin. The other six are fanning out. If any of them have tracking skills, it won't be long before they notice our trail up here."

Sam realized they had very little time. The thick trees of the forest below would shield them from view for a bit, but not for long. He grabbed the double strand of rope hanging from the birch, handing it to Sergei. "You wanted to do a little more exploring? Looks like you'll get your wish."

Sergei turned a worried glance toward the forest. "I didn't mean now."

"Sorry," he said, drawing his gun. "Not a lot of options."

Sergei climbed down.

"You're next," he said to Remi.

She dropped down.

A moment later, a half dozen armed men crashed through the forest into the clearing. So far, they hadn't been seen. He doubted their luck would hold.

"Hurry," Sam whispered to Gustaw, aiming at the approaching men. Gustaw slung his rifle over his back, then lowered himself into the shaft.

"*Da oben!*"

A shot whizzed by Sam's head.

He returned fire.

The men below scattered.

Sam grabbed the two strands of rope, ripped off another shot, holstered his weapon, then slid down. The second he landed, he gave a tug, and the rope snaked down into the cavern at his feet.

Sergei watched as Sam coiled it, then slung it over his shoulder. "How will we get out?"

"Quiet," Sam said. He motioned toward the rocks that separated them from the outside. Last thing he needed was for the gunmen to realize how very little stood between them. At least if they came down the air shaft, he could pick them off.

A moment later, they heard the sound of running outside as the men converged on the cave entrance. "*Da oben!*" someone shouted again, then something more that Sam couldn't understand.

"Up there!" Remi translated. "They're calling for someone to bring a rope."

Sam took the flashlight from his pack, hoping to find a place of defense when he heard the unexpected scrape of rocks at the cavern entrance.

"Sam . . ."

He was alarmed to see the light bleeding through the rocks, re-flecting off the barrel of a gun. "Hurry!"

They scrambled over the other side as the sharp crack of gunfire peppered the cavern.

Sam grabbed Remi's hand, and they raced down the tunnel, Sergei and Gustaw at their heels. At one point, the echo of gunfire was so fast and so loud, Sam had to look to reassure himself that the Guard hadn't made entry. For now, the tunnel behind them was clear.

As they followed the tracks around the curve, Sam glanced back, trying to listen. The gunshots had stopped, replaced by shouting. "Can you hear what they're saying?"

No one could. They hurried down the tunnel, stopping at the point it divided into two. Sam looked both ways, then turned to Gustaw. "I vote left. What do you think?"

"There's more of a chance of an outlet toward the castle. Why else would the Nazis have gone to the trouble of tunneling down below it?"

"It's not even finished," Sergei pointed out.

And it wasn't. Sam glanced down the long stretch of reinforced tunnel to the right. Who knew what the Nazis were contemplating when they built it? A deeper place to bury the Gold Train? Or something else entirely?

It didn't matter. What did was finding a way out. Whether it led to the castle or a dead end, he wasn't sure. "To the left," he confirmed, hoping anyone chasing them would think they'd gone down the finished tunnel.

They continued at a run, the sound of their pursuers echoing toward them. They were growing closer. Soon, the smooth floor gave way to loose rock and uneven terrain, slowing their progress. At one point, Sam felt the movement of air across his face, along with the familiar smell of must and mold. He hoped that meant they were nearing another tunnel entrance, but the scent quickly disappeared. As the shouts and footsteps of the Wolf Guard grew louder, Sam drew his gun, covering them from the back.

Remi stopped at the turn. "Sam."

"What's wrong?"

"The tunnel. It ends here."

37

Sam rounded the corner, the beam of his flashlight bouncing off a thick wall of rock and rubble that filled the tunnel. Someone had blown up that entrance as well.

"What now?" Remi asked.

"Back the way we came."

"But—"

"I think there may be a way out." He led them to where he felt the air moving and smelled the musty odor of dead leaves. A deep crevice angled off to the right. "Here. Smell that?"

Remi stepped closer, breathing deeply. "Yes."

"What is it?" Sergei asked.

Sam reached into the crevice, pulling out a handful of debris. "Remember the smell of leaves where we came in? That's what this is."

"Another air shaft?"

"Possibly."

Gustaw looked in. "I don't see any sunlight."

"The dead leaves got in there somehow."

A shout echoed down the tunnels, and they all turned, startled at how close it sounded. Sam turned back to the crevice, shined his light into it, examining the cracks and fissures within view. Plenty of finger- and toeholds, and narrow enough that they could brace themselves without need for a rope. What he didn't see was any light at the top. "It's a risk, but it's our only option. If we're lucky, it's our way out."

He turned to Gustaw and Sergei. "Follow Remi. I'll bring up the rear."

Sergei eyed the narrow space. "What if it doesn't go all the way through?"

"At the very least, we can climb up and hope they'll miss us."

He gave Remi a boost and she disappeared inside. Sergei followed, then Gustaw. Sam was just about to climb in when he heard a shout of *"Da!"* behind him. He looked back. A half dozen men raced in his direction, their flashlights bouncing along the tunnel. One of them saw him and fired.

Sam shot back as Gustaw lowered his hand toward him. Sam grabbed it, pulling himself into the crevice, as a barrage of gunshots hit the tunnel.

Bracing himself in the narrow space, he waited for Gustaw to move before climbing up after him, grateful to hear Remi's voice call- ing down, "There's light. It leads out."

The passage angled sharply to the left, then up, where sun filtered down. By the time he emerged from the tunnel, he heard the gunmen clambering up.

Outside, Sam looked around. The air shaft they'd just emerged from was completely hidden in the low brush growing at the edge of the forest. No wonder it'd never been found.

"Look," Sergei said, pointing down the hill toward a sign near the railroad tracks. The sixty-fifth-kilometer marker. "I guess we can safely say the Gold Train isn't in this tunnel."

"Or," Sam said, "it's buried beneath all that rubble we saw down there." He reloaded his revolver, then aimed at the air shaft, waiting to pick off anyone who emerged. "What's the fastest way out of here?" he asked Gustaw.

"To the west," the miner said over the low rumble of an approaching train. "But the Guard. They patrol these woods. If you shoot, they'll hear."

"Any other option?" Sam said, never moving his gaze from the opening. "I *am* open to suggestions."

"Block the opening?" Sergei replied.

Before Sam could tell him there wasn't enough time, it grew suddenly quiet in the shaft. He put his finger to his mouth. Grass around the hole rustled with movement. Sunlight glinted off the steel barrel of a handgun as well as the brown hair of the man holding it. The gunman looked around, his gaze widening when he saw Sam aiming at him.

Sam fired. The sharp crack echoed through the forest.

"It's blocked now," Remi said as the man fell down into the shaft.

"Not for long," Sam replied, still hearing movement below. "Should buy us a few minutes, though. Let's get out of here."

They ran through the trees toward the tracks. Sam, hearing voices, glanced back, seeing a dozen armed men in the woods behind them.

"The train!" Gustaw called as a blue locomotive rounded the bend.

A shot whistled past them as they raced down the hill.

The four neared the tracks as the rails began to creak from the approaching drive wheels of an old 2-4-2 locomotive that struggled to pull a long freight train up the steep grade. The first few flatcars, empty and rattling, were followed by several tankers and a long line of boxcars, most covered with graffiti.

Sam leaped from the trees bordering the tracks, realizing if they didn't cross to the other side, they'd be trapped. Luckily, he saw several boxcars that were empty with their doors open. Then a quick glance to see if the engineer and fireman were concentrating on the track ahead, and he took off running.

"Quick! Get in!" he called above the clatter of the wheels against the rails.

Sam ran and leaped to the floor of the boxcar, rolled to his knees and jumped to his feet in one motion. Then he leaned out and caught Remi by the wrist as she ran and pulled her in. Sergei followed as Gustaw tossed his rifle into the car but fell slightly behind.

Sergei grabbed Sam around the legs, allowing him to lean farther out the door and grasp Gustaw around one arm and haul him into the boxcar.

Sam found his gun, moved to the doorway, leaning out, as the Guard ran out to the tracks behind the last car. When they caught sight of Sam, they raced after the train, far too late.

Sam pushed away from the door, turning toward the others, glad to see everyone appeared unharmed. "Any chance you know where this stops next?"

38

Put the gun away," Tatiana said to Viktor. "They're gone." She
glanced down the hill through the trees at the handful of men
who were catching their breath after chasing the train.

Wolf Guard.

She would have dismissed them outright if not for Rolfe's involvement with them. "I'd be interested to know how long they've been in
Rolfe's pockets. Every time I turn around, that man surprises me."

"Speaking of . . ." Viktor nodded toward their left.

She glanced in that direction and saw Rolfe with a half dozen
Guardsmen tromping through the woods. His attention was fixed on
the heavy brush where the Fargos had emerged and where a couple of
the Guard were trying to extract the body of one of their fallen com-
rades.

Rolfe said something to the men, then continued on. When he
reached her side, he stood next to her, his eyes on the departing train.
"Not too bad. We only lost one man," he said.

"Which would not have happened if you'd done as I asked and not
shot at the Fargos. What'd you expect? That they were going to ignore the bullets flying past their heads?"

He gave her a thorough appraisal. "Whose side are you on? Not mine, apparently."

"When it comes right down to it, mine. However, I'm not the only one searching for this treasure. Which makes it difficult when I have to work with—" She stopped at the look of warning from Viktor. He was right, of course. Making an enemy of Rolfe Wernher at this point wouldn't be wise. "Let's just say I'm not used to being the one who *isn't* in charge."

"So I've gathered."

Time to deflect attention away from her. "Are you sure you can trust those men?"

"In case you haven't noticed, I don't trust anyone."

"Then why are they working for you?"

"Their ability to gather forces anywhere in Western Europe at a moment's notice, and their willingness to skirt the law, has been indispensable." When Leopold and his men reached them, Rolfe gave a benign smile. "Any chance the Fargos found something down there?"

"Unfortunately," Leopold said, "we believe so."

"'Believe'? What's that supposed to mean?"

"We've long suspected the chamber was in one of these tunnels. Until today, we've never found it."

"And the Fargos did?"

"No doubt. What we don't know is whether or not it was sealed when they entered or if anyone else had been there before them."

Leopold's radio crackled as someone called in. He listened, then turned to Rolfe. "The train is headed to Wrocław."

"Can you get it stopped before it gets there?"

"Possibly."

"Good. Find them. I want to know everything they have in their possession."

Leopold walked off, relaying Rolfe's orders into his radio. Tatiana waited until he was out of earshot, then leveled her gaze on Rolfe, not about to let him skip over what she needed to know. "You were saying . . . ?"

"About what?"

"About what the Fargos found down there. Clearly, it's not the ransom. All they had was one backpack. So what is it?"

"I really don't have time—"

"If you want to do business in *my* country, you'll make time."

Rolfe glanced at Viktor, then back at her. "I'll tell you, but it goes no further."

She waited.

"Lose your bodyguard."

A flick of her head, and Viktor walked off. Even then, Rolfe hesitated. She crossed her arms. "I'm waiting."

"What do you know of the Romanov Ransom?" he asked.

"That it was stolen by the Nazis, stored in the castle at Königsberg, then secreted away at the end of the war."

"I mean, what it was intended to be used for."

"I have no idea."

"To fund *Unternehmen Werwolf*," he told her. "To start the war again."

She hid her surprise over this bit of news. "I'm listening."

"The sole purpose of the Wolf Guard was to protect the Romanov Ransom so that it could be used to bring back the Third Reich. The plan was so secret that only a few in power knew." His gaze flicked toward Viktor, and even though he was still out of earshot, Rolfe lowered his voice even more. "They *divided* the code into three parts so that if any one part was captured, it would be useless. The plane that went down in Marrakesh belonged to a Nazi pilot who was an Allied spy."

"The pilot knew of the code?" Tatiana asked.

"Possibly. He'd found the first part in Königsberg, which would lead to the second part."

"In the Project Riese tunnels." She realized how very little she actually knew about what had happened to the Romanov Ransom after it'd been stolen from the Catherine Palace in Russia. If there was one thing she was good at, though, it was prodding for information. "Are you telling me that there's more to this than what Durin found in the courier bag on the plane?"

"I am saying that we have nothing until we get *all* three boxes gathered in one place. Only then will it lead to the location of the Romanov Ransom."

"Not even an educated guess?"

"I know this much. The war was over, and the Nazis were scurrying like rats to get out. Every treasure they hid was meant for their eventual return. The Romanov Ransom was the exception. It was smuggled out of Königsberg for one purpose only—to bring about Operation Werewolf."

She glanced over at Leopold and his men, off in the distance. "That doesn't make sense. They're part of Operation Werewolf. So where's the treasure?"

He laughed. "They're the Wolf Guard, a big difference. Their primary duty is to protect the hidden caches that lead to the Romanov Ransom."

"How do you know all this?"

"My father, who believed in the Nazi idealism, spent his life researching it."

"I never would've taken you for a Nazi."

He regarded her with a look of scorn. "I have no desire to resurrect that failed ideology. I'm in it for the money."

"Do they know that?" she asked, nodding toward Leopold and his men.

"I've never pretended to be anything other than a capitalist, but why would I tell them?" he asked. "As long as it continues to be mutually beneficial for both parties, our respective motives and beliefs matter little." A distant train whistle caught his attention. He picked up his radio, keying the mic. "Why is that train still moving? I don't care if you have to blast everyone on that thing. Just get me what they took from the tunnels."

Tatiana waited until he walked off before waving Viktor over.

"What's your plan?" he asked.

"Find the Fargos and whatever they took from the tunnels before Rolfe does."

39

"Tell us something good, Selma," Sam said into the phone over the steady rumble of the train as it sped along the tracks.

"I wish I could, Mr. Fargo. But we're still missing quite a bit of information. The letters we found in the courier bag appear to be just that."

Lazlo added. "I'm still trying to figure out the reasoning behind carrying the letters in the courier bag if they're of utterly no importance."

"Exactly," Selma said. "But, enough about our end. What do you have on yours?"

"You're not going to believe it but we have a key and a tin."

"'Tin'?"

"Typewriter ribbon tin," Sam clarified.

"The same as—"

"The same."

"Interesting."

"There has to be some significance. There were no typewriters, to speak of, in the tunnel. And someone went to the trouble of putting one of those tins in the courier bag. So why are they there?"

"Send me photos of the one you found. Top, bottom, inside. I'll see what I can find. In the meantime, you were saying something about a key?"

"Old antique type. Brass. I'll send a photo of it as well. Other than that, we'll be heading to Wrocław, waiting to—" He looked out the open door of the boxcar.

"What's wrong?" Selma asked.

"The train's slowing down." He moved to the door for a better view, but they were on a curve, and he couldn't see far enough up the tracks to see if anything was going on.

Gustaw joined him. "This isn't anywhere near the next stop."

"Selma, I'll have to call you back. We have a problem." He shoved the phone into his pocket. "Any idea where we are?"

"I'm familiar with the area," Gustaw said. "They had to have called for help. They couldn't have gotten here this quick."

"The Guard's that big?" Remi asked, coming up behind Sam.

"They are. Especially around any of the sites rumored to have hidden Nazi treasure. That is, after all, one of their reasons for being."

Sam eyed the low, grass-covered hill, and the forest beyond, thinking about the length of the train. It'd take a few minutes for this many cars to come to a complete stop. "Why wait? We should get off here."

He looked over at Remi, who gripped the side, the wind whipping at her auburn hair. He wasn't worried about her. Sergei and Gustaw, on the other hand . . . "Think you can manage that jump?" he asked the both of them.

Gustaw nodded.

Sergei glanced out, looking a bit unsure. "Yes . . . Maybe . . ."

Sam stood back. Gustaw tossed his long gun out, then leaped. Sergei hesitated, and Sam put his hand on his shoulder. "I'll tell you when . . . Go!"

Sergei jumped, then rolled down the hill.

"Your turn," Sam told Remi.

"Tuck and roll, Fargo!" Remi called out as she jumped.

Sam tossed his pack, then followed, landing a few feet away from her. He looked over, saw Sergei start to rise. "Stay down." He drew his gun, then crawled through the long green grass, up the side of the hill, looking below the passing boxcars.

Gustaw grabbed his long gun, belly-crawling next to Sam.

"What do you think?" Sam asked him, talking loud enough to be heard over the train. "If the Guard is the one who is stopping the train, we're going to need a better place to hide."

"If we can get across the tracks to the forest, there's a back road I know of. We're not too far from a friend who can help."

Sam eyed the tree line on the other side. They'd be exposed on the hill leading up to the woods, which was a lot farther from the track than he liked. Not that they had much choice. Behind them was a wide-open field. He waved Remi and Sergei over. "We need to get across before that train clears the curve. Otherwise, if they're anywhere in the area, they'll see us."

After the last car rumbled past, they raced across, up into the trees. Sam found a thick stand of shrubs and directed everyone behind it.

The squealing of the train brakes faded as it finally slowed to a stop. Above them, birds chirped and leaves rustled in the breeze. In the distance, Sam heard a high whistle. Human. And then another.

"The Guard," Gustaw said. "One of the ways they communicate. No doubt they're checking the train."

From the sound of the whistles, Sam estimated that they were at least a quarter of a mile away. He crawled out, catching sight of the last train car on the tracks up ahead, before turning back to the others. "No sign of patrols. Stay low, we'll have a better chance. They've got a lot of cars to search."

"This way," Gustaw said, and they followed him up the hill into the woods, breaking every so often to listen. The whistles between the patrols grew fainter the farther they traveled. After a half hour, the trees grew thick enough to provide decent cover. Now all they needed was distance.

40

Rays of sunlight broke through the treetops, lighting up the forest floor, as Sam, Remi, and Sergei followed Gustaw. An hour after that, they came to a cabin in the woods. "There it is," Gustaw said, pointing.

It was slightly bigger than the one he lived in. No smoke from the chimney. A bad sign, Sam thought.

"Wait here," Gustaw told them. "I'll see if he's home."

They watched as he broke cover and walked up the dirt drive to the cabin. He knocked on the door, the sound carrying down to them. After a moment or two, he walked around to the side, then disappeared around the back. Five minutes later, he returned.

"He's not there."

"What about a car?" Sam asked.

"I checked. Nothing. It's possible he'll return."

The faint whistle of the train drifted up to them. It was moving again. Which meant the Guard was done searching.

"They've got to know we're in the woods. Let's keep going. The more distance between us and the train, the better."

Gustaw nodded. "Our only option at this point is to head higher into the woods or try to get to one of the towns between here and Wrocław. They'll set up checkpoints, so we'll have to find a way past them. Once we do, there are plenty of people who are against the Guard who will help."

They continued on. After fifteen minutes, they heard the rumble of an approaching vehicle—a large one, by the sound of it.

Sam motioned everyone to the ground. He peered through the bushes, seeing a red World War II Opel Blitz truck bouncing down the road. Used for cargo or soldiers, this truck had been refurbished, the once-open cargo bed completely enclosed with hard siding. White lettering on the door read *CC's Antykwariat*.

"Antique dealer," Remi said.

"I've seen the shop in town," Gustaw added. "The man who owns it as well. I think he'll help."

The truck pulled into the drive of a nearby cabin, backing in. The driver, a tall white-haired man with a gray, neatly trimmed beard, got out of the truck.

"Worth a try," Sam said, watching as the man unlocked the back of the truck, rolling up the door. If they didn't do something soon, the Guard would catch up to them. "Ask if he can give us a lift."

Gustaw called out.

The man turned, his green eyes regarding them with curiosity as they approached.

Gustaw spoke rapidly. The only word Sam understood was *American*.

The man eyed each of them, rattled off a response to Gustaw, then settled his gaze on Sam, asking, "Got yourself into some trouble?"

"You're American?" Sam said, surprised. "Running antiques in Poland?"

"Started off collecting cars and branched out a bit. Interesting work that keeps me busy. Never know what'll turn up from one day to the next. So what is it I can do for you?"

"We're looking for a ride into Wrocław."

"I'm headed that way. If a couple of you don't mind riding in the back . . . Not enough room up front."

"About that," Sam said. "Might be better if we all hid in the back."

The man stroked his beard a moment. "Exactly what sort of trouble are you in?"

"Don't suppose you've heard of the Guard?"

His brows went up. "How'd you cross paths with them?"

"Sort of a long story."

"Give me the condensed version while I load the truck. Get us out of here that much faster." He unlocked the cabin door, dropped the keys into his pocket, then rolled the dolly in.

Sam, Sergei, and Gustaw followed while Remi kept watch out front. A few boxes were stacked by the door next to a table and, beside it, two wooden crates. "What goes in the truck?" Sam asked.

"Everything. Couldn't get it all in the first trip. This is the last of it." Sergei and Gustaw carried the table out as Sam helped move the two crates onto the dolly, all while giving a quick version of their hunt and the Guard's pursuit.

Once everything was removed from the house, the man locked the door, then met them at the back of the truck. "It's a good thing I happened along, then, isn't it?"

"Definitely," Sam said. "So you'll help?"

"Gladly. But we're going to want to move those boxes to the other side of the truck bed."

"What's wrong with them?" Sam asked.

"They're covering the trapdoor to the false bottom."

Sam eyed the truck, only then realizing that the rear bumper and side panels concealed the hidden compartment beneath the raised floorboards so that it couldn't be seen from the outside. "You think we'll all fit?"

"Three of you, it'll be tight. It was used to smuggle supplies so the

Nazis couldn't find them. Occasionally, children and resistance fighters were smuggled out as well. Someone will have to ride up front."

"I'll do it," Sergei said. "I'm probably the last person they're looking for. And I speak Polish."

Sam jumped into the back of the truck. "Let's get this show on the road."

41

Remi slid onto her back into the hidden compartment in the truck bed next to Sam, who was next to Gustaw. Sergei and the driver lowered the floorboards over them, then moved the boxes into place, the space turning suddenly dark. As the truck started down the road, she wondered how terrifying it must have been for the children hidden there during the war.

After several minutes—the road, thankfully, fairly smooth—she felt the truck slow, then stop. A few moments later, she heard someone talking and strained to listen as the antique dealer, speaking Polish, said, "Is something wrong?"

"There was an escape. Dangerous criminals in the area. We're searching every vehicle."

"Nothing back there but boxes and old furniture. It's been locked the whole time. I can't imagine how they could get in, then lock it."

"We'd like to look. For your own protection."

Remi slid her hand toward Sam's as she heard the sound of someone walking toward the back of the truck. "Do you have a key?" the man asked the driver.

"I can open it for you."

"Just the key. Please."

The engine shut off. "Here it is."

"Thank you." She heard someone walking toward the back, then the sound of keys jangling as the person unlocked the cargo door, then rolled it up. Light filtered in through the cracks in the floorboard a moment before the back of the truck dipped as someone stepped inside. Remi felt Sam tensing beside her as he gripped his gun with both hands. She tried to even her breathing, sensing that the man was standing directly over them.

"Anything?" someone from the outside asked.

"Just furniture," the man above her said.

"Let's go."

The truck rose slightly as the man jumped out, then walked back toward the cab. "You haven't seen anyone around, have you?"

"I saw several people walking through the forest about a kilometer or so back, but they didn't look like criminals. There was a woman with them."

"That could be them. We heard a woman was helping. How long ago was this?"

"No more than five, ten minutes, I'd say."

"Thank you."

The truck started, the engine sputtering before it turned over, then accelerated down the road. After a few minutes of driving, he called out, "I think we made it. No one's following."

Even so, Remi didn't relax until they arrived in Wrocław and the four of them were out of the truck. He'd parked in the street behind the antique store, and she was grateful that no one was around to see them emerging from the hidden compartment below the floorboards. "We can't thank you enough," Remi said. "We owe you our lives."

He smiled at her, his green eyes alight. "My pleasure. I'd heard rumors that the Guard was active in these woods. But this is the first time I've ever seen them."

"We hope," Sam said, "you'll never encounter them again."

They followed him into the back of the darkened shop. He turned on a light, and Remi was surprised by the quality of the antiques as she ran her fingers along a spinning wheel that was from the turn of the nineteenth century. "These are beautiful."

"Feel free to look around."

"We really do need to get going," Sam said.

As the man walked them to the front door, Sam paused by a glass case near the cash register. "Quite a few old keys here. Do you know anything about them?"

"A bit."

"We have one we found in the tunnels," he said, slipping his pack from his shoulder and taking the key from one of the pockets.

The man took it from him, moving toward the window for better light. "Very distinctive bow."

"'Bow'?" Sergei asked, trying to see what he was talking about.

"The grip," he said, holding it up. "Looks a lot like one I've seen around here fairly recently. Some are more decorative than others, which is why I have so many. Old keys appeal to collectors . . ." He eyed the keys in the glass cases, then looked around the shop. "Where did I see it? . . . Ah, yes. Over here." He crossed the room to an old writing desk, turning a lock and pulling out a key, which he brought over to them, placing it side by side with the key they found in the tunnel.

The bow of it was similar, though not as extravagant, as theirs. The bit that slid into the keyhole was also different.

Remi examined the desk. "Where was that made?"

"Good question," he said, returning the key to Sam. "I bought it from a man who restores old furniture. Wilhelm Schroeder. He has a shop in Münster. He'd definitely know something about the locks and keys of old furniture."

Sam unzipped a small pocket in his pack, dropping the key inside. "Guess that's our next stop. Gustaw, you're welcome to come."

"Thanks, but no. I need to get back. I'll be fine."

"You're sure?" Sam asked.

"I've been fighting the Guard this long on my own. And now that you have what they're after, I expect things will ease up—around my property at least."

"There's still the Gold Train to be found," Remi pointed out.

"True. And now we know which tunnel it isn't in. So there's that." He nodded at Sam's pack, where the tin and key were hidden. "Let me know what that leads to. I'll be interested to find out."

"Almost forgot," Sam said. He took out the cash and the gold bar. "The paper money might not be any good, but I'm pretty sure the gold's gone up a bit since then."

"Thanks," Gustaw said, hefting the gold bar in his hand. "I can put this to good use."

He caught a ride home with the antique dealer, and Sam, Sergei, and Remi took a taxi to the airport. Once there, they purchased Sergei's ticket to Kaliningrad, since he had to return to work, then walked him as far as security clearance. Sam shook hands with him. Remi, however, gave him a hug. "We can't thank you enough. Give our love to your Cousin Leonid."

"I will," he told her.

After watching him clear security, they left, texting their crew that they were on their way.

"That's strange," Sam said, reading the return text.

Remi glanced over but couldn't see it in the glare of light. "What is?"

"The pilot says our jet's been moved to a private hangar."

"Why?"

"He doesn't know, but he's telling us to get there right away."

42

The main hangar door was closed, but a side door was open, and Remi could see one of their two pilots standing just inside it. "He looks worried," she said.

"Let me go in first."

As Sam was about to enter, a man in a gray suit walked out. "Mr. and Mrs. Fargo? So glad you could make it."

"And you are . . . ?" Sam asked.

"Forgive me. Tomasz Gorski, with the Internal Security Agency. We have a few questions about your activities in Wałbrzych."

He indicated they should precede him into the hangar.

Sam went first, Remi followed. Both stopped short at the sight of ten uniformed, armed men standing just inside, as well as the Fargo flight crew seated nearby. The crew gave Sam and Remi nervous smiles, but before she or Sam had a chance to ask if they were okay, Tomasz closed and locked the door behind them.

"What's going on?" Sam demanded.

"All in good time. I'm just waiting for the commander of—"

"Are we under arrest?" Sam asked.

"Of course not."

"Then why the armed guards?" He nodded toward the group of men. "And the locked door?"

"For your protection."

Remi moved closer to Sam, resting her hand on his arm, feeling at once how tense he was. He leaned into her, whispering, "Feel free to lay on the charm."

Remi tried for a doe-like expression. "Captain—"

"*Lieutenant,*" he corrected. "But, please. Call me Tomasz."

"Lieutenant," she continued. "Perhaps if you took a moment to explain to us *why* we're being detained?" She gave him her sweetest smile, noticing a slight softening in his expression. "Please?"

"What I can say is, we're aware you have been to several restricted areas and possibly removed items from those areas without approval from the government. Therefore, we'd appreciate your cooperation so that we can quickly resolve this matter and get you on your way. Once the commander arrives, of course."

Sam crossed his arms. "And how long will that take?"

"Soon."

Remi eyed the armed men, noting each with his finger relaxed along the trigger guard of his weapon, ready for action. She focused on the lieutenant again. "The only reason we neglected to get the proper authorization was because circumstances forced us to take shelter in the very tunnels we're being accused of entering. People were shooting at us."

He gave a bland smile but didn't comment.

Time to change tactics, she thought. "I'm sure that you can appreciate that after our . . . *narrow* escape, I'd like to freshen up." When he seemed unmoved by her request, she added, "Or is there some reason we can't wait on the jet?"

"Forgive me, Mrs. Fargo. Of course. You are not prisoners here."

"Thank you." She and Sam started toward the plane.

"But I must ask your husband to leave his backpack behind."

They stopped, looking back at him. "Why?" Sam asked.

"We know you have guns. And there is the matter of what was taken from the tunnel . . . I should have specified that you'll need to be accompanied by a guard. In case there are more weapons in your hold." His smile this time was patronizing. "My source tells me this is probably the case."

Sam slid the pack from his shoulder, setting it on the ground, just as someone knocked at the hangar door. Several men pointed their weapons that direction as Tomasz asked the visitors to identify themselves. Apparently satisfied by the response, he opened the door.

A tall man, wearing fatigues and with a holster carrying a high-caliber pistol, walked in, followed by the man and woman who'd tailed them at the Amber Museum.

Remi edged closer to Sam as he eyed the couple, then pinned his gaze on Tomasz. "What's going on?"

"Finally!" came a woman's voice from just outside the door. The group parted and let her through. She glanced around the hangar, saw Sam and Remi, then gave a stiff smile. "Clearly, you're the Fargos. I understand you've met my associates in Kaliningrad?"

"And who are you?" Sam asked.

"Commander Petrov. But, please, call me Tatiana."

43

The door," Tatiana said to Tomasz, her tone one of authority. He quickly closed it as she turned to Sam and Remi, "You'll have to forgive our rather unorthodox method of contacting you, but, as the good lieutenant undoubtedly explained, we were worried about your safety."

She walked toward them, pausing to pick up Sam's backpack. "I'm sure you must have questions. I know I do, particularly about what you found in the tunnel. So," she said, holding the pack out to him, "I propose we go inside the jet and discuss—assuming you don't mind?"

Sam exchanged glances with Remi, then took the pack. "What about my crew?" Sam asked.

"Give us a few minutes of privacy and then bring them aboard?"

Sam glanced over at them. "You're okay out here?"

They nodded in return.

"Let's get this over with," he said.

Tatiana motioned the man in fatigues to follow them up the stairs while the couple from Kaliningrad remained behind.

Once on board, Sam led them to the table, dropping his pack on the top. Before he even had a chance to ask what was going on, she said, "Again, my apologies for delaying your departure, but I didn't know how else to get you alone without any possibility of someone overseeing us."

"Why would that be an issue?" Sam asked.

"Because your hunt for the Romanov Ransom has brought the attention of Rolfe Wernher, who will do anything to get it, including killing you and your wife. I couldn't have that on my conscience."

"What about them?" Sam asked, nodding out the window toward the man and woman from Kaliningrad. "What's their part in all this?"

"They were supposed to follow you to determine why you were in Kaliningrad."

"They shot at us."

"It wasn't them," the man behind her said. "The group who came after you were part of the Wolf Guard, sent by Rolfe Wernher." He glanced at Tatiana, then back at Sam, saying, "We were, however, responsible for the shooting at the apartment in Marrakesh. That was before we realized who you were. For that, we apologize."

"And you are?" Sam asked.

Tatiana glanced behind her, then back at Sam. "My partner, Viktor Surkov."

"Partner?" Remi said. "I wasn't aware that was a rank in the military."

Exactly what Sam was thinking.

The woman had a pained smile. "The subterfuge of my . . . exalted rank was necessary in order to receive the help we needed from the Polish government. They're not exactly going to roll out the red carpet for a couple of police investigators, especially when they find out we're using the cultural property as our—"

"Investigators?" Sam said. "For which agency?"

"FSB," she clarified. "Viktor and I have been working undercover for the last six months, cultivating contacts with Rolfe as part of our investigation. No one out there can know."

"You have identification?" Sam asked.

"Not with us. We were, after all, in the middle of an operation, so you can imagine what might happen if someone ran across it."

Sam's gaze flicked toward her so-called partner, who certainly held himself in a manner of someone with military training. But he'd also seen ex-military who were employed by criminals. "There has to be some way of verifying it."

"There isn't," she said. "If an inquiry is made through any law enforcement branches, it signals an alert. In fact, we're breaking protocol just by talking to you. What I need, what I'm hoping for, is your trust."

"Trust," Remi said, "isn't something we give too easily. Especially considering you're not giving us any way to check."

"It has to be that way," she said. "We don't know if Rolfe or the Wolf Guard have anyone working on the inside of any of these agencies."

"Why come to us?" Sam asked.

"There's no delicate way to put it, except to say that you've stumbled into the middle of what had been a meticulously planned operation. As a result, your lives are in danger."

"From whom?"

"Rolfe Wernher and another, larger organization called the Wolf Guard. They're working together."

"Operation Werewolf."

"You've heard of them. No doubt from your friend Gustaw here in Poland and Miron in Kaliningrad."

"Miron?" Remi asked. "We haven't been able to reach him since we've left. You've been in touch?"

Tatiana nodded. "Right after you fled Kaliningrad, the Wolf Guard picked him up on the orders of Rolfe. They were in the midst of beating him to find out what he'd told you. A little subterfuge on our part—along with his cooperation—we were able to track you to Poland. He's fine, by the way. In hiding until we can be assured of his safety."

Sam wanted to believe them if only because her story answered a lot of questions. Even so, he wasn't about to risk the lives of Remi and his flight crew on the say-so of one woman he'd never met until today. "What's your opinion, Remi?"

"I think I'd like a little more proof. If I'm not mistaken, Sergei mentioned that he'd heard of this Petrov crime family. Why is that?"

"Good question," Sam said. "Come to think of it, Selma told us about your crime boss father being murdered by a rival gang. Can you explain that?"

"Very simple," Viktor replied. "We created that crime family as part of Tatiana's cover story. We knew Rolfe Wernher wouldn't trust her unless she had a pedigree that matched his own. We ran a few well-placed articles in the newspapers and on the internet." He pointed to Remi's tablet on the table. "If you look it up, you'll see that Tatiana Petrov recently stepped into the role of her notorious crime boss father, Boris Petrov, known for his drug running and arms dealing."

Remi reached for the tablet and started searching. "Here it is," she said, showing Sam. He scanned the search results and saw a number of headlines detailing the crime family.

"My so-called father's name," Tatiana said, "was used in a previous operation several years earlier, and, as you can see, older articles already existed. Search further and you'll find arrest records, property records, and a few blurry photos. Rather than come up with a new legend, we piggybacked off the old one."

The story was entirely plausible. What they didn't have was a way to verify it. And yet, Sam's instinct was that they were telling the truth. "Isn't Rolfe Wernher a German national? Why the complicated game to get him?"

"To start," she replied, "he's trying to expand his operation of drugs and firearms into Russia. We have enough of that going on as it is. The last thing we need is more of the same."

"His gang," Viktor said, "killed two Russian citizens during a robbery of a jewelry store in Germany."

"We cultivated our first informant from that case," Tatiana added. "Durin Kahrs."

Sam glanced at Remi, saying, "He tried to kill our friends. He's—"

"Dead," Tatiana said. "We know. But before his unfortunate run-in with the other end of your weapon, he was . . . How do you say it?" She looked at Viktor.

"Double-crossing?" he said.

"That's it. Double-crossing Rolfe for money."

"The courier bag?" Sam said.

"Exactly. When we learned that he'd possibly found it, we approached him and offered double what Rolfe was paying for it. Unfortunately, your friend Zakaria was kidnapped, and we lost the bag." She turned, nodding toward her partner. "That's where Viktor's expertise comes in. He's worked extensively with Interpol in recovering stolen art. When my agency found out that there was a possibility of the Romanov Ransom actually being found, we brought Viktor on board to pose as my personal bodyguard."

Sam eyed the man. "Interpol?"

He nodded.

"His connections," Tatiana said, "allow us access to some less-than-orthodox methods, such as the one we used this afternoon, turning my rank into a commander who has need of a private hangar."

"Interesting," Sam said. "I have a friend who did a lot of work with Interpol back when he was in the FBI. Runs a security firm these days."

"Donovan Archer?" Viktor said.

"You know him?"

"Very well."

"Then you won't mind if I verify your story with him?"

44

Viktor didn't answer Sam right away. He seemed to think about it, then said, "You want to contact Donovan? I don't mind, but it's up to Tatiana."

She made a dismissive gesture. "As long as he doesn't make any law enforcement inquiries, I have no objections."

Sam slid his phone across the table to Remi. "See if you can get Donny on a video call."

Remi found his number in the contacts and called. "Donovan, sorry to wake you."

"Remi? Is everything okay?"

"Fine," she said, handing the phone to Sam.

Donovan, his blond hair sticking up on one side, stared back at Sam on the screen. "Fargo. Some reason I have to look at your ugly mug at this hour?"

"Quick question," Sam said. "Someone here says he knows you. I need to know if I can trust him."

"Who is it?"

"One second." Sam turned the camera toward Viktor.

"Donovan," Viktor said. "Good to see you."

"Whoa. And here I thought Fargo's mug was bad to wake up to."

"You're looking . . . somewhat awake."

"You realize what time it is here? Put Fargo on again."

"Well?" Sam asked.

"Viktor Surkov," Donovan said, stifling a yawn. "Worked a few art theft cases with me at the Bureau in conjunction with Interpol. Good investigator, terrible poker player. You can trust him."

"Thanks. Get some sleep. You look terrible."

Sam ended the call, then looked at Tatiana and Viktor. "I trust Donovan. Therefore, you have our cooperation. What do you want from us?"

Tatiana's glance strayed to his pack. "Preferably, what you found in the tunnels."

"We'd like to get a few photos first, but they're yours." Sam unzipped his pack, removing the key and tin from it. "Any idea what they're used for?"

She picked up the tin, turning it over in her hands. "According to Rolfe, the tins have something to do with finding the location of the Romanov Ransom. But he needs all three of them."

"This one makes number two," Sam said. "We were on our way to Münster, following up a lead—we hoped—on the third. You're welcome to what we have."

"Perfect. But I'll need to come back for them. Preferably, tonight."

"I'm not sure I understand."

"What I need to do is steal them from you."

Definitely not what he was expecting to hear. "How will that help?"

"Buy Rolfe's trust. He'd be suspicious if I suddenly showed up with whatever this is." She returned the tin to the table, her smile apologetic. "In order to make this real, I'll have to bring along Rolfe, or someone in his entourage, and I'd rather not have either of you present. Is there any chance you can leave this in your hotel room and go out for a while? A late dinner?"

Sam thought about it for a moment, weighing the risks. "What sort of security can you guarantee? We've already had one midnight visit from this group."

"So I heard. I didn't find out until afterward. There'll be four of us. Viktor, the two agents you met in Kaliningrad, and I."

Sam and Remi glanced out the jet's window at the pair standing near their flight crew.

"*Those* two?" Remi said, the tone of her voice echoing how he felt. "You're kidding."

"Believe it or not," Viktor said, "Nika Karaulina and Felix Moryakov are actually very capable. The problem was, they were under the mistaken assumption that the two of you were not."

Sam watched the agents a moment longer. "We'll give them the benefit of the doubt," he said. "So where do you want to do this? We've already checked out of our hotel room in Wałbrzych. A good thing, since the security there was lacking."

Tatiana nodded at Viktor, who pulled a card from his pocket. "I'd recommend this place," he said. "It's high-end enough to not raise suspicion, but more secure than the last place you stayed. More important, you can disappear into any number of restaurants literally right outside the door. We'll make sure that Felix and Nika are shadowing you the entire time."

Sam took the card, showing it to Remi. "Feel like going out tonight?"

"Date night in Wrocław?" She smiled. "I always have my Jimmy Choos on standby."

45

Rolfe stared at the text from Tatiana a moment longer. "Why," he asked Leopold, "am I paying you when that Russian is doing your work?"

Leopold, who'd just finished disassembling and cleaning his Glock and was now using a cloth to wipe the oil from each piece, barely spared him a glance. "What is it she's saying?"

"She tells me that she has a location on the Fargos."

This caught his attention, and he looked up. "I'm curious as to how she managed that. We had every road leading out of that forest blockaded."

"And yet still they somehow slipped past you. At least she has a solid lead."

Leopold's jaw clenched. The man hadn't liked Tatiana to begin with, and Rolfe suspected he was liking her less and less. He tossed the oilcloth onto the table, then began to reassemble his weapon. "Where are they, then?"

"That's what I'm asking now." Rolfe sent the text, then waited for a response. It took a long time coming, but when it did, he smiled. "She saw them walking into a hotel in Wrocław."

"Ask how she found them."

"You don't trust her?"

"Why should I?"

Rolfe texted her. A moment later, he received the response. "Apparently, the Fargos have been in touch with that old man in Kaliningrad. She has someone monitoring his cell phone."

"Convenient."

"Or smart," Rolfe replied. But Leopold had planted the seed of suspicion, and Rolfe couldn't let it go. He decided to call her. "Tatiana," he said when she answered. "Where is this hotel?"

"I'm checking into it now. Easier to break in when I'm a guest."

"Is that wise?"

"They've never seen me," she said. "How can it hurt?"

"I'll meet you there. Where is it?"

"Seriously?" She gave a cynical laugh. "You must take me for a fool to give out that information. All so your trigger-happy Wolfmen can come through here, shoot up the place, and bring in the authorities? We aren't in the middle of the woods. We're in the center of town. This calls for subtlety."

"My men had no problem breaking into their last hotel."

"And how did that work out for you?" she asked.

The dig infuriated him. "Do you honestly believe I'm going to let you walk off with what they found?"

"Unlike you, I keep my word. If they found these items in the tunnel, I'll bring them to you. What I need is a way out of here when I do get them. I can't exactly use a rental car, which can be traced back to me, or a taxi, with a driver who can act as a witness."

"What is it you're planning?"

"I expect they have to eat at some point. If—*when*—they do, we'll go in. I'll give you the location then."

"And what if they decide on room service?"

"I doubt it. The restaurant in this hotel is less than adequate.

Should that be the case, however, I'll let you know, and you can do it your way. As long as I'm not around when it happens."

"I'll wait for your call."

He disconnected, then told Leopold what she'd said.

"The Russian's playing you," Leopold told him. "She'll get what she wants and leave."

"Which will do her no good," Rolfe said. "She doesn't have access to the first tin. What good will the second do her?"

"And what if she withholds it from you in order to negotiate a better deal?"

He didn't like the feeling of paranoia that Leopold was feeding him, but he wasn't about to admit that the very thought had also occurred to him. "Let's see if she delivers before we make that judgment."

"So we wait?"

"Do you have a better idea?"

"Yes. I call the men I have stationed in Wrocław to be ready." Leopold picked up another box of ammunition and placed it into his gear bag, then grabbed the car keys. "And we drive there now so we're that much closer."

They were about halfway to Wrocław when Tatiana texted, telling him that if he wasn't on his way, he needed to be. It bothered him that she hadn't suggested the idea sooner. Was she trying to play him, as Leopold suggested? He went over every detail of their relationship but couldn't find anything that stood out as being overtly suspicious. Besides, he'd had her thoroughly vetted. At the moment, there was little he could do but wait.

It was after eight when Tatiana called. Rolfe put her on speakerphone. "They've just left," she said. "We're watching from the next floor up in the same building."

"And that would be . . . ?"

She named the hotel. "Wait at the south end. We saw them walking north. I don't want them to see you." She disconnected.

Leopold called his men to tell them where to set up. "I know right where it is." About two minutes later, he pulled behind a parked car with its emergency flashers on. Two young men loaded something into the trunk, then closed the lid, returned inside, leaving the amber lights blinking. "What are you doing here?" Rolfe asked. "She said the other end."

"Maybe so, but I didn't survive this long in the Guard by listening to other people. You can see the front of the hotel from here. That's good enough. And if we see the Fargos, even better."

After several minutes, Leopold grew restless. "Get behind the wheel. I'm going to have a look around."

"She might call."

"I won't be far. She's not getting out of here without us, is she? And if she does, I have at least half a dozen Guardsmen in the area."

He got out, then walked across the street, strolling along the rows of restaurants, pausing at one as though to look at the menu posted at the door. Rolfe moved to the driver's seat, then turned his attention to the hotel, growing impatient. Control seemed to be slipping from his grasp, and he tried to pinpoint when that had actually started. Durin. It had started with Durin and his backroom dealing. And now there was Tatiana and her meddling. He didn't like that she had inserted herself into his hunt for the Romanov Ransom. How had she even known about it?

He searched the area for Leopold. Finally, he saw the man leaning against a streetlamp, his cigarette glowing in the dark as he smoked. His gaze seemed to be fixed on the window of a nearby restaurant. No doubt the man was capable—after all, he ran a widespread network far more mobile than anything Rolfe had at his disposal. That made him useful, but that also made him dangerous. Especially considering that the Wolf Guard's sole purpose was to keep the treasure safe from anyone who went after it.

He'd have to watch the man. But as long as their purposes were aligned, he was willing to overlook any blurring of who was actually in charge.

What he couldn't overlook was the nagging suspicion that Tatiana was up to something. Even so, he couldn't fault the logic in monitoring that old man's phone, especially if it ended up getting them the second tin box.

What really bothered him was, she was always first.

Surely he wasn't jealous that a mere woman was besting him at his own game? Or was it something more?

Before he had a chance to decide, Tatiana phoned.

"I have it. We'll be walking out the door in two minutes."

He looked around for Leopold, didn't see him, so called. "Where are you? They have it. They're on their way."

"I'm heading back now. By the way, we have a slight problem."

"What's that?"

"I found the Fargos."

"Where?"

"Sitting inside that restaurant down the street. The one with the outdoor patio."

Rolfe could just make out the tables and chairs in the dark, and then Leopold quickly walking away from the place. "So what's the problem? We knew they were going out to eat."

"Because there are two Russian agents sitting at a nearby table. I saw both at the Amber Museum following the Fargos. Only one reason I can think of." He stopped at the curb, waiting for traffic to clear. "Your Russian crime princess is a police agent."

46

Remi watched as Felix, one of the Russian agents, received a text from Tatiana. "They're waiting to be picked up in front of the hotel," Felix said, putting enough money on the table to cover dinner. "I want to make sure they get off okay."

Felix walked to the door, Sam, Remi, and Nika right behind him. They stood in front of the restaurant, the two Russian agents watching the hotel. Sam glanced that way, then looked down the street in the opposite direction. Remi followed his gaze, catching sight of a parked vehicle with its emergency flashers on, then, behind it, another car, its blinking amber lights reflecting off the windshield. Nothing too suspicious until she saw a tall man coming up behind the car on the passenger side. He turned, looking their way, his gaze sliding right past Sam and Remi to Felix and Nika.

"Sam," Remi said. "Did you—"

"I saw it. Call Tatiana," he told Felix as he handed Remi his backpack. "They know we're here."

"Of course they do," Felix said, taking out his phone. He pressed her number, then put the phone to his ear, as the vehicle sped off toward the hotel. "You were supposed to be going to get something to eat."

"They weren't looking at us," Sam said. "They were looking at you."

"It's going to voice mail," Felix said.

"Text her," Sam called out as he raced toward the hotel. "Tell her they know."

He broke into a run. Remi threw his backpack over her shoulder and ran after him. Within seconds, the Guard's car pulled to the curb in front of the hotel, the brake lights glowing red. Tatiana and Viktor were there, waiting. Tatiana slid her phone from her pocket, looking at the screen, as someone jumped out of the front passenger seat. He grabbed her arm, jerking her toward the car. Viktor lunged forward, trying to stop him. A gunshot cracked as Sam ran into the street, dodging cars as he crossed. Viktor fell. The man, using Tatiana as a shield, aimed at Sam.

Remi stepped off the curb, racing across, as the man fired again, pulling Tatiana into the car. The vehicle sped off, tires screeching. A smell of burnt rubber assaulted her as she searched for Sam, heart clenching when she found him on the ground, hunched over Viktor. "Sam!"

He didn't move.

Remi's heart constricted as she ran toward him, praying he was okay. "Sam!"

He looked up at her, his hands covered with blood. "Remi . . ."

"Are you—"

"I'm fine. It's Viktor."

"Leopold . . ." Viktor said, ". . . shot me." Viktor was bleeding from his left shoulder, and Sam was putting pressure on the wound.

"We're so sorry," Sam told him. "We didn't see them until too late."

"Not your fault . . . At least she gave us a bargaining chip."

"A what?" Nika asked, coming up behind Remi.

Viktor opened his hand, revealing the key. "She threw it at me as they sped off."

"What does it belong to?" Nika asked.

"We'll figure that out later," Sam said. "First, we need to get Viktor some medical attention."

"I'm fine."

"Sure you are," Sam said as he and Felix helped him to his feet. "Let's keep you that way."

"Tatiana's phone," Viktor said as he slid his own phone from his pocket. "If she still has it, we can follow her." His hand shook as he opened the app that would locate the device. They watched as the screen lit up with a map, a small icon indicating her phone was not too far from where they were. It wasn't moving. He and Sam both glanced that direction. Clearly, Rolfe and Leopold must have anticipated they'd be followed so they tossed it from the window. "I need to find it. There are numbers on there . . ." He winced in pain when he tried to move.

"Easy, there," Sam said.

Remi heard sirens. "The police are coming."

Viktor looked around at the gathering crowd. "Take the key," he told Sam.

"No," Nika said, grabbing it before Sam could. "We should keep it."

"Nika," Viktor said. When she failed to turn it over, he spoke to her in Russian.

Sam couldn't understand a word, but he definitely understood the terse tone. She glanced down at the key in her hand, then closed her fingers around it, saying, "Tatiana's *our* concern, not theirs."

"Give it to him. I trust him to do the right thing."

It was a moment before she opened her hand, allowing Sam to take it.

The sirens grew closer. "You and your wife should go," Viktor told Sam. "We can direct the investigation to keep you out of it. Better for you to find answers to help Tatiana than spend hours being questioned."

Sam took another look around, searching for Guardsmen lurking nearby. No one seemed out of place, the expressions he saw on the faces of bystanders a mix of curiosity and concern. "You're sure you're okay?"

Viktor, looking paler by the second, nodded, as Felix supported him. "I'll be in touch. Find that phone," he said as the first patrol car pulled up. "Get out of here."

Sam wiped his bloody hand on his pants, took his backpack from Remi, then casually stepped with her into the crowd of onlookers. The two weaved their way through, people parting around them, then pressing together again, unaware they were even involved. As the police were stepping out of the car, they were nearly a half block away, melting into the pedestrians who either weren't aware what was going on, or had lost interest.

When they reached the corner, Sam stopped. "Tatiana's phone was sending out a signal from around here."

"Aren't those things notoriously inaccurate?"

"It gives the general vicinity. It's a start. You take this side of the street, I'll take the other. But keep an eye on what's going on over there. If anyone looks like they're coming this way, we're out of here."

Sam crossed over as Remi glanced back toward the crowd, grateful that no one seemed to be watching them. When she turned back, Sam was already on the other side, walking along the curb, checking the street and the sidewalk. She did the same, hoping that if they did find it, it hadn't been run over too many times. After several minutes of searching, she was about to suggest that they call, hoping they might hear it ring. When she looked over, Sam was bending down behind a parked car, picking it up.

"Found it!" he called out. He waited for a car to pass, then crossed back over. The screen lit up when he tried to gain access. It was locked. He glanced down the street toward the hotel, seeing someone pointing their direction. "Time to get out of here," he told Remi, leading her around the corner, stopping as they came face-to-face with two men, both armed with knives.

47

Sam recognized the man on the left from the alley in Marrakesh. The other, a stranger, leered at him. "I was hoping to run into you again," the stranger said, his accent reminding Sam of Gustaw's. "Too bad I missed you on the train."

"The feeling's mutual," Sam said, stepping between the men and Remi. No way could he get to his gun before either man threw their knives at him. He angled his body, allowing his backpack to slip from his shoulders, catching the strap with his right hand. "What is it you want?"

"The key," he said. "Hand it over."

"And you think I have it?" Sam replied, eyeing the man's knife.

"The Russian woman told us."

Sam swung the heavy pack against the robber's arm. The knife flew from his grasp, striking the door of a parked car, then falling into the gutter.

The second man jumped forward. Sam blocked that strike with his pack, using the weight to push him back.

The first man scrambled to the curb, reaching in the gutter for his knife, as Sam slammed his partner's head into the vehicle's hood. The metal dented, and Sam grabbed his collar, pulling him back, swinging him down on top of his partner.

As the two stunned men lay there, Sam took Remi's hand, leading her down the street. He glanced back, seeing both men trying to pull themselves from the ground.

"WHAT WENT WRONG?" Remi asked as she and Sam reached their car.

"If I had to guess, Felix and Nika's presence at the restaurant."

"That doesn't make sense. How would Rolfe or his Wolf Guard even know who they are?"

Exactly what Sam was wondering. One possibility came to mind. "The Guardsman must have been in Kaliningrad. He could've seen them at the museum. Maybe he was one of the men who shot at us at the castle."

"Poor Tatiana."

"She got the key to Viktor," he said, checking the rearview mirror as they took off. So far, their assailants weren't following. "Like he said, a bargaining chip. It worked to get back Zakaria."

"You think it'll work a second time?"

"Definitely be harder. They'll know what to expect, which means we'll have to stay one step ahead of them. Before we do anything, I want to look in on Viktor. Let him know we found the phone."

"I better check in with Selma before she starts worrying." The call went to voice mail, and Remi left a message.

They were just pulling into the hospital parking lot when Selma called back. "Mr. and Mrs. Fargo. Glad to hear you're okay. I take it the theft was successful?"

"Not exactly," Remi said. "You tell her, Sam."

He related the night's events, finishing with, "We're hoping you have something on your end that'll help. Any luck breaking the code to those letters?"

"I better let Lazlo tell you."

Lazlo cleared his throat. "Quite the difficult beast, don't you know. As mentioned before, I'm not even certain it is in code. There seems to be no rhyme or reason to what it all means."

"But," Remi said, "wasn't that the very reason you thought it *was* in code?"

"Originally, yes. Now, however, I'm starting to wonder if it's something else entirely. It's almost as if someone went to the trouble to include the letters to throw anyone off, should they discover them."

"What about the typewriter ribbon tins?" Sam asked him.

"Without having them in our possession, it's difficult to tell. But, from the photos, they seem like ordinary ribbon tins that were manufactured in Berlin and used during the war. Common, in fact. I don't suppose you had a decent look at the ribbon?"

"Enough to know it was just a ribbon," Sam said. "That, and the ink was dry."

"No messages hidden in the spool?"

"After Tatiana told us about her conversation with Rolfe, we looked. There was nothing."

"Unfortunate, that," Lazlo said, giving a glum sigh. "Of course, it wouldn't be unusual to find one in any location where a typewriter might have been even if said typewriter is no longer there."

A logical assumption, Sam thought. Except that Rolfe and his Wolfmen were willing to kill to get them. "What about this furniture restorer that antique dealer mentioned? Any luck finding him?"

"Unfortunately," Selma said, "his name is quite common. We've called everyone listed in the public directories, leaving messages where we could. We're waiting to hear back."

"Let us know when you find out anything."

"Will do. Take care."

Remi disconnected. "What do we do in the meantime?"

Sam pulled Tatiana's phone from his pocket. "Get this thing to Viktor and find out what she's been up to."

Nika and Felix were waiting in the lobby of the hospital when Sam and Remi walked in. "Any word?" Sam asked.

"Lucky for Viktor," Felix said, "the shot went clean through and missed the bones. We should be allowed to see him soon."

"Good. Any chance you can get us in? We have a few questions."

"What sort of questions?" Nika said. "We'd be glad to help."

"I'm sure you can. But I'd rather wait, just to keep him in the loop."

He and Remi took a seat as someone wheeled a patient past them down the hall. After about fifteen minutes, a nurse approached, asking for Felix by name. He stood.

Her first attempt to inform him of Viktor's progress was in Polish. After a few exchanged words, determining that he didn't speak Polish and she didn't speak Russian, she said in stilted English, "He does well. He asks to see you. This way."

They all started to follow. She shook her head. "Only two."

Felix glanced back at them, his gaze landing on Sam. "You come." Then he said something in Russian to Nika. She sat down, looking upset that she wasn't included.

He followed Felix into the room. Viktor was hooked up to a monitor that beeped quietly in the background. There was a tube coming from the upper left side of his chest, snaking down to a white plastic box hanging from the side of the hospital bed. His eyes were closed until he heard them enter. ". . . Good . . . You're here . . ."

"Of course we are," Felix said. "How are you?"

"Collapsed lung . . . Procedure to insert the tube is like getting shot all over again . . . They're insisting on keeping me here . . ."

"So listen, for once."

Viktor glanced at Sam. "Not quite how we expected this to turn out, is it?"

"At least you're alive."

"Tatiana, though . . ."

"I found her phone. If we can get in it, we might have a chance of finding her."

Viktor seemed to perk up at that.

"Contact Rolfe . . . Tell him we have the key . . ."

"And you know what it's for?"

"Not yet. But I have someone working on it now."

"Good." He closed his eyes a few seconds, then looked at them. "We should have anticipated . . . *I* should have . . ."

"No," Felix said. "We did the best we could. Now we try to find her."

Sam moved closer. "Do you have the code to get into her phone?"

He nodded, then recited the numbers.

Sam typed it in. "That works. Now, about Tatiana . . . We'd like to help. We can call friends. Government agents, even."

"No . . . No outside help," Viktor said. "We handle our own."

Sam was surprised by his refusal. "I don't understand . . ."

Viktor glanced at Felix, then turned to Sam, his expression troubled. "There's something about this that I haven't told you . . . Or Felix." He took a ragged breath. "Something . . . important . . ."

48

The monitor beside Viktor's hospital bed beeped steadily as Sam waited.

"Felix," Viktor said. "Close the door . . . please . . . I'd rather not have anyone overhear."

Once it was closed, Felix taking a position in front of it, Viktor turned his attention to Sam. "Because you're Donovan's friend, I know I can trust you . . . And I want Felix to also hear . . . Tatiana isn't the only Russian involved with Rolfe Wernher. She's merely the latest. It's how we knew to cultivate Durin . . . And now that we've verified that the Wolf Guard is still operating in Europe, the stakes are even higher. They are, no doubt, how Rolfe has managed to eliminate witnesses in every case brought against him . . ." He closed his eyes, the sound of the monitor beeping as they waited. Finally, he opened them again, saying, "Until the shooting in Königsberg castle, we weren't even aware they'd infiltrated Russia. Now . . ."

Sam glanced over at Felix, then back at Viktor. "You can't mean to leave her there?"

"Of course not," he said. "But in the past, every time we made a move, they found out . . . We have to be careful who we include. I hate to believe that anyone we have inside Rolfe's circle is giving information . . . Or, worse yet, that the few of us who know on the outside are . . ." His voice grew softer, his eyelids starting to fall. But he roused himself, looking at them again. "The possibility exists . . . So you see my dilemma? There are many more lives involved than just Tatiana's . . . She knows the risks . . . knows our hands are tied. But . . . she knows . . . someway, somehow . . . I'll get to her . . . Have to do it below the radar . . . Without help . . ."

"From a hospital bed?"

"A flesh wound . . . They'll be releasing me in the morning . . . I hope . . ."

"And if they don't?"

"Perhaps . . ." He looked at Sam. "We saw how you went after your friend, Zakaria. I thought that you . . ."

Felix took a step forward. "You can't mean send an American?"

Sam, hoping to cut through the tension in the room, said, "I'd be glad to help in any way I can."

"No," Felix replied. "It's as Nika said. Tatiana is our concern. Not the Americans'."

"You're right," Viktor said, his breathing more shallow. "Except that the Fargos are . . . in a unique position to help . . . without raising suspicion. They did it once . . . Not too out of the realm of their nature to do so again . . . without exposing anyone on the inside." He looked at Sam, trying to keep his eyes open. "I have no idea if this key is important . . ."

"We're hoping to find out," Sam said. "Even if we don't, we'll make them believe it's important."

Viktor nodded. "Thank you." He closed his eyes a moment. "I think whatever they've given me . . . for the pain . . . is starting to work . . ."

"We'll let you rest," Sam said.

"Felix . . ." It took some effort for Viktor to open his eyes. "Help the Fargos . . ."

"Yes, sir."

When it was clear he couldn't fight the pain medication anymore, they left, Felix following Sam down the hall.

Remi stood when they walked into the lobby. "How is he?" she asked Sam.

"Fine. Sleeping now."

"Thank goodness."

Felix looked around for Nika. "Where is she?"

Remi nodded toward the doors. "She went for a walk. I'm sure she'll be back soon. She was very upset."

About two minutes later, Nika walked in the lobby doors. "Well?" she asked Felix. "What did he say?"

"He's asking that the Fargos help."

"Is that wise? We're wasting time as it is. Tatiana could be hurt."

Felix glanced down the hall toward Viktor's room, then back at Nika. "It's what he ordered."

She crossed her arms. "Is there some grand plan?"

"I have none," he said.

She turned her gaze to Sam. "And you?"

"To start? Call to let him know we have this key. And that we'll exchange it for Tatiana."

Nika opened her mouth to speak but then clamped it shut. Instead, she started pacing.

"Call," Felix said.

Sam took out Tatiana's phone, found Rolfe's number, and called.

It went to voice mail. Sam waited for the recording, then said, "Sam Fargo. Call if you want the key. In exchange for Tatiana, unhurt."

He disconnected.

Remi exchanged glances with him, her expression worried. "I hope she's okay."

"She's smart," Sam said. "She threw that key for a reason."

Nika continued her pacing until the phone rang a few minutes later. She and the others gathered around Sam as he answered. "Fargo . . ."

"Apparently, you have something I want."

"Who's this?"

"Leopold."

"Leopold? Where's Tatiana?"

"Sitting across from me as we speak."

"She's not hurt?"

"The gag might be a little tight, but no. She made it clear that we'd be hearing from you about this key that you found."

"I'd like to speak to her."

"We all have things that we desire, don't we? About that key—"

"Tatiana! On the phone!"

Sam heard an annoyed sigh, then, "Take the gag from her mouth so she can speak to the American."

"Sam?"

"How are you?"

"I'm fine. Viktor?"

"Fine," he said, relieved to hear her voice.

"Thank—"

"Touching," Leopold said. "I've heard my fill. Have you?"

"How do you want to do this?" Sam asked.

"I can tell you how I don't want to do it. I've heard all about the exchange in Marrakesh. So to avoid any possibility of losing control to you, we'll make the exchange tomorrow night outside Berlin." There was a muffled sound as though he'd muted the phone. A moment later, he said, "I'll be in touch to arrange for the exchange. Tomorrow night. After midnight."

"Why so late?" Sam asked.

The line went dead.

49

Sam and Felix decided they'd make the three-and-a-half-hour drive to Berlin, where they'd meet up to wait for Leopold's call. The moment he and Remi were alone in their car, Sam telephoned Rube. "We have a slight problem."

"Any chance it involves an undercover Russian agent and a German crime boss?"

"I see you've been talking to Selma. What you might not know is that the Russians are working some inside operation to take Rolfe Wernher down. They're willing to sacrifice Tatiana for the cause."

Remi leaned over, talking into the phone. "She saved our lives more than once. We can't let that happen."

"I'm going to let you in on a little secret," Rube said. "The Russians aren't the only ones working to take this guy down. The Germans have had their sights on him for a long time. And we've got our hand in it as well. This guy is running these Wolf Guard members throughout Europe as his own personal henchmen."

"We've run into a few . . . About Tatiana . . . ?"

"That's the thing. If we go barreling in there to rescue her, it's likely to blow a few covers and endanger both German *and* U.S. operatives. So the Russian lives aren't the only ones that'll be at stake. They're under orders to ignore all but the prime mission. Tatiana isn't part of that."

"And what's this 'prime mission'?" Sam asked.

"I can tell you this. It's not just Rolfe Wernher. It's also this Wolf Guard. There's a whole hierarchy from this group who will gladly step in and take over his business. We'd like to take them out, too. But if these covers are blown, that's not going to happen."

"We can't just leave her there. As Remi said, she saved our lives on more than one occasion."

"I get it. I'd feel the same way. But if you weigh the lives of all the operatives in place versus the one . . . My hands are tied."

"Is there anything you can tell us?"

"Depends," Rube said. "Is there any way to stop you from going after her?"

"Not a chance." He glanced at Remi and saw her give a nod of approval.

"It might be a bit, but I'll get back to you."

They were checked into their Berlin hotel by the time Rube called back. "Here's what I have so far. The address to his villa and the code to his alarm. There's a door leading from the garage that tunnels down beneath the garden, then up to the house. More than likely, that's how he'll get her in without being seen. Follow it to the left. Third floor."

"We know for sure he took her there?"

"My contact says he definitely brought someone in not too long ago. And I also found out the reason for the midnight exchange tomorrow. He's hosting a party for dignitaries earlier tomorrow evening at his villa. So I doubt anything's going to happen before then. Do me a favor, though. Wait for your Russian FSB friends to go in after her."

"We will. Calling them as soon as I hang up."

SAM DUCKED DOWN behind a parked car, then motioned Remi over. "There it is," he said when she was at his side.

"It's going to be hard to get to without being seen."

He pulled his binoculars from his pack for a better look. The long narrow street allowed parking on the left side for the private residences, but no parking along the right, keeping the street and sidewalk in front of Rolfe's villa clear. One advantage was that it was surrounded by a low stone wall topped with wrought iron railing, giving him a clear view in. The disadvantage was that it also gave a clear view of anyone walking along the sidewalk just outside the fence. Armed security guards stood near the wrought iron gate that opened to a circular drive at the front of the stately mansion. Even if they could get in through the main gate, there were guards roaming within, and the few trees on the vast expanse of lawn wouldn't allow any cover.

Unfortunately, there was no access over the back wall, which was topped with shards of glass to keep out intruders. On their first drive past, Sam hadn't seen any way they could get into the back without being noticed. The front wasn't looking much better. The only possibility he could see was the service entrance farther down the street, where a boxwood hedge ran the length of a drive around to the back of the house. He handed the binoculars to Remi. "I think that's our only chance to get in."

"You're not seriously thinking of going in now . . . are you?"

"No time like the present," he said.

"What about Felix and Nika? They're expecting us back."

In fact, the two were sitting in a hotel room in downtown Berlin waiting for Sam and Remi to return with their preliminary findings on what they'd seen on the drive-by of the villa. "My feeling? Better to ask forgiveness than permission. If there *is* someone on the inside working against Tatiana, they're going to be expecting us after midnight, since that's the time we've planned. No one's expecting us to come in right after dusk."

"For very good reason," she said, handing the binoculars back to him. "There's no way we're getting to that service entrance without being seen. Even the woman pushing that baby carriage is getting the once-over."

He took another look, seeing the woman and carriage passing the main gate. The guards watched her for a few moments as she stopped to adjust something inside the carriage. When she moved on, their attention shifted back to their surroundings. "I have an idea," he said.

BY THE TIME Sam and Remi returned to the street, the golden sunset was fading into the shadows of twilight, bringing with it a gentle wind that stirred and rattled the dry leaves in the gutter. The only other sound was the soft squeak of the blue baby carriage that Sam pushed as Remi walked alongside him, her arm linked through his. She leaned down to adjust the downy white blanket over Sam's backpack. "Sleeping like an angel," she said.

"If it starts crying, it's because we paid way too much for this thing. Two hundred euros? It looks well used to me."

"Imagine how much it would've been new," she said. "It's a top-of-the-line perambulator."

"That's what they call these things?" He lifted his hands from the handle momentarily.

She laughed. "You realize that if you push this like you're allergic to the thing, no one's going to believe we're new parents."

"If anything, those guards will empathize with my new position in life. Dirty diapers? Late-night feedings?"

"Obviously, you're not ready for fatherhood yet."

"I don't see you lining up for maternal duties anytime soon—including pushing this carriage."

"You look less threatening that way. Besides, there's plenty of time, should we decide to go that route."

He stole a glance at her, somewhat surprised. "I didn't know you wanted kids."

"Not at the moment. But people change."

He tried to imagine Remi as a mother but couldn't. At least not yet. "You're not really . . . ?"

"Quiet," she said, looking into the carriage. "It took us this long to get him to sleep."

He had to admit she played the part convincingly, and they settled into a relaxed pace as they neared the main gate. Just as they stepped into view of the guards, the wind gusted, lifting the blanket, exposing Sam's pack, and, nestled next to it, Remi's gun.

One look and they couldn't miss seeing it.

Without missing a beat, Remi leaned over, speaking German to their pseudo-infant, gently patting it as she tucked the blanket safely around the pack and her gun. When she rose, she leaned her head into his shoulder, her smile so serene even he believed she was staring at her firstborn.

The guards barely spared them a glance as they passed by, and, before he knew it, they were rounding the bend toward the service entrance drive that led along the back of the house. The locked gate was framed on either side by stone walls, the one on the right sloping down to accommodate the wrought iron fence along the front of the villa. Sam pushed the carriage alongside the wall so it couldn't be seen from the main guardhouse. The service gate itself was solid wood, no doubt to allow privacy toward the rear of the house. There was also a matching wooden door, also locked. A sign in red was posted on it. "And?" Sam asked.

"'Deliveries by appointment only.'"

"Best news I've heard all day. That means they don't regularly post someone here."

"We hope."

Sam peered through the space between the gate and the wall it was anchored to. "Looks empty."

He knocked, just to be sure. When no one answered, he tried to open it, but it was locked. Nothing on this side indicated it was alarmed, and he made short work with the pick from his wallet, then drew his gun. "Get the baby. We're going in."

50

S am held the door as Remi slipped in behind him.

"What about the baby carriage?" she asked, handing him the pack. "We can't just leave it there."

"If we bring it in and someone sees it, they'll know we're inside. Out there, we stand a chance of someone thinking it's abandoned."

"Not if they knew how much it cost."

"*Now* you're worried about the price?" He closed the door, then dropped down next to Remi behind the boxwood hedge. The main gate and guardhouse were to their right, toward the front of the villa. To their left, the solid glass-shard-topped wall. Right now, their only advantage was that the lights on the perimeter weren't yet on, and the four-foot-tall boxwood was high enough to allow them cover if they ducked down while they walked. As they neared the rear of the house, the sound of an engine turning over broke the silence.

They stopped, Sam looking around for a place to hide.

Headlights appeared on the drive ahead, lighting up the hedge and a few hollows beneath it. He pulled Remi down to the ground. "Underneath as far as you can get."

She rolled in, flattening herself on the ground, gripping her gun in one hand, aiming it toward the truck. Sam shoved the pack at her feet, then dove on top of her, using his free hand to move the branches from his face, then positioning himself, gun at the ready. Not a moment too soon, as the truck rumbled past, then stopped at the closed gate. Sam's German was spotty, but he recognized the word for *Garden* emblazoned on the side of the truck's door. Working late, he thought as the gate swung open, a steady beep sounding as it moved. The truck started forward again once it was clear. Sam caught sight of an electric eye near the gate as it closed, the beep starting up once more until the gate was secured.

He waited a few moments, the sound of the truck fading away as it drove off. "You okay?" he asked Remi.

"A bit flatter than I was a few minutes ago."

He slid off, then helped her out.

"How's the baby?" she asked.

"Still sound asleep," he said, grabbing the pack and slinging it over his shoulder. "Let's find Tatiana."

The drive led to a separate garage, with quarters above it, located behind the main house. A delivery van, its rear door open, was backed up to the garage.

"Caterer," Remi said, translating what was written inside the logo on the door.

The party, of course. That explained why the other truck was there so late. Apparently, it had left a delivery of dozens of potted plants that were being set up around an outdoor terrace by a handful of security guards who should have been patrolling this side of the grounds. "Rube's right," Sam said. "Looks like Rolfe's getting ready to entertain."

"And we didn't receive an invitation? I am *so* crossing him off the list for the baby's first birthday."

"The door Rube told us about has to be in there." Sam nodded toward the six-car garage and the rooms above it. The windows were all dark. He eyed the back terrace. "A good time to get in. He must be short-staffed, or in a hurry, to use security to move those things."

No sooner had the words been spoken than they heard a steady beep, this one softer and coming from their right.

The main gate, Sam realized, rising up just high enough to see over the top of the hedge. A sleek black Rolls-Royce pulled in, followed a moment later by a white Mercedes. He looked back toward the terrace, where the guards were moving plants. There were only about a half dozen pots left, which meant they didn't have much time. "I think the party's starting without us. We better hurry."

Moving toward the garage, they stopped at the end of the hedge. Sam looked out, waited until the guards were turned away from the service drive, then signaled for Remi to follow him.

The door was alarmed but unarmed. In fact, it was unlocked. Sam had to assume it was due to the party, and when they entered, he realized that's exactly why. There were boxes of catering supplies stacked along the wall. Just inside, a windowed door to the left led into the garage, where several cars were parked, among them a red Ferrari, a yellow Porsche, and the sedan that they'd used to kidnap Tatiana. If there was a door that led underground to the main house, he couldn't see it, and he backed out to the short hallway, then up a staircase. At the top, another hallway with several doors, all unlocked, clearly the servants' quarters.

"She's definitely not here," Remi said after they checked each room.

"Looks like we'll have to find that entrance to the house."

They were halfway down the stairs when someone walked in the hall below and turned on the light. Sam slid his pack from his shoulder, hiding his gun behind it, as a short, stout woman glanced up at them, her look of surprise turning to one of anger as she asked them something in German.

Remi, on the stair behind him, replied.

"Nein," the woman said, pointing toward the side door that led into the garage. *"Die Uniformen sind dort."*

"Danke," Remi said.

The woman started to turn away, then asked something else.

"Marta," Remi said.

The woman looked at Sam, her brows raised in inquiry.

"Hans," he replied.

She simply stared at them, making Sam wonder if he'd totally misunderstood. *"Schnell! Schnell!"* she said, waving her hands at them before picking up a box on the floor, then walking out the door once more.

"Dare I ask?" Sam said.

"That would be Helga. The guests are early, we're late, and our uniforms are hanging in the garage."

"Not quite how I was expecting to get into the house, but it'll do."

51

If not for the uniforms, they might not have found the door. It was hidden behind the rack. Just as Sam was about to punch the code into the alarm pad, their new boss returned, insisting on helping them pick out their uniforms. That done, she shooed them up the stairs, then left them to change clothes.

Remi pulled her hair back into a ponytail, then looked at her reflection in the mirror. "Nice to know that the company Rolfe hired to serve his guests isn't sexist."

Sam glanced over at her as she slid her holster onto the belt of her black pants, then pulled the matching jacket over it. The slightly too big uniform covered it nicely. "A shame. You would've looked cute in one of those little skirts and white aprons."

She made a scoffing noise as she folded her clothes, about to shove both into his pack on top of his tools and rope. "Get everything you needed from here?"

"Got it." He'd taken a knife, small flashlight, and a couple of the more likely lockpicks, but that was it. Like Remi, he wore his holster toward the small of his back, and he checked his own reflection to make sure it couldn't be seen.

She shoved her clothes into the pack. He did the same, then zipped it closed. "How quickly they grow," he said, hefting it over his shoulder.

Remi walked to the window, pulling a curtain to look out. "You better brush up on your German. It's getting crowded down there."

Sam glanced out. There were at least a couple of dozen well-dressed guests mingling on a terrace beneath propane heaters. "You think they'll miss us if we skip the party?"

"Somehow, I doubt it."

"Let's go do this."

Unfortunately, Helga was waiting for them at the bottom of the stairs—and somewhat impatiently, judging by the expression on her face. She motioned them to move quicker. Sam lifted his backpack, mumbling, "One moment," hoping it passed for something German. Then he slipped into the garage, getting one last look at the door. A red light on the alarm keypad blinked steadily. Hoping the code Rube provided was still good, he left his backpack on the base of the rack. There were still several uniforms left hanging on it, and he wondered if some of the hired help hadn't shown up.

"*Schnell!*" the woman said, waving her hand for them to quicken their pace. They followed her out, and she led them down a graveled path, around the garage, to the manicured garden. Shorter boxwood hedges surrounded fountains, flowers, and topiaries. Farther down the path, an expanse of lawn stretched out just beneath the terrace, accessed by twin staircases, one on either side.

Two armed security guards walked past, giving them a quick look, before continuing on toward the perimeter, as Helga rushed them up the staircase to their right. At the top, she said something to Remi, then quickly walked toward the main house, where uniformed staff, carrying hors d'oeuvres, mingled among the guests.

Remi touched Sam's sleeve. "This way, Hans. Apparently, we're here to serve champagne." She nodded toward a long table on one side of the terrace, where a bartender filled crystal flutes.

Sam, following Remi's lead, picked up a tray. "Somehow, we need to get back out to the garage and that door."

"How?"

"Playing it by ear, Marta." He casually moved to the edge of the terrace and saw a line of cars, headlights glowing in the dark as they idled in the street, waiting to enter to drop off even more guests. The guards who'd been removed from the perimeter to carry the potted plants earlier that evening were back on patrol. Sam turned toward the guests, now numbering over three dozen, surprised to recognize a couple of faces in the crowd. "Take a look at ten o'clock."

Her gaze slid to the left, her brows going up. "American Ambassador Halstern and his wife. And that congressman . . . What's his name . . . ?"

"Jones."

"What're they doing here, of all places? Halstern, I get. But Jones?"

"I seem to recall some recent trade agreement with Germany."

Remi smiled at a man who approached, taking two flutes from her tray. "Lovely. Always nice to know our politicians are fraternizing with crooks."

"We're assuming they know he's a crook. At least Rolfe isn't around. Do me a favor. Try not to position yourself anywhere near them in case he suddenly makes an appearance and they recognize you."

"I doubt any of them will see past our uniforms."

"If we get caught, you better make sure they *do* see past them. They might be our only chance out of here."

"So what's the plan?" Remi asked.

"We serve champagne until we can go down the opposite staircase and get back to the garage. Too many guards on this side. If we get separated, you glue yourself to the Halsterns. Whether they're supporters of his or not, I doubt they'll allow Rolfe to start an international incident by killing an American on his back porch."

"Fingers crossed."

Sam hefted his tray, about to take a step in that direction. "How do I say—"

"*Champagner,*" she replied.

"Got it." He wove his way through the guests, feeling the warmth from the propane heaters as he passed by. "*Champagner?*" he said, holding the tray out. He'd picked a path that would purposefully avoid Ambassador Halstern. And just when he thought he had a clear path, the Ambassador and his wife suddenly appeared in front of him.

52

The Ambassador grabbed two flutes from Sam's tray, handed one to his wife, who barely spared Sam a glance before both turned back toward the couple they were talking to.

Sam worked his way around the guests until the tray was empty, spotting Remi coming up on his left. He took the stairs down, holding his empty tray at his side, hoping he looked like the hired help taking a short break rather than someone about to burglarize an exclusive German villa. Wondering where Remi was, he turned, saw her starting down the stairs behind him, then stopping when someone called out, "Marta!"

Helga, the woman who'd cornered them in the garage, stood at the top of the stairs, hands on her hips. And though Sam couldn't quite hear what she was saying, it was clear that she was demanding to know what Remi was doing.

Remi held up her empty tray with her right hand, saying something to the woman, as she moved her left hand behind her back, waving for Sam to continue on.

He hesitated, then hurried down, knowing that Remi would've never signaled for him to go on if she'd thought there was the least bit of trouble. A moment later, she was exchanging her empty tray for one full of hors d'oeuvres, before making her way back into the crowd. Little he could do about that. Deciding that she was probably safer up there than with him, he ditched his tray in the bushes, walked back to the garage, then moved the uniform rack. After double-checking his phone for the code that Rube provided, he punched it in, breathing a sigh of relief when the red light turned green.

Just as he slipped in, a man entered the garage and walked up to the uniform rack. Sam was stuck. He couldn't close the door without being seen or heard and so he pressed back against the wall, looking through the crack in the door, gun aimed. Just when he thought he'd been seen, the man grabbed a uniform, then turned away and walked out.

Sam pulled the door closed, then took his small flashlight from his pocket, the dim blue glow reaching just a few feet in front of him. The hallway sloped down, no doors on either side as he followed along, judging it to be at least the length of the open lawn, then the terrace above him. A door at the end blocked his way, its red light indicating it was alarmed.

He used the same code. The door opened into another hallway that branched off in three different directions. He took the left, followed it to the stairs, then up. At the third level, a guard stood at the door.

No doubt, he'd found Tatiana.

Now all he had to do was take out the guard.

He pulled a coin from his pocket, then tossed it low across the floor. The guard, hearing it hit the wall, took a few steps in that direction. Sam crept up on him, shot his arm around the guy's neck, then locked it with his other arm, squeezing against his carotids as he pulled the man off balance. The guard, unable to speak, grabbed at Sam's arm, trying to free himself, his feet thrashing out as he tried to turn away. Within seconds, the guard's strength waned, and his body jerked as the oxygen supply to his brain was cut off. The moment he went limp, Sam dropped him to the floor, then found the keys to the door and opened it.

The only furnishing in the room was the chair where Tatiana, bound and gagged, was seated. Her eyes widened in surprise when she saw him dragging the guard in.

Sam removed her gag, then took the knife from his pocket to cut her ties. "Are you okay?"

"Fine." She rubbed at the rope marks on her wrists. "I take it the trade for the key didn't work?"

"We didn't get that far," he said, cutting through the rope around her ankles. "As far as Rolfe knows, that deal's going down at midnight." He tossed one of the ropes to her and she helped bind the guard's feet while he took the hands.

"Why midnight?" she asked.

"He's a bit preoccupied. Looks like some political fund-raiser thing."

"No wonder he was in such a hurry to get home, never mind they seem to have forgotten about me. If not for that, who knows where I'd be."

The guard started to stir. Sam gave his gun to Tatiana so he could place the gag in the man's mouth. "Let's get out of here before he comes to."

53

"Why do you waste your time with such things?" Leopold asked.

Rolfe drained the last of his wine from his glass, then glanced out the window down to the terrace below, where his guests mingled beneath propane heaters. If not for the constant scrutiny he was under, he'd let them drink themselves to oblivion, never once stepping out there. "It's important to keep up appearances," he said.

Suffering through the occasional social event so that he could appear philanthropic had served him well over the years. It created an illusion of legitimacy. When those occasional investigations into his extracurricular activities veered a little too close, there was never a shortage of high-ranking people willing to vouch for him, never mind overlook the whispers of his involvement.

"Americans?" Leopold commented.

Rolfe followed the direction of his gaze. "The Ambassador to Germany and his wife."

"Why?"

"U.S. connections are always good. I have special interests over there."

"Legal?"

"Depends on one's viewpoint."

Leopold turned back to the guests on the terrace. "What does a party like this cost?"

"Enough," he said. In truth, too much. What he wasn't willing to share was that paying the Guard to help him with the hunt for the Romanov Ransom had taken far more capital than he'd ever anticipated. In fact, he had a new appreciation for how it was his father had burned through the family fortune.

"You should have canceled," Leopold said.

"I don't have that luxury. I've worked too hard networking for my contacts. Canceling the party would start the sort of gossip I can't afford right now."

"'Gossip'?" A look of disgust swept over Leopold's face. "I'd be more worried about a potential kidnapping charge than what anyone thinks about his invitation being pulled."

Rolfe didn't bother mentioning that the only one who could be identified by any witnesses at the scene was Leopold. Instead, he looked at his watch. "You have at least an hour's drive. Get Tatiana out through the tunnel. The sooner you and your men get there, the better. We don't want the Fargos to have the advantage." He started out the door.

"One thing you haven't discussed—how you're going to keep Tatiana from talking once the exchange is made."

He looked back at Leopold. "You don't think we're actually going to let her live, do you?"

"And you think Fargo will turn over the key without getting her in exchange?"

He had a point. The Fargos had proven themselves to be more than troublesome. "Get the key, then put a bullet in each of their heads. Just make sure that no one gets out alive."

"Not a problem."

Leopold followed him out the door when Gere suddenly appeared in the hallway, still trying to hide his limp.

"What are you doing out here?" Rolfe asked.

"I tried calling you, but it went straight to voice mail."

"I have the ringer turned off on my phone. What's wrong?"

"I just checked in with security. There's an abandoned baby carriage outside the service gate."

"And I care because . . . ?"

"I checked the video surveillance. The man and woman pushing it definitely looked like the Fargos."

54

emi left the terrace, passing through a windowed sunporch that ran the length of the house, on her way to pick up yet another tray of canapés. Just as she pushed through the swinging kitchen door, she felt her phone buzzing in her pocket. Her taskmistress, Helga, in the midst of giving orders to the staff about the way the trays were being filled, looked over as Remi read Sam's text.

"Nein!"

Remi apologized, returned the phone to her pocket, breathing a sigh of relief.

He and Tatiana were on their way out.

Helga handed her a tray, then swooshed with her hands, urging her out the door. Remi pushed it open with her shoulder, walked through the sunporch just as someone burst through a door almost in front of her.

She halted in her tracks, the canapés sliding in the tray, watching as Rolfe and Leopold stormed toward the very terrace doors she was heading for. Both men stopped just inside, their gazes fixed on something in the distance. Unable to get past them without being seen, she turned back to the kitchen. At that very moment, the door swung open and Helga appeared, ordering Remi out to the party.

Deciding it was safer out where there were a hundred witnesses, she approached the doors, coming up behind the two men.

"I want the grounds searched," she heard Rolfe saying quietly. "No one gets out until they're found."

Suddenly, Helga was at her heels, urging her to move quicker. Moment of truth, she thought, mumbling, "Excuse me," in German, both men stepping aside as she, then Helga, passed through the door.

Her only thought at that point was to get to her phone and warn Sam. She dared a glance back and saw that Rolfe had stepped out onto the patio, but Leopold had returned inside, no doubt to issue orders without causing a scene.

Within a few seconds, she noticed the guards doubling up, patrolling the perimeter, their routine pace turning to hurry, with several of them walking toward the terrace.

"I'd love one. Thank you."

Remi forced her gaze from the garden to the blond woman standing in front of her.

Ambassador Halstern's wife.

The woman looked past her toward Rolfe, who had moved to the balustrade. There was no sign of recognition when her gaze met Remi's. In fact, her expression was almost blank, dismissive. "A few hours earlier than I was led to expect," she said, reaching for a second hors d'oeuvre. "No matter. I'll be the distraction."

Before Remi had time to react to or process what she'd heard, Mrs. Halstern turned away, walking toward the table where the bartender stood, filling champagne glasses. Remi, keeping her back to Rolfe, made her way to the far stairs, hoping she hadn't heard wrong.

Mrs. Halstern *knew*.

At the top of the stairs, Remi glanced back. Mrs. Halstern was laughing at something her husband had said. She looked at Remi, gave the slightest tilt of her head, then turned back to the Ambassador.

Remi started down the steps, scanning the garden, hesitating at the sight of two guards patrolling the same gravel path she'd need to take to get to the garage. One of them looked up at that very moment, his expression turning wary. He stopped in his tracks, calling out, asking what she was doing.

Seconds ticked by as she eyed both men, one looking at the tray in her hand, the other focused on her face. Trying to appear slightly embarrassed, she shrugged her shoulders, then in a loud whisper said, "*Zigarettenpause.*"

The one guard nodded as though he'd suspected all along. The other eyed her pockets as though trying to determine if she really had any cigarettes. Suddenly, a loud crash and the sound of breaking glass mingled with a scream carried down from the far side of the terrace.

Both guards took off running in that direction.

Remi tossed her tray into the bushes, then bounded down the stairs, gravel crunching beneath her feet as she raced to the garage. Glancing back, she saw Mrs. Halstern being helped to her feet from the vicinity of where the champagne table had once stood. Remi nearly slid in the gravel as she rounded the corner, taking a quick look around to see who might be watching. The back of the catering truck was still open, though a few boxes remained. At least it blocked the view of the garage door as she opened it, slipped in, then closed it behind her, leaning against the wall for a few moments not only to catch her breath but to listen in case anyone else was there.

She glanced up the staircase, saw it was dark, then entered the door on the left into the garage. Sam's backpack was still there behind the uniform rack in front of the door, the light on the alarm keypad blinking red. Remi took out her phone, texted him that Rolfe knew they were there.

With nothing left to do but wait, she returned to the garage door and peeked out, catching sight of another guard who had appeared in front of the catering truck. She ducked back as he looked toward the garage. A moment later, she heard footsteps outside. She reached for her handgun, eyeing the doorknob as someone on the outside turned it to enter.

55

Sam, Tatiana at his heels, keyed in the alarm code and opened the tunnel door a couple of inches, peering through the uniforms to see Remi standing near the garage door, looking outside. Her hand was at the small of her back, about to draw her handgun from beneath her jacket. Gun in hand, he stepped out, motioning for Tatiana to keep quiet as he closed the door behind them, his eyes on his wife.

Remi suddenly relaxed her grip as Helga's round face appeared in the garage window. The woman entered, surprised to see Remi there. Although Sam had no idea what she said to Remi, he understood Remi's response. Something to do with cigarettes.

"*Nein, nein,*" Helga said, then straightened, her gaze sliding past Remi into the garage. When she saw Sam and Tatiana standing behind the uniform rack, she pushed Remi aside and approached, the tone of her voice demanding.

Sam looked at Remi for guidance. Before she had a chance to respond, Helga narrowed her gaze at Tatiana. "Friede?"

"*Ja,*" Tatiana said, nodding.

Helga grabbed a uniform, shoved it at Tatiana, scolding her.

Whatever Tatiana said in response seemed to satisfy her and she pointed to the boxes stacked against the wall. When Tatiana nodded, Helga turned on her heel, squatted like an Olympic weight lifter, hefted two boxes as though they were empty, then walked out the door.

Sam picked up his backpack from the floor. "She didn't sound happy. I take it she thought you were one of the missing employees?"

"Friede, apparently. She's upset because someone fell and broke all the champagne flutes on the table. She wants the extra glasses brought up to the terrace. Oh, and my pay is being docked because I was two hours late."

"She's going to be even more upset when we leave."

"Which," Remi said, "could be a problem. Or didn't you get my text?"

"No signal came through in the tunnels. What text?"

"Rolfe knows we're here. Every security guard out there is on alert."

He walked to the door that Helga had left open, looking out. "No way we're getting down that drive without being seen."

"How did you get in?" Tatiana asked.

"The service entrance gate." Unfortunately, he couldn't see that far down the curved drive from where they were. "No doubt it's guarded now."

Tatiana moved to his side. "What if we joined the party? Surely he wouldn't kill us in front of all his guests?"

"No. He'd kill us before we ever got there. Easier to say we were mistaken for burglars than let us get close enough to call for help."

"Besides," Remi said, "there's a constant patrol walking the stretch of lawn between here and the terrace."

Sam looked over at the cars in the garage. "Check to see if the keys are here."

They did. Not one set.

"We could hot-wire the van," Remi said.

Sam looked out the window. "Actually, we won't need to. The keys are hanging from the rear door." He turned to Tatiana. "Put your uniform on. I think it's time we helped Helga load her boxes into the van."

Tatiana pulled on a pair of pants and jacket, both far too big for her slight frame. With no choice, she rolled up the pant legs so she could walk without tripping, then grabbed a box, following Remi and Sam out the door. The same guard who'd been patrolling the area glanced over at them, his gaze landing on the boxes as they loaded them into the back of the van. When he turned away, Sam grabbed the keys from the lock. Another guard appeared, and the two met up, their attention fixed on the three at the rear of the van. Both started walking in that direction.

"I think that's our cue," Sam said. "I'm going to start the van before they get too close. Maybe if they think we're loading up to leave, it won't look so obvious."

Remi stood to one side near the rear, pointing at the garage, doing a convincing job of acting like she wanted him to back the van closer. He shifted to reverse. The guards seemed to buy it, their steps slowing. But then one of them put his hand to his ear, adjusting his earpiece. Suddenly, both men broke into a run.

Sam shifted to drive, checking the side mirror. "Now!" he shouted. The weight in the back of the van shifted as the two women jumped in. Sam hit the gas, the tires screeching as the van lurched forward, Remi barely closing the rear door in time. He approached the curve, letting his foot off the gas when the wheels lost traction. Up ahead on the left, between him and the gate, another guard stood near the hedge, his gun pointed at them. Sam floored the gas. The guard fired, then dove, his shot going wide. Sam glanced at the side mirror, saw several guards running behind the van.

"Get down!" he called. The two women dropped to the floorboards as a volley of shots rang out. Leaves flew up beside the van like a hedge trimmer in action. The closed gate loomed ahead, the guards standing in front of it, guns out. Sam shifted to the right, overcorrecting, the van coming up on two wheels, then settling. Both guards fired. The windshield fractured, obscuring his vision, as he gunned it straight toward them. The guards dove, one to the left, one to the right. Sam blasted through the gate, wood boards flying as the van hurtled through.

56

Remi, Tatiana, and the boxes they'd loaded flew backwards into the cargo hold as Sam slammed on the brakes, then made a turn onto the street. Remi grabbed one of the cargo straps hanging from the side. "Any chance you were sampling that champagne we were serving?"

Sam took the corner a little too fast, sending her against the side of the van. "Sorry," he said. "Must have been all the alcohol."

He looked back at Tatiana, who was also clinging to one of the cargo straps, looking a bit shell-shocked. "Ignore my wife," he said, turning back to the road. "She's a little sore that she had to watch the baby while I had all the fun."

"The what?" Tatiana asked.

Remi cleared her throat as she made her way to the front passenger seat. "Do you really want to get into who was the better parent?"

"Did I mention how good you look in that uniform?"

The van jarred as they hit a pothole. Remi turned a stern glance his way.

"Sorry," he said. "That one, I really didn't see. He checked the side mirrors just before turning down an alley. "Keep an eye out. The van's a bit obvious."

"You think?" Remi said. "The giant catering sign on the side? Or the bullet holes in the shattered windshield?"

He laughed, glad to see her sense of humor had returned.

Even Tatiana smiled. "You two are incorrigible."

"Makes for a good marriage," Sam replied as he pulled up behind their rental car.

They got out, Remi glancing at the damage to the front of the catering van as they walked to their car.

They drove straight to the hotel where Nika and Felix were waiting. Sam knocked on the door of their room. Nika opened it after only a moment. "Sorry we're late," Sam said. "Stopped by to pick up another passenger."

He stepped aside to let Tatiana in the door first.

Nika's eyes widened. "Tatiana . . . ?" she said, her voice filled with disbelief. "How . . . ? I don't understand."

"The Fargos saw an opportunity and took it."

Nika stared a moment longer, then shook herself, saying something in Russian as she gave Tatiana a hug. "I can't believe you're here."

Felix closed the door behind them. "We were just talking about what we were going to do—I wasn't sure we could pull this off. I—" He hugged her, then stepped back, uncomfortable with the show of affection. "Good to have you safe."

"Thank you, Felix."

"You're not hurt?"

"Other than a few bruises, I'm fine."

He nodded. "Have you called Viktor?"

"Not yet," Tatiana replied. "We were—" She took a deep breath, then sat on one of the beds. "Sorry. It's just now hit me how very close we were to not making it."

"It was the key," Felix said. "That was brilliant."

Sam and Remi backed to the door, Sam saying, "We'll talk in the morning. Give you time to call Viktor and get some rest."

Tatiana nodded. "I don't know how to thank you both."

"No thanks needed," Sam said. "You looked out for us. We wanted to do the same for you."

They left, driving back to the hotel that Selma had found for them. After checking in, they called Rube on speakerphone, informing him of the night's events.

"Glad it worked out," Rube told them. "I'll get a more detailed briefing from you tomorrow—in case there's anything we need to know for the investigation."

"Actually," Remi said, "there is one thing I'm curious about. The Ambassador's wife. She knew we were there. She even created a distraction for us. CIA, by chance?"

There was a second's hesitation on Rube's end, then, "Wow. Didn't realize how late it was there. You two should get some sleep. Big day tomorrow."

"Guess that answers that question," Remi said.

"Good night, Rube," Sam said, then disconnected. He walked over to the bar. "I don't know about you, Remi, but I think we deserve a celebratory drink."

"As long as it's not champagne," she replied, moving to the window and pulling the curtain.

He looked over at her in surprise.

"After spending the night serving whatever cheap brand Rolfe bought for that party," she said, "I'd rather have a good brandy. Enough to sleep in tomorrow morning."

"A girl after my own heart." He selected the brandy, and poured two glasses just as his phone vibrated. He picked it up, reading the text from Selma. "Looks like you and our flight crew will be getting up early tomorrow after all. Selma found the address we need."

Remi lifted her glass to his. "Here's to discovering what that key leads to."

"I'll definitely drink to that."

57

―――――

Your car is ready," Gere told Rolfe from the doorway.

Rolfe ignored him, watching as the last guest's vehicle exited from his property, the red brake lights momentarily lighting up the faces of the two guards at the gate. "Let's hope everyone bought our story," Rolfe said.

Leopold glanced up from the computer monitor, where he'd been reviewing the surveillance videos. "How could they not? With that catering woman screaming that her van had been stolen, and the guards firing at it as it fled, there's no other explanation than a few rogue catering employees. You're lucky."

"How? They got away."

The man turned back to the computer. "Imagine trying to explain what the Fargos were doing, stealing a van from your villa. Good thing the police don't have access to the surveillance."

"I told them the system's been malfunctioning." Rolfe moved away from the window, eyeing the monitor, recalling the sight of the catering van crashing through his gate. "The question now is, what to do about the Fargos?"

"I'd be more worried about your princess and what she plans on doing. Letting a kidnapped Russian agent escape might put a damper on your plans to go after the Fargos. Or anything else, for that matter."

Gere cleared his throat, no doubt as a reminder that he was waiting. Rolfe glanced over at him, giving a dismissive wave. "I'm coming."

Leopold waited until Gere left. "Almost done. What are you planning?" he asked.

"I've survived this long by having contingencies in place—several in non-extradition countries."

"I assume you're crossing Russia off that list?"

"Is that supposed to be amusing?"

"Very." Leopold pushed away from the desk, then stood. "Your surveillance videos are erased."

"One piece of evidence they can't use against me."

"So where are we going?" Leopold asked as they left the room and started down the stairs.

"I have private quarters just outside Berlin that can't be traced to me. We'll regroup there until it's time to leave the country."

"And then what?"

"Figure out where the Fargos are going next." Not that he was about to tell Leopold everything. What he didn't mention was that if he was forced to leave the country, he intended to use the Romanov Ransom to support his lifestyle. He wasn't sure if Leopold planned to keep the portion Rolfe had promised him—the forty percent that was Tatiana's—or if he planned to turn it over to the Wolf Guard. It mattered little. With Tatiana on the loose, law enforcement was sure to start closing in, and they needed to get out. "That key is the clue to the third tin. Since we failed to get it back, I'm open to ideas."

"For sixty percent," Leopold said, "I'll implement one."

After tonight's events, Rolfe was at a complete disadvantage, and he decided to make one last attempt to maintain his hold on the larger share. "You really think I would turn over sixty percent?"

"Assuming you want the Guard's help, yes."

Resisting the urge to pull out his gun and kill the man right there, Rolfe tried to think of a way to finish this hunt on his own. Nothing came to mind. Keeping his expression calm, he waved Leopold through the door.

When Gere saw them walking out, he hobbled forward, opening the back door for Rolfe, before sliding in behind the wheel and starting the car.

Leopold walked around to the other side and got in, his expression that of a man who knew he had the upper hand. "Do we have a deal?" he finally asked once they took off.

"That depends on how you plan to accomplish this."

"Easy. We do to one of the agents what the Russian princess said they were doing to the old man."

Rolfe looked over at him.

"You recall how she said she threatened the old man's family to get cooperation?"

"Clearly, it was a ruse."

"Yes, but in our case, it won't be," Leopold said. "My men have been following the two agents since we spotted them in Wrocław."

"That means you know where Tatiana is. We can stop her."

"The last thing you want is to stop her. As long as she and the Fargos believe they're safe, they'll discover what that key is for and find that third tin."

It took a moment for Rolfe to put aside his anger so that he could concentrate on what Leopold was proposing. "We sit back and wait. What does that do for us?"

"The woman's in our pocket."

"Tatiana?"

"No. The one from Kaliningrad," said Leopold. "Nika. My man cornered her at the hospital."

"Then how is it that the Fargos got into my villa and rescued Tatiana without us knowing?"

"Because the last Nika had heard, they were all coming at midnight, as I'd directed. Fargo didn't tell them he was changing the plan."

"You think she'll continue to cooperate?"

"I know she will. All we have to do is sit back and let the Fargos figure out where that key leads. Once they find the tin, she can give us the code." Leopold sat back and smiled, "We have a deal, then?"

Rolfe thought how easily they'd be able to kill the Fargos once they had what they needed. "Most definitely."

58

That morning, Sam called Tatiana to let her know they'd found the furniture restorer who might have information on the key. "We're heading out right after breakfast. You're welcome to come with us. The jet is waiting."

"Thank you," she said, "but the three of us are driving back to Wrocław to visit Viktor. You'll let us know what you find out?"

"Of course. Give him our regards."

"I will."

Before Sam and Remi made it out the door of their hotel, they received a text from Selma. Apparently, Brand and Karl had discovered something unusual about the logbook from the downed airplane and wanted a video call.

They immediately skyped the boys. Brand answered. "Sorry to interrupt your trip, Mr. Fargo, but there's something here that doesn't make sense, and Selma said you'd be able to help."

Sam glanced at Remi, before turning back to the screen. "You have our complete attention."

"The logbook," Karl said, holding it up. "At first glance, it looks like an official record. But there are notes, sketches, the sort of thing that make us think it might be a duplicate."

"A duplicate?" Remi asked. "Why would they keep two log-books?"

"Because the official one would've been turned over to their superior officers," Sam replied. "The duplicates often have corrections, personal notes . . . Sort of a rough—"

Remi looked over at him when he stopped talking. "Sam?"

"I was going to say 'rough draft.' If they were turning over the logbook to superiors, they'd want to make sure it looked good. No mistakes. But . . ." He thought of everything they'd learned so far, especially the history in Kaliningrad. He looked at the screen, seeing Karl holding up the book, wishing he could read the German writing. "Miron told us that Lambrecht was a double agent. He was helping the authorities follow some of the Nazi officers who were fleeing Europe after the war. If Lambrecht turned over the official book to the Nazis, this one might have information about his spying."

"Spying," Karl said, looking at the book, turning the pages, nodding his head. "We had a feeling the logbook had something to do with the ratline, but we weren't sure. That might fit with what we found . . ."

Brand moved into the video feed. "Definitely. We were trying to figure out what 'use the first' meant," he said. "'First' is underlined twice. So there's got to be some importance."

"And," Karl said, "'Romanov Ransom' is also underlined twice."

"Okay," Sam said. "They intended that the two be noticed. What else?"

Karl answered. "We think the pilot was on his way to Tunisia when the plane went down, presumably to deliver the courier bag."

"Do you know to whom?"

"Someone named Häussler. But that's all we know."

"Not all," Brand said. "We found Lambrecht's name mentioned in some of our other research. He'd found out something important about the ratline and was delivering the evidence when his plane went down somewhere in North Africa. We just don't know anything about this Häussler. We're looking into it now."

"Good work, you two," Sam said. "Give Selma a call and let her know everything you've discovered. Have her get back to us the moment she finds anything."

They disconnected. "Häussler," Remi said, picking up her coat. "I wonder what that's all about."

"I'm sure we'll find out in due time," Sam said. "Right now, I'd like to get to Münster and find this furniture restorer."

THE FLIGHT TO MÜNSTER took a little over an hour, and the drive into town about half that. Once Sam found a parking spot, he and Remi walked to the city center, up a cobbled street toward the main square and St. Lambert's Church. They searched for the man who was supposed to meet them, eyeing the tourists who seemed to be looking up at the church tower—not at the clock, but at the three iron cages hanging above it. Although Sam and Remi had been there before, like the tourists, their gazes were drawn to the cages where the bodies of the Anabaptist rebellion leaders had been placed on exhibition after the yearlong siege in 1536.

"Sinister-looking, aren't they?" someone said from beside them.

"Definitely," Sam replied, looking over to see a blond-haired man in his late forties eyeing the two of them. "Wilhelm Schroeder?"

"Call me Will," he said, pronouncing the W like a V. He glanced up toward the church towers as the bells started ringing. "But you're not here to talk about the architecture. I understand you have a key that you'd like me to examine?"

"We do."

"Very good. We can talk in my shop." He led them across the square, behind the church down a narrow street and into an alley to an unmarked door. "I knew you'd never be able to find my little shop. I'm actually a lawyer by day. The shop is in the basement of our law offices. Furniture restoration is a hobby of mine. It helps me relax."

The moment he opened the door and led them down a short flight of steps, they were hit by the scent of sawdust mixed with tung oil. "This is my latest project." He stopped to show them a dark walnut armoire with an intricate geometric pattern carved into the doors, reminiscent of a Gothic church. "French. From the nineteenth century," he said, leading them past the armoire to a small office area filled with bookshelves, a desk, and on the wall over the desk, a painting of a lone wolf in the forest.

He opened the shutters, letting in some light before turning toward them, looking expectant. "So, where is this key?"

59

Sam took a quick glance around the room, noticing two other wildlife paintings, neither of which featured a wolf. He dug the key from his pocket.

Will took it, then sat at his desk, holding it beneath the lamp, examining both sides. "Very nice. It does indeed appear to be similar to the key from another desk that I had the pleasure of restoring . . ." He swiveled his chair around, searching the titles on a bookshelf behind him, then pulled out a volume, *Early 19th Century Furniture*, turning through the pages until he came to a section filled with photos of old keys.

"I believe," he said, running his finger down the photos, "we're looking for Lieschblume's work. He specialized in locks for the various furniture makers of the time." He turned the page, scanned it, then turned another, pointing to a photo of a key in the lower right corner of the page. "Here it is. See the very distinct fleur-de-lis pattern stamped on the shaft? That was the trademark of the Lieschblume Locksmith Company at the turn of the early nineteenth century. They supplied locks and keys for high-end furniture. Your particular key," he said, setting it on the page next to the photo, "appears to be of the same make. What makes your key special, though, are the extra teeth on the bit." He picked up the key and pointed to the end of it. "More teeth means the lock was slightly more secure than the one your antique dealer showed you from his desk."

"What do you think it's from?"

"Hard to say. A desk, a trunk, or maybe a wardrobe. The more decorative Lieschblume keys, such as the one you have, were used almost exclusively for furniture. Very fine furniture, I might add. Not for the commoner, which makes your quest a bit easier."

"Every little bit helps," Sam said, glancing over at Remi, who was standing behind Will's chair, her gaze on his paintings.

"The intricate detailing of the scrollwork on the grip usually had a matching ornamental plate around the keyhole on the furniture piece. They were custom made to the specifications of their clients." He set aside the key and started turning pages in the book until he reached one filled with writing desks, some with a writing surface that could be closed and locked. He pointed to the decorative plate around the keyhole. "For instance, if we had the key to this desk in hand, we'd see that the design on the bow or grip of the key would match the design on the plate."

Sam took another look at the key. The scrolling of the grip, in comparison to the one in the book, seemed far simpler. "You're saying that we could match the pattern in the bow to the decorative plate covering the keyhole? And we might be able to identify the key that way?"

"Exactly. In some cases, they were family crests. In others, simply a commissioned design."

"Which does us little good unless we know who commissioned it."

"I can't be positive, but it reminds me of the crest from the principality of Salm-Salm. Two fish, back-to-back."

Now that he pointed it out, Sam and Remi could see how the design might be two fishes. "Where would this be?"

"Anholt castle in Isselburg. A little over an hour's drive from here.

If you like, I can call the solicitor on retainer for the Salm-Salm family and explain what it is you're looking for. We went to law school together. If anyone can get you an audience with the prince, or someone from his house who knows anything about this, he can."

"We'd appreciate it," Sam said, picking up the key and placing it in his pocket.

"Thank you for your help," Remi added. "I think we can find our way out to the square." She made a beeline to the door.

Sam followed quickly behind his wife. At the end of the alley, Remi turned left. "The square's the other way," he said.

"Just want to see something . . ." She stopped in front of a door, reading the placard next to it.

"Entrance to law offices?"

"Interesting . . . Bachman, Dreschler and Dreschler. His name's not even on here."

"Junior partner?"

"Or the Guard? You did notice that wolf painting, right?"

Sam was already heading back down the alley, looking through the basement window to see what Will was doing. But there he was, whistling away as he hand-sanded the side of the armoire.

SAM PARKED IN a gravel lot, and the two walked toward the park-like grounds, catching sight of the castle through the trees. The still moat reflected not only the red-bricked castle, and the Baroque gardens to the left of it, but also the dark, threatening clouds above—until the breeze rippled across the water, blurring everything on its surface.

"It's beautiful," Remi said.

A light sprinkle started to fall, and Sam looked up at the sky, quickening their pace. "Hope we can find what we need and get out of here before the weather turns."

They crossed the footbridge, then passed through an arched entry into a courtyard, their footsteps echoing as they walked in. To their right was the wing of the castle that had been turned into a hotel. Directly in front, mounted high on the courtyard wall, was a simplified wrought iron version of the Salm-Salm family crest of two fish, back-to-back. "Just like the key," Remi said.

Sam looked around and found the tour office to their left. Wilhelm had made arrangements for them to meet up with Laurenz Hippler, who worked on-site and managed the castle grounds for the family. Inside, a middle-aged woman, wearing a white blouse and black slacks, sat behind a glass window, attending a cash register. "Sam and Remi Fargo," he said. "Mr. Hippler, please. He's expecting us."

"One moment," she replied, picking up the phone and punching the extension. "*Herr und Frau Fargo sind hier . . . Danke.*" She hung up the phone. "He will be right down."

"Thank you."

About one minute later, a gray-haired man, wearing a dark blue suit and tie, came down the stairs from the end of the hall. "Mr. and Mrs. Fargo. A pleasure to meet you," he said, shaking their hands. "I understand you're trying to match a key to a piece of furniture? A bit of a mystery, of a sort?"

"We are," Sam said.

"I spoke with the family and they've agreed to let you look. As long as you understand that nothing can be removed from the premises. At least not without their permission."

"If we find what we're looking for," Sam said, "I think a few photos will do."

"That shouldn't be a problem. So where is this key?"

Sam took it from his pocket, holding it out to him. "Any ideas what it might belong to?"

The man's eyes widened slightly as he stared at the key. He looked at Sam, almost in disbelief. "I know *exactly* what it belongs to."

60

S am and Remi followed Laurenz out of the office, down the
stairs, then across the castle's courtyard. He looked over at the
key Sam held. "That is amazing. Where did you find it?"

"In Poland," Sam said, deciding it would be much easier to keep it
vague. "An old Nazi office."

"Who knows how many Nazis were in and out of the castle in
those days. Anyone could have taken it. It does, however, answer the
question of what happened to it. During the war, most of the furniture, paintings, and valuables were moved to an underground, shell-
proof mine. A wise move, since more than seventy percent of the castle
was destroyed during the air raids. As you can see, it's since been re-
built."

"What does the key belong to?" Remi asked as Laurenz opened
the door to the castle.

"The writing desk that originally belonged to Marie Christine,
sister of Prince Carl Theodor Otto. From the seventeenth century. But
a lock was added to it sometime after the First World War. The key
has been missing for as long as I've been here."

He led them through a door into a small room with a fireplace whose surround was made of Delft blue tiles, then on past into a library filled with thousands of volumes locked behind glass doors. "I'm only assuming it's the key since the desk is the only piece of furniture I know of in the castle that is missing one. Here," he said, stopping in front of a windowed alcove to the left that was barricaded from public access by a velvet rope. Inside was a desk, stationery, and writing instruments, set up to show what it might have looked like centuries ago. "Here it is. Shall we see if it fits?"

Sam handed the key over. Laurenz removed the rope barricade, then stepped around the desk, inserting the key into the lock and turning it. "Perfect fit. Though I'm not sure how this will help you."

Sam and Remi watched as he opened the drawer, Remi saying, "We need to know what is inside it."

"The drawer? Empty, I'm afraid. We had a locksmith open it long ago, when they decided to allow tours. I don't recall anything of value ever being mentioned. Just some of the writing tools you see on the desktop."

He stepped out of the narrow space so that they could see for themselves. Sam examined the desk, as well as the empty drawer. "Any hidden compartments?" Sam asked.

"I don't believe so. But feel free to check for yourself."

Sam felt around inside the drawer, then beneath the desk. "Remi, take a look. You seem to have better luck with this sort of thing."

Remi took his place but, after a few minutes, shook her head. "Nothing."

"What is it you're searching for? I'm familiar with many of the family heirlooms. Perhaps I can help."

Sam showed him the cell phone photo of the tin.

"That would explain it," Laurenz said. "The display here was for historical value, as you can see from the pen and ink set. Had they found a typewriter ribbon, they would have either thrown it out or taken it to the office where the typewriter was located."

"Any chance you have a typewriter and ribbon set up anywhere?"

"Unfortunately, no. You have my curiosity piqued, though. What's so important about a typewriter ribbon tin? I can't imagine it'd be worth all that much on the antique market."

"Probably not," Sam said. "In this case, it was one of a set of three. We think that, together, the three tins are part of a code or message. Possibly the items were used in some sort of spy operation. We checked for hidden messages on the spools. Nothing."

"As a history buff, I happen to know a bit about that sort of thing. May I see the photo again?"

Sam brought up the picture, then handed him the phone.

He looked at the tin, his expression one of mild curiosity as he enlarged the picture, staring at it for a few seconds. "Are there more photos of the tins?"

"Several. Feel free to look."

The man swiped his finger across the screen, accessing the next photo, enlarging it, then moving on to the next, until he'd looked at each in that file. "Interesting . . . It's definitely not a method I've seen . . . but it makes sense . . ."

"What does?" Sam asked, unable to see the actual photos and what he seemed to be focusing on.

"If I had to guess, these tins were chosen precisely because they appeared innocuous. What was your first inclination when you found them?"

"To see what was inside."

"And not pay attention to the tin itself beyond a cursory glance, no doubt." He showed them the photo of the underside of one tin. "Pay particular attention to the manufacturer's stamp on both the tins. At first glance, they appear identical."

Sam took the phone, noting the small diamond stamped on the bottom. The rust made it difficult to see, but there was definitely something in the center of the diamond. He enlarged it, showing it to Remi. "Numbers."

"Yes," Laurenz said. "Now, look at the other."

Sam swiped through the photos to the second tin from the Project Riese tunnels. The bottom of this one, having been in the desk in the cave, had no rust at all, and it was easy to see what was stamped inside the diamond. "Roman numerals."

"Exactly," Laurenz replied. "*That* is your message."

"Two-thirds of our message," Remi said. "We're still missing the third tin."

Sam took one last look at the photos before putting the phone in his pocket. "Any idea what it might mean?"

"I can't help you there."

Sam shook hands with him. "Definitely more than we knew before we got here. Thank you. We appreciate your time."

Remi shook hands as well. "At least the key is back where it belongs."

"For which we'd like to thank you," Laurenz said. "We have a very nice restaurant that overlooks the water. Take a tour of the castle and stay for lunch. Our treat."

"As much as we'd like to," Sam said, "we really have to get going. Thank you again for your time."

SAM CALLED SELMA the moment he and Remi stepped out the door and started walking back to the car.

"The key led to the third tin?" Selma asked.

"No. The key was a red herring."

"A red herring that saved Tatianna's life," Remi chimed in.

"Right as usual, Remi," Sam said as he eyed her. "But, even better, the manager at the castle noticed differences in the manufacturer's stamps on the bottoms of the tins. Take a look. See if you can get Pete or Wendy to clean up the rust on the digital images," he said, referring to Selma's assistants. "Maybe if we get a clear view of the characters, we can figure out what the code is."

"Say no more."

He pocketed his phone, taking one last look at the castle before getting into the car. "Let's hope they figure it out."

Remi looked at the map on the car's navigation screen. "We're not too far from the Netherlands. Winterswijk is right across the border."

"Winterswijk—why does that town sound familiar?"

"The Mondrian House museum is there. Really, Sam, how is it you don't remember these things?"

"Could be the thousands of museums you've dragged me through over the years. Mondrian . . . Which artist is he?"

"Primary colors, cubist painter."

"Don't we have a Mondrian cow in our kitchen?" Sam asked. A porcelain figurine sat on a shelf above the stovetop.

"You're trying to change the point," Remi replied. "I didn't hear you complaining when we were at the British Museum."

"That's different. We were looking for King John's Treasure. There was a purpose."

"We're not too far. Date night in Winterswijk? We could go to the Strand Lodge for dinner. Remember how wonderful the food was?"

Sam suddenly pulled over to the side of the road. "Not this time."

"What's wrong?" Remi asked.

"Get Selma on the phone. I just realized what the tins are for."

61

"Wait," Sam said as Remi started to make the call. "Make it a videoconference. This is important."

"Are you keeping me in suspense on purpose?" she asked as the phone rang twice before it was answered, the video screen showing Selma at her desk.

Selma looked up at the camera over the top of her reading glasses, saying, "Mr. and Mrs. Fargo. I hope you're not calling about the digital image. We're not that fast."

"I take it back about the key being a red herring," Sam said. "If it weren't for the key, we would've never found out that the tins are the key to a code. And why we need all three."

"That fits with what Lazlo's been thinking. The information on this Häussler name that Karl and Brand read about in the pilot's logbook."

Selma turned the camera so that it included Lazlo, who was sitting next to her at the desk, his attention focused on the paper he was holding. When he didn't respond, she nudged him with her elbow. "Oh. Sorry," he said, eyeing the camera. "I believe the chap we're looking for is one Eckardt Häussler, a cryptographer working with the Allies during and after the war. If this is who Lambrecht was on his way to see, then, yes, it has something to do with a code. Regrettably, one I've not yet been able to decipher."

"I may have the answer," Sam said as the first few drops of rain splattered against the windshield. "Is it possible the numbers on the tins are part of an Enigma code? Or, rather, the key to the code that was used?"

Lazlo's brows went up. "You may very well be right."

"The Roman numerals on the one tin tell us which three of five rotors were used and in what order. The second tin—assuming we can clean up the digital image to read what's on the bottom—would be the ring settings."

"And the third?" Remi said. "The one we're missing?"

Lazlo answered, "That would have the order of the wiring, the plugs. But with the third tin still missing, we have no way of knowing what's stamped on the bottom. And, I'm afraid, the key to the other two—or, rather, what we'd need to decipher the letters—would be on that third tin."

"Which is why I'm calling," Sam said. "We found an Enigma machine—possibly the one they used—in the tunnels in Poland."

"But it was destroyed," Remi added.

"Mystery solved," Lazlo said. "That's got to be why Lambrecht was on his way to Häussler. Trying to figure out how to decipher the code without it. Unfortunately, that doesn't help us much now."

"Can't we use a different machine?" Remi asked Lazlo. "There has to be a number of them in private collections and museums. If we can get one, you can decipher the letters."

"Not that easy," Sam said.

"Quite right," Lazlo replied. "Assuming your theory is correct, even though we know which variant of the machine—three rotors versus four—and in which order—the start positions, et cetera, et cetera—we're still missing one important variable—the order of the plugs wired into the machine, no doubt stamped on the bottom of that third tin."

"The wiring?" Remi looked over at Sam. "The machine was smashed, but I distinctly remember seeing the wiring still plugged in."

"You're sure?" Lazlo asked.

"Positive. But I didn't pay attention to the order. Did you, Sam?"

"I was paying more attention to the smashed rotors, but I definitely noticed exposed wires. The good news is, we know someone who can get some photos. If we're lucky, it'll narrow down the options."

"Brilliant," Lazlo said. "Any chance I can speak to him first? Might make things a lot easier."

"Not a problem," Sam replied, slipping his phone from his pocket. "I'll give him a call while we still have you on video."

A moment later, he had Gustaw on the line, and introduced Selma and Lazlo. Lazlo explained what they needed, finishing with, "Pay particular attention to the front of the machine, where the plugs and wiring are. If you can get photos before it's moved, and from multiple angles, that should help. In case any of the plugs were dislodged when they tried to destroy it, it's possible we can re-create the position."

"Anything else?" Gustaw asked.

"I think that should do it," Lazlo said.

"What about the Guard?" Sam added. "Any chance you can get in there without being followed?"

"I saw a few in town yesterday, so they're still here," Gustaw replied. "But no alerts on the cameras."

"I'd rather be safe than sorry," Sam said as Remi nodded her agreement. "We're just outside Münster. We can fly into Wrocław."

"What about the Russians?" Selma asked. "Wouldn't that be quicker?"

Remi added. "Good idea. They're still in Wrocław, waiting for Viktor to get out of the hospital."

"Russians?" Gustaw said. "Did I miss something?"

Sam gave a quick explanation, ending with, "I'll call Tatiana now and have her get in touch with you. I'm sure she'll be happy to help."

62

Tatiana knocked on the doorframe of Viktor's hospital room. "You're awake."

"Come in," he said.

"How are you?"

"About *this* close to making a break for it. They say one more day."

She glanced at the IV drip hanging above him and the bandage on his chest, where the tube keeping his lung inflated had only recently been removed. "Listen, for once."

"I might if they serve decent food today. What brings you to my lonely hospital room?"

"I just got off the phone with the Fargos. They're asking help for Gustaw Czarnecki. They want to make sure he's not in any danger."

"Help for what?"

"To go back into the tunnels. There's a broken Enigma machine in the chamber they found that they think might be related to these tins."

"Enigma machine?" He was quiet a moment. "A code, of course. That sounds easy enough. The man seemed capable to me."

"I'm sure he is. But they're worried about this Wolf Guard. I've checked with a few of our intelligence agencies. Not one realized they were operating in Russia. They assumed it was strictly a loosely based group within the borders of Germany."

He gave her a slight smile. "I see a medal in your future for exposing them."

"I'm serious." She glanced out to the hallway and even though it was still empty, she closed the door, then moved to his bedside. "They had someone at Königsberg castle, right under your nose. And don't forget about what happened in Poland. They stole that map before we'd even realized where they were. And the night I was kidnapped . . ."

As much as she wanted to forget what happened, she couldn't. The steady beep of the heart monitor had a calming effect as she tried not to think about the terror of that night, not knowing if Viktor was alive and certain she was going to be killed.

"Tatiana . . . ?"

"I'm fine," she said.

"No, you're not."

He was right, of course. "I've been doing a lot of thinking about the Guard. Rolfe might believe he's running the show, but I'm not sure that's entirely true. Leopold is far more dangerous. This organization of his is . . ."

"Is what?"

"Far more widespread than any of us realized. It has to be."

"I agree. But what does this have to do with the miner?"

"What if the Guard gets wind of what he's doing? If the Fargos are correct, that this Enigma machine they found in the tunnel relates to the code they're looking for, it's imperative that they get this information. As long as the Guard is out there, we need to ensure that Gustaw is protected while he's trying to get it."

"True."

"We're close enough that Felix and I can drive up, meet him, and make sure he safely gets in and out."

"I'd think you'd want to keep yourself free to run the investigation. What if you get word of where Rolfe is hiding? Wouldn't it be better to have Nika with Felix?"

"In this case, I don't know . . . I was thinking about giving her some time off."

"Why?"

"If you saw how emotional she's been, jumping at every little thing, you'd agree with me."

"I haven't seen her since I landed in here. But she seemed fine while we were waiting for the ambulance. Her usual stubborn self."

"She was a mess last night. And no better this morning. Felix said it started here at the hospital. The only thing I can think is that both my kidnapping and your shooting have affected her even more than any of us realized."

"Maybe putting her to work is exactly what she needs."

"Maybe . . ."

"Send her. It's an easy assignment. Standing guard over a tunnel. What can go wrong?"

63

What *could go wrong?* Viktor's question echoed through Tatiana's mind long after she assigned Felix and Nika to accompany Gustaw out to the tunnels to recover the Enigma machine. The Guard could go wrong, she thought, recalling how easily they'd followed the Fargos, breaking into their hotel and putting the couple in danger.

They were everywhere.

This last thought worried her the most, and she called Felix. "Just checking to see how you're both doing," she said when he answered.

"We're fine. The map to his cabin is straightforward. Gustaw said he'd meet us where the pavement ends."

"Do me a favor. Wait for me. I want to go with you."

"Are you sure? It's nothing we can't handle."

"We shouldn't underestimate the Guard. You know what happened in Kaliningrad. They're even more prevalent where you are. Why take chances?"

"No argument there," Felix said. "We'll see you in a while."

TATIANA QUIETLY OBSERVED Nika on the ride up to Gustaw's property. Other than the dark circles under her blue eyes, she seemed fine, and Tatiana hoped that the young woman had merely been suffering from a mild case of post-traumatic stress brought on by Viktor's shooting.

At Gustaw's cabin, the three got out of the car. As Felix walked up to greet the miner, Tatiana turned to Nika. "How are you?"

"Fine," Nika said. "Why?"

"A lot has happened. You've seemed . . . upset."

Nika glanced toward Felix, then back. "I'd think you'd be more upset. You were the one kidnapped, after all."

Tatiana studied her a moment. Same brusqueness Nika usually showed. Still . . .

"Thought there were only two of you," Gustaw remarked.

"My apologies," Tatiana said. "I decided to come at the last minute."

"And you are . . . ?"

"Tatiana Petrov. We spoke on the phone."

Gustaw nodded.

"With the threat of the Guard, I thought it a good idea to bring more help."

"Lucky for us, I haven't seen any signs they're back in any large numbers. Let's hope it stays that way." He had two packs on the porch, handing one to Felix, then shouldering the other himself. "The sooner we get started, the sooner we can get the photos to the Fargos."

The four hiked through the woods until they reached the entrance to the tunnel. A half hour later, he was leading them into the hidden cavern where they had found the Enigma machine. "There it is," he said, pointing.

Tatiana drew her gaze from the mummified Nazi on her right to the smashed box on the floor near the desk. Just as Sam Fargo had described, someone had tried to destroy the machine. "I'll get the photos," she said, pulling the camera from her pocket. She took pictures from every angle, some with the flash, some without, paying particular attention to the plugs and wiring.

Felix picked up the rotors on the floor beside the machine, placing them on the desk. As she took photos of the rotors, Nika crouched beside the Enigma, her back to them. Tatiana glanced over, noticing Nika holding her phone over the machine. "What are you doing?" Tatiana asked.

"Good idea to have backup, don't you think?"

"Definitely." Tatiana took one last look around. "This should do it. Unless there's something else we need here?"

Gustaw suggested they take the machine and rotors with them just in case, and once they gathered the pieces and placed it into his pack, they headed back to the entrance, where Gustaw climbed out first in order to pull them up with the harness system he'd rigged. As he assisted Tatiana, she'd convinced herself that her worry for Nika was more in her mind than anything else—until she glanced down into the tunnel and saw Nika holding her phone, the screen lighting up.

Waiting until everyone was out, she turned to Nika, saying, "What were you doing on your phone?"

"I thought I received a text. It was nothing."

"Let me see it."

Nika's face paled. "I swear, I wasn't doing anything."

Tatiana held out her hand. "Your phone. *Now.*" Nika unlocked the screen, then handed it over. Tatiana looked over the text and attached photo, hoping to come up with a logical explanation for what she was seeing. There was none, and the look of guilt on Nika's face confirmed her worst fears. ·

64

Sam and Remi were landing in Berlin, on their way to see Karl and Brand, when Tatiana emailed the photos of the Enigma machine to them. Sam immediately forwarded the photos to Selma. A moment later, Tatiana called. "I have bad news," she said when Sam answered.

"What's wrong?"

"The photos . . ."

"They came through fine. We sent them to Lazlo the moment we got them."

"It's not that. It's Nika. The Guard got to her."

"Hold on," he said, "I'm placing you on speaker so Remi can hear." He pressed the button. "What happened?"

"They got to her the night of Viktor's shooting. They threatened to kill her family if she didn't turn over anything she found out."

Remi looked up at Sam, saying, "Her family? Did anyone check on them?"

"We sent agents out. I haven't heard back. Unfortunately, I didn't find out until after Nika sent a photo of the Enigma machine's wiring to Leopold. She's been in touch with them from the moment you left the hospital at Wrocław."

"So every time I updated you," Sam said, "she forwarded that information to Leopold. The Guard knew our every move."

"Exactly. From the furniture maker in Münster to the trip to the castle with the key."

"Clever," Sam said. "Letting us do the legwork. Forewarned, forearmed. Since they have the information from both tins and the Enigma machine wiring, we have to assume they're on the same trail."

"What are you going to do?" Tatiana asked.

"Not much we can do until Lazlo finishes working on the Enigma code. In the meantime, we're meeting up with Brand and Karl to see what they've found. Something to do with the logbook."

"That's good," Tatiana said. "Neither Rolfe nor Leopold know about the logbook."

"Let's hope it stays that way. We'll keep in touch."

BRAND AND KARL seemed amped up on coffee when Sam and Remi arrived. "You have to see this," Karl said, drawing the two to the dining room table, where butcher paper covered the entire surface, charts and notes written across most of it. "We've gone over every page of the logbook. Most of it's standard, but in the margin toward the end someone wrote 'Strassmair has it' next to the letters *RR*, which are circled." He picked up the book, opening it to show Sam. "We're guessing that *RR* stands for *Romanov Ransom*."

"No doubt," Sam said. "Strassmair, though . . . that's one of the names we heard recently."

"Königsberg castle," Remi replied. "The table, with his signature on the orders for the trucks to remove the treasure."

"That's what it was." Sam glanced at the chart drawn on the butcher paper. "What's all this?"

"The ratline trail," Karl said.

Brand dug through a small stack of papers, pulling one out. "Strassmair is on one of the lists of Nazi officers suspected of escaping through the ratline. It's possible he ended up in Spain. We're going through our research papers now, trying to trace his route from there, but we've hit a dead end."

"At least it's a start," Sam said, reading the notations on their chart. "What else do you have?"

"This," Karl said, showing Sam the logbook again. "Right after the notation *RR*. What if it's the key to those two letters?"

Sam eyed the book. "What do you mean?"

Karl pointed to a notation underlined. "First."

"First what?" Sam asked.

"Brand thinks it refers to how the code should be read."

Remi looked over Sam's shoulder, taking everything in. "Does Lazlo know?"

"We just spoke with him. Now that he has the photos of the Enigma machine, he's going to take another look."

And, sure enough, Lazlo called fifteen minutes later. "The boys were right," Lazlo said. "The notations in the logbook are the key on how to read the coded letters. Now that we have everything set in the Enigma machine, it didn't take long at all. It was the first letter of each sentence."

"What did you translate?" Sam asked.

"That we know where the Romanov Ransom was taken."

"Where?" Sam and Remi asked at the same time.

"South America."

Sam exchanged glances with Remi, asking, "Any chance you can narrow it down? That's a big continent."

"Argentina."

"That fits," Brand said. "A lot of Nazi war criminals ended up there."

Sam quickly looked over the pages of the logbook, wondering if there was anything they'd missed. "Lazlo, what are the chances that Rolfe and Leopold know this information without the logbook in their possession?"

"Assuming they aren't somehow already in possession of this knowledge? After all, they certainly seem to know what the tins are for."

"Good point."

"It's really only a matter of time," Lazlo said. "Anyone with the least idea on how cryptology works has probably already tried deciphering the first letters of each sentence. I certainly tried it. Of course, it didn't work until you recovered the Enigma machine settings. And now that they have those—"

"How?" Karl said. "I thought—"

"A long story," Sam said, turning to the last page of the logbook, where Strassmair's name was circled. "I'll let Selma tell you. Right now, I'd like you and your brother to concentrate on finding out whatever you can on this Strassmair person."

"Anything in particular?"

"Where he was from, any family he had. In other words, anything that will help us pinpoint where in South America he might have gone." He closed the book, placing it on the table. "In the meantime, it looks like our next stop is Argentina."

"What about Rolfe and the Wolf Guard?" Remi asked.

"Let's hope they're not as astute as Lazlo is at deciphering codes."

65

Rolfe paced the room, looking over at Leopold, who was sitting at the computer. "What's taking so long?"

"Nika's photo is not the best," Leopold said.

"She only took one picture?"

"More than likely, she only managed to send the one before she was caught. A shame they discovered her. She was a valuable asset for a while."

"Not too valuable. The whole trip to Anholt castle was a wild-goose chase. The key didn't lead to the third tin."

"Doesn't matter, since Fargo guessed what was on it. If not for Nika, we wouldn't have known about the smashed machine found in the tunnel—never mind gotten a photo of the wiring."

Rolfe walked over to the computer, trying to determine if Leopold had made any progress. "How are you doing this without the actual machine?"

"The computer program *is* the Enigma machine. It was designed to duplicate an actual machine by taking the information entered and scrambling or unscrambling, as the case may be. All I need is to input which rotors were used and the order of the plugs. And, of course, the coded message. In this case, it's from the two letters found in the courier pouch. Or, rather, the first character of each sentence in those letters."

"How is it you know this?"

"It's been passed down to the head of the Guard since it was first known."

It occurred to Rolfe just then that had he not joined forces with the Guard, he'd be at a loss when it came to interpreting the exact method of using the information from the tins. At least he was getting something for the exorbitant split he was handing over.

Rolfe studied the screen while Leopold typed. All he saw was a bunch of garbled words. Nothing made sense. "How long do you think it'll take?"

"It will be considerably faster if you leave me alone."

He started his pacing again, occasionally looking over at Leopold to see how he was faring. Watching him work, Rolfe wondered again at his luck in meeting the man.

Or was it luck?

Rolfe had always assumed he'd been the one to find Leopold. Suddenly, he wondered if it hadn't been the other way around. While he wasn't the gambling sort, if he had to lay odds on the chances of running across the one man who knew everything there was to know on how to find the Romanov Ransom . . .

He stopped in his tracks at the dawning realization that his luck on finding Leopold was anything but.

So where did that leave him? Now that Leopold had the tins and the photo from the Enigma machine, there was only one thing standing in the way of him taking the information that he needed, then leaving: Rolfe was bankrolling this venture.

So, for the moment, there was a mutual need.

A sobering thought. Once the treasure was found, that need

ended. And though he'd avoided thinking about that until this very moment, he realized it was time to start planning the endgame. He wasn't about to lose any part of the treasure to the Wolf Guard.

Or lose the whole thing. Shifts in loyalty could occur for any number of reasons.

"It's done," Leopold said.

"And?"

"The treasure was taken to South America. Argentina, to be exact."

"Do we know where?"

"Not yet. But based on what I know about the travels of most of the high-ranking Nazis, they landed in Buenos Aires. What I don't understand is why the Wolf Guard wasn't aware that the treasure had been taken there."

His comment surprised Rolfe. "Why would they know?" Rolfe asked. "Clearly, it was a secret, or why bother with the tins and protecting where they'd been hidden?"

"Except," Leopold said, leaning back in his chair as he stared at the computer screen, "the Guard also operates in South America."

"Since when?"

"Since the end of the war. A number of Guardsmen escaped using the ratlines."

"That explains it, then," Rolfe said. "They weren't interested in guarding anything beyond their own lives."

"No . . ." He pushed away from the desk, then stood. "The Guard branched out to every continent for the specific purpose of furthering the Führer's plans. No one knew which country to expect the uprising, in case of spies. If the treasure had safely arrived in Argentina and made it into the hands of those in charge of Operation Werewolf, the Guard would've been called into service." He looked at the computer, then back at Rolfe. "Something had to have happened to the treasure, and the men carrying it, before it reached its final destination. It's the only explanation why it became lost. If nothing else, we may be able to find information that will help us locate where the treasure was last seen."

"So all you need to do is check with the Guard in Argentina?"

"Something like that. In this case, I think it best that you stay behind. They're dangerous. Not as organized. There may be issues."

"Issues, I can deal with." Not a chance he was staying behind to let Leopold take possession of the treasure. "I'll make the flight arrangements."

66

While Sam and Remi waited on the jet, Remi received a message from Selma. "Apparently, Brand and Karl found records that Ludwig Strassmair had a sister who arrived in Buenos Aires with her family a few years before the war ended. She suggests we begin our search there."

"I'll have the pilot update the flight plan," Sam said. When he returned from the cockpit a few minutes later, he took a seat across from Remi at the table, watching as she spread several documents in front of her. "What's all this?" he asked.

"Speculation on what might be in the Romanov Ransom. Selma did a little research for me."

"Counting the chicks before they hatch?"

Remi's brows arched. "Knowing what it consisted of could tell us the size, which could help us figure out where it's hidden."

"You're not still holding out hope it's the Amber Room, are you?"

"The possibility always exists. But, no," she said, giving a sigh of disappointment. "I think that if the treasure made its way from Europe to South America in the possession of Nazi war criminals, it would have to be small enough to be smuggled in luggage. Something like this," she said, sliding one of the papers toward him.

He picked it up, looking at the list. "Missing Fabergé eggs . . . ? That *would* be a find. Aren't some of these in private collections?"

"Most, yes. But according to Selma's research, out of all the eggs owned by the various Romanovs, there are only four that haven't surfaced, at one time or another, between the Bolshevik Revolution and World War Two. Not surprisingly, all four belonged to Maria Feodorovna." She nodded toward the paper.

He scanned the names of the eggs. Hen with Sapphire Pendant Egg, the Royal Danish Egg, the Empire Nephrite Egg, and the Alexander III Commemorative Egg.

"And what else have you determined?"

"That if it really *is* treasure that the Dowager Empress Maria Feodorovna turned over to the Bolsheviks, the possibilities of what else might be included are . . . big. The missing Romanov fortune in totality is worth billions." She slid over several more pages, showing paintings and photographs of the empress wearing bejeweled tiaras and necklaces. "It's possible that when she fled the Bolsheviks, she managed to take everything with her, including the four eggs."

"How is it that history paints her as having died a relatively poor woman?"

"Even more reason to believe that everything she owned was paid in a ransom, don't you think? When her son and the royal family were executed, the Romanov women had a fortune of jewels sewn into their clothing. And this was while they were being held prisoner. Unlike her son and his family, Maria was living in the Crimea, far from the revolution. The royals tended to keep their prized possessions close by whenever they traveled. Certainly if they feared they might be in danger. My feeling? If this ransom truly exists, it contains her personal wealth."

"That's a pretty big assumption."

"Not really. I may not have children of my own, but if I did, there's no price I wouldn't pay for their freedom. I'd do the same if it were you."

"Good to know," Sam said, when his phone suddenly rang. He looked at the screen. "Tatiana." He put the call on speaker. "Everything okay?"

"With us, yes," Tatiana said. "But there've been a couple of developments since our . . . incident with Nika."

"Speaking of," Sam said, "what's going on with her?"

"She's in protective custody while the investigation is being conducted. The bigger question is, will she serve time?"

"Custody?" Remi asked. "So she's been arrested? But her family was being threatened."

"Which they'll take into consideration, Mrs. Fargo," Tatiana replied. "Her actions have endangered everyone in this investigation, including you. Which is why I'm calling. Hold on one second . . ." There was a muffled noise in the background, and then she returned. "Sorry. Felix just walked in. He just found out that Viktor is going to be discharged from the hospital this afternoon."

"Glad to hear it," Sam replied. "You were saying something about 'developments'?"

"Yes. Our sources have informed us that Rolfe and Leopold are—or will soon be—on their way to South America. Argentina to be exact."

Definitely not good news, Sam thought. "No chance of taking them into custody?"

"If they were flying out of any of the major airports, I wouldn't be calling. But they're probably traveling in a private jet. Under assumed names, probably. Worse, and the main reason for my call, is that our sources are telling us that the Guard is active in South America. No doubt Rolfe and Leopold will be receiving help from them."

"Thanks for the information."

"Have you considered not going?"

Sam glanced up in time to see Remi's knowing smile. "Never entered our minds," he replied.

An audible sigh sounded from Tatiana's end of the phone. "I wish you luck, then. We'll be headed that way at some point but probably not in time to be of much help with your search. Our goal is to shadow Leopold and Rolfe and meet up with our contacts in that part of the world. We'll be in touch with any information."

"Thank you," Sam said. "We appreciate it." No sooner had he disconnected than the pilot announced they were cleared for takeoff.

"Buenos Aires, here we come . . ."

67

BUENOS AIRES

An afternoon of research led Sam and Remi to discover that Ludwig Strassmair's great-grandnephew Dietrich was listed as the owner of a home about an hour's drive from the city center. They pulled up in front of the bungalow that evening and found several boys playing soccer in the street out front.

As Sam and Remi walked toward the neat yellow and white house, a Spanish television announcer's voice drifted from the open window. Sam knocked at the door, which was opened by a dark-haired woman in her late twenties. "We're looking for Dietrich Fischer," he said, then repeated the question in Spanish.

"Who are you?" she asked in thickly accented English.

"Sam and Remi Fargo. We're . . . researching old World War Two history, and his name came up as being a relative of . . ." He looked at Remi.

"Ludwig Strassmair," she said. "We think Dietrich might be able to answer questions about his relatives for a documentary."

The woman said nothing for a moment, her gaze moving to Remi, then back to Sam, as though weighing whether or not she could believe either of them. "He left about two years ago," she finally said. "We rent the house from him."

"Any idea how to get in touch?" Sam asked.

"The only address I have is a post office box, where we mail the rent check."

"A phone number?" Remi said. "Something in case of emergencies?"

"No. I have an email address for him, but the last email I sent over a month ago has yet to be answered. I'm not sure there is internet where he is."

"Which would be . . . ?" Sam asked.

"Somewhere in the middle of the jungle."

"Any idea where? Or what he does there?"

"Maybe someone at the property manager's office might know. I'll get you their card."

THE PROPERTY MANAGER, a man in his forties, gave the same information as the woman. Just as Sam wondered if they'd hit a complete dead end, the man said, "If it's really important, the fastest way to get in touch with him is by messenger. No internet, and cell phone signals are sketchy, but if you're willing to pay, it's possible to get a message out to him."

"We're willing to pay," Sam said. "Let us know what we need to do."

"Not what you need to do. Where you need to go."

"And that would be . . . ?"

"Better to show you." He brought up a map of Argentina on his computer screen and pointed to a location near the north. "The village borders the river on the outskirts of the jungle. The water is how most people get to the village. It caters to guided river travelers. But it's also a longer route."

Sam eyed the winding river on the map. "There's a shorter route?"

"Two days shorter. Through the jungle, unfortunately."

"What exactly does Dietrich do?" Remi asked.

"I've heard he's a pilot. Boats, we assume."

At least they had a starting point, Sam thought. "Any chance you can print this out for us?"

"Not a problem." He hit the button, and his printer whirred to life, dropping a sheet of paper into the tray. "If you don't mind my saying so, I'd highly suggest hiring a guide. The jungle isn't without its hazards. That area is rife with drug runners."

68

The guide recommended to Sam and Remi by the property manager was a young man named Nando Sandoval. After hiring him, and acquiring supplies, they drove out the next morning to his address outside of town. The pavement stopped after a few miles, dust kicking up behind their four-wheel drive as they drove slowly down the dirt road, trying to read the addresses on the brightly colored, flat-roofed houses. As they neared, Nando, a wiry man in his early twenties, waved at them.

Sam pulled up in front of the house, rolling down the window. "Ready?"

He nodded. "Let me get my gear. I'll be just a minute."

Sam parked, got out, and opened the tailgate. Nando returned shortly with his gear. As Sam loaded it into the back, Nando waved to a woman on the porch. "My wife," he said. "She has fresh coffee, if you'd like."

"We're good," Sam said. "Had ours before we left."

"One moment, then." Nando returned to the porch, kissed his wife, took the stainless steel, insulated coffee cup she held, then walked back to the car, waving at her as they took off.

"Nando," Sam said as he made a U-turn, heading back down the road. "I've heard that name before."

"Nando Roberto Sandoval is my full name," he said, his face lighting up with pride. "After the two rugby players whose plane went down in the Andes Mountains in the nineteen seventies."

Sam recalled reading about the event. Two months after the crash, two of the rugby players made the many days' trek through the snowy mountains to Chile, bringing back help for the remaining fourteen survivors. "Amazing story," he said.

"My father thought so," Nando replied. "I think I've always loved the outdoors because of it. The beauty and danger. It's why I became a guide. Well, when I'm not working at my family's tire shop."

"We're glad to have your help," Remi said.

THE DRIVE TO the location where Nando had made arrangements for them to leave their car took several hours. According to Nando, they had at least a three-day walk through the jungle to the remote village where Dietrich was supposed to be living. When they had their gear, the three set off on foot, following a trail into the jungle, an ever-changing world of color amidst an orchestration of birdsongs and the percussion of buzzing, clicking, biting insects. They made considerable progress on the first day through the stifling humidity and heat.

Progress slowed halfway through the second day when the trail narrowed. But then it suddenly widened into a well-marked path.

Nando seemed surprised. "This is new."

Sam didn't like the looks of it. "You two wait here," he said. "I want to check this out before we go farther. Something doesn't feel right."

"No argument from me," Remi said. "I can use a rest."

Nando slid his pack from his shoulders. "I've heard about drug runners in the area, but they've usually been farther south."

Sam unsnapped his sidearm. "Just in case, stay off the trail until I get back."

After he left, Remi looked around for a dry place to set down her pack and rest where she and Nando wouldn't be seen from the trail and where they wouldn't be eaten by ants. "Maybe farther in," she suggested to Nando.

"I'll check this side, you check that side."

Remi pushed through a wall of vines, stepping off the trail, seeing something that looked promising just a few feet in. The thick, raised roots of a tree would keep them off the rain-slicked ground, and there were no ants anywhere near it. About to call out to Nando that she'd found a decent spot, she stopped when she heard voices coming from the trail in the direction they'd just traveled.

She stilled, wondering for a moment if it was Sam. No. He'd gone off the opposite way. Setting her pack on the roots, she retraced her steps to the wall of vines, peering through just as three men, automatic rifles slung across their backs, walked up the trail.

Nando appeared on the other side, looking out at her. She held up her hand, warning him to stop, go back. He didn't move, his expression telling her that he was confused about what she was trying to tell him.

Realizing he couldn't see the men from where he stood, she pointed in their direction.

He nodded just as a monkey screamed above him. The men stopped, looking in that direction. The moment they saw Nando, all three pulled their guns.

"Who are you?" one asked in Spanish.

Nando froze, then slowly raised his hands, telling them his name.

"Who else is with you?" one of the men demanded as the other two turned their weapons to cover both directions of the trail.

Remi stepped back into the shadows, ducking down, fully expecting Nando to look toward her. But he shook his head, saying, "No one. I'm a student at the university. I'm hiking alone."

They didn't believe him. One reached out, grabbed him by his collar, while another shoved the barrel of his rifle against Nando's chest. The third turned about, searching for signs of anyone else in the area.

Apparently satisfied that Nando was truly alone, one said, "Search him."

They did, taking his machete.

"Bring him along."

The first man shoved Nando forward, forcing him down the trail.

And just as Remi drew her gun, figuring she could take them out as they headed down the trail, two more men arrived, and, from the sound of it, there was at least one or more farther down the trail.

And all of them were headed in Sam's direction.

69

Sam didn't like the look of the trail, even more so now that he'd had a better view of it. When he saw the trip wire up ahead, his suspicions were confirmed. Drug runner trail, if ever he saw one.

So much for this path, he thought, turning back. He hadn't gone more than a few feet when he heard voices coming toward him. Men talking loud enough to be heard over the cacophony of insects and birds.

He drew his gun and stepped off the trail, ducking behind a broad-fronded fern. Finger on the trigger, he tried to hear what they were saying, their heavily accented English making it difficult to understand—until one voice stood out. And this one he recognized—Nando, their guide.

The first two men walked into view, followed by Nando, and then a third man, who seemed to relish shoving his gun into the guide's back.

Sam listened, trying to find out what happened, and where Remi was.

His patience paid off when he heard Nando saying, "Where are you taking me?"

"Shut up," the man at his back said.

"Just leave me here. I'm alone. One man against six. How can I possibly harm you?"

"By sending someone after us." He shoved Nando, causing him to stumble forward. "Now, shut up before I change my mind and kill you where you stand."

"Hold up," the lead man said. "Wait for the others."

A minute later, three more men came up from behind, each carrying a fully automatic rifle. Sam knew the moment he saw them, saw the way they covered the trail on either side as well as front and back, that they were highly trained. Had it not been for Nando's warning—and Sam was sure he'd worked their number into the conversation as a warning—Sam might have tried to take out the first three before he realized there were more men. He might get off two decent shots, but they'd have little difficulty taking him out before he got off a third.

He'd be dead.

Parting the fronds slightly, he watched as they walked past. When they stopped to step over the trip wire, Sam caught sight of a tattoo on the forearm of the man bringing up the rear.

A wolf's head.

What were the chances?

He waited for them to pass, listening until their footsteps and voices faded in the distance. Confident that no one else was on the trail, he stepped out, then made his way back to where he'd left Remi, grateful that there was no sign of any struggle or that she'd been harmed.

"Remi?" he whispered.

Nothing but the sound of the birds and insects filling the air around him.

"Remi?" he said a little louder.

A rustle to his right. And then the welcome sight of his auburn-haired wife as she emerged through a curtain of vines. "They have Nando," she said, stepping into his arms.

"I saw."

"I was right here, across from him, and he told them he was alone. We have to go after him."

"We will," he said. "Where's your pack?"

"Over here," she said, pushing back through the vines.

He followed her to the banyan tree where she'd left her gear.

"Drug runners?" she asked.

"Maybe. I saw a wolf's head tattoo on the arm of one of the gunmen."

"You're kidding . . ." She looked over at him. "They can't possibly be related to the group in Europe? I know Tatiana warned us, but—"

"Why not? Argentina's known for being a safe haven for Nazis after the war. Why wouldn't they have a branch of the Wolf Guard here, too?"

"You're right," she said, picking up her pack. "But first things first."

"Get Nando out of there."

Remi smiled, leaned over, and kissed him. "And that's why I love you, Sam Fargo."

THE TRIP WIRES made Sam and Remi's progress slower than Sam had anticipated, but he soon realized that they were marked with stones off to one side of the trail, allowing them to pick up speed. After a couple of hours, they heard raindrops hitting the treetops above them. "A good time for a break," he said, pulling off his hat, wiping the sweat from his brow. "Let's see if we can't find somewhere to rest."

They found a place far enough off the trail to avoid being seen and, they hoped, to stay dry. The rain added to the already thick humidity, and, within a few minutes, rivulets of water started running down the branches.

Remi, watching a tree frog make its way up a nearby tree trunk, wiped her sweat-soaked forehead with the scarf she'd tied in her hair. "What do you think they'll do to him?"

Trying to stay positive, he didn't tell her his worst fears. That he'd be tortured to find out what he was doing in an area he shouldn't have been. "It's a good sign they didn't kill him right off."

"You think they'll hold him for ransom?"

"Hard to say." The rain finally stopped. Sam held out his hand to her, pulling her to her feet. "Let's get moving."

Unfortunately, the edge of the trail wasn't clear-cut and finding anything that resembled a footprint after the rain wasn't going to be easy. The moist forest floor was layered with fallen leaves, creating a spongy surface that seemed to bounce back after each step. If the men veered from the path, he and Remi might miss it if they weren't careful.

After another hour of walking, the trail ended at a clearing. There was a momentary silence in the jungle as they stepped into it. A monkey screamed at them from a nearby tree and scampered off, and suddenly it was back to normal, the constant chirping, clicking, ticking, and buzzing surrounding them like a white noise machine.

Sam slapped at a mosquito on his neck as he took a look around. "I don't know about you, but dinner and a glass of wine right now would be nice."

"How does hot water sound?" Remi asked, opening her canteen and taking a sip, before handing it to him.

"Not something I want to hear unless it's followed up with the words *long shower*."

"Sorry, Fargo. The closest we're going to get is the tropical kind."

"Let's hope it's done for the day." He took a drink, eyeing the area around the clearing before returning the canteen. They walked a few feet farther, about to turn around, when he noticed where some animal had dug a shallow hole in the ground, the center still filled with water from that afternoon's rain. There, in the mud at the very edge, was a partial footprint. He walked over, crouched down, taking a closer look.

"What is it?" Remi asked, coming up behind him.

"Someone's been here since the rain." He pointed at the print, before glancing in the direction of travel. "That way," he said, nodding to their right. This trail was more obscured. Sam led, parting the thick leaves of a canna, holding them until Remi stepped through, blocking them with her arms. The late afternoon sun angled in through the canopy above, turning the steam rising up from the ground into a silver mist. The thick humidity trapped the cloying smell of decay as they trekked along, sweat dripping down their necks and sapping their strength. It was slow going, trying to follow the trail of broken leaves and vines. By the time the sun neared the horizon, plunging the jungle into a mass of noise-filled shadows, they had a hard time seeing any evidence that they were on the right path.

Just as Sam was about to suggest that they'd have to stop for the night, they pushed through the thick foliage, coming across a crumbling, vine-covered wall. Just visible, dead center on the bricks, the paint faded and peeling, a swastika—and above it, the skull and crossbones of the Wolf Guard.

70

Sam and Remi peered through a tree fern at the faded swastika painted on the ruins. "Any chance," Remi said quietly, "that we're looking at graffiti instead of some Nazi hideaway?"

"Anything's possible," he said. "But the stonework looks more European than South American." At least what was left of it, he thought, eyeing the heavy philodendron vines creeping over the crumbling stones of the remaining roofline. Had it not been for the thickness of the walls, no less than three feet, the jungle would have destroyed the structure long ago. "Whatever this place was, it was built for defense."

"Like a bunker?"

"One way to find out."

Unable to see into the ruins, he drew his gun and motioned for Remi to stay where she was. He took a closer look, watching for any booby traps or trip wires. As far as he could tell, the drug runner's trail veered around the ruins. All that was left of the stairs leading up to the doorway were loose stones, roots, and fist-sized vines.

After a quick check of the inside, the remnants of three partial walls, he waved to Remi and she joined him, picking her way up the root-bound stairs. She stood there for several moments, looking around at the lush, green vines that had grown up along the inside of the walls, spilling over the top to the outside. Off to the right, the late-afternoon sun filtered through the lace-like hollowed trunk of a strangler fig, the host tree it had killed having rotted out long ago. "It's really quite beautiful," she said.

"Especially now that it's empty of any Nazis." Staying close to the wall, Sam moved to the edge, looking in the direction of the trail. Satisfied that they wouldn't be seen, he returned to Remi's side. "As good a place as any to spend the night."

"You think this really was a World War Two Wolf Guard holdout?"

"Or a hideout for Nazi officers being hunted," he said, removing his pack and leaning it against the stone wall.

Remi did the same. "I suppose a fire is out of the question?"

"So is chilled pinot grigio and fresh fish for dinner," he said, taking off his hat and setting it on his pack.

After protein bars, they sat side by side against their respective packs. Remi leaned her head back, looking up. "The stars are out," she said. "Too bad the moon is full or we'd have a better view."

Sam followed her gaze, seeing only a couple of stars through the canopy of leaves. "I'll take the first watch," he told her, getting up, moving out to the edge of the wall again. He looked out into the jungle, listening. The constant sound of birds and insects, prevalent during the day, had been replaced with a different chorus of insects and night creatures moving around. From the northeast, another sound—faint singing. He was almost able to make out the words being sung . . .

If he could hear their music, they were much closer than he'd thought.

He backed toward the ruins, returning to Remi's side, gently shaking her shoulder. "Remi . . ."

She opened her eyes. "It can't be my turn already."

"I hear music."

"Music?"

"Let's go have a look."

"What about trip wires?"

"We'll carefully have a look."

THE GOOD NEWS was, the trail was wider, and the full moon shining down made it easy to navigate. The bad news was, the trail was wider, and the full moon lit up everything in its path. That meant they had to move low and slow, with the hope that no one was standing guard.

The singing Sam heard grew louder, covering any noise they were making as they neared even if someone could hear them over the constant buzz of insects and crickets. Soon, they heard talking and laughing, noise loud enough to give the impression that this group wasn't worried about anyone stumbling on their location.

Probably because they were the type to shoot first, ask questions later.

"Over here," Sam said, crouching behind the long, sword-shaped leaves of a bromeliad. When Remi joined him, he pointed toward the clearing. "Look due east. See it?"

"I see a lot of trees."

"Just beyond that. You can see the glow of a fire. Let's try to get closer."

They hadn't gone more than a few feet when Sam saw the signature pattern of rocks hidden beneath a large fern. He pointed, Remi nodded, and the two stepped over the wire, working their way farther east. They found a patch of bromeliads—pineapples, by the looks of the softball- and larger-sized crowns growing from the plants. Hoping the fruit would help camouflage their heads, he and Remi crouched down, looking through the bromeliads' leaves. The six men who'd kidnapped Nando sat in a clearing around a fire, while Nando, feet tied, hands bound behind him, sat against the trunk of a tree.

"One thing in our favor," Sam said quietly. "Their compound has to be at least a day's walk from here or they wouldn't be camping for the night. Assuming that's where they're headed."

He scanned the area, his gaze returning to the gunmen, who sat in a circle around the fire. As highly trained as they seemed on the trail, he was surprised by their relaxed attitude, not only in leaving their hostage positioned behind them but in not posting a guard to watch the perimeter. Of course, any area frequented by drug runners armed with fully automatic weapons tended to be a good deterrent to intruders. And they were relying on the trip wires to serve as warning.

Two of the men started singing again while another passed around a bottle. Sam looked at Nando, eyeing the tree he was seated against, the thick jungle behind him, and then the unripe pineapples growing everywhere. "I have an idea . . ."

71

Remi listened while Sam outlined the plan, then detailed exactly what they'd need to do in order to pull it off.

"You're in?" he said.

"You have to ask?" If there was one thing she knew, it was that her husband weighed everything, including the risks. "When do you want to start?"

"The first part we can do now. The rest let's wait until at least a few of them have dozed off. I like the odds better that way."

They worked their way back down the trail, passing the first trip wire, then stopping at the second. Remi kept watch in the direction of the camp while Sam picked up the stones marking the location of the wire, moving them beneath another fern about twelve inches closer to the clearing. "Let's hope it trips them up," he said, examining his work.

"Pun intended?"

He gave a quick grin. "As long as *we* don't forget where it is."

"Good point." Something rustled in the leaves behind them and they both pivoted, aiming their guns at a five-foot boa constrictor gliding out onto the trail. The moonlight glistened off its smooth scales as it slithered past, disappearing from view into the plants on the other side. Remi lowered her gun, eyeing the pile of stones. "Let's hope this works."

"Have my plans ever failed?"

"There was that time in—"

"Never mind. Let's go see what our friends are doing."

They returned to their hiding place behind the thicket of pineapples. The men were passing around a bottle of amber liquid, their talk growing louder the more they drank. One glanced back at Nando, the man's comment causing the others to look back at him, then laugh. After nearly an hour and another bottle, they seemed to do less talking and more staring at the fire. Eventually, five of the men leaned back against their packs to sleep while the lone guard—his back to Sam and Remi—lit a cigarette, the smoke drifting up to join that of the dying campfire.

"Now?" Remi whispered.

"Now."

Remi, close enough to smell the faint, acrid scent of the guard's cigarette, made her way around the edge of the clearing toward Nando's tree. When she felt enough time had passed for Sam to be in position, she crept out to where Nando was tied, crouching down behind him. It wasn't until that moment that she realized he was actually awake and trying to loosen his ties.

"Nando," she whispered. "We're here."

His hands stilled.

She pulled the knife from her belt and cut his ties. When he started to rise, she grasped his hand, holding him back. "Not yet," she said, leaning out just far enough to see around his shoulder. The guard hadn't moved. Her glance shifted to the right, where she knew Sam was waiting. A moment later, Sam threw a baseball-sized pineapple down the trail. The thump, as it hit the ground, and the rustle of leaves, as it rolled, drew the guard's attention.

The man stood and ventured toward the sounds, stopping at the edge of the clearing. Remi gripped Nando's hand even harder. "Keep still," she whispered.

The guard gave one last look into the jungle before returning to his spot by the fire.

Sam threw a second, larger pineapple at one of the trip wires. An explosion ripped through the air, debris flying up. The guard jumped to his feet, slinging his rifle from his shoulder, aiming toward the trail. The other men scrambled for their weapons. One started toward Nando.

"Leave him!" the guard said. "He's not going anywhere. Follow me."

They ran toward the trail in the direction of the explosion, each man jumping over the first trip wire. The moment the last one disappeared from view, Remi let go of Nando's hand. "This way."

Nando followed her into the thick foliage. "Where are we going?"

"To find Sam."

She pointed toward the trail that led toward the ruins, keeping low. Nando followed behind her. When they reached the path, Remi stopped at the sound of rustling leaves up ahead. She aimed her gun. Relief flooded through her as Sam emerged on the other side. He held up his hand, motioning for them to stay where they were. He looked across the clearing, then waved at them. "Go!"

Remi took Nando's hand, leading him down the moonlit path, watching for the pile of stones that indicated another trip wire. She stopped, pointed, then carefully stepped over it. Nando followed suit while Sam brought up the rear.

"The prisoner!" someone shouted. "Gone!"

"Maybe he set off the explosion?" another asked.

"Impossible. He was tied. You three, head south. You two, with me toward the ruins."

Remi looked back at Sam.

"Keep low," he said quietly. "Nando, let Remi go first. We moved some of the trip wire markers."

He nodded, stepping behind Remi, matching his pace to hers, stopping when she did at the next wire. They stepped over it, Sam following. When they reached the ruins, Sam took a quick look around. "Inside. If we're lucky, they'll pass us by."

Another explosion rocked the air. The ringing in their ears dulled the sound of someone screaming in agony. A gunshot cracked, and the screaming stopped. "Keep going!" the first guard shouted.

The moment they entered the ruins, Sam went for his pack, digging out the extra ammo and the speed loaders for his gun and the box of rounds for Remi's.

"They're coming," Nando said to Sam. "Shouldn't we try to outrun them?"

"Three-foot stone walls," Sam said. "It's the closest thing we have to a bunker." He handed the box of ammo to Remi. "What do you say we go for that nice chilled champagne when we're done?"

"Perfect plan."

"See you at the bar, then."

Nando, who was leaning against the wall, shook his head. "How is it you two can joke at a time like this?"

"Passes the time," Sam said, giving the place one last look. His gaze caught on the top of the ruins and the thick vines that grew up the side, providing plenty of cover at the one window that looked out in the direction of the trail. "You're the sharpshooter in the family," he told Remi. "What do you think?"

She followed his gaze, then tugged on the vines. "Looks doable. Where are you going?"

"The window. They'll be looking for us on the ground before anywhere else," he told her. "Don't give your position away unless it's absolutely necessary."

"Got it."

She holstered her gun, slipped the box of ammo into her pocket, and he gave her a boost up.

Nando watched as she climbed to the top. "What about me?"

Sam took up a position near the window on the right side, where the leafy vines created decent cover. "Keep your head down. If we're lucky, this'll be over soon."

Remi stretched out along the top of the wall, the sharper stones digging into her as she drew her gun, aiming toward the trail. "And if we're not?" she asked, glancing down at Sam.

"The champagne will have to wait."

72

The reflection of the moonlight cast a blue glow on the thick vegetation—a cruel illusion of coolness in a jungle that refused to let go of the day's heat. Sam wiped the sweat from his brow before it dripped into his eyes, then leaned into the wall, listening. The air vibrated with the sound of a million insects. Beyond that, nothing. Using the barrel of his gun, he nudged the leaves aside until he had a view of the trail. Nothing moved. He heard Remi shifting on the wall above. "Anything?" he whispered.

"No—wait. Movement. Two o'clock."

Sam shifted his gaze to the right, searching until he saw the leaves move just off the trail. He tracked it with his sights, finger pressing on the trigger, waiting . . . waiting . . . A head popped up. He fired. The man fell back. Suddenly, someone jumped out on the opposite side, muzzle blast lighting up as he sprayed the walls with gunfire. Bits of rock flew up, hitting Sam in the face as he pressed back.

Crack! Crack!

Those shots came from above. "Time to move, Remi."

Remi slid to the edge, swinging her legs down. Nando got up, catching her by her waist as she dropped to the ground.

Sam turned his attention back toward the trail. "Get him?"

"*Them.*"

"That's my girl." Nothing moved out there. "Don't suppose you saw the other two?"

"No."

"We need to flush them out."

"I have an idea . . ."

He glanced over at Remi and saw her looking at his pack, trying to figure out what she was thinking—until he realized what she was focusing on. "Anything but that."

"It worked in Madagascar." Remi picked up his panama hat, twirling it on her finger, a slightly devilish look in her eye as she looked at him.

"That's my favorite hat."

Her brow furrowed in mock sympathy. "We'll be *very* careful."

"Not careful enough," he said, hoping he could find the other two gunmen first. Unfortunately, nothing moved out there. He waited a few more seconds, just in case. "Fine. Just. Be. Careful."

Remi looked around for a suitable stick.

Nando watched with interest. "What are you planning on doing with that?"

"Not us. You," she told him, placing the hat on top of the fork-like end, balancing it.

"Me?"

"You're going to hold it in the window just high enough." She moved the stick in an up and down motion. "If we're lucky, they'll shoot at it." She glanced over at Sam, then quickly back to Nando. "Or, rather, the hat."

"How will that help?" Nando asked.

"Muzzle blast," Sam said, hoping one of the men would make a move before they had to resort to sacrificing his hat. "The reason why Remi had to move from her sniper position. Like a beacon in the night." He and Remi were going to have to move outside the ruins if they had any hope of taking out the last two kidnappers. The steps leading up to the doorway were high enough to hide behind. He looked to the right, where the buttressed roots of a tree snaked out toward the crumbling wall, providing decent cover. "Remi, take the stairs. I'll take the right side."

Remi dashed out the doorway. Nando held the stick and hat, his expression one of uncertainty.

"You'll be okay," Sam said.

"How will I know when to show the hat?"

"After I fire a few rounds from the window. When I'm ready, I'll let you know. Just raise it high enough in the opening so that the moonlight hits it. Make it look like someone's underneath. Got it?"

Nando nodded. "Got it."

"Good." Taking one last look through the vines, he noticed a fruit bat swoop down from beneath the broad leaves of a tree not too far from where Remi had taken out one of the men. "Get ready."

He fired twice in that direction, then quickly moved back, out of sight, making his way to the right side of the wall. Nando crouched beneath the window, hat low. Sam peered through an opening in the wall, finger on the trigger. "Now!"

Nando bobbed the hat up and down.

Sam's gaze swept over the landscape. Nothing happened.

"Higher!"

The hat went up.

Twin muzzle blasts flashed again and again as the gunmen peppered the stone walls. Sam fired twice. One of the men cried out, his rifle flying from his hands as he fell back. Remi hit the second man, vines rustling as he fell into the branches.

"Nando, move the hat again. See if we get a response."

The hat danced in the window. When nothing happened, Sam

made his way inside the structure, climbing up the wall where Remi had been earlier, looking out over the jungle and trail.

"Sam?" Remi asked.

"Counting bodies . . . So far, three . . ."

"Don't forget the one who died on the trip wire."

"That makes four." He spotted the fifth body where he and Remi had shot the last two, near the trail. "Number six is missing," he said, spying a blood trail leading away from them.

"Do we go after him?"

"It will take him at least twenty-four hours before he can return with help. I say we put some distance between him and us. The farther away we are from here, the better."

73

Rolfe, still jet-lagged, poured the last bit of coffee from the carafe into his mug before returning his attention to the map that Leopold was looking over. They were holed up in a suite of a downtown Buenos Aires hotel, the remnants of their room service breakfast on the cart waiting to be picked up. "And why is it we think they'd be contacting this Dietrich person?"

"He's the last-known relative of Ludwig Strassmair."

"All well and good," Rolfe said, "but my understanding was that Strassmair, being a Nazi, was estranged from his sister's family. Why on earth would he have entrusted the treasure to one of them?"

"He wouldn't have. But the possibility exists that he contacted his sister's family when he arrived. They might know something about his last days in Buenos Aires."

"You're assuming they even spoke."

"Hoping. Something we won't know unless we find Dietrich."

"And what are the odds of that?" Rolfe asked, examining the area Leopold had circled. "Even with the number of Guardsmen you say are here, that's a lot of land to cover."

"Except a lot of that land is controlled by the Guard. Advantage, ours."

"Controlled, how?"

"They run arms and drugs for support. Trust me when I tell you no one is moving across that land without them knowing about it."

"You're sure?"

Leopold looked up at him. "I have no reason to question their authority and competence. Their training is my training."

"Then how is it that Dietrich managed to stay off their radar?"

"I said they controlled the land down here," he said, tapping the map. "Dietrich is reported to be living and working outside their control. At the moment, anyone looking for him will be heading through Guard territory."

"And the man they picked up last night? Have they determined whether or not he's searching for Dietrich?"

"No," Leopold said, when his cell phone lit up from an incoming call. "They were under orders to wait until we arrived at their compound. The less people who know about our true purpose here, the better."

"At last, we agree on something," Rolfe said as Leopold picked up his phone from the table.

He looked at the number, then answered. "Yes . . . ?" His pale eyes narrowed as he listened to whatever was being said. He answered in Spanish, a language Rolfe didn't understand. The man ended the call, almost slamming the phone down on the table.

"What's wrong?" Rolfe asked.

"The man they picked up escaped."

"How?"

"He had help, obviously. Five of their men are dead. The sixth barely made it out alive." Leopold drummed his fingers on the table-top, upset by the turn of events.

As well he should be, Rolfe thought. Apparently, the Guard

wasn't as infallible as they'd have everyone believe. "One man against six? What was it you were saying about anyone traveling in Guard territory?"

"He told them he was alone, a student. Clearly, they believed him or they wouldn't have let their guard down. It's possible he was exactly that."

"You're deluding yourself. Someone who happens to be studying in the very area we need to travel escapes, kills five Guardsmen? It has the Fargos written all over it."

"You may be right."

"*May* be? They've been one step ahead of us on everything. Which needs to change. I'm not paying you all this money to let them get to the treasure first."

Leopold pulled the map closer. "The survivor said the man they captured was heading north. There are villages here and here . . . That's where I'm going."

"You're going?"

Leopold folded the map, putting it into his pocket. "You're certainly welcome to come. Unless, of course, you'd rather stay here and trust that if I find Dietrich before the Fargos do, I'll pass that information to you."

"Trust?" Rolfe said. "I want to know what you plan to do about the Fargos?"

"I've already dealt with that. The entire compound is aware they may be in the area. They're starting the search for them as we speak."

"And Dietrich?"

"They'll be looking for him as well. The good news is, thanks to the Fargos and their intervention in this kidnapping, we have a promising lead on where Dietrich might be. If the Fargos make contact, the Guard will be ready. They won't last long."

"Good. When do we leave?"

"Within the hour."

74

After putting considerable distance between themselves and the ruins, Sam, Remi, and Nando set up camp. When it was Sam's turn to sleep, he leaned back against his pack, covering his eyes with his hat to eliminate the sunlight filtering through the thick canopy of leaves. The next thing he knew, something was nudging his foot. He shifted position. When it continued, he reached up, shoving his hat back, squinting at the silhouette of his wife, looking down at him.

"Rise and shine, Fargo. We have a lot of miles to cover before nightfall."

He lowered the hat again.

She kicked the bottom of his boot with a bit more force. "Up and at 'em."

"Okay, okay . . ." When he sat up and looked around, he realized they were alone. "Where's Nando?"

"Exploring."

That got him to his feet. "He shouldn't be out there alone."

"Nothing to worry about," she said, pointing. "Just on the edge of camp."

Sam looked that direction, seeing Nando just a few feet outside the clearing, bending down, picking up something from the ground, then reaching up and shaking a vine. A few minutes later, Nando returned with an armful of passion fruit. "Breakfast!"

"Perfect," Remi said.

They sat down to a meal of protein bars, passion fruit, and water. The tart, wrinkled dark purple fruit had a scent that was a cross between overripe apple and banana. A refreshing addition to what they'd been eating the past few days, Sam thought, tossing the rind out into the jungle.

He took a drink from the canteen, then turned his attention to Nando. They'd had little opportunity to talk the night before. "You okay?" he asked.

"Fine," Nando said.

"Tell Sam what you told me while he was sleeping."

"They're called the Wolf Guard. I heard them talking around the campfire last night. They're all being called in for the arrival of a captain of the Guard from Germany."

"I suppose we shouldn't be surprised," Sam said. "The tattoo I saw on the man's arm . . . As big a Nazi enclave as Argentina was after the war, it makes sense they'd have a branch of the Guard here."

Remi tightened the top on the canteen. "Must mean we're on the right track? That Ludwig Strassmair came here?"

"At the moment," Sam said, "all it means is that we've got more Nazi wolves to deal with, and Leopold is probably headed this way." He looked at his watch. It was after eight. "Let's get moving. The sooner we find Dietrich, the better."

THEY REACHED the village the following afternoon, chickens scattering as they traveled along the dirt road leading up to the first few houses. A woman sweeping the porch of a green bungalow paused to watch them.

"Might as well start here," Sam said. He smiled at the woman, then, in Spanish, asked if she knew Dietrich Fischer.

She shook her head and went back to sweeping.

The three continued up the road toward a man loading something into a donkey cart. When they reached him, he was tying a canvas over baskets piled high in the back of the cart.

Sam repeated the same question he'd asked the woman.

"Dietrich?" the man said. "No. But if anyone knows of him, it would be Avi."

"Would you know where to find him?"

"*Sí*. At *el avión*."

"The plane?" Remi said in English.

"*El Avión, la cantina*." He pointed farther down the road. "You will find a lot of the men there when they come down from the river. That is where Avi tends bar."

The cantina was about a half mile up the dirt road. There was no sign in the window, but there was a faded painting of a 1940s era propeller airplane on the front.

Sam pulled open the door, looked inside, then held it for Remi and Nando. The brown-haired, blue-eyed bartender looked up from the drink he was making, saw them, and nodded. Behind him, an old plane propeller was attached to the wall, with shelves around it holding liquor bottles. The three approached as the man squeezed a slice of lime into a drink, the citrus scent drifting toward them. Sam held a chair for Remi as he and Nando took a seat on either side of her.

Sam ordered three beers, then asked, "Any chance you know where we can find Avi?"

"And you are?"

"Sam Fargo, my wife, Remi, our friend Nando."

"He expecting you?"

"No. But we're hoping he can help us. His name came up as someone who might know someone we're looking for."

The bartender slid the drink toward the man at the end of the counter, then held a glass beneath a tap. "Something I can answer for you?"

"Maybe you can pass a message on to him? We're looking for Dietrich Fischer."

The man stopped mid-pour, his gaze widening.

"You've heard the name," Sam said. "Perhaps you know where to find him?"

"In regards to . . . ?"

"A relative of his. Ludwig Strassmair."

"I'm Dietrich. I'm just not used to anyone using my given name unless it's trouble. Definitely not in combination with my great-great-uncle's name." He finished pouring the beers, handing Sam one of the glasses. "What is it you want to know?"

75

W e heard you were a pilot," Sam said, taking the first glass and passing it to Remi.

Dietrich laughed as he filled two other glasses with beer. "A nickname from some of my regular customers. Because of the plane painted on the front and the way it looks inside," he said, nodding at the wooden ceiling fans shaped like plane propellers. "But you're not here to talk about how I decorate my bar."

"No," Sam said as he heard the door behind them open. Light spilled in across the floor as two middle-aged men wearing cowboy hats, their faces deeply tanned, walked in. They nodded at Dietrich before their gazes flicked to Sam, Remi, and Nando, dismissing them, as they moved to the far end of the counter, sitting next to the other man seated there.

"One second," Dietrich said, then pulled two beers, bringing them over to the men. He returned a moment later. "You were saying?"

"This uncle," Sam replied, "what can you tell us about him?"

"Why are you asking?"

It didn't occur to Sam until that moment how it might sound, announcing that someone's relative was not only a Nazi war criminal but also one who had hoped to resurrect the Third Reich. Trying to be diplomatic, he said, "You're aware of his history in the Nazi Party?"

"Unfortunately, yes. My grandfather made sure my mother knew, when she was old enough to understand, and she told me."

"We believe Ludwig Strassmair fled from Europe to Argentina in order to resurrect the Third Reich and bring the Nazis back to power. The plan, called Operation Werewolf, was a closely guarded secret. Still protected even to this day."

"That explains a lot."

Not the reaction Sam was expecting. Even Remi's brows went up at his response. "You know about Operation Werewolf?" she said.

He took a look around the bar, then lowered his voice. "It's why I'm here. To find my great-uncle and give him a proper burial."

"Your Uncle Strassmair?" Remi asked, surprised.

Dietrich's expression darkened a moment. "Not that uncle," he said. "My grandmother's brother. My Uncle Klaus. But maybe you need to hear the whole story. Or at least what I know of it." He glanced over at his other two customers, asking, in Spanish, if they needed anything. When they shook their heads, he directed Sam, Remi, and Nando to a table at the opposite end of the room, poured himself a beer, then took a seat with them where he could see the door and the bar.

"The short story is," he said, "my great-grandparents fled Germany during the war to protect their middle son, Klaus, after their oldest was killed fighting the Nazis in the resistance. After the war, my great-grandmother's brother, Ludwig Strassmair, showed up, offering to pay a good sum if Klaus would accompany him on a trip to Chile. The plane never made it. My grandfather believed it went down in the Andes Mountains, or it would have been found before now. It was after the plane was lost that people started making inquiries about what Ludwig Strassmair discussed with my great-grandfather. It's also how I ended up here, of all places."

"Did your grandfather know anything?" Sam asked.

"I know what he *didn't* tell them. He only allowed Klaus to go with Ludwig as a paid companion. He felt guilty for taking the money, but they desperately needed it. And, of course, after the plane was lost, he suspected there was some other reason that Ludwig was taking the trip—something he didn't know about, especially after these inquiries were made. There was no doubt in his mind that the people asking were Nazis." He leaned forward, resting his arms on the table. "This last fact I didn't find out until right before he died. Even my mother didn't know. Once I was old enough, I did some digging on my own. My search eventually brought me here."

"For what reason?"

"A number of reasons, actually. The night Klaus and Ludwig left, there was a murder at the shipping office where Ludwig worked. The newspaper reported it as a robbery, but my grandfather didn't believe it." He glanced over at the men at the bar, then back. "My grandfather said that the man deserved to die like the wolf he was. It wasn't until I started researching the Nazi war criminals and read about Operation Werewolf that I realized he wasn't speaking metaphorically. That, in turn, made me wonder about the drug runners in this area after I heard the locals referring to them as *los lobos*."

"The wolves," Sam translated. "We ran into them on the way here."

"They have a compound in the jungle about three days west of here."

Remi said, "I'd think this would be the last place you'd want to be."

"I'm just the bartender. They're so used to my presence, they tend to look right through me. It's one of the reasons why I've stayed on." He looked up at the door, then back. "I figured I might be able to turn over information about their movements to the government. My way of getting back for what happened to Klaus."

"Rather dangerous, don't you think?" Sam replied.

"Maybe so, but these men transport their drugs right past us on the river. The people in this village deserve better."

Sam agreed with him. "Did you ever find out anything else on the downed plane?"

"There seems to be conflicting evidence that some sort of cover-up took place after the plane went down."

"What sort of cover-up?"

"About who was on board. One of the reports I read said that there were only five civilian passengers and three crew, but another said six civilian passengers. Apparently, someone on the ground crew recalled seeing a man boarding when the plane was about to take off and yet there is no official record of a sixth passenger."

"Odd," Remi said. "Do you think that tied in with the murder at the shipping office?"

"Possibly," Dietrich replied. "Of course, there was also the physical evidence. A propeller." When all three of them looked at the one mounted on the wall behind the bar, he laughed. "Not that one. That was found in the jungle nearby. A much smaller plane, and much more recent. I'm talking about one found high up in the Andes near Mount Tupungato. It was from an Avro Lancastrian, the same type of plane Klaus and Ludwig were in."

Sam and Remi exchanged glances. "Pretty conclusive evidence, I'd think," Sam said.

He shrugged. "No one's ever found anything else, including me. I've led dozens of expeditions to help fund my searches. When my money runs out, I return here, tend my bar, then head back up, listening to the stories from other climbers, hoping I might hear about more debris. So far, nothing . . ."

"Any chance you can show us where it was found?"

"The actual location? Not easy to get to. The conditions are extreme, between the high altitude, glacier, and unstable weather, even if we rented a helicopter to get from the base camp to the location, we could spend days up there searching. But the cost—between the helicopter, equipment, and the time, it's expensive."

"If you're willing to lead it, we're willing to fund it."

"Beside Klaus, what exactly is so important about this plane that complete strangers are interested in it?"

"Something called the Romanov Ransom."

"Which is what?"

After Sam told him, Dietrich leaned back in his chair, whistled, and looked at the three of them. "Looks like we have some plans to make."

76

The next afternoon, Sam stood outside Dietrich's bar, talking to Selma on his satellite phone. "You've got our list?" Sam asked.

"Already sent it to your flight crew," Selma said. "They did an inventory check right before they took off from Buenos Aires. I found a store in Mendoza that has the rest of what you need."

"And the helicopter?"

"I called the company that Dietrich recommended and spoke to the pilot this morning. He'll pick up the four of you downriver, then fly you into Mendoza from there."

"And he's agreed to be on standby?"

"Since he's based out of Mendoza, he said it wouldn't be an issue. The only thing that might come up is that his wife's expecting in the next few weeks. He'll make arrangements with his brother to take over should she go into labor early."

"Check that off the list. What else?"

"I heard from Rube," Selma said. "Tatiana and Viktor have followed Leopold and Rolfe to Buenos Aires. They were seen at the property manager's office. Leopold knows that you're looking for Dietrich. He's on your trail."

"Not surprising. When we rescued Nando, one of the drug runners got away. Good news travels fast."

"I'll give Rube your location. Good luck, Mr. Fargo."

Sam disconnected, then returned inside the bar, joining Remi and Nando at a table. "Everything's set," he told Remi.

"And Nando?" she asked, looking up from the map she'd been studying. "How's he getting home?"

"We can arrange for a car service once we get to Mendoza."

"Actually," Nando said, "I was hoping I could go up with you. I want to help."

"If you had more climbing experience, I'd agree. It's dangerous."

"And so are the men coming after you. I'm strong. I've always dreamed of going up to the mountains where my namesake saved so many. Maybe I'll be good luck?"

Remi gave a supportive smile. "Hard to argue with that."

Sam's instinct was to tell him no. And yet, the fact Nando had saved Remi in the jungle by refusing to tell the kidnappers that she was in the vicinity was enough to convince Sam that he had the fortitude to persevere even in the face of danger. "Dietrich? You're familiar with the area. Exactly how difficult are we talking?"

The bartender eyed Nando. "He seems fit. Considering that we're bypassing the worst of it on a helicopter, an extra body at base camp will be welcome. It should be safe enough there."

"And," Remi said, "he cooks. So it's agreed? I'll call Selma and make sure she adds Nando's list to what we'll need in Mendoza."

"Why do I get the feeling she already has it?" Sam asked.

Remi gave a not-so-innocent smile. "I have no idea what you're talking about."

AT SAM'S INSISTENCE, Dietrich left a false travel plan with one of his employees who'd be running the bar in his absence—in case anyone came around, asking. Three days later, they set up base camp at the foot of the glacier in the Andes Mountains. That evening, Sam and Remi stole a moment alone from Nando and Dietrich, who were sitting at a table, playing cards, in the largest tent, which would serve as their headquarters and dining area. This time of year, the area below Tupungato was a colorful and bustling tent city, with dozens upon dozens of men and women prepared to make the trek up into the Andes. In the short time they'd been there, Sam had heard several languages. Spanish, German, French, and Italian.

"Quite the tourist attraction," he said, nodding toward the twinkling lights of the tent city.

Sam put his arm around his wife as they looked up toward the summit. The half-moon cast a pale blue glow across the snow-covered valley below, the steep peaks silhouetted above them, as the stars glittered against an ink black sky. "If the plane continued on the direct route from Buenos Aires to Santiago . . ." He pointed up and to their left.

Remi looked that direction. "That's a lot of ground to cover."

"You have anything better to do?"

"Turns out, I'm free for the next few days," she said as Nando and Dietrich joined them.

"You're going up tomorrow?" Nando asked.

"Not too far," Sam said. "Take it slow, get acclimated."

"It's not like the jungle," Dietrich said. "A lot less oxygen up here."

Nando laughed. "And a lot more snow."

THE NEXT MORNING, Sam, Remi, and Dietrich set out, arriving several hours later at the area where Dietrich thought the propeller had been found. "Granted, I wasn't here when they made the discovery, but I returned here with the man who was. This was the location he pointed out to me."

Sam looked around the valley, seeing nothing but the spires at the foot of the melting glacier. Unless the plane had completely disintegrated on impact—which was highly possible—there didn't appear to be anywhere a fuselage could be hiding, even one partially intact. "What direction do you think the plane was traveling?"

"Over there," Dietrich said, pointing to their right. "I figured if it came from that direction, it might have clipped a propeller on that ridge, knocking it off. But there's nothing. I can't tell you how many times I've been through this area, even with a metal detector."

Sam took out his binoculars for a better view, looking at the high ridge Dietrich had pointed out. The sun glared against the snow, and it took a moment for his eyes to adjust. Dietrich was right. The plane could have clipped the propeller there. He scanned the valley again, a different idea forming. "What if it didn't come from that direction?"

"Then where?" Dietrich asked.

"Up there." He pointed straight ahead to the summit. "What if the plane clipped the propeller on the summit as it was flying over it? As many years ago as it went down, that propeller would have moved with the glacier."

"Where's the rest of the plane, then?" Remi asked, the icy wind blowing against the fur trimming the hood of her red parka. "Even if the plane was in pieces, you'd think the debris would have traveled together."

"You're assuming it crashed on this side of the summit."

Dietrich and Remi both looked at him in surprise, before Remi said, "But the propeller was found way down here. That's a long way from the summit."

"Gravity," Sam said. "Think about it. Clipped at the top, propeller bounces down the summit on this side as the plane continues on its crash course on the other side. That propeller had a lot of years to make it down here. Every time the ice melted, in fact."

"Good theory, Sam," Remi said.

"Only if it turns out to be true."

"It won't," Dietrich said. "I've been up there. I've looked. There's nothing on the other side."

"If we're lucky, you've missed something."

The next day, they climbed to the top of the glacial ridge, and Sam realized not only that Dietrich was right but Sam's theory was highly flawed. For one, they were staring at sheer cliffs, which held very little snow, and definitely no place that could hide an entire airplane. Two, the plane would have to have been on an upward trajectory to make it over the cliffs of the next ridge, which was higher than the one they were currently standing on.

"Next hypothesis," Remi said.

Sam stared for several seconds longer, then turned back, looking down along the glacier, trying to picture how that propeller could have landed on it. His gaze swung to the high cliffs on their right, and he pictured the plane flying past, clipping it instead. "Maybe we're wrong about that downward trajectory from here, where we're standing. What if it *was* up there?"

The two turned and looked as Sam pointed to the higher cliff on their right. He traced the direction in the air, and they followed along, as he said, "Starboard wing, barely clears that cliff, knocks off the propeller, which lands down here, where we're standing. Plane continues on its downward spiral . . ." He eyed the cliffs, and ridges beyond the ridge where they stood, noting a few narrow passes that a plane could have hurtled through. "And lands somewhere over there, through the pass on the left."

"You're sure about the angle?" Dietrich said. "Because using that theory, depending on exactly which angle the plane was traveling when it hit, any of those passes could be the one. That's a lot of miles to cover between here and there."

"Exactly," Sam said. "And why we have a helicopter and pilot on retainer."

77

The Fargos were looking for a pilot."

"You're sure?" Rolfe asked Leopold, who was studying the information he'd just received from a lengthy text. "What on earth are we doing out here in the middle of the jungle, then?"

"This is hardly the middle of the jungle," Leopold said without looking up.

"Close enough," Rolfe replied, eyeing the Wolf Guard compound with distaste. They were seated in a Quonset hut, camouflaged on the outside to avoid being detected from the air. They'd spent the last couple of nights here in order to interview the survivor who'd managed to escape the assault by whoever it was who rescued the tour guide. And while they were no closer to learning anything, there was no doubt in Rolfe's mind who it was. The very thought angered him, and he pulled at the collar of his shirt, sweat dripping down his neck. "Back to this pilot—how do you know that's who they were looking for?"

"Because the men I sent out to make inquiries about this so-called student they found wandering in the jungle were able to confirm he was actually a guide who was hired to take a married couple to find the man."

"So we were right."

"More important, the man they were looking for was a descendent of Ludwig Strassmair."

"Then why aren't we going after him?"

"No need. He was the owner of a bar in a village to the east of here. I've already sent someone out there."

"And how long until we hear back?"

"Anytime now."

The news struck Rolfe as highly suspicious. "How far is this village?"

"Does it matter?"

"No," he said. Because, right now, it didn't. It was more important to find the Fargos and figure out what they were up to. Later, he'd have to take into consideration exactly how much it was that Leopold was keeping from him. Clearly, more than he was letting on.

Rolfe got up, walking to the open door, wondering if it was possibly cooler outside. He watched the Argentine Guardsmen in the yard, resting beneath camouflaged netting. Turning back toward Leopold, who was now talking on his phone in Spanish, Rolfe pulled out his own phone and hit RECORD, so he could translate Leopold's side of the conversation, to make sure he wasn't being left out of the loop.

He stood there, pretending to read email, until Leopold finally ended the call. "Well?" Rolfe asked, looking up from his phone.

"We found them. Or where they went. Mendoza."

"Mendoza?"

"It's a popular destination for anyone headed toward the Andes."

"Why would they be headed from the jungle to there?"

Leopold gave him a look that bordered on incredulousness. "Naturally, they have to be looking for a plane crash site."

"You're sure?"

"Ludwig Strassmair was killed in a plane crash. They must have a lead on where it went down or they wouldn't be there."

At last, Rolfe thought. That much closer to the Romanov Ransom.

And eliminating the Fargos.

78

"Y ou'd think this high above the tree line," Remi said as the helicopter climbed in altitude, "a downed plane would be much easier to spot."

"Except for the decades of snow covering it." Sam adjusted the volume on his headset as he pointed out the starboard side of the helicopter, telling the pilot, "That looks promising."

Dietrich, sitting next to Remi in the back, glanced in that direction. "How can you even tell? From up here, it looks like endless peaks and valleys."

He was right about that. On the other side of the summit, there was nothing that stood out but snow and gray rock.

Remi leaned over for a better look. "Talk about the proverbial needle in a haystack," she said.

"Where's your faith, Remi?" Sam replied. "Assuming the plane was on a direct route from Buenos Aires to Santiago, this fits with the route."

"That doesn't make sense," she told him. "The propeller—"

"Was found on the other side behind us. And no other debris was found with it, odds are that something had to happen for the plane to lose its propeller and yet still be high enough to clear everything below us," he said as the pilot navigated the area on the other side of the summit. The barren rocks confirmed to Sam that the plane had to have been much higher or there'd be more debris on the other side, never mind a lot on this side as well.

"We've searched three of those passes," she said, sounding tired.

"And we've got three left. Hang in there. It's a good theory. Or it will be if I can figure out what the angle was." He shifted in his seat, looking back at the glacier, then the high cliff next to it. "Bring it up again," he told the pilot. "Back over the cliff."

The helicopter rose, then circled around, hovering above the cliff in front of them. Flurries of snow stuck to the glass as Sam looked out, trying to picture how an airplane could lose one of four propellers in the glacier below and not end up against the cliffs just beyond it. The only way he could see was if it skimmed the higher cliff next to the glacier, clipping the propeller, which fell to the glacier below. If so, the plane was more than likely already on a crash course. But not heading straight down . . . "It had to have cleared those distant peaks," he said. "One propeller out of four, left side of the cliff, lands on the glacier . . ."

"But which peak?" Remi asked, looking that direction.

"And which side of the plane?" Dietrich said. "That would make a difference."

"Starboard, would be my guess," Sam replied. "It all depends on the angle when it hit. A glancing blow on that cliff top might send it up again, so it could clear the peaks on the other side of the glacier field. At least that would be the most likely reason it cleared."

Remi sighed. "You're not exactly narrowing it down."

"Agreed."

Dietrich shook his head. "Even on a crash course? One direction, hitting the cliff, losing the propeller . . ."

Sam realized in that one moment what he was missing, all because the propeller was found in the glacier. They'd assumed the plane had been traveling west, the logical route. They were looking at the glacier field like it was some marked highway. "What if that plane had been flying northwest or even due north?"

"Why would it?" Dietrich asked.

"Any number of reasons. Jet stream, weather, faulty instruments."

"Okay," Remi said. "And what would that do?"

"It means if the plane was heading down in a crash course toward the northwest, it could've hit the starboard side against the cliff, knocked off the propeller, then continued down through that pass," he said, pointing to the only place low enough to allow the plane through—in the opposite direction they'd been searching.

Their pilot, Julio, looked over at Sam. "That way?"

"Yes."

FOR THE NEXT three days, with Julio piloting the helicopter, Sam, Remi, and Dietrich searched the pass for the downed plane, each evening returning without finding anything.

The next morning, they expanded their search even farther. Julio circled the helicopter around a craggy peak of barren rock and snow, when Sam saw something that caught his eye. "Make another pass again," he said. "Lower, this time."

"I'm going to need to refuel soon."

Julio was right. Too dangerous to cut it close out here, with the unstable wind patterns. "One more pass, then we go back."

Julio nodded. What looked like a shadow jutting out from between the two peaks was taking on the appearance of something a lot smoother than the snow-covered, rocky terrain.

Remi leaned over, peering out. "Sam . . ."

"Sure looks like something there."

Julio hovered over the area. "Decision time." He tapped at his gauge.

"Come in from the other side," Sam said, trying to get a better look through his binoculars. "I have a good feeling about this."

79

There was no doubt when they made the next pass.

"Look at that!" Dietrich said. He pulled out his phone and took several pictures, while Remi did the same with a camera and telephoto lens. The plane was wedged in a crevice between two peaks, the glacier holding it, having melted just enough to partially expose the nose, fuselage, and left wing. Because the shadow of the mountain helped camouflage the gray Avro Lancastrian, blending it into the rocky landscape, if they'd flown over it in any other direction, they probably would have missed seeing it altogether.

"Time to head home," Julio said.

Dietrich looked around, almost in a panic, as the helicopter started moving away. "Where are we going? We need to get down there."

"Tomorrow," Julio replied. "Unless you want to spend the next week hiking back."

Sam eyed the fuel gauge, glad to know their pilot was keeping a close watch. "Now that we know what we're dealing with, we can come back better prepared."

Julio nodded toward the mountain peak on the right of the plane as they took off. "I don't like the looks of that."

Neither did Sam. He glanced down at the plane again. Sunlight glistened on the rivulet of water running down one side of it. The warming trend that helped to expose the missing plane was a doubled-edged sword, he thought, looking back up at the mountainside. Packed with snow and with a melting glacier at the base, it was an avalanche in the making. They'd definitely want to avoid disturbing the right shoulder of the mountain. "Let's hope the weather is better. We'll have to find somewhere to land tomorrow below the plane. I think it'll be safer to climb up."

As far as Dietrich was concerned, tomorrow couldn't come fast enough.

BACK AT BASE CAMP, Sam, Remi, and Dietrich hiked from the helipad up the hill, almost half a mile through the scattered tents, until they reached their campsite. The scent of beef simmering in spices greeted them as they entered the tent. Nando, busy stirring the stew, looked up. "You're back. How was the trip?"

"We found it," Dietrich said. "We just couldn't get to it today."

"But we have pictures," Remi said, taking the memory card from the camera and transferring the photos to her laptop.

Nando gave the stew a quick stir, then walked over to see the photos. "That's amazing. No wonder no one's found it before. It looks a lot like the rock from the mountainside."

"We got lucky," Sam said, taking a seat next to Remi. "A few feet over, one way or the other, we might've missed it." He pulled out his own computer to look up the weather report. The storm coming in had been upgraded, which meant more snow and stronger winds. But the front had stalled, and it wasn't supposed to move in for a couple of days. That would leave them with more than enough time for exploring the plane.

They studied every aspect of the area, and though it was hard to tell from the images alone, there appeared to be an open spot, about a quarter mile down from the plane, where the helicopter could safely land. "Let's hope this is as level as it looks," he said.

In the morning, they hiked down to the helipad, where Julio was waiting. As usual, Sam asked after his wife.

"She's feeling—what's the word in English?—the ants."

"The *ants*?" Remi said as they lifted off.

"Yes. Not when you feel them crawling on you but you feel like them. Moving."

"*Antsy.*"

"That's it. She is very antsy. Wanting to move around."

"Not that I'm the expert," Remi said, "but I've heard that if she suddenly starts wanting to clean and rearrange everything, it's getting close."

"I'll make sure to check in on her after I get back to refuel. And have my brother be on standby to get you," he said, aiming the helicopter to the northwest as light snow flurries hit the windscreen, quickly melting. The snow stopped by the time they arrived at the crash site, though the sun was hidden behind the clouds. Thankfully, the area Sam thought might be level enough to land was nearly perfect, and, before they knew it, they were waving good-bye to Julio as he lifted off.

"I hope that baby of theirs holds out for another day," Remi said.

Sam's attention was on the snowpack, above and on the right shoulder of the pass, just over the plane. "I hope that snow holds out for another day."

80

Before Sam would let them climb up to the plane, he used his binoculars and examined the mountainside. Deciding that it looked stable, he gave the okay, and the three made the steep climb.

The snowpack beneath the belly of the plane was solid enough to make sure the craft wasn't going anywhere. Unfortunately, the ice pack was also a good two feet above the base of the door, preventing easy access.

"What about around the back?" Remi asked. "Maybe there's an opening at the tail."

Sam had already looked, from the air. "If the tail is even still there, it's buried under several feet of snow. This is our best bet."

They had to use a combination of small shovels and ice picks, but they finally had the area cleared to get to the door.

Sam and Dietrich pushed and pulled together, and the hatch opened. Remi followed them in. Snow blocked most of the light coming through the starboard windows, and she shined her flashlight around. The impact from the crash had sent everything tumbling. That the plane landed relatively intact was a miracle in itself, she thought, looking at it in awe. The entire right side of the plane where the wing had been was now a wall of ice, as was the tail.

The bodies, though . . . Hard to see them and not imagine the terror. She tried not to look too closely past the ice crystals covering each mummified corpse as she counted. Six.

"Klaus . . ." Dietrich examined each body, quickly assessing, all clearly adults, then moving on to the next. "I don't see him . . ."

"Could there have been survivors?" Remi asked. "Maybe they left the plane?"

"Anything's possible," Sam said, pulling aside one of the seats that had ripped from its bolts anchoring it to the floor in order to get to the cockpit ladder. He climbed up, disappearing from view. "But I doubt it. There're more bodies up here. Fits with the unofficial report for the number of crew and passengers, or, rather, a sixth passenger . . ." He stepped down, looking back at them, his expression solemn. "I'd say one of them up here is about the size of a twelve-year-old. I'm sorry."

Even though Dietrich had known the young boy was on the plane, he still looked stunned. "I don't understand. What's he doing in the cockpit?"

"Hard to say," Sam said. "He could have ended up there on impact, depending on where he was sitting. Maybe they let him up there to observe. Young kid, planes . . ."

"May I?" Dietrich asked, nodding at the ladder.

"Of course," Sam said, jumping down and moving aside.

Dietrich climbed up, entering the cockpit. Remi glanced at the frozen bodies strewn about the fuselage, then quickly looked away, grasping at Sam's gloved hand, taking solace as he squeezed back.

"There's a gun up here." Dietrich climbed down. "Why would there be a gun?"

"A gun?" Sam said, glancing at Remi. "Where?"

"The floor. Next to the pilot's seat."

"Let me take another look." Sam climbed into the cockpit.

Remi followed him, remaining on the ladder, watching as he searched. "It's like a perfectly preserved crime scene," she said.

"We should get pictures. It'll help determine what caused the crash."

The pilot's frozen body was crumpled against one side of the cockpit. Another man against him, the flight engineer. The gun was near their feet, wedged between the floor and the cockpit controls. A smaller body about the size of an adolescent boy was on the floor, headfirst toward the nose, and Remi was grateful she couldn't see his face—any of their faces, for that matter. "Why would there be a gun up here?" she asked.

"Could have been the pilot's," Sam said. "Possibly fell out on impact." He shined his flashlight on the two adults before focusing on the body of the young boy. The thick ice crystals hid any details that might tell them anything about how they died—at least from Remi's point of view—not that there was any doubt in her mind. If the crash didn't kill them, they undoubtedly froze to death.

Sam looked at his watch. "It's past time to leave. Let's get out of here."

Remi climbed down, then waited for Sam. Dietrich was looking around at the rear of the plane. "No tail. Where do you think it is?" he asked Sam.

"Probably broke off on impact. Something to look for tomorrow when we come back."

Dietrich nodded, then followed them out. The three hiked down the mountainside, reaching the rendezvous point just as the helicopter appeared overhead, then touched down. "Sorry I'm late," Julio said as they boarded. "I was concerned about my wife when she didn't answer her mobile. She was at the store and didn't hear it ringing."

"No worries," Remi said, speaking loud enough to be heard. "We're late, too. Is she okay? Your wife?"

He nodded. When everyone was inside, buckled in and headsets on, he lifted off. "Discover anything?"

"Lot of bodies," Sam said.

That was enough to temper any excitement over the find, and the rest of the trip was made in silence. Dietrich, Remi noticed, was staring off into the distance, even as they landed. She reached out, put her hand on his, and he looked over and smiled at her.

Sam helped Remi out, then waved at the pilot. "Same time tomorrow?"

"Same time." Julio waited for them to clear, snow whipping around like a mini blizzard.

Remi waved as he lifted off, then linked her arm through Sam's. As the three walked back to the tent, her gaze lingered on Dietrich, wondering how he was taking this. Once in the tent, he sat off to one side, looking deep in thought. Before she had a chance to see if he was okay, Nando told Sam that Selma had called a couple of hours earlier. "She tried reaching you on your satellite phone, but couldn't get through. Something about your Russian friends. The cell phone signal up here isn't very good, so I didn't hear everything."

"I'll give her a call," Sam said.

The satellite phone was notoriously unreliable if there wasn't direct line of sight to the sky, and so he stepped outside the tent. While Nando served up their dinner, Remi tried to engage Dietrich in conversation. But he was clearly distracted, and so she was glad when Sam returned a few minutes later. "Anything important?" she asked him.

"Tatiana and Viktor followed Leopold and Rolfe to Mendoza but lost them somewhere in the city. They think the Guard is hiding them but have a lead on where they might be."

"I hope they're not out there alone."

"The Argentine Federal Police are helping. Even so, don't go wandering out without a gun. I wouldn't want any surprises before they meet us here, once we finish up."

"Let's hope they're successful," she said, glancing at Dietrich, who barely touched the stew, pushing it around on his plate. He seemed uninterested in the news and, after several minutes, excused himself, saying that he was turning in early. "I'm worried about Dietrich," she said later as she and Sam climbed into the sleeping bags in their tent.

"Give him time to process the reality of it," Sam said, "he'll be okay. You'll see."

"I hope so."

As usual, Sam was right. By breakfast the next morning, Dietrich seemed perfectly fine, eager to get back to the plane. "No baby yet?" Dietrich asked Julio as they climbed onto the helicopter.

"Not yet. My brother's on standby if I have to leave."

"Swing around the back," Sam said when they neared the crash site. "I'd like to see if there's anywhere that tail might have ended up."

Julio nodded. A moment later, they were circling the area at the rear of the site. "A lot of ice down there," Julio said. "Used to be one glacier, separated over the years."

"If that tail's there," Sam said, "it's buried where we can't see it. Take us down. Time to get a more thorough look at what's in that plane."

81

Julio brought the helicopter around the peak, bringing it down to their makeshift landing pad. "Don't forget," he told Sam. "The storm is coming in, so we'll need to get an earlier start back."

"What time?"

"Say, two-thirty, three at the latest."

"See you then."

Considering that the day had begun with a crystal clear sky, not a cloud to be seen as they climbed the hill, it was hard to believe the storm would arrive on time. Glistening droplets of water dripped from the plane's propellers in the warmth of the sun, and the three wore sunglasses against the glare on the snow.

Once inside the plane, they spent the next several hours meticulously documenting everything they found, starting at the front and working their way back. Out of respect, they left the search of the cockpit to Dietrich. By the time he finished, Sam and Remi had worked their way to the ice wall on the right side near the missing wing.

"Find anything?" Sam asked Dietrich as he climbed down the ladder.

"I'm not sure, but it looks like the pilot was shot in the head. I don't see any other reason for the hole in his skull."

"It certainly explains why the plane crashed," Sam replied.

"Have you found anything down here?"

"We've identified three of the men." Two were intertwined on the floor at the front of the plane against a third man, who had no ID. The other three passengers, two men and a woman, were draped over the seats. "That man there," he said, pointing to one of the three on the floor, "is your Great-uncle Ludwig Strassmair. I expect the woman has a purse somewhere. We just haven't found it yet."

Dietrich stared at what he could see of Strassmair for a few moments, then turned away. "What about the treasure? You think it's here? You think that's why he was on this plane?"

"So far, it's not looking good. We only found one suitcase. Nothing but clothes."

He nodded, looking around. "Only one?"

Sam shined the light on the rear of the plane, revealing the wall of ice where the tail used to be. "My guess is, the cargo was in the tail of the plane and that it's located between here and wherever the tail landed. It might be close."

"Or not," Remi said. "Look how far that propeller was."

"Where's that positive thinking, Remi?"

"Back at base camp. Nando mentioned something about fresh-made empanadas for dinner."

"Speaking of," Sam said, looking at his watch, "we should start heading down the hill. Julio's due anytime now."

"So we return tomorrow?" Dietrich asked.

"If the storm blows through quickly," he said, picking up his backpack and strapping it on, then helping Remi with hers. "If the weather report's accurate, it'll be the day after."

They left the plane, heading down the mountainside. The wind gusted through the pass, the frigid air having dropped several degrees from earlier that morning. By the time they reached the rendezvous point, it was even colder. Sharp winds began to attack, quickly changing direction, and never in a repeating pattern.

The minutes ticked by. As the clouds grew thicker and darker, Remi leaned in close to Sam. "Let's hope he gets here soon."

"I'm sure he will," Dietrich said.

Thunder rumbled in the distance. Sam glanced up the sky, searching.

Remi, apparently, noticed his concern. "What's wrong?"

"Hate to say it, but Julio should have been here by now. He's way too experienced to try to get out here this late, in this weather."

"Wouldn't he call?" Dietrich asked.

"Assuming he could get through, it's possible he did." Sam took out his satellite phone and tried to call Julio. When there was no answer, he nodded at the plane. "Lucky for us, we've got shelter and food."

"Protein bars," Remi said as the three trudged through the snow back to the plane. "Hardly a consolation."

"They're *gourmet* protein bars. The label says so."

"Keep telling yourself that, Fargo."

"I'll phone Nando and let him know we're probably not making it to dinner." They stopped at the nose of the aircraft. When he tried to make the call, nothing happened. "You two wait in the plane. I've got to move out farther. Something's blocking the line of sight." What, he wasn't sure. Possibly the two mountain peaks they were standing between or interference from the storm.

Remi hesitated. Sam reassured her he wasn't about to wander that far from the plane. Not in this weather.

When Dietrich took Remi's arm, helping her up through the door, Sam worked his way down the mountain until his phone was able to pick up a satellite signal and he could successfully call Nando.

"I can barely hear you, Mr. Fargo. We were worried when it got dark and you weren't back."

"'We'?"

"Julio called. His wife had the baby. He was sending his brother. I assumed he was on his way to get you. He didn't make it there?"

"Not yet," Sam said, shouting over the wind. "We're taking shelter in the downed plane. Call Julio's brother. Tell him to come back in the morning when it's clear."

"If it's clear," Nando said. "The weather report isn't looking good. You're sure you'll be okay?"

"We'll be fine."

Sam pocketed his phone, then climbed back up to the plane, keeping his head down against the wind, which was even stronger now than it had been just a few minutes ago.

Remi watched him from the doorway, the flashlight turned on to light his way. "Did you reach anyone?"

"Nando," he said, pulling himself into the fuselage. He and Dietrich pushed the door closed, the wind whistling through the crack. "On the good news front, Julio's wife had the baby."

"That explains why he's not here. He—"

Sam held up his hand. "Hear that?"

"Thunder?" Remi asked.

"I think our ride's here."

They pulled open the door, the three running out toward the front of the plane. A tiny speck in the sky just over the pass was almost hidden in the snow flurries, the sound of the rotors barely audible over the wailing wind.

With gloved hands, they shielded their eyes against the spotlights as the helicopter swept overhead. It suddenly swung back on a course directly toward them, the pilot struggling to control the craft against the ever-stronger wind.

It rose sharply for a few moments, fighting a losing battle with the gale. The rotors blasted the frigid darkness. Then, barely in the air, the nearly uncontrolled helicopter pounded the driving snow, magnifying the thunder, on the ridge and steep side of the mountain.

Suddenly, there was an unbearable roar that swept down the deeply blanketed slope that engulfed the helicopter. It became lost under a white storm of ice and vanished.

The three stared in shock as the ice-packed snow beneath their snowshoes began to pulsate, and Sam realized it wasn't thunder at all.

"Run!" he yelled. "To the plane!"

82

"Avalanche!"

Bits of snow and ice rained down on them. Remi ran without question. Dietrich froze, his attention fixed on the wall of snow slipping down the mountainside.

"Hurry!" Sam shouted. He followed Remi under the wing, Dietrich coming to his senses, following right behind them. The noise grew louder as ice chunks pelted the fuselage. Snow slid in from both sides as Sam shoved open the door.

Remi climbed in, then looked back just as a sea of white swept Dietrich from his feet. "Sam!" she yelled, pointing.

He grabbed Dietrich's arm, pulling him up. The two men scrambled into the plane, then struggled to close the door before the snow poured in, Remi leaning into it alongside them. The fuselage creaked and groaned from the weight, the deafening roar turning into muffled silence as the level rose past the windows, shrouding them in darkness. The three stood there, leaning against the door, their breaths coming fast.

"Remi?" Sam asked.

"I'm fine."

"Dietrich?"

When he didn't answer right away, Remi reached for him. "Are you okay?"

"Yes . . . What—what about that pilot?"

"Hard to say," Sam said. "But his helicopter was in one piece right before the avalanche. If he's as experienced as Julio, he'll find a place to ride out the storm."

"What if something happened to him? Or the helicopter?" Dietrich asked. "How will they even know to come looking?"

"Satellite phone," Sam said, taking it from his pocket, the screen lighting up his face as he turned it on, showing it to Dietrich, before powering it off to conserve the battery. "Not that it'll do us much good now. At least not until we dig out."

"And if we can't dig out?" he asked.

"Avalanche beacon. But we'll be okay. I'm hoping that from the angle of the mountain, most of the snow fell on the other side."

Remi eyed the door, unable to see anything out the window. It might as well have been a starless night looking back at her. "Not looking good so far."

"Being optimistic again, Remi?"

"Practical."

"Wait until we dig our airhole. You'll see. So what is it you have in that magic backpack of yours to tide us over the next couple of days?"

"Caviar and champagne," she said, pulling out protein bars and water bottles.

Dietrich reached into his pack. "I have chocolate."

"You," Remi said, eyeing the shiny silver wrappers, "are my new best friend."

"One night covered," Sam said. "But we'll have to ration, and hope it blows through soon. In the meantime, let's get to work on that snow tunnel. The longer it snows, the farther we'll have to dig out. I'd hate to run out of oxygen before then."

He took his flashlight and climbed up into the cockpit.

Remi also climbed up, but just far enough to take a look, forcing her gaze past the shadowed frozen bodies to the snow-covered cockpit glass above. All was dark. "You think we'll be able to dig through?" she asked softly.

He glanced over at her. "Depending on how deep it is, it's our only chance."

About to climb down, she saw Klaus's boots just a few inches from her face and she paused. "What about Klaus?" she asked in a low voice, her expression one of sadness, no doubt thinking about the fear the young boy had felt as the plane was going down. "It seems almost sacrilegious to be stepping over him . . ."

This time, Dietrich overheard her, saying, "I don't think he'd mind. He'd want us to live."

"I agree," Sam said, climbing down after Remi. "Let's have another look in the fuselage and see if we can't come up with some wood to shore up that snow tunnel."

"Out of what?" Dietrich shined his flashlight around. "There's not much down here."

"That broken seat, for one," Sam said, nodding at its back. "Maybe others are loose. Pre–World War Two construction. No doubt they used wooden frames," he said, pressing down on the nearest seat.

Remi held the flashlight as Sam and Dietrich tore apart the leather upholstery, separating the ties and frames from several seats.

When they had enough wood, Sam climbed up into the cockpit, carrying his compact shovel and snow probe. He had two worries. The first was that he hoped his calculations on the avalanche were correct, that it had fallen mainly to the right of the plane. There was no telling how far they'd have to dig otherwise. The second and bigger worry, one he hadn't shared, was that the current storm might create a second avalanche by adding weight to an already unstable base.

Using his shovel, he broke the glass, knocking away any shards left in the frame. Snow fell down to the floor as the two men started digging through the hole in the window. Remi propped the flashlight so that it shined into the cockpit, then started scooping the snow to the cabin below.

It was slow going, and in some places they had to hack away at the concrete-like snow, careful not to dislodge the braces they'd placed. Finally, Sam's shovel broke through. Frigid air blew through the hole, snow swirling in from the storm raging outside.

Remi and Dietrich cheered, breathing in deep, and the three celebrated by splitting a protein bar and a chocolate for dinner, then toasting with water bottles.

After their meal, the three settled against their packs, leaning into one another to conserve warmth.

"What if they can't find us?" Dietrich asked.

"It'll be a long walk back," Sam replied, "but at least we have snowshoes."

Remi elbowed him. "He's kidding, Dietrich. Of course they'll find us. Right Sam?"

"Exactly," he said, putting his arm around her, knowing he wouldn't be able to sleep after seeing the force of the wind and snow blowing in, straight toward that same mountain shoulder and the source of that first avalanche. There was no doubt in his mind. If the storm kept up, a second avalanche was imminent. He only hoped it didn't strike until after they were rescued.

orning took its sweet time arriving. Remi shifted in the crook of Sam's arm, taking a deep sigh.

"You're awake," Sam said.

"I'm not sure I ever slept." She sat up, turning on her flashlight. "It's still dark in here. I was hoping for daylight." She looked over at Dietrich, who was seated to her left. "How about you? Any rest?"

"Not much," Dietrich said. "It sounds like the wind is dying down somewhat."

Not enough for Sam's liking. The constant whistling through the tunnel they'd dug up in the cockpit had lessened a bit in the early morning hours, giving him hope that there wasn't too much weight added to the snowpack on that right shoulder. But it had started up again at daybreak and didn't show any sign of lessening.

"Maybe we should try to call," Dietrich said, standing, clearly anxious. "I'll go. I don't mind a little cold. Maybe I could climb out far enough to get a signal."

"It's not the cold," Sam said, realizing he had no choice but to be up front. "That wind was blowing snow straight into that peak all night. As long as there's a risk of avalanche, we're better off staying right where we are."

"So we just wait?" Dietrich asked.

"Not much choice. No sense getting out before our rescuers can start searching. Looks like we'll be here for a while. I don't suppose anyone brought cards?"

"Poor planning on our part," Remi said.

A long stretch of silence followed, broken only by the wind whistling through the tunnel up in the cockpit. Even though the storm showed no sign of letting up, the tunnel they'd dug remained clear, and they took turns checking on it, making sure their braces were holding under the weight of the new snow.

Sam went up to check one last time before they settled in for that night's ration of protein bars. So far, so good, he thought, able to see a few stars in the black sky. The wind was still fierce, but he hoped it would soon die down.

"How is it?" Remi asked as he joined them back in the hold.

"Snow's stopped."

"That's good, then, right?" Dietrich said as the wind gusted through the barrier.

"Let's hope so."

Remi glanced at Sam, saying nothing. Her expression told him that she knew the bigger danger with all that new snowfall was the wind blowing it against the mountainside. He still held out hope, but as they sat there eating, they heard a low rumble and felt a vibration that seemed to penetrate them, followed by a swoosh of air coming from the cockpit as the avalanche covered them.

Sam grabbed his flashlight and shovel, rushed up the ladder, removing the barricade they'd erected to keep out the cold and snow.

"How bad is it?" Dietrich asked as he looked around.

"The tunnel collapsed." He started digging.

"Of all the bad luck," Dietrich said, stepping in to help. "This?"

"Definitely lucky," Sam said.

"How?"

"We were close to the plane for the first avalanche. Had we been any farther away, we'd be buried at the bottom of the mountain. This avalanche, we're safe inside. Doesn't get much luckier than that."

"And to think," Dietrich said, "I wanted to climb out there to try to call for help."

"Which shouldn't be a problem now that the risk is over," Sam said, using his shovel to scoop down into the hold the snow that Dietrich was digging out.

Icy wind whipped into the cockpit when they finally cleared the tunnel. Unfortunately, most of the wood they'd salvaged from the seats had snapped from the weight of the new snow.

"We're going to need some way to shore this up," Sam said, glancing over at Remi, who was watching from the ladder while she held the light for them.

She shivered as she eyed the narrow space and the bit of black sky through the hole. "This may be wishful thinking," she said, "but any chance we can make a call?"

Sam dug the satellite phone from his pocket, powered it on, and held it near the tunnel. "Not looking good," he said.

"The storm?" Remi asked. "Or the signal?"

"Both. The wind's strong, signal's nonexistent. But the biggest danger's over, so no harm riding it out until morning." He pocketed the phone, looking back at her. "Let's get this tunnel fixed. We have a few more seats we can tear apart, but I'm not sure there's going to be enough wood."

"What about that suitcase we found?" Remi said. "I'll get it."

The suitcase worked better than he'd expected. "That's a good start," Sam said, working the two halves into place. "We need something else to brace it."

"Snowshoes?" Dietrich suggested.

"We're going to need those to trek through that snow, once the storm ends." He climbed down, looking around the fuselage. "Let's see if we can't loosen up a couple more of those seats."

Sam and Dietrich pulled together on one seat back, which broke almost too easily, sending Sam back into Remi, knocking the flashlight from her hand. It hit the ground and spun beneath the seats near the front. She got down on her knees, retrieved it, but stopped and reached for something else.

"What is it?" Sam asked.

"Another suitcase under here. I can't get it out."

84

The suitcase was wedged between the seat and the floor, inconveniently on the starboard side, where the wing had been sheared off. A wall of ice bearing down on the seat prevented them from being able to move the suitcase, and the space was too narrow for Sam or Dietrich to get to. The two leaned into the seat, pulling up, trying to make more space for Remi. "Can you get it?" Sam asked.

"It's not budging," Remi said. "Wait. It moved. I can feel something. The buckle. We're not going to be able to get it out."

"Maybe there's something inside we can use." Sam braced his feet against the seat behind them, applying leverage.

"Do that again," she said. "I've almost got it."

Dietrich moved in close to Sam, both men pushing. Finally, they were able to shift the seat above the suitcase enough so that Remi was able to unbuckle it.

"Any luck?" Sam asked.

"I can only get my fingers in. The bottom of the seat's stopping it . . . I feel something . . . Papers . . ." She pulled out a few and held them up.

Sam took them from her. "Anything else?"

"More papers," she said. "And something soft beneath. Clothes, probably. Whatever it is, I can't quite reach it."

"So much for our great find," Sam said, handing the papers to Dietrich before reaching down to help Remi to her feet.

"Anything interesting?" she asked.

Dietrich took the flashlight, reading the typescript, an odd expression on his face. "Isn't that what you were telling me about? *Unternehmen Werwolf . . .*"

"Operation Werewolf," Sam said. "The reason the Wolf Guard exists."

"Maybe it tells something about the Romanov Ransom?" Dietrich said.

"A mystery that'll have to wait," Sam replied. "Let's get back into that cockpit and finish bracing our tunnel."

"What about the papers?" Dietrich asked.

"Give them to Remi. I promise she won't start reading without us."

"Me?" Remi said, looking far too innocent for her own good. When he and Dietrich finished bracing the tunnel and returned down to the hold a few minutes later, she aimed the flashlight on her pack, taking out the papers. "A little light reading to catch up on. Part of it at least." She handed them to Dietrich, no doubt to help get his mind off their situation.

Sam waited while Dietrich read. "Any talk of the treasure?"

"Not by name." Dietrich scanned the first page, then turned to the next. "This seems to be a synopsis of more detailed plans to sabotage the peace efforts. Bomb Russia and blame it on the Americans, bomb America and blame it on the Russians—apparently, they were waiting on the money to finance it. The goal was to start the war again . . ." He looked up at them. "If the treasure was on this plane, then I guess it's a good thing it went down."

"Except for Klaus," Remi said.

He nodded, returning the papers to Remi, who read them herself, then returned them to her pack.

They spent the remainder of the night keeping warm, taking turns on checking the tunnel, telling stories about the various places they'd been. Dietrich had never traveled beyond South America and was fascinated by their adventures. "How is it you two met?" he asked.

"The Lighthouse Cafe," Sam said. "A bar in Hermosa Beach, California."

"In fact," Remi added, "we were on our way there when we landed here. Sort of."

"Listen." Sam turned on the flashlight, aiming the beam at the cockpit. "I don't hear any wind."

"Not again," Remi said, shivering. It seemed colder now than it had been the previous night.

Dietrich got up. "My turn. I'll check." He took his flashlight and climbed up the ladder. They heard him moving around up there. "It's still open. But the wind has stopped."

Sam joined him in the cockpit, looking through the tunnel. "He's right," he called down to Remi, who was holding on to the ladder behind him.

"When can we get out?" she asked.

He looked at his watch. "My guess is, they'll be waiting for morning to start the search. We'll call first thing."

The three settled in for the night. The cold seemed even harsher. When morning came, Sam climbed up, disappointed to see that the snow had once again covered their tunnel. He grabbed the shovel and started clearing the entrance. This time, though, when he broke through, it was to a clear, sparkling sky.

"That's a welcome sight!"

Once the three were free of the plane, snowshoes strapped on, they worked their way down the mountain far enough to get a clear signal on the satellite phone. Sam called Nando.

"Good news!" Nando said before Sam could get a word in edge-wise. "Julio is already on his way. He's insisting on piloting the search and rescue himself."

"We'll be at the rendezvous point. What about his brother?"

"Fine. Made it back, but wracked with guilt."

"Tell him not to worry."

"I will!" Nando said. "We're celebrating tonight. Big dinner. And your friends said to tell you they're waiting for you."

"Who is?"

"Yes. See you soon!"

Nando disconnected before Sam could clarify further. He stared at the phone a second.

"Well?" Remi asked.

"He's more excited about our rescue than we are. Celebratory dinner. And our friends are waiting for us."

"Tatiana and Viktor?" Remi asked.

"I hope that's who he meant." Sam tried calling him back. This time, there was no answer. "Odd. I'll call Selma. Maybe she'll know."

Selma, however, had no idea what he was talking about. "As far as I know, Tatiana and Viktor are still in Mendoza. That's got to be who he meant."

"Of course it is. I'll give them a call."

"I'll see what I can find out on my end." But neither Tatiana nor Nando answered their phones. He left voice mails on each, then pock-eted his phone. "I'd feel better if we knew which friends he was talking about. Especially considering Tatiana and Viktor are the only ones who know we're up here."

"Surely," Remi said, "Nando would suspect if two strange men showed up at camp?"

"Let's hope so," he said as the air began thrumming from the ap-proaching helicopter.

Dietrich pointed. "There it is!"

Sam looked up. "Better late than never," he said, watching as the helicopter approached, flying over the top of the ridge, circling back and then down the pass—something Julio had never done.

Remi even noticed. "Why's he coming that way?"

"Good question," Sam said, shielding his eyes against the glare, trying to see if it really was Julio piloting. It definitely wasn't the same craft.

The helicopter seemed to shudder as it hovered over them, before banking sharply. Remi reached out, grabbing Sam's arm. "Something's wrong."

85

The three watched as the helicopter picked up speed again, circled around the peaks one more time, then landed near the rendezvous point. When the door opened and Julio appeared, waving at them, Sam, Remi, and Dietrich continued down the mountain.

"Is everything okay?" Sam asked Julio. "Looked like you were having some trouble up there."

"Combination of an unfamiliar craft and a sharp downdraft," Julio said. "I wasn't about to trust anyone else. I had to borrow this after my brother's accident. I can't tell you how sorry he was."

"He's not hurt?" Remi asked.

"He's fine. Our helicopter not so much. But it got him home, and you're all okay."

"More than okay," Sam said, making a mental note to have Selma get started on replacing the damaged helicopter. He threw their packs into the back before helping Remi. Once they were in the air, he tried calling Nando and Tatiana. Again, neither answered, and so he checked in with Selma, who had the same results. Concerned, he asked Julio if he'd spoken with Nando at all.

"Earlier this morning."

"He say anything about friends stopping by?"

"Not a word."

Sam eyed the base camp below as the helicopter neared. "Do me a favor, Julio. Fly a little slower as you make the first pass. I want to get a better look at our tent."

He lifted the binoculars, focusing as their large orange dining tent came into view. He scanned the area around their campsite. No one seemed to be around. "If our 'friends' are there, I don't see them," he told Remi. "Then again, I don't see Nando, either."

"I'm still worried," Remi said.

"Good reason for it," Sam replied, pointing near the helipad. "That man at the northeast corner. Possibly a sentry."

"There, too," Remi said. "A little farther to the south."

"How can you tell?" Dietrich asked.

"Besides that we're expecting it? The way they're standing, right hand in the right pocket, most likely holding a gun. Notice we're all wearing bright colors," Sam added. "They're dressed in white. Blends in with the snow."

"Guess my false travel plans didn't work," Dietrich said.

"Might have bought us a few days." Sam scanned the area with his binoculars, telling Remi, "I don't see Rolfe or Leopold."

"Maybe they didn't want to get their new white snowsuits dirty."

"Somehow, I doubt we're that lucky. There's got to be more sentries. Leopold doesn't send a couple men out and hope for the best."

"This isn't his territory," Dietrich said. "Maybe he doesn't have enough people."

"Every time we've dealt with him, he's always had several men patrolling the outer perimeter. No reason to think any different. Take us down, Julio," Sam said, then looked back at Dietrich. "Remi and I will go on up. If we can get around those sentries, it shouldn't take us too long to get Nando and meet you here."

Dietrich nodded. "You sure you don't want me to come with you?"

"I'd rather you wait with Julio. If we're lucky, we can get in and out without anyone noticing."

"How?"

"They're not watching the helipad, so they might not even know we were stuck in the avalanche or coming in on the helicopter. If there's the slightest problem, you two get out of here and get help."

"You got it."

When the helicopter landed, Sam jumped out, then helped Remi, the two running up the hill to a position where Sam could see the sentries. The first was behind a rock and about a hundred yards away, the second about twenty-five yards beyond him. "Let's come up from above them," Sam said. "They're busy watching the tents below." If he had to guess, Rolfe and Leopold were probably below, searching for them. Their camp was higher, overlooking the tent city. Sam hoped that meant they had plenty of time, but he wasn't about to chance it. He drew his gun. "Ready?"

Staying low, the two followed a craggy trail of rocks and boulders. As they neared, the first sentry turned, drawing a gun from his right pocket. Sam grabbed Remi's hand, pulling her behind a boulder. The sentry fired. Bits of rock flew up, the shot echoing around them. Sam returned fire as he and Remi ran through the snow down the trail, the echo sounding like ricocheted shots cracking off the mountain peaks.

"So much for getting to our tent unobserved," he said. "Keep an eye out for that other guy. I'm going to find a way to get over there without them seeing. I need to take this guy out."

"I vote we take them both out." Remi had drawn her gun and aimed at the last location of the second sentry. "It'd be nice if he made a move. I have no idea where he went."

"Let's see if we can't flush him out. Fire a shot his way when I tell you to. Then give me enough time to get into position and do it again. If he doesn't move, the other one will. We'll use the echo to our advantage."

She leaned over and kissed him. "Be careful, Fargo."

"Likewise."

Sam waited until the first sentry edged up high enough to where Sam could see his shadow on the snowbank behind him. "Now."

Remi fired, her shot cracking across the surrounding mountains. The moment Sam saw the first sentry duck, he dove behind a boulder across the trail, then ran between the rocks just above the man's position. Sam glanced in Remi's direction. When she looked his way, he gave her a thumbs-up. She nodded, and he worked his way through the rocks, wedged himself against a boulder, then peered around the side, waiting, listening for Remi. She fired again. The first gunman rose, aimed in her direction.

"Hey!" Sam yelled, firing twice.

The man turned, fired several times. The shots hit the boulder in front of Sam, snow and rock flying up. Sam shot back, ducked, and crawled through the snow until he reached a space between another pair of rocks. Two shots left, he was going to have to make them count. And hope that Remi had the other gunman covered.

Wind gusted through the rocks. Sam strained to listen, hoping to hear his opponent's movement. There it was, faint, the crunch of snow, a few feet to his right. Sam edged his way around the boulder just as the gunman broke cover. Sam squeezed the trigger. The man fell back, red spreading across his white snowsuit.

Sam had just retrieved the man's gun when he looked back and saw the second gunman working his way toward where Remi was hiding.

"Behind you!" Sam shouted, aiming.

Remi spun around, firing at the same time as Sam, their shots echoing around the mountains like machine guns. The sentry twisted, then stumbled, his weapon falling from his lifeless fingers.

Sam and Remi heard gunshots from the camp below.

"Nando?"

"I'm checking now," Sam said, looking out toward the base camp. He took his binoculars, scanned the camp, unable to find who was shooting. He focused on the front of their dining tent. One of the door flaps was strapped open, and he watched a few moments, seeing Nando walk past the doorway. "He's there. Looks fine. I don't see anyone else in the tent or around it."

"You know Leopold and Rolfe must have heard those shots."

"You're right. Can you get that guy's gun and see if he has any extra magazines? I think we may be in for more trouble."

Sam swept his gaze from their tent, past the group of tents down the hill. Not a lot moving. Most of the occupants were probably taking advantage of the clear weather, out climbing the summit. "If they're down there, I don't see them. Let's get Nando out of here."

Just to be safe, they decided their best bet was to approach their campsite from the rear. They picked their way through the snow, grateful that it was wasn't deep. Sam leaned toward the tent, trying to hear inside, but a gust of wind ruffled the nylon canvas, muffling all sound. When the wind died down, he heard Nando singing along with a song on the portable radio.

That, Sam decided, was a good sign, and they continued around the corner into the tent. Nando, his back to them, was swaying to the beat of the pop music as he stirred something simmering in the large pot on the cook stove, the scent of savory spices filling the air.

"We're back," Sam said.

Nando, spoon in hand, turned, a smile lighting his face, until he looked past them out the door. "Where's Dietrich?"

"Waiting at the helicopter. Which is where we need to go. Right now."

"Why? What's wrong?"

"We're a little worried about how friendly our friends are."

"The ones Tatiana called about?"

"You spoke to her?"

"Yes. She said she couldn't talk but told me to tell you your mutual friends were on the way. They were following."

"Definitely time to go," Sam said, taking a few steps in. "When did you talk to her?"

"Not since . . ." Nando stared at Remi, slowly raising his hands.

Sam looked that direction and saw Rolfe and Leopold in the doorway, both holding guns.

86

Rolfe motioned with his gun for Remi to move toward Sam and Nando. "Search them," Rolfe said.

Leopold holstered his gun, then checked each of them for weapons, taking a gun from Sam's holster and the second gun Sam had picked up from the dead sentry. He did the same with Remi. "Clean," he said, moving off to the side, tucking the weapons into the pockets of his parka.

"Staying for dinner?" Sam asked Rolfe.

"We would," he replied, his glance sliding toward Nando, then back to Sam, "but we have a few loose ends to tie up. Like eliminating any obstacles that stand between me and my treasure."

"If you think you're going to find it without us, you're mistaken."

Leopold took a step toward them, his hand on his holstered gun. "Is there some reason we don't just get it over with?"

"Patience," Rolfe said, his gaze locked on Sam's. "You were saying? About the treasure?"

"Right," Sam said. "The treasure. Where was I . . . ? Oh, yes. We have it. You don't. And if anything happens to us, you'll never find it."

"He's lying," Leopold said.

"Who are you going to believe?" Sam asked. "The one with the proof—me—or the one with the hidden agenda?"

Leopold gripped his handgun tighter. "What hidden agenda?"

"Wolf Guard? Fourth Reich?"

"Forget him," Rolfe said, never taking his gaze off Sam. "What proof do you have that you even found it?"

"Remi," Sam said. "Show them."

As she started to reach for her pack, Rolfe lifted his gun, pointing it at her. She stopped. "Papers," she said. "Tucked inside to keep them dry."

"Slowly, Mrs. Fargo."

Remi unzipped her pack, removing the papers they'd found on the plane, holding them out. "See for yourself."

Rolfe took them from her, scanning the topmost page before handing them to Leopold, who quickly looked them over. "They look real. But how do we know they're not forgeries?"

"Right," Sam said. "Because onionskin paper and typewriters are so easy to find these days. We just whipped up these copies in the few minutes we had—in case you showed up."

"Enough!" Leopold grabbed Remi by the arm, pulling her toward him. "Collateral. Until you show us where that treasure is."

Before Sam could move, Rolfe stepped between them, leveling his gun on Sam. "Don't do anything stupid."

"Trust me, I won't," he said, his eyes on Remi. She tried to pull free, but Leopold held tight. "Hurt her, and I promise your death will be painful."

Leopold's pale eyes narrowed. "You think you're going to kill me?"

"No doubt," Sam said. "I just haven't decided how. Yet."

A loud hissing behind them startled Nando. The bubbling stew boiled over, brown liquid hitting the burner, steam and smoke rising up.

Rolfe turned toward it. Sam lunged, grabbing at Rolfe's gun with one hand while slamming his other hand upward, cracking the man's elbow. As Sam wrested the gun from Rolfe, Leopold swung Remi around, trying to reach for his holstered weapon. Remi rammed her shoulder into his side, then dropped down, giving Sam the clearance he needed.

Sam fired. Leopold staggered back, a look of disbelief on his face, as Remi pulled free. Sam fired again. As the Guardsman dropped to the ground, Rolfe lunged toward Sam. Nando grabbed the stewpot, then swung it. Rolfe screamed, stumbling back.

"Get the gun!" Sam said.

Remi dove for the weapon that fell from Leopold's lifeless hand. She pointed it at Rolfe, who tried to rise to his knees, about to make a break for it, when Tatiana and Viktor appeared in the entrance. Tatiana shoved him down with her foot until he was facedown in the snow, screaming in pain. "Going somewhere?"

87

—————

S orry we're late," Tatiana said once they had Rolfe cuffed. "Viktor and I had trouble locating your tent. We took out a couple of Leopold's men down the hill. We figured he and Rolfe wouldn't be too far. Unfortunately, they'd taken a completely different route."

"We ran into a couple more at the helipad," Sam said.

"Apologies," Viktor said. "We must have missed those two."

Tatiana glanced down at Rolfe, who was writhing in pain, a look of satisfaction on her face. "This is one time I'll be happy to testify in court."

ROLFE WAS turned over to the Argentine authorities after he had been taken to the hospital because of his broken arm and the burns on his face. Several days later, Tatiana was able to get an expert to verify and link the Operation Werewolf papers found on the airplane to Ludwig Strassmair. As a result, the Argentine government offered to assist the Russian government in the recovery of the downed Avro Lancastrian and whatever else might be found on it.

With a break in the weather, and after assessing the danger of any further avalanches, the teams flew out to start a full search of the plane and surrounding area. One group was assigned to forensics, to determine the cause of the Avro plane crash and to recover the victims. The other team, composed of local experts, accompanied by Tatiana, Viktor, the Fargos, Dietrich, and Nando, started the search for any historical evidence, beginning with the suitcase in which Remi had found the Operation Werewolf papers.

Once the remaining seats were removed, they were able to retrieve the suitcase, hoping to find further evidence of the plot to use the Romanov Ransom. "Remi, you found it," Dietrich said. "You do the honors."

Remi glanced at Sam, who nodded at her, and she picked up the suitcase, carrying it out into the light, placing it on a table. She lifted the lid, finding a brown folder containing a number of yellowed sheets of paper, which she handed to Dietrich. "More from Operation Werewolf, I'd say."

Their attention turned to the cloth covering whatever else was in the case. Remi carefully lifted one corner, along with the soft wool just beneath, revealing a green egg that looked to be carved from jade and decorated with gold and diamonds.

"An Easter egg?" Dietrich said.

"Empire Nephrite Egg," Tatiana replied, her voice filled with awe. "Fabergé."

Remi stepped aside, looking at Tatiana. "You should do the honors."

Tatiana hesitated, almost afraid to touch the cloth covering the second egg. Finally, she reached out, lifting it, the sun striking the gold vertical lines and diamonds set around the white-enameled egg. She turned it about, feeling the weight of it in her hands. "This is the Alexander the Third Commemorative Egg."

She replaced it in the case, then ran her fingers across the third, a platinum hen-shaped egg speckled with diamonds, sitting in a gold basket. "And the Sapphire Hen." She picked it up, examined it for a few moments, the sunlight striking the deep blue sapphire in the hen's beak as she gently returned it to its bed of wool. "Three out of the last four that were unaccounted for. What an incredible find."

"Which one's still missing?" Remi asked.

"The Royal Danish," Tatiana said. "It contains the miniature portraits of Maria Feodorovna's parents. Each of these are nearly priceless. One Fabergé egg recently sold for over thirty-two million dollars."

Dietrich whistled.

Tatiana closed the lid of the suitcase. "That's quite a recovery fee the four of you will get."

"The Fargos, you mean," Dietrich said. "I was just here to find Klaus."

"You and Nando deserve it as much as we do," Sam replied. Dietrich looked at him in confusion. "You didn't think we were keeping all of it? You were right there with us."

"I—I don't know what to say . . ."

Remi smiled at him. "You don't need to say anything," she replied as Viktor called to them from behind the plane.

The four walked beneath the now cleared wing, toward the back of the plane, where Viktor, Nando, and the other workers were busy excavating the area where it was believed the tail might be located. It turned out the plane had actually touched down higher on the ridge, the tail breaking off at that location before the main fuselage came to rest in the pass. One of the workers had uncovered a piece of the tail.

With nothing else to find in the plane, the Fargos spent the next several days expanding their search where the tail piece had been found. About four days in, Viktor held up a chunk of wood with a metal brace attached to it. "Luggage?" Viktor asked.

Sam examined the scrolling on the metal, thinking it looked more like a decorative embellishment from the early 1900s. "Or a wooden chest." He called Remi and Dietrich over to help excavate the snow and ice. Hours later, when they were about to give up for the day, Sam kicked at a piece of rock embedded in the glacier. It skittered a few inches away, landing next to something that looked like a spot of blood in the snow. It wasn't until he bent down, brushing at the snow with his gloved finger, that he realized it was, in fact, a large blood-red ruby pendant hanging from a platinum and diamond necklace.

He carefully extricated it from the glacier, then held it up in the sunlight, the diamonds sparkling like ice crystals.

Nando stared in awe. "What is it?" he asked.

"Part of the Romanov Ransom."

88

Over the next few weeks, they recovered dozens of loose precious stones, a fortune in gold, as well as diamond necklaces, tiaras, and bracelets. When the items were turned over to Tatiana, she estimated that the finder's fee, split among the Fargos, Dietrich, Nando, and the Argentine government, was worth millions each.

Dietrich, however, was more interested in why the plane went down, and, of course, giving a proper burial to Klaus in a grave next to that of the boy's mother and father. A week later, after the brief ceremony, he, Sam, and Remi stood at the gravesite. "My grandfather," Dietrich said, "and his father, always believed that they'd find Klaus."

Remi laid roses on the freshly turned earth. "They're together again."

"I'm glad. I can't thank you enough for helping to bring him home."

After a moment, Sam clasped him on the back. "We'll be in the car when you're ready."

Dietrich nodded as Sam and Remi walked off.

The following day, Sam and Remi were relaxing at their hotel before their trip home. Remi gave a sigh of contentment. "A good trip, Fargo, don't you think?"

"Very good."

"And to think this all started on date night."

"Which I'm going to make up to you," he said, when someone knocked on their door. He crossed the floor of their suite to answer it.

Dietrich was there, an odd look on his face.

"What's wrong?" Remi asked, getting up from the couch.

"The autopsy report came in. I wasn't even aware they were doing one."

"They had to," Sam said. "At least if they wanted to find out why the plane went down."

"Come in," Remi said, drawing him to the couch. She took a seat next to him. "What does it say?"

"All but two died from injuries received on impact."

"Does it give a cause of death for those two?"

Dietrich looked down at the papers, almost as if he didn't believe the report himself. "The unidentified sixth passenger died of a stab wound to the heart. The pilot from a single gunshot wound to the head . . . It's just . . ."

He handed the papers over. Sam, noticing the report was written in Spanish, gave it to Remi. She scanned the document, then glanced up, a look of astonishment on her face. "I didn't expect this . . ."

"Expect what?" Sam asked.

"That they'd make a determination on who shot the gun. It's not conclusive, but they think there's a cut and stippling on the hand of the person who fired it. *Klaus.*"

"Klaus?"

Remi nodded. "They believe that he's the one who killed the pilot."

Dietrich nodded. "That's why I came over. I just . . ." He let out a sigh. "I guess what I mean is that all this guilt I carried over the years, knowing my great-great-uncle was this horrible Nazi . . ."

Remi put her hand on his arm. "That was never your fault. Ever."

"Maybe not," he said. "But that's how I felt."

"Well, then," Remi said. "You have to feel a *lot* better reading about Klaus. The boy's a hero. Who knows how many lives he saved by keeping Operation Werewolf from happening?"

"I don't think I would've been brave enough to kill the pilot and bring down the plane."

"Don't sell yourself short," Sam said, walking over to the bar. He poured three glasses of Rémy Martin and brought one over to Dietrich and Remi before picking up his own. "The way I see it, you inherited the same genes as young Klaus. That deserves a toast."

"I'm not so sure," Dietrich said.

"Are you kidding?" Remi replied. "Who was it who decided to set up a cantina in Wolf Guard territory, hoping to gather evidence of their drug running? On top of that, you never gave up searching for Klaus. Even knowing the type of people who were trying to stop you and how dangerous they were. Klaus and your grandfather would be very proud of you."

Dietrich stared at his drink before looking up at them. "I never really thought about it like that." He smiled suddenly, lifting his glass. "To Klaus?"

"To Klaus," they both said, touching their glasses to his.

89

S am, wearing a suit and tie, waited by the door for Remi. When she hadn't appeared within a few minutes, he looked at his watch. "The limo's waiting," he called out.

"On my way," she said, her voice coming from the second-floor hallway. She walked down the stairs a few minutes later, dressed in a Ralph Lauren black jacquard-weave tuxedo jacket with black satin lapels, a silk ruffled shirt, and her favorite jeans.

Sam couldn't take his eyes from her. "You look beautiful."

"Thank you," she said, kissing him as she reached his side. "Nothing too good for the Lighthouse."

Sam opened the front door, holding it for her, then backtracked to pick up a chilled bottle of Billecart-Salmon Brut Rosé champagne. "Wouldn't want to forget this," he said. "A little something to tide us over on the long ride."

Remi gave him a dazzling smile. "What are we waiting for? That champagne's calling my name."